Rachael Stewart adores conjuring up stories, from heartwarmingly romantic to wildly erotic. She's been writing since she could put pen to paper—a fact the stacks of scrawled-on pages in her loft will attest to. A Welsh lass at heart, she now lives in Yorkshire, with her very own hero and three awesome kids—and if she's not tapping out a story she's wrapped up in one, or enjoying the great outdoors. Reach her on Facebook, Twitter @rach_b52, or at rachaelstewartauthor.com

Christy Jeffries graduated from the University of California, Irvine, with a degree in criminology and received her Juris Doctor from California Western School of Law. But drafting court documents and working in law enforcement was merely an apprenticeship for her current career in the dynamic field of mummyhood and romance writing. She lives in Southern California with her patient husband, two energetic sons and one sassy grandmother. Follow her online at christyjeffries.com

TEMPTED BY THE TYCOON'S PROPOSAL

RACHAEL STEWART

WHAT HAPPENS AT THE RANCH…

CHRISTY JEFFRIES

MILLS & BOON

First Published in Great Britain 2020
by Mills & Boon, an imprint of HarperCollinsPublishers,
1 London Bridge Street, London, SE1 9GF

Tempted by the Tycoon's Proposal © 2020 Rachael Stewart
What Happens at the Ranch... © 2020 Christy Jeffries

ISBN: 978-0-263-29894-9

0121

TEMPTED BY THE TYCOON'S PROPOSAL

RACHAEL STEWART

For my editor, Carly.
For believing in me when I struggled to believe
in myself and making this another dream come true.
This one is for you!
Rachael x

CHAPTER ONE

'SOPH, WE HAVE a situation.'

Normally those words from her extremely capable assistant hotel manager would have had Sophia Lambert on edge, but not today. Today, she needed the distraction. In fact, she'd take a month of situations just to get through January and keep the past at bay.

Taking a breath, she turned from her computer screen to give Andrew a smile and felt it freeze midway.

Whatever it was, it wasn't good. Andrew was unflappable and yet his age-old wrinkles were creased tight, his warm eyes bright with concern.

Maybe this would be a distraction too far...

'What is it?'

'The McGregor child has gone missing.'

'Missing?' Her semi-smile became a frown. The McGregors were staying in the penthouse suite, one of the most luxurious suites London had to offer and as such rarely used. Only the richest of the rich could afford its extortionate nightly rate and the billionaire businessman McGregor was one such man.

A widower too. Not that Sophia knew this first-hand; the trusty grapevine of the hotel trade was responsible for that. His financial status and the tragic tale of a hit-and-run that took his wife three years ago, and almost took his child too, had spread far and wide thanks to the world's media. She could just imagine how fast news of his child being missing would spread...

'She came back with her nanny just after lunch and before they made it to her room...' He shrugged, the move stilted with unease. 'Poof—vanished.'

Sophia shook her head and pushed herself out of her seat. 'A little girl can hardly vanish.'

Although, if she was honest, she'd disappear if she was in the care of that particular woman. She hadn't had the pleasure of meeting the illustrious McGregor yet—he hadn't arrived—but she'd met his little miss of a daughter and the battle-axe caring for her.

She approached him in the doorway. 'We have twelve floors, one hundred and thirty rooms, cupboards, trolleys, luggage; if the girl wants to hide, she's in the right place. There's no need to think the worst.'

He scratched his brow. 'I hope so.'

'Come on.' She started off down the corridor that led into the main foyer. 'Where have you tried?'

'The toilets, the public rooms downstairs, the lifts and stairwell.'

'Okay, who's on the search?'

'Everyone who's not needed out front. I even have the maids who were due to clock off hunting and Marie has taken Ms Archer back to the penthouse to calm her nerves.'

Marie was a good choice. Calm, efficient, matronly even, and a fabulous head housekeeper. 'Good.'

'But it's been half an hour; we'll have to call the police soon.'

'We'll find her.' Sophia paused to rest a hand on his shoulder. 'What about CCTV?'

He nodded. 'We've checked. She was last seen heading towards the conference room on the second floor.'

'And you've tried there?'

'Of course—no joy.'

'But there's no sign of her leaving the building?'

He shook his head. 'Absolutely none.'

'There we go; she has to be here somewhere. We just have to think like a child and we'll find her. I'm going to head up to the conference room; you carry on the search down here. Call me if you find her.'

'Will do.'

They branched off and Sophia took to the stairs. She wasn't ready to worry yet. Things and people went missing in hotels every day and it was their job to see it resolved, to keep the guests happy. Which included Little Miss Trouble and her elusive father.

The conference room looked deserted, tables and chairs all stacked neatly to one side ready to be laid out for a company's belated Christmas function. One table had already been set up, a red cloth covering it, with flowers, glassware and napkins all arranged to the organisers' exacting standards. But no child.

She turned to leave and then something caught her eye. She looked back, eyes narrowing on the tablecloth. She could have sworn it had fluttered.

'Hello?' She took a tentative step towards it. Another flutter. Definite this time. 'Hello?'

This time she got a small giggle in response and her heart lifted. 'Is that you, Miss McGregor?'

'I don't have time for this, Connor. Why wasn't it on our radar?'

Jack scowled at the hotel doorman. It wasn't intentional—his mind was on the call—but it got the door opened promptly and he was off, striding across the foyer. He pressed the button to call the lift and threw his focus down the line, surveying the room with unseeing eyes.

'We hadn't even heard of them before today,' Connor was saying. 'Apparently it's some new start-up that's done well enough to outbid us.'

Fantastic. This was all he needed. The plan had been to fly into London, stay for a week—two at most—get the takeover signed and get out again. He hated the city at the best of times. Too cold, too grey, too loaded with the past.

'Well, get digging. I want to know all there is by close of play t—'

'Er…excuse me, Mr McGregor.'

Jack frowned and turned towards the voice. A quick appraisal of the man's uniform and badge told him he was the assistant manager and he looked nervous, his hands wringing before him.

'Hang on, Connor… Yes?'

'I'm afraid, sir…' he bowed his head slightly '…we have a…situation.'

The guy had to be kidding. Was this really going to be his life today? Connor had used the exact same words not twenty minutes ago.

'What kind of situation?' He couldn't think for a second what it would be. Was his room not ready? Had there been a double booking? Nothing could be worse than Connor's unwelcome news. 'Well?'

The guy stopped wringing his hands and placed them behind his back, his chin lifting. 'It's your daughter… I'm afraid she's gone—'

His walkie-talkie sounded as Jack's stomach took a dive, and the manager jolted as he scrambled to pull the device out of the pocket of his hotel-issue blazer. 'Yes?'

Jack couldn't catch what was said over the blood ringing in his ears, his patience hanging by a thread. What the devil was going on? What *had* Lily done now?

The guy physically relaxed before him, his body deflating as he blew out a gust of air. 'That's great news. Thank you!'

He repocketed the device and smiled up at him. 'I'm very happy to report all is well.'

Jack just frowned. 'Excuse me?'

'Sorry, Jack,' Connor piped down the phone line, 'like I was saying—'

'Not you...*you*.' He glared at the manager, now flushing crimson.

'Pardon me, sir. It's just...it seems your daughter decided to play a little hide-and-seek with Ms Archer this afternoon. However, she has now been found and—'

He cursed, his head and heart racing with a multitude of what-ifs that didn't even matter now that she was found, but they existed anyway. 'How long was she missing?'

'Well... I... It was...' He started to wring his hands again. 'I'm not sure. Perhaps Ms Archer can explain. I'll take you to your daughter, shall I? She's with Ms Lambert, our hotel manager.'

Jack gave him a brusque nod. 'Connor, I'll call you back.' He cut the line and followed after the manager, who was already walking away faster than his advancing years would suggest possible.

Jack shook his head and pulled at his tie, easing it away from his neck as his skin prickled and perspired, the stress building in spite of her safety. This really was not his day. And as far as Lily's nanny-cum-tutor went, maybe it was time to find another—something Lily would no doubt appreciate.

But he paid her to look after Lily twenty-four-seven and in the last two weeks alone she had misplaced her a dozen times. He really was at his wits' end, let alone his nerves.

Finding another would take time—time he didn't have. What he really should be doing was explaining the dangers to his daughter, making her realise her safety was more important than whatever distraction she had sought out this time. And he could just imagine how much of that she would take on board. She was too much like her mother: free-spirited, impulsive, a sitting target for another hit-and-run or, heaven forbid, a kidnapper seeking a ridiculous ransom sum.

And how exactly did he tell his five-year-old daughter that her father's success made her a target? That for all he worked to ensure their financial stability and a quality of life that far exceeded anything he had ever known, she was to be caged by it too. Maybe it was high time he employed a security detail. He'd avoided it thus far, trying to retain some normality for his daughter, but he wasn't sure how many more of these incidents, these disappearing acts, he could take.

'They're just this way, Mr McGregor...' the manager said, ending Jack's troubled inner ramblings as he pushed open a door and gestured for him to enter.

He gave him a grim nod, being too strung-out to speak. And it wasn't this guy's fault his temper was frayed. It was all—

He didn't get to finish the thought. He was too surprised to do anything but gawp.

And he *never* gawped.

Before him was a festive table. A festive table with a pair of nude stilettos attached to dainty ankles and slender calves poking out beneath its deep red tablecloth.

What the devil?

Within minutes of meeting the little girl, Sophia found herself lying on her back beneath the beautifully laid table staring at its underside, while Miss McGregor flashed a torch at it.

'Isn't it pretty?' The little girl rolled the *r* as she waved her hand at the star constellation the torch projected.

'It is...and clever... Is this what you've been doing all this time? You know Ms Archer has been quite worried about you.'

The girl gave a dramatic frown, her eyes, dark in the

low light, now appeared both serious and disappointed at once. Here it came—the excuse. There always was one with children and Sophia had a sneaky suspicion she was going to be reeled in regardless.

'She never lets me look at the stars. She says it's a waste of my noggin.' She prodded her forehead with one forefinger as she stared Sophia down. 'That I should be learning my maths and reading.'

'Well, I'm sure Ms Archer just wants what's best for you.'

She looked back to the lit-up stars. 'I'm going to be an astronaut; I don't need maths…or the books she wants me to read.'

Sophia gave a soft laugh. 'Maths will certainly help you if that's what you want to be when you grow up.'

'Really?'

'Really.'

She sighed heavily, her bottom lip jutting out. 'Maybe I will try a little '

'What on earth?' The heavy booming voice took over the girl's and her eyes widened as she switched off the torch.

'Uh-oh, Daddy's mad.'

Daddy's mad… Oh, no.

Sophia imagined the scene from Mr McGregor's eyes and felt the heat radiate out from her middle, her cheeks burning bright. All he would see were her calves and her shoes, like something out of *The Wizard of Oz*… Only her shoes weren't red; they were nude and attached to her. No witch, just a blushing hotel manager about to face the music.

Not that there was anything to be apologetic or embarrassed about. She'd found his daughter and really he ought to be grateful for that, not—

'Lily, come out here this minute.'

'I'm sorry,' the little girl whispered to Sophia, her hair a bobbing mass of dark ringlets as she clambered onto her knees and crawled out backward. She made it look so simple, almost graceful, and Sophia ought to do the same.

She really ought to.

Really, *really* ought to.

But there was something vulnerable about being caught lying on your back beneath a table, the oddity of the situation leaving her quite incapable of thinking straight.

'What do you think you're doing, running out on Ms Archer like that?'

Sophia couldn't make out the girl's response, just a short, sharp sniff. The next thing she knew, the tablecloth was being flicked up and the most dramatic pair of grey eyes speared her. 'Ms Lambert, I presume?'

She looked down her nose at him, literally, since she was still lying back on the floor and wishing the ground would swallow her up. Particularly as the eyes spearing her were far too attractive and far too hard all at once.

Get with it, Sophia.

She cleared her throat and rolled onto her knees, mimicking his daughter's method, only she was very much focused on tugging her dress as low as possible over her behind and doing her utmost to avoid not only his eye but his entire body.

Even in his crouched position he exuded a panther-like grace. All power, sinew and strength, in a dark suit complete with tie…and the effect he was having on her pulse really wasn't helping her focus on words. Words of any shape or form.

'It's a pleasure to meet you, Mr McGregor,' she said, finally standing and lifting her gaze, only to wish she'd kept it lowered. Yes, she knew he was a widower. Yes, she knew he was the father to a young daughter. Yes, she knew he had a reputation for being a bit of a looker. But for some reason she'd had him pegged as being older, his reputation stemming from money and power, not a seriously impressive frame and a face that belonged on the cover of a magazine.

His body too, she was sure—

She swallowed and cut the thought dead. It was entirely inappropriate and in no way helping her function in a manner befitting her professional role. He was a guest for goodness' sake, a very important guest, the kind she should be impressing, not… What exactly was she doing?

'Jack.' He offered his hand and she jumped a little.

Great. Now she just looked scared. And judging by the way his brow lifted and his lips—his very full and teasing lips—quirked he'd not missed her overreaction either. *Even better…*

'Sophia.' She forced a smile and quickly slotted her hand in his, but his eyes stayed locked with hers, their intensity making her feel exposed, as if he could read every debauched thought racing through her mind and her cheeks flushed all over again.

Another swallow, another breath and a shake of the hand. At least she hoped she'd shaken it because the warmth zinging along her fingers, through her wrist, her arm and settling somewhere around her tummy made it hard to focus on the actual giving of a handshake.

He didn't seem disturbed though; his eyes were sharp as they assessed her. For what she couldn't really tell, but she had a fair idea what a panther's prey felt like seconds before it pounced.

Maybe it was his unruly dark hair, the rich colour to his skin and the slant to his dramatic grey eyes that had her heading down the wild-cat route. Whatever the case, she was off on some weird tangent where professionalism continued to evade her.

'I like Sphea. Can she come for tea, Daddy?'

What? No! Sophia's laugh came out a strangled mess, thankfully drowned out by a sudden bellow from the man before her. So the panther was capable of laughter. Fascinating. And distracting. Especially when she should be drawing a line under that right now. She did not socialise, fraternise or any other *ise* with the clientele.

'I think Sphea has far more important things to be taking care of...'

The way he mimicked his daughter's pronunciation of her name had her entire insides turning to mush and she opened her mouth to agree but nothing came out.

'Unless, of course, that is not the case?'

He turned to pin her with that far too astute gaze. 'Then you would be more than welcome this evening, as a thank you for finding my little runaway.'

Sophia looked from him to the little girl staring imploringly up at her, eyes the colour of her father's, and erupted in a nervous giggle which she abruptly quit as her eyes caught sight of Andrew in the open doorway. He was positively beaming, reading whatever he fancied into her crazed behaviour. *Great.*

She would sort that, just as soon as she turned down Mr McGregor's very kind and far too appealing offer. But how exactly could she turn down their most lucrative customer without causing offence?

Stick to work—something he'd understand...

What are you doing, Jack?

Looking down into the alluring blue gaze of Sophia Lambert, he really had no idea. She was the hotel manager, not some new friend his daughter had taken a shine to. He blamed the crazy suggestion entirely on Lily of course. If she hadn't put the idea out there, he certainly wouldn't have thought of it and he definitely wouldn't have found it as appealing as he did.

Hot off the back of the little display that had greeted him when he'd first entered the conference room, he wasn't so certain he was thinking with his brain either. Two slender calves, a pair of stilettos and the knowledge that the woman had got down to his daughter's level, no airs and graces, tugged at him even now.

Sophia blinked, and blinked again, her cheeks a delightful shade of pink as her eyes adjusted to some unknown thought and then she drew in a breath and crouched down to Lily's height.

His view was reduced to her auburn hair, knotted high, her escaped curls that brushed over the creamy skin at her nape and the dusting of freckles that disappeared into the high neck of her navy dress. He cleared his throat, surprised to find his mouth as dry as the Sahara.

'It's so kind of you to offer, Lily,' she said softly, 'but I'm afraid I need to work.'

'Now you sound like Daddy.'

He cringed inwardly as Sophia sent him a brief look. It wasn't how he wanted to be; it was how he had to be. You didn't get to run a billion-pound company taking it easy. You didn't get to provide a financially stable home without putting in the hours. Lily had so much more than he'd ever had, and his work saw to it she always would.

'Well, you see this big building—this hotel?' Lily nodded at her. 'If I don't work, then this place doesn't work. I make sure important guests like you are taken care of and have a good time.'

'You're the boss lady?'

Sophia laughed, the sound reaching all the way inside him and teasing at the edges of his mouth.

'Yes, I'm the boss lady.'

'One day I want to be the big boss lady...on the moon.'

Sophia laughed again, her hand reaching out to stroke Lily's cheek. 'Then remember what I said about your maths and your reading.'

'Maths *and* reading?'

Sophia nodded and Lily looked up at him. He was waiting for the eye roll; instead she hooked her tiny hand through his and looked back to Sophia with a firm nod. 'Okay.'

'Good girl.' She ruffled Lily's hair before rising up, her eyes finally coming back to his. They were still bright, but her cheeks had calmed, only a hint of pink remaining beneath the delicate sprinkling of freckles.

'I trust you have everything you need in your room,' she said smoothly, the difference in her marked. She was in work mode now and he found himself wanting the other version back, the version that had just spoken so kindly to his daughter.

'But if there is anything at all that you require, please don't hesitate to call down.' She gestured for them to leave the room. 'Shall we, Mr McGregor?'

'Jack, please.' Normally formal terms of address didn't bother him; he was used to it. In her case, though, it seemed he couldn't let it go.

He was treated to another flush of colour in her cheeks, something he was fast becoming attached to, and she cleared her throat. 'Jack.'

Better. Much better.

Her eyes evaded him now as she sought out her assistant manager. 'Andrew, could you see Jack and Lily to their room, please, and relieve Marie.'

'Of course.'

Jack looked to the elderly gentleman and knew who he'd rather be escorted by. Perhaps his lack of interest in the dating scene was taking its toll. It wasn't as if opportunities didn't present themselves but what had first been an avoidance of women, especially in the months following Elena's death, had now become a habit. Life was far less complicated when it was just him and Lily to think about. Him, Lily and work.

'It was a pleasure to meet you, Mr— *Jack*, and Lily. I hope you enjoy your stay.' She turned and swept from the room, no backward glance. And he wanted one.

'Daddy?' Lily tugged on his hand and he looked down at her.

'Yes?'

'I think you should change her mind.'

He laughed, but inside he completely agreed with his little girl.

And what was that about?

He had no idea.

But the desire was there, all the same.

CHAPTER TWO

SOPHIA RUBBED THE back of her neck and stifled a yawn. Before her, the computer screen started to blur, facts and figures forming indistinct lines and making her squint. It was gone ten and she should have left work long ago but all that waited for her was an empty apartment and her thoughts. Neither of which she could bring herself to cope with.

Tomorrow would be better. Tomorrow it would be February, marking the end of another anniversary. Ten years since the death of her sister. A decade of guilt and grief. Time was supposed to heal. Make it easier. Soothe the horrors of the past. Whoever said that was either an idealist or a liar.

A short rap on the door put an end to her depressive stupor and she looked to it.

'Yes?'

The door opened and Andrew poked his head around. 'Isn't it time you left?'

'I will, soon.'

He nodded but didn't make to leave, his eyes narrowed on her instead. 'Mr McGregor seemed nice.'

Sophia's heart gave an involuntary flutter, just as it had every time she'd found herself reflecting on their little encounter that afternoon. 'Yes, and were they happy when you left?'

'Well, I think Ms Archer would've been happier to see the child disciplined more, but as far as their accommodation goes they're happy enough.'

'Good.'

'So, I'm off…' He hesitated on the threshold. 'You will go home soon?'

Sophia gave him a reassuring smile. 'Yes, *soon.*'

'Okay, goodnight.'

''Night.'

He pulled the door closed and Sophia looked back to her computer screen, starting to kill the applications still running. She was about to shut down her internet browser when the face of Jack McGregor came back to her, the instant effect he'd had on her pulse just as effective now.

She'd never felt anything like it. Ever. She was a twenty-four-year-old woman with zero relationship experience, zero experience of men really, unless you counted the odd fumbling kiss in her teens. She'd pretty much considered that part of her physical make-up dead, any frisson of excitement lost in her well-controlled exterior and the persistent ache left by the loss of Amy, her happy-go-lucky sister.

But she'd felt it looking into his eyes, she couldn't deny it. Not just the thrill, the kick to her pulse; there had been a connection she couldn't shake. It had taken her all to reinstate the professional front, turn down his offer of dinner and leave.

Was it the fact he had suffered too? The loss of someone he had loved? Was there some weird underlying connection drawing her to him?

She wasn't an old romantic. When her friends had dreamed of fairy-tale weddings, two-point-four children and happy-ever-afters she'd thrown herself into her studies, making sure she was the best she could possibly be, that she achieved and achieved. Not that it had made her home life easier.

No, she'd been invisible to her parents. It didn't matter what she did, what awards she won, what promotion she earned. She could never bring back her little sister, the one she should have been taking care of when it happened—an accident she herself had instigated.

That same wrenching motion took hold of her gut and

her hand went to her stomach, her lungs dragging in air. It would pass. The nausea always did soon enough. But the force of it was always the same, the pain no less than it had been when she was fourteen.

But today…today she'd had a glimpse of an entirely different emotion, one that gave her hope that she had no right to feel, and her fingers moved to the keyboard, almost of their own volition, his name appearing letter by letter. She hit the enter key before she could reconsider and there he was, filling her screen: images across the top, article after article listed below.

What are you doing, Sophia?

It was likely he had no interest in her. Why would he? He was a billionaire businessman leading a life set so far apart from her own…but it didn't stop her looking, didn't stop her seeking the distraction he so readily represented, or preventing the spark he lit within her.

She smiled at the screen, her body indulging in the escapist fantasy he represented and for the first time in her life she understood the dreams of her peers in their teens.

Shame she was far too wise for dreams, far too weathered to find passion, fun and whatever else Jack had inspired in her. But sitting there in the privacy of her office she could pretend she was normal, that she was capable of more, that maybe, just maybe, she didn't have to be dead on the inside too.

Jack was at a loss.

He'd dealt with Connor and the unexpected hurdle in their takeover bid. He had calmed Ms Archer to the point that she hadn't chosen to pack in the job altogether and he'd decided to give her one more chance. And he'd been on hand at bedtime, coaxing Lily into her pyjamas and bed without too much fuss. But his daughter's last words as he'd bade her goodnight echoed with his own internal plea.

Please can we see Sphea again?

He rarely had an interest in anyone outside of Lily, outside of work. The last time he had tried for more he'd been a disappointment, long before the hit-and-run, long before Lily even. He'd tried to make Elena happy, he truly had, but it had never been enough—*he* wasn't enough.

He raked his fingers through his hair and leaned forward in his chair, reaching out for the whisky decanter on his desk and pouring a decent measure.

The fact was he never wanted to be in that position again. He'd grown up with nothing. Put into care at the age of six when his mother had shown more interest in getting her next fix than feeding her own son. He'd spent his childhood acting out, angry at the world, at her, for being alone, unwanted and unloved. There had been the promise that his mother would get better, that she would have him back, until finally she'd died of an overdose when he was nine. No, he'd been destined for a troubled childhood of foster homes and he'd soon realised that if he ever wanted to gain control over his life he needed to take charge of his own destiny and that meant becoming financially independent.

He'd thrown himself into his studies, working hard to ensure he could stand alone, and on that journey he'd met Elena. A foster child like him, they'd been homed together at thirteen and grown close, their family history so similar it had given them a bond that no one could take away.

He'd sworn he'd take her with him, he'd look out for her; she too would escape the bad hand they'd been dealt. She'd loved him and he had loved her too, in so much as he could. Though over time it had become more like friendship—to him at any rate—only he hadn't realised it quickly enough.

The day she'd asked him to marry her he'd known it. He'd known it and couldn't bear the pain of telling her. And then she'd produced the pregnancy test, a shock to them both, and he'd known he could never tell her.

He'd set aside his own feelings to do right by her, as he'd always promised, and they'd married, they'd had Lily, and he had worked harder than ever. Longer hours, more trips away. Part avoidance. Part habit. But their relationship had suffered; she'd wanted more of him, more family time, more couple time, more love.

The night of the accident he'd been working late—another failed promise to come home in time for dinner. She'd left the food on the table, taken Lily in the buggy and headed out to the park. It was how he'd found the house when he'd returned home from the hospital, a sleeping Lily in his arms. Quiet. Dark. Cold.

He threw back the whisky, needing its burn to neutralise the churn in his gut.

Elena had been lonely. He'd *made* her lonely. She'd loved him and he'd repaid her with...what?

No, he didn't deserve another's love. Save for Lily's. He'd take that and give her back his all. She was his priority. The only one he needed to be concerned with.

So why did he want more time with Sophia? Why would he want to get mixed up in something that could only complicate things?

He clenched the whisky glass tighter in his hand and stared out unseeing at the impressive London skyline. The view that made the hotel penthouse one of the best in London was wasted on him right now. And just what would Ms Lambert say to that?

He conjured her up in his mind's eye—the appeal of her creamy, freckled skin, her over-bright blue eyes and that mass of red hair he could only imagine splayed out upon his pillow...and felt the heat of attraction he hadn't experienced in so long burning away the chill, the emptiness... and in Elena's city of all places. *Their* city.

His throat closed over, his hand pulsing around the whisky glass as guilt swelled just as quickly, forcing hatred on its tail. Because he did hate London. It had been their home and she had died there. But it wasn't hate that had engulfed him the second he'd laid eyes on the fascinating hotel manager. No, it had been far more potent and far more disturbing than that.

It was also the reason he couldn't sleep. And drinking alone in his penthouse wasn't improving his mood. He should have gone to the gym rather than hit the bottle, but two whiskies in and exercise was out.

Perhaps the hotel bar would be preferable. The in-house pianist was talented and at least the gentle hum of people might distract him from the inner workings of his brain that seemed determined to flip-flop between the pain of the past and the potentially disruptive Ms Lambert.

Eleven o'clock. So much for leaving just after Andrew had bade her goodnight.

Instead, she'd lost herself in the enigma that was Mr McGregor—Jack.

Married to his childhood sweetheart, father to one girl and an orphan who'd come from nothing and made billions. It was the perfect fairy tale and the tabloids had capitalised on it, not holding back on the personal details they divulged either, worst of which was his mother's demise in a drug den, and that his father was unknown.

Her heart ached for him even as she read on. It seemed he fared better these days. No salacious gossip pertaining to his private life, no pictures of his daughter, no rumoured love interests since the passing of his wife. It was all business- or charity-related news and her admiration of him swelled.

Just what would it be like to sit across a table from this man and learn what made him tick, what made him the man he was today, to achieve all he had, to continue to achieve when he'd lost the closest person to him. His wife. The odd picture existed of them together at events. She had been beautiful, a statuesque blonde to his tall, dark good looks. But now she was gone, taken from their daughter before she'd had a chance to see her grow.

Sophia's eyes burned with unshed tears and she rubbed at them, refusing to submit. It didn't help to cry. She'd learned that over the years. It didn't change anything; it didn't bring anyone back.

She took a breath and let it shudder out of her. Tired. She was just tired. Time to go home and pour a nice glass of red and a stupidly hot bath. No more distracting herself with Tall, Dark and Handsome and his own personal tragedy. She had enough tragedy of her own to bear.

She pushed out of her chair and finally shut down her computer. Shouldering her handbag and hooking her coat over her arm, she headed out. At least it was late so maybe sleep would be forthcoming for a change and the nightmares non-existent.

She was halfway across the foyer when her eyes were drawn in the direction of the bar, to one lone figure in particular. Even from this distance she knew it was Jack.

He was leaning back in one of the plush armchairs, drink in hand, one leg crossed over the other, his ankle resting upon his knee. He'd lost the suit jacket and tie, his shirt now unbuttoned at the collar and framing his broad shoulders, his posture the only relaxed thing about him because his eyes told another story. Trained on the pianist playing in the corner of the soft-lit room, they were intense, inward, thoughtful, a frown creasing his brow as he stroked his forefinger across his lips.

She should move but her feet felt glued to the floor. And then he stilled, the finger pausing over his lips as his eyes shifted and connected directly with her own. Her belly came alive, tiny little flutters erupting all the way to her throat.

She tried for a smile, swallowing back the nerves and whatever else her body was in the mood to feel. She gave a nod which was meant as a silent goodnight, but instead of leaving she headed for him. What possessed her she didn't know, but the second his lips curved upwards her body gained a will of its own.

He stood as she neared. 'Sophia, it's good to see you again.'

His words lit her up from top to toe, whether he meant them or not. And how could he when she was no one special?

'And you.' She gestured to the drink he'd placed on the small round table beside him. 'Enjoying a nightcap?'

'The bar's finest. Can I tempt you to join me?'

Her eyes darted to his, an impulsive 'no' dying on her lips as she heard herself say, 'I wouldn't want to intrude.'

'You're not.'

She looked back to the foyer, to the exit just beyond and where she should be heading.

'Unless you count the fact you're taking my mind off my thoughts, which isn't a bad thing, believe me.'

His honesty called her eyes back to his and then she saw it, in the lines around his eyes, in their stormy glint—the same kind of pain, the same need for distraction that she felt.

'It's late and I really should go.'

'A quick one then…just to say thank you for today?'

She couldn't say yes. He was a client. This was her hotel. It wasn't the done thing. Only the same reasoning she'd used earlier was weaker now, in the lateness of the day, the intimacy of the bar and its lighting, with him filling her vision and drowning out the past. Perhaps for both of them.

'Okay.' She nodded, her lips wavering into a smile. 'A small Shiraz…please.'

His grin reignited the nervous flutter in her belly. And it was nerves. Just nerves.

'Great, take a seat.'

She did as he asked, sitting in the vacant chair positioned at an angle alongside his own and tried to relax.

Relax? You should be leaving. No good can come of you indulging yourself in the fantasy world he represents. It's not real. Not for you.

'It's on its way.'

His voice was real enough; she mentally fought back as he returned, closing her mind to everything but his presence.

'I hope I'm not keeping you from anything?'

She laughed at the very idea and watched him settle back in his seat. It was disconcerting, bizarre even. It was her hotel and yet he looked more at home here than she did, perched on the edge of her seat as if at any moment she might bolt.

She shifted back, resting her coat over the arm of her chair and crossing her legs. She wanted to appear just as at home, just as calm, just as in control, when she knew she wasn't.

'If by that you're asking whether I have a partner waiting up for me...' She lowered her bag to the floor, her eyes coming back to his as she straightened up. 'No, you don't need to worry about that.'

'Good.'

Good?

She narrowed her eyes. 'Are you flirting with me, Mr McGregor?'

Heavens, where had that come from?

Not only the question but the realisation that she wanted him to flirt with her. She was in trouble and sinking deeper, when she should be at home, running that bath and forgetting her problems in the sanctuary of solitude.

His long, deep laugh put the brakes on her escape plan, the sound provoking her already racing pulse. 'It's Jack, remember, and I suppose I was…'

Sophia tilted her head to the side, her curiosity aroused by his tone, his hesitancy. She couldn't imagine Jack being less than one hundred per cent sure of himself. Maybe she wasn't the only one struggling with this surprising connection. It actually made her feel better. Not a lot, but enough to ask, 'Why do I get the impression you've surprised yourself with that admission?'

He held her eye, silent for a beat. 'In all honesty, I'm a little rusty.'

Her smile was slow, growing with her confidence. 'You and me both.'

And there she went again, encouraging him when she knew she shouldn't, but she couldn't stop.

'I can't believe a woman like you could be all that rusty.'

'A woman like me never really got started.'

The air seemed to crackle in the silence that descended, a stream of unspoken thoughts passing between them.

'Jack, I—' She broke off as her drink arrived. She glanced up at her head barman with a smile. 'Thank you, Peter.'

'You're welcome.' He walked discreetly away, for which she was grateful.

She picked up the glass, took a much-needed sip and re-gathered her wits to tell him what needed to be said. That she didn't do flirting, or any kind of dating for that matter. Certainly not with the clientele, or anyone come to that. But as her eyes returned to his, now almost black in the low light, she found her voice failed her.

'Jack, you…what?' He gestured at her with one hand, drawing her eye to those long, lithe fingers that looked so capable, so strong, and the heat spread from her core to her cheeks and she swallowed, hard.

'I'm not sure this is wise.'

'No,' he said softly. 'You're probably right.'

Disappointment sneaked its way in, and she found her second sip of wine far harder to take than her first.

'And yet you still came over?'

Her cheeks flushed deeper. 'It would have been rude not to.'

'Is that the only reason? You didn't want to appear rude?'

She felt her eyes widen, her heart pulse in her chest. No, it wasn't, was it?

The fantasy she'd been harbouring in her office collided with reality, her lie catching in her tone as she said, 'I wanted to see how Lily and Ms Archer were faring after their little adventure.'

'They're fine, thank you for asking.' His lips quirked, the spark in his eyes telling her he'd seen her lie for what it was. 'However, me, not so much.'

Her brow pulled together. 'Really, in what way?'

'It seems my daughter's high opinion of me has taken something of a knock.'

She could sense where this was heading, knew she should put a stop to it, but the thrill of it, of what he might admit, had her pushing for more. 'And why's that?'

'She's taken quite a shine to you and she's not impressed that I failed to secure her a thank-you dinner.'

She chuckled softly. 'Why does it sound like both you and your daughter are used to getting what you want?'

'Because we are.' He shrugged, his easy grin setting her belly on fire. 'What can I say? People are powerless in the face of our McGregor charm.'

'The McGregor charm?' She laughed again. It seemed Jack had the ability to lift her mood so completely with his boasted charm, no matter how strung-out she was.

'What?' He raised his brow at her, his eyes dancing. 'Are you questioning its existence?'

'Moi?' She pressed her palm to her chest in mock sincerity. 'I wouldn't dare.'

Now he laughed, the sound resonating through her and making her feel so very alive.

'You could help me get out of trouble very easily, you know.'

She stilled, her smile as genuine as she felt. 'Is that you asking me to dinner again?'

'Is that you saying you will agree this time?' he quipped, his hopeful expression weakening the last of her resolve.

'Dinner with you *and* Lily?'

'Yes, she can be our chaperone.'

'Are we in need of a chaperone?'

Too quick. Too feisty. Too full-on, Sophia!

Something flashed in his gaze, something akin to the heat streaking right to her toes as she realised she couldn't take back her reckless words and knew she didn't want to either.

'So, what do you say?'

She didn't know whether she should be disappointed or relieved that he didn't answer her question. Not directly at any rate.

But what should she say?

No, because the chemistry between us is scaring the life out of me.

No, because I'm messed-up and in no place for whatever this is.

No, because...just because.

'You know, I really am starting to question my charm.'

His grin, filled with the very charm she'd brought into question, seared away any intention of saying no.

And what was there to say no to when she thought about it rationally?

She enjoyed his company. She'd enjoyed Lily's company that afternoon. Would it really be so bad to go to dinner?

What was the worst that could happen with his daughter present?

She smiled and raised her glass to her lips, enjoying the anticipation heating the air between them. This was fun. So much fun. And fun wasn't something she'd had in a long time.

'Come on, one dinner and you'll make both mine and Lily's day.'

She knew she'd regret it later, but…

'Okay, Jack, dinner it is.'

CHAPTER THREE

AS FAR AS Fridays went, today was certainly up there with the worst and she was late. Really late. She'd agreed to meet Jack in the foyer at six-thirty but it was now gone seven and she was having to call his room to delay it another thirty minutes at least.

'Jack, I'm so sorry,' she rushed out as soon as he answered. 'I'm still tied up.'

'It's okay.'

In the background she could hear an excited Lily asking if it was Sphea and she closed her eyes briefly, shutting down the guilt.

'I can deal with this,' Andrew said before her.

'No, it's fine,' she mouthed, adding into the receiver, 'Maybe we could do this another night?'

She cringed after she said it, her ears straining for his response. She knew she was running scared, but she'd had time to sleep on it, a day to think without him in front of her...

'No, we'll do it tonight, just let me know when you're ready.'

Her shoulders relaxed and tensed up again just as quickly. 'But it's already past seven. Surely Lily needs to eat and get to bed.'

'Let me worry about her and you get yourself sorted.'

She said, 'Okay,' as she hung up although she was far from okay. The truth was her common sense had returned the second she'd been outside of Jack McGregor's field of charm, and she'd known she couldn't indulge this strange fantasy that had overcome her.

She was Sophia Lambert, destined to live and die

alone for what she'd done. It was the very same reason she couldn't go back home and visit her parents. To see Mum and Dad, the way they would embrace her and pretend to forgive. She couldn't. Just. Couldn't.

And the more she kept her distance from people, the less likely she was to suffer a similar loss again. It was how she lived her life, how she had to live it.

'Seriously, Sophia, if I'd known you had plans I never would have brought this to you in the first place,' Andrew stressed, wearing his own look of guilt. 'We're more than capable of dealing with it.'

He was right. They were. And yet here she was, insisting it be her. Seeking a delay that gave her the distance she needed.

'I know you are.' She strode forward and gave him a reassuring smile. 'But you should have clocked off an hour ago. You know Cassie will be waiting for you.'

Cassie, his wife, always planned a candlelit dinner on Friday nights and Sophia knew how much both she and Andrew valued that tradition.

'*Go,*' she insisted, spying the continued hesitation in his gaze.

He shook his head in surrender. 'Okay, I'm going, but get this delegated and get yourself off. You need fun too.'

His grin was warm, but she could see the concern that cast a shadow over it. She didn't need Andrew to worry about her. She was fine. At least she would be after the night was done and she could go back to life as normal. Why had she even agreed in the first place?

Silly question. She couldn't think past the chaos that kicked up inside when she was around Jack.

She watched Andrew go, wondering what it would be like to have that kind of companionship and unconditional love to go home to. Was she a fool to reject it at every turn?

Her phone rang again and she pushed the thought aside. Just work—focus on that.

And she did.

It was almost eight by the time she caught a breather to think about Jack and his daughter. Her inner self laughed at her. *Who are you kidding? You've been forcing yourself not to think about them all evening.*

And Lily didn't deserve such behaviour. Neither did Jack. It wasn't his fault she was in a tizz over the way he made her feel.

She picked up the phone and dialled his room, anxiously rubbing at her neck as she waited.

'Hello?'

The fine hairs beneath her fingers pricked up, her heart tripping over itself and all from his simple hello.

'Hi.' She swallowed. 'It's Sophia.'

'Hey.'

She could hear the smile in his voice, imagined him standing before her and basking in its glow. And there she was, drowning in a sea of sensation and losing her mind all over again.

'I'm ready if you are.' She sounded breathless, her lungs struggling to function past the churn of nerves...or was it excitement?

'Great, I'll see you in the foyer in five.'

'Great,' she parroted, lowering the phone and staring at it as if she couldn't believe this was happening. Any of it.

The evening truly was set. She was going to dinner with a guy who was the stuff of heroes in one of her favourite romance novels and his charming daughter—*Single Dad meets Lonely Hotelier*—she could see it now in all its fanciful glory and pinched herself back to reality.

For the first time in her adult life Sophia was going to take a risk and let go for a night. She was going to have some fun, safe in the company of Lily, and then tomorrow she would move on. Simple.

Only when she got to the foyer there was no sign of them. The lift pinged its arrival and the doors opened.

There he was, dominating the opening, her eyes so caught up in him that she didn't notice the lack of mini-McGregor. Not until he was striding for her, the designer cut to his deep blue suit complementing his smooth, confident stride, his white shirt open at the collar, his grey eyes sharp against his dark skin and pinned wholly on her.

She frowned, looked to his left, his right, behind. She wet her lips. 'No Lily?'

He paused before her, his smile bordering on sheepish. 'I took your advice and fed her early. She's now tucked up in bed as she should be and I'm all yours… I mean…well, you know what I mean.'

Her cheeks coloured, the warmth spreading through her belly and smothering her nerves. 'You should have eaten with her, not waited for me. We could have postponed.'

'No chance.' He grimaced, his hand running through his hair that refused to be tamed and her palms tingled, itching to try. 'The only way I could get Lily fed and into bed was by assuring her we would still go out to dinner.'

She gave a shaky laugh. 'She has you wrapped around her little finger.'

'Don't all daughters?'

She thought of her own father and banished him from her mind just as swiftly. 'I hope she wasn't too disappointed?'

'No, she just sees it as a reason for us to get together again.'

Her heart skipped a beat. Pleasure, quickly followed by panic. 'Again?'

He chuckled. 'Do you have to look so unsettled by the idea?'

'Sorry, I'm just thinking… I'm sure you have more important things to be doing while in London.'

'Let us McGregors be the judge of that, hey?'

His light-hearted tone and the appreciative heat of his gaze worked together to lure her into feeling almost worthy of this evening, of a date with someone as impressive as him.

'Shall we?'

It took her a second to register his gesture to leave, another for his arm to curve around her and for his palm to settle against her lower back. The warmth of his touch soothed away her anxiety and slowly she turned on her heel and walked with him to the door, her head awash with questions.

Would it hurt, just for one night, to pretend it was all possible? To pretend it was a date? A real date? To go with the flow, go with…? His fingers fluttered against her lower back, reminding her of their presence, their effect, and her breath caught with her silent agreement.

When going with the flow felt this good, how could she possibly fight it?

'I hope you like Chinese.'

'Hmm?' was all she could manage as she focused on keeping her legs moving and not turning to jelly beneath her.

'This restaurant used to be a favourite of mine,' he added.

'Uh-huh.' *Oh, goodness, Sophia, is that really the best you can do?* 'I'm so hungry I could eat pretty much anything right now.'

She flicked him a look, saw his eyebrow raise at her impulsive statement and snapped her eyes back ahead. He thought she meant him. *Him.*

She nearly swallowed her tongue and threw her attention to the night doorman instead. 'Evening, Henry.'

'Miss Lambert.' He held the door open for them both and smiled. 'Have a good evening.'

'Thank you,' Jack said, his focus returning to Sophia. 'I'd tell you to put your coat on but my driver's waiting for us and the car will be warm.'

He looked to a sleek black car parked up in the circular courtyard, its driver, dressed in livery, already pulling open the rear door.

Wow. The number of times she had greeted or bade farewell to influential clients in this entrance, dreamed of how their lives would be, so different to her own, and now here she was, doing the exact same thing.

Her grip on reality really was wavering, but in that moment, as she thanked his driver and slipped inside the luxurious interior of his car, she didn't care.

Reality could wait a few more hours at least...

Jack waited for her to get settled into the back seat before joining her a respectful distance away, but her presence radiated down his side, his pulse hammering in a way it hadn't since...since for ever.

He watched her out of the corner of his eye as she played with her fingers upon her lap, her attention on the outside world as his driver pulled out into the traffic.

She wore a similar dress to the previous day, only now she'd lost the ID badge. Her hair was once again knotted up high, her make-up sparse and natural, and her ears were adorned with small pearl droplets that drew his attention to her long, slender neck. She had an effortless poise about her that made her as elegant as any date he'd had before.

Though this wasn't a date. Nothing of the sort. It was a thank-you meal to keep his daughter happy.

He just had to keep reminding himself of that fact.

'Something tells me you work late a lot?' It was a question aimed to distract himself from his thoughts, but as she looked to him, her eyes sparkling with humour, he could no longer deny the reason he was here was because, above all else, he wanted to be.

And he wanted it to be a date, to take her out to dinner regardless of whether it was wise or sensible, without guilt.

'Something tells me you do too.' Her voice was light, teasing, and he found himself grinning.

'Fair point.'

She returned his smile, her fingers ceasing their nervous play. 'I take it you're in London on business?'

'Yes, that's right. I was hoping it would be a week, but it's looking more like two now.'

She frowned a little. 'You're in a hurry to leave then?'

'Is it that obvious?'

'You were the one who said you *hoped* to be gone sooner,' she reminded him, not missing a beat. 'I assume that's because you're *wanting* to be gone.'

She waved a hand through the air and he had to stop himself from frowning as he thought about the reason he wanted to be gone. He didn't want to think about it. He didn't want anything to put a damper on their evening, not now they were heading out together. Alone. Just the two of them.

And there came the guilt again...the timely reminder of Elena and his biggest failure. He glanced out of the window and London looked back at him, full of its memories. He breathed through it and schooled his expression.

'I was,' he said, facing her again. 'London isn't... London isn't exactly a city I'm fond of.'

Her eyes scanned his face, her curiosity at his remark obvious, but he did the same, taking advantage of her attention to drink her in, her natural beauty, her appeal that warmed him all the way to the bone, and he realised that London looked slightly less grey now. 'But perhaps staying longer isn't such a bad thing.'

Her eyes met his and he added carefully, 'Lily certainly likes the idea.'

She nodded, her smile full of affection. 'She seems like a great kid.'

'That she is.'

'Do you travel a lot with her?'

'Quite a bit.'

'So where's home when you're not travelling?'

Home? Nowhere. Not since London, not since Elena. A cold sweat instantly spread, the hairs at his nape prickling against the crisp collar of his shirt and sending his eyes back to the outside world, safe from her astute gaze.

He clenched his hand into the soft leather seat and tried to keep his voice neutral. 'We don't have one as such. I have headquarters in various continents and I move between them depending on where I'm needed most.'

She was quiet for a while and he took the time to regain that sense of ease, to put the past to bed for a few hours at least.

'She must be well travelled for a… How old is she?'

'Five—she's six in a few weeks.' And she was excited about it too, birthdays becoming a bigger deal now. His heart and body softened as he remembered their conversation just last night and how they had to count the number of sleeps remaining.

'Ah, a birthday—how lovely! And what has she asked for?'

'A pony.'

Sophia's laugh tinkled through the car, taking away the last of his unease with it. '*Every* little girl goes through that phase.'

'You too?'

'Oh, yes, my sister and I…' A slight tremor entered her voice and she shook her head, her throat bobbing as her eyes flitted away for a second, and when they came back there was a sheen that hadn't existed before. But still she smiled, the gesture such a contrast to her sudden sadness.

'We begged for one, just one to share if we couldn't have one each.'

He couldn't take his eyes from the look in hers. 'And did you get your wish?' he asked softly.

She shook her head and he knew the sheen of tears had nothing to do with the pony. He wanted to ask her what was wrong, but he didn't want to make it worse. He didn't want to upset her. He tried to think of something else to say—anything to fill the void, to distract her—but the look in her eyes haunted him. It made him want to delve deeper, have her talk, and in turn he could offer…offer what? Comfort? Distraction from whatever this was?

His eyes fell to her lips and he felt the pull swell exponentially, felt it wrap around them, drawing them closer. Did she feel it too?

'So…' her voice drew him up sharply, his eyes lifting to hers to catch the way her lashes fluttered, her breath shaky as she visibly sought to regain control '…is she getting a pony?'

He gave a laugh that sounded more like a bark as he tried to relax into his seat. What was wrong with him? He was used to beautiful women up close and personal, but never had he felt so out of control of his senses.

Maybe it was the hint of trauma, of darkness he glimpsed in her too. The one thing he could understand, feel connected to.

'Hardly.' He raked a hand over his hair and looked to the window, to the far less evocative passing world. 'They don't exactly fit in a suitcase, and she has no need for one, not when I bought her an entire stud farm last year.'

'You bought her what?' she choked out, half-laughing, half-incredulous, calling his gaze back to her.

'Last year she asked for a horse,' he explained with a shrug, 'and it seemed like a wise investment opportunity.'

'I don't think she was thinking about its investment potential.'

He grinned now. 'No, that much is true, but she has one of the racehorses named in her honour and she gets to sit on him occasionally.'

'Right…okay…' She gave a downward smile, her head nodding as her eyes twinkled under the passing streetlights. No sadness now.

'What?'

'Nothing.'

'What?'

'Don't you think she was looking more for a pet, a friend of some sort?'

'Perhaps.'

'Maybe she thinks asking for a pony will give her that. I'm surprised she hasn't asked for a puppy.'

'Oh, she's asked for one of those too.'

'And it's a no?'

'Again, not suitcase-friendly and it wouldn't be fair to lug it from country to country, not to mention the vaccinations, the pet passport, the poo…' He shuddered. 'No, it's a definite no.'

A crease formed between her brows and she looked desperate to say something.

'What is it?' he probed when she wasn't forthcoming.

'It's nothing.' She caught her bottom lip in her teeth and looked to the window.

'Nothing again, hey?' He had to drag his eyes from her mouth, from the plump flesh caught in her teeth, taunting him with the urge to run his thumb over it, release it…kiss it. He cleared his suddenly tight throat. 'Well, if that's your "nothing" face, I'd love to see what you look like when you *are* thinking something.'

She gave him a guilty smile, snuffing out the desire with rising curiosity. Just what was she thinking?

'It doesn't feel my place to say.'

He tensed. 'Now I really am curious.'

'Well…it can't be easy on her, travelling all the time.'

'She's seeing the world. There aren't many five-year-olds that can claim to have visited as many incredible cities as she has.'

'But what does she do for schooling?'

The tension ratcheted up. 'She's taught by Ms Archer.'

Her brow lifted. 'She's home-schooled?'

'You say that like it's a bad thing, but what other option is there when we travel so much?'

'It's…well, it's just…when does she get to see other children, have play dates, that sort of thing?'

He frowned at her, the tension making him snap. 'My daughter wants for nothing. She's kept safe, she's well educated, and I'd like to think well-rounded too.'

She shook her head softly. 'But it must be lonely for her? Especially if you don't have a base, a place to call home.'

Surely home was where he was. It was why he took her everywhere with him. He wouldn't be the poor excuse for a father that he'd once been, always absent, always late.

'It's a well-known fact that children are quite resilient to change.' He knew he sounded petulant, defensive, but she'd got his hackles up.

She studied him silently and he wondered whether she would argue more, dreading what she would say next, but instead she nodded.

'I'm sure you're right. What do I know after all?' She shrugged. 'I'm not a parent and she is lovely, really truly…'

She looked back to the window, but her words hung over him. No one had ever questioned his parenting before, not since Elena and her desperate plea for him to be around more. And now he was never far away from Lily—they had weekends and bedtimes.

He could sense Sophia's thoughts still whirring away

and the need to defend himself, to explain, had him opening his mouth to speak but she got there first. 'So what have you got against London?'

It was the last thing he'd expected and he was ill-prepared for it, the direct hit winding him as his chest squeezed tight, the fateful night replaying in his head in freefall. The blood left his face and he saw her own eyes widen, her hand reaching out to softly touch his arm, sending an aftershock rippling through him, a confusing mix of heat teasing at the chill.

'I'm so sorry,' she whispered. 'I shouldn't have asked.'

He was slow to respond. Slow to quash the swirl of emotion inside, slow to adjust to the warmth spreading beneath her touch. He never spoke of it. London. The past. Elena.

'I read about your…your wife.' Her eyes wavered over his face, projecting and evoking so much emotion that he couldn't break free of it to speak. Thinking about Elena was one thing. Talking to Sophia of her was another.

'I don't talk about it.' His voice was tight, dead, and he watched her nod, the sheen returning to her gaze.

'I understand.'

And then he saw it reappear in her gaze, heard it in her words. She didn't simply understand; she felt it. She felt it as only someone who'd been there could. She'd lost someone too. He knew it just as clearly as if she'd told him so herself. And he forgot his own pain in hers.

'Who was it?'

Her lips parted in surprise, a subtle frown marring her brow. 'Who?'

'You've lost someone too.' He covered her hand upon his arm as she shook her head, her pain tugging at a part of him he'd long since thought dead. 'I can tell, Sophia. You don't have to talk about it, not if you don't want to, but…'

She took a shaky breath, her fingers trembling beneath his as she swallowed and lifted her chin a little. 'My sister.'

'When?'

She blinked back tears as she looked to him and the air caught in his lungs, her beauty all the more powerful for her sorrow. 'Ten years ago.'

'And yet it feels like yesterday?'

She nodded, the knowledge passing between them, the shared understanding, the bond growing.

'It doesn't matter how much time passes,' he said, the words easing out with their connection, 'how many times I return to London, to where we lived together…' He shook his head. *We? * More like *she*… He'd never been around. Absentee husband. Absentee father. His throat closed over. He couldn't face up to his failings, not in front of Sophia, not when her soft blue gaze offered up sympathy he had no right to accept.

He closed his fingers around her hand and squeezed gently, throwing the focus onto her. 'I'm sorry you lost your sister.'

She gave a small smile. 'Isn't it funny how we all say we're sorry, like we're in some way to blame for their death?'

His blood ran cold. He *was* to blame for Elena's. If he'd just come home in time for dinner, if he hadn't taken that last phone call, if he hadn't ignored her ringing him…

'I guess it's just a catch-all term, a way to express our sadness at the news of someone's passing, the pain of those left behind, but you hear it so much you become numb to it.'

'Yes.' He felt her fingers flex beneath his seconds before she pulled away, saw her eyes cloud over as she twisted her hands together again.

'What happened?'

She stilled and he cursed his lack of tact. He never should have asked. But he wanted to know. He wanted to reach out for her once more, to pull her hand back, to offer and take comfort. Even though, to all intents and purposes, they were nothing more than strangers.

Only she didn't feel like a stranger and he had no idea what to make of that. He felt exposed, vulnerable, as if he'd opened up a part of himself that he always kept well hidden. And he could sense she had too.

Maybe that was why he couldn't let it go. Why, when his brain told him to change the subject, to pull away from the personal, something more powerful had him wanting her to open up. To talk to him.

He was a hypocrite. He didn't want to talk about Elena and yet he was pushing her to talk about her sister. 'I'm sorry. You really don't have to talk about—'

'It was a sledging accident, ten years ago yesterday in fact...' Even though her eyes were on her hands, he could visualise the pain in them as she spoke, her words whisper-soft. 'It was my fault too. I'd taken her out on my own while Mum and Dad were busy with friends. We were only supposed to be gone an hour, but we were having too much fun, and she begged me for a go on her own, just one... It seemed harmless enough. I'd done it a thousand times before, so I sat her in and gave her a push—' She broke off, her body shuddering, her head lifting to look out of the window. 'She came off and hit her head on a rock hidden in the snow.'

His gut turned over with sickening force as the scene played out in his mind. 'How old was she?'

'Seven.' It shuddered out of her.

Seven. Barely older than his Lily. His gut rolled anew, her pain feeding his own, and he couldn't hold back any longer. He reached out for her hand. 'It doesn't make it your fault. It was an accident, a tragic accident, surely you can see that?'

'But if I hadn't taken her out, if we'd only stayed indoors, if I hadn't said yes to that last ride, if I hadn't pushed her...' Her voice trailed off and he grasped both of her hands in his.

'Hindsight is a powerful thing, Sophia. We can learn

from it, but you shouldn't let it torment you. It can't change the past.'

He should try telling himself the same too. Only he deserved to suffer. She didn't. Maybe it was the guilt that bound them and not the loss. No matter how undeserving hers was.

Her eyes snapped to his, adjusted, and then she was breathing deeply and blowing it out. 'And you really didn't need to know any of that. Sorry, let's just—'

He squeezed her hands, silencing her apology. 'I wanted to know.'

The silence settled around them, neither needing to speak, and the desire to draw her into him was there, aching in his arms, his chest.

She shook her head a little. 'I really don't do this normally.'

'Do what?' Though he could see what she meant in the surprise widening her eyes.

'Talk about the past, the accident...'

'It's not good to keep it all locked inside.'

Says the man who never talks of Elena.

'It seems we have quite the pasts to share,' she said quietly.

'Yes... I suppose we do.'

But her past...hers was the true pain of loss, shrouded in a guilt she shouldn't feel. Not like his guilt. His was deserved and it was the reason he couldn't accept her sympathy. Or anyone's love, for that matter.

With Elena he'd not only proved himself incapable of loving another, he'd proved himself unworthy of it too. He hadn't deserved her, and he certainly didn't deserve Sophia now.

He withdrew his hands and sat back in his seat once more.

He didn't deserve anyone.

CHAPTER FOUR

Sophia was in heaven.

It was the only way to describe the candlelit luxury of her surroundings and the calibre of the man sitting opposite her. No amount of reminding herself that this was temporary, just a thank-you meal to keep his daughter sweet, could dissuade her from getting wrapped up in him and his world.

As for the restaurant, everyone in the service industry knew of it with its numerous awards, accolades and several-months-long waiting list. She shouldn't really be surprised that Jack of all people had managed to secure a last-minute reservation, although people like him probably had a table kept in their name just on the off-chance they'd swing by. They'd certainly made him—*no, the two of them*—feel like royalty the second they'd arrived.

She spooned up her decadent chocolate dessert and in spite of being stuffed to the brim she couldn't resist its rich, salty-sweet goodness. Much as she couldn't resist discreetly devouring the sight of the man who'd recommended it. And with the wine, the pleasurable food and his stimulating conversation she was getting less discreet by the mouthful.

Now, as her eyes lifted to his, she paused, the spoon hovering halfway to her mouth. He was watching her, the dark intensity in his gaze making her pulse dance.

'What?' she asked, lowering the spoon just a little.

'You like your food.'

It was an observation, a simple statement of fact, but her cheeks burned. Her mother's teasing coming back from their childhood: *Did you inhale it?*

'I'm sorry.'

She placed the spoon back on the plate and smoothed her palm over her belly, her eyes falling away from his. Thoughts of her family always made her stomach swim. Seconds ago, she'd been floating in the clouds, loving every second, now she plummeted back to earth with a bump.

His grin was as swift as the shake of his head. 'Don't apologise.'

He leaned forward, his elbows pressing into the table as he rested his chin on his folded hands, that intense gaze still on her and making her forget the momentary nausea. 'It's a nice change, eating with someone who doesn't play with their food.'

'Are we back to talking about Lily again?'

He gave a soft laugh. 'No, she's as eager as you... I meant—' He broke off, another shake of his head.

'You meant...?'

Leaning back in his seat, he took up the napkin and raised it to his lips. Her eyes traced the move, the swipe of the cotton against their teasing curve, their appealing softness... What would it feel like to press her own lips against them, to catch the lower one in hers, to lick...? Promptly, she lifted her spoon and stuffed it inside her own mouth. There would be no kissing, no licking, no nothing.

She feasted on the dessert, slowly savouring the taste explosion as she tried to douse the heat unfurling low in her belly. But it was no use. It continued to flare, stoked by the way his own eyes watched her devouring the heady chocolate.

'I was going to say...' his voice had turned gruff, its edge at odds with the calm way in which he folded the napkin onto his plate '...it makes a change from the women I'm used to eating with.'

She felt the oddest spark of jealousy and quickly stamped it out with another spoon of heaven. Her taste buds sang while her brain talked her down. He wasn't hers to get jealous over. He never would be. It was ridiculous even to feel it.

But she had.

So much for not getting carried away. First kissing fantasies, and now jealousy! She wanted to roll her eyes at herself.

'Do you date often then?' The question came out smoothly, controlled, just as she'd hoped, but his sudden frown had her worrying she'd overstepped.

'No.'

It was abrupt, severe. Was he thinking of his wife again?

In the car she'd felt his grief, seen it echoed back at her when she'd told him things she'd never told another soul because she'd been powerless to stop the words from flowing. She'd felt the connection, the understanding, the ability to let go of it just a little with someone who had also loved and lost.

'Not a lot anyway. I don't really have the time,' he added, softer now. 'Work takes up most of it, Lily the rest.'

Her heart eased a little, her smile lifting with it. 'I can believe it.'

'What about you?' He held her eye, the candlelight flickering in the darkened depths of his, making her forget how to breathe, how to blink, his attention making her feel almost drunk with it.

'Me?' She was stalling but, despite how much she'd already opened up to him, she wasn't ready to confess the sorry state of her love life. Not that she'd ever considered it 'sorry' before…

'Yes,' he pressed. 'You're beautiful, intelligent, quite the catch. I'm sure you must get invited out often.'

Beautiful. Intelligent. Quite the catch.

Now she laughed, her head shaking incredulously as she covered her mouth with her hand. 'You, Mr McGregor, really are a charmer.'

'I only speak the truth.'

Did he? Was that really how he saw her?

She didn't like the way her body reacted to the idea. No, correction. She *loved* how her body reacted, and that was the problem.

'Sorry. I've made you uncomfortable.'

Was she really that obvious? Or did he just have a knack for reading her?

'You haven't. Or, rather, you have, but it's not your fault,' she assured him, taking up her wine glass for a confidence-boosting gulp. She had no need to lie. It wasn't as if she was there to impress him. And soon he would be gone, and she would be forgotten, so she might as well be honest. 'Truth is, I've never dated.'

His eyes widened, his shock permeating the air and making her cheeks burn anew in spite of her confident mental reasoning seconds before.

'Never?'

She shook her head.

'I take it you've always been in relationships instead. Friends that became more?'

His voice drifted off at the continued shaking of her head.

'No...*relationships*?'

She swallowed another sip of wine, knowing full well that her skin likely matched the blazing colour of her hair now. And she could hardly backtrack; she'd already said too much.

'I've always worked hard,' she tried to explain, grateful that her voice was level enough, her eyes still fixed on his, 'whether it was studying for exams at school, university or pushing my career, and I haven't had the time for it.'

'But...there must have been someone...at some point?'

She shook her head. 'You can consider yourself my first date—date-that's-not-a-date,' she swiftly added.

He studied her for so long, his face unreadable and, boy, was she trying. He was probably assessing her V plates right now and labelling her as some kind of freak.

'It's not that weird, surely?' She took another swig of wine. 'It's not like I've sprouted three heads.'

She was trying to lighten the mood and was relieved when he laughed. She wanted their easy footing back. They'd enjoyed it all through dinner when they'd talked of work, Lily, favourite foods, nothing serious. Not like in the car...

She shifted in her seat as she felt a line being drawn in the virtual sand. One side safe, platonic, friendly. The other... She wet her lips.

She knew which side her body wanted to be on.

And it wasn't the same as her single, solitary head.

'No, definitely not three heads...' His eyes fell to her recently glossed mouth. 'But you are quite fascinating, Ms Lambert.'

Jack watched her lips part, her cheeks flush deeper, their freckled warmth a delightful contrast to her sparkling blue gaze. Did she really have no idea how beautiful she was? That the reason her confession stunned him came from his disbelief that a woman with her qualities had avoided anything close to a relationship all these years? And what a waste that was...

'Fascinating?' She averted her eyes for a second, reached for her wine glass and took another sip, the rich red liquid disappearing swiftly now that their conversation had taken a more personal turn.

'You, Jack...' she waved the glass at him '...really are a master of flirtation... Rusty, nuh-uh.'

She shook her head as she made reference to their conversation the previous night, but he didn't comment, only asked the question he was eager to have answered now. 'How old are you?'

'Okay, scratch that last one,' she scoffed. 'Didn't your mother ever teach you not to ask a woman her age?'

She paled as soon as the words were out, her wine glass deposited and her hand reaching across the table to rest upon his arm. 'I'm so sorry. I shouldn't have... I forgot, I didn't think—'

'Hey, it's fine,' he assured her, cutting off her panicked apology that she needn't give. 'I've been fielding questions like that for years; it's second nature now. Am I to take it you've been reading up on me?' He cocked an eyebrow at her, projecting a jovial arrogance in the hope that she would see that her words didn't sting.

The colour returned to her cheeks just as quickly, her hand pulling away to stroke the back of her neck. 'Maybe... just a little.'

'A little?'

'Okay, a lot... I happen to find you quite fascinating too, Jack.'

His eyes were lost in the blazing sincerity of hers, his ears ringing with the heat of her admission. *Touché.*

'You fancy taking a stroll before I take you home?'

He wasn't ready to be out of her company and was relieved to see her smile.

'I'd like that and... I'm twenty-four.'

'Twenty-four?' He raised his brow. 'That's quite an achievement, to get where you have at your age.'

'Now you sound patronising.'

He laughed at the scowl she sent him and gestured over her head for the bill, his eyes coming back to her, appreciative, sincere. 'No, I'm just impressed. I have almost ten years on you to get where I have.'

'Yes, well, I can't see me getting anywhere close to you in another twenty, let alone ten. Try as I might.' She winked on the last, her easy laughter carrying across the table and warming him through.

'Your parents must be proud?'

The second his words registered, he felt the sudden chill that came over her, her words wooden as she said, 'I guess.'

'You guess?' Had she lost them as well as her sister? Had he inadvertently put his foot in it too? 'I'm sorry, are they...are they not around any more?'

She took a breath and looked away, a hand smoothing over her hair. 'No, they're very much around...we're just not close.'

'How come?' He couldn't understand it. The way she'd handled Lily, the love she had for the sister she'd lost, he'd expected them to be close. He certainly hadn't expected to put her on edge. And though he wanted the blush back in her cheeks, the fire in her eyes, the laughter, he wanted to understand more.

'We drifted apart when...when Amy died.'

She lowered her eyes to her lap, to where her hands now were, and he knew she twisted them together just as she had in the car.

He reached across the table, his hand resting beside her wine glass, and her eyes came back to him.

'They must miss you,' he said. 'I can't imagine losing Lily, to know that she is somewhere in the world and not be close to her.'

'I'm not sure.' She looked back to her hands as she paused. 'I think I'm a constant reminder of what they lost.'

He shook his head, but she wasn't looking at him.

'We don't really talk. We used to, before... Everything was different then, but after... I just couldn't face them, I didn't want to see the blame in their eyes, you know.' She gave a shrug and looked to him, her tormented gaze tugging at him.

'They wouldn't have blamed you,' he said softly.

She gave a shake of her head and reached out for her wine glass. 'It's how it felt. It was far easier to stay out of their way.'

'And so you locked yourself away?'

'Pretty much. Now it's just the norm.'

'Don't you have any other brothers, sisters?'

'No. Just me.'

Her voice was strained. His own, low and husky as he asked, 'Is that why you work so hard?'

Her eyes flicked to his, a surprising smile playing about her lips. 'Are you psychoanalysing me, Jack?'

His chest tightened. 'I guess I am.'

She shook her head some more, her smile indulging him. 'I have a need to prove myself, to succeed, to make my life worthy, if the therapist in you needs to know...' She looked away from him and her smile fell, her voice turning distant. 'I was the one who survived after all. I owe it to Amy to achieve.'

'There's achievement and then there's happiness, Sophia.' He pulled her attention back to him, his eyes searching hers and looking for the truth. 'Are you happy?'

She shrugged but he knew it was a front for what was really happening beneath the surface, behind her swirling blues.

'What's not to be happy about?' Her voice was steady, level, defiant. 'I'm the youngest hotel manager Devereaux Leisure has ever seen; I can afford my own apartment in London and I don't need a man or flatmate to do it. There aren't many twenty-four-year-olds who can claim the same.'

'But are you happy?'

He knew the answer; he could read it in her forced nonchalance, the way her fingers shook a little as she raised the glass to her lips and finished her wine.

'I'm happy enough.'

'I think Amy would want you to be happy above all else… Your parents too.'

Her throat bobbed, her eyes glistened, and he suddenly felt like the worst man in the world to make her suffer. He'd gone too far.

'Okay, Mr Know-It-All,' she suddenly fired at him. 'Tell me, are *you* happy?'

He should have expected it, her turning the tables on him. But he felt no more prepared, no more capable of giving an honest answer. And he didn't need to give one as the bill arrived. He placed his card on the small metal tray without looking, his eyes locked with her probing ones.

And he realised, for the first time in a long time, he did feel a sense of happiness, of being where he belonged, sitting across from a woman who sparked such feelings that he was torn between running for the hills and taking her home. And the latter could only ever end badly. She deserved more than what he could ever give her.

So why aren't you bringing an end to it now? Why aren't you walking away?

He couldn't explain it. It was impulsive—the need to be with her, to get to know her—and impossible to resist.

That realisation should have had him running too. Instead, he was looking into her eyes and telling himself it would be okay. He just had to be careful. Controlled. Sensible.

He ran a billion-pound empire so they were qualities he possessed in spades, and he should be able to rely on them now. But as he continued to lose himself in her gaze, he started to doubt even himself.

'Sir?'

It was the waiter, offering the card machine and judging by the amusement he could spy in Sophia's gaze it wasn't the first time he'd tried to get his attention.

Careful. Controlled. Sensible. Restrained.

He punched in his PIN with each word.

He started to rise. 'Shall we?'

'Good to have you back in the room, Jack.'

Her eyes sparkled with her teasing, her humour reaching right inside him and warming him through, pushing out the panic, the worry, the warning sounds in his head.

He offered his hand to her and she slipped her fingers into his, getting to her feet, all the while her eyes locked with his.

She was beautiful, she was funny and, without thinking any further, he leant in, his mouth brushing beside her ear. 'You make me feel happy.'

CHAPTER FIVE

AS THEY STEPPED out into the brisk winter's night Sophia shivered. Not from the chilling wind that whipped around them, but from the memory of his touch against her ear. It had hardly been there at all—just the brush of his lips. But the power of it...

'Are you cold?' He frowned down at her, clearly spying the tremor and misreading its cause. 'Maybe a walk isn't such a great idea.'

'No, no, it would be nice to get some fresh air. I don't make enough time for it these days.' She pulled her thick woollen coat tightly around her and smiled up at him. 'But if you want to wuss out?'

He grinned, his arm hooking around her waist and setting off a new string of fireworks inside.

'No way.'

Was he as surprised as she at the protective gesture? If he was, he didn't make any show of it. Instead, they walked in step with one another, completely at ease as though they'd been doing it for years, when in reality she'd never walked like this before, a man's arm around her.

She bowed her head against the wind and the odd spot of rain starting to fall, her thoughts turning to his late wife and whether this was something they had done often. Maybe even the exact same thing, dining at the same restaurant, taking a walk around Hyde Park after?

A multitude of scenarios played out in her head, her internet search having provided the perfect image of Elena and their projected happiness together. Her heart panged inside her chest and she hunched her shoulders, fending it off.

'What are you thinking about?'

She felt his eyes burning down into her, but she couldn't look at him, couldn't tell him the honest answer either.

'Sophia?'

Her softly spoken name tugged at her and she found herself looking up at him, forcing a smile. 'I guess you don't get to do this often either?'

'What, take a walk?'

'Yes.'

'I do, as it happens. Lily and I take a walk every Saturday morning, even in the rain.'

She grinned. 'Ah, muddy puddle days.'

'Indeed.' His eyes narrowed on her. 'You know, for someone who doesn't have children, you sure know what they like.'

'My friend Samantha has a five-year-old boy. I figure mud is just as appealing at that age whether you're a boy or a girl. Nothing beats donning wellies and making the most of the puddles.'

He laughed, the deep rumble working its way through her. 'Don't tell Lily that; she'll be dragging you outside in all your hotel finery, wellies or not.'

She laughed too, the joyful image he painted coming alive in her brain. 'Any time.'

'Any time?' he repeated, clearly not believing she was serious.

A smile continued to tease at her lips, the idea of doing exactly that with both Lily and him far too appealing. Appealing and just as unrealistic. Her breath stuttered in her chest and it took her a second to recover.

'Don't look so surprised about it, Jack,' she murmured when she could. 'I'm not afraid of a little mud.'

No, she was more afraid of enjoying their company a little too much.

He pursed his lips and nodded. 'Or crawling underneath tables to play hide-and-seek with my daughter...'

In spite of her unsettled thoughts, she laughed some more. 'She was actually star-gazing.'

'With her torch?'

'I take it you've done that with her before?'

'She's a little obsessed.'

'There are plenty worse things she could be obsessed with. Take slime, for example; it gets *everywhere*.'

'Oh, no, we've been there too. You should have seen the clean-up fee they charged on my last hotel suite.'

Her eyes snapped to his. 'Am I to expect the same?'

'Oh, dear...' He cringed, his boyish hesitation tickling at her. 'I'd forgotten who you were for a second.'

She had too. She wanted to be someone different; she wanted to be the kind of woman who would date someone like Jack.

He stopped walking, encouraging her to do the same. 'Forget I mentioned it?'

'That depends...what's it worth?'

His eyes darkened, his hands lifting to cup her upper arms and hold her still. The wind, the rain, the passers-by, all fell away. 'Name your price.'

Price. She'd asked for that and her cheeks warmed against the cold night air while her mind seared with her answer: *a kiss*.

It was written in her face, in her eyes, she was sure. But she had no right to ask for such a gesture, no right to even think it. It was foolish and...no, she couldn't.

She turned back towards his car. 'The rain is picking up; we should head back.'

He was slower to follow, as if he too had been caught in the same momentary fairy tale, but then he was there, his arm back around her waist, bringing his warmth and his comforting presence.

But they'd had their meal, the night would be over soon and tomorrow both Jack and Lily would be back to being just guests in her hotel. The sooner she accepted that, the sooner she could protect herself from getting too attached.

Don't you think it's a little late for that already?

'So, what do you say, Sophia?' Jack said into the sudden quiet, and lustful heat wedged its way into her throat. He wanted to know her price...

'Will you have another dinner with Lily and me?'

Phew. No, not phew. She went from overheated to cold and back to overheated in a heartbeat. Another dinner was worse than some flirtatious demand. Wasn't it?

She gave him a quick look, saw the wish for her to say yes in his imploring greys, and lowered her eyes back to the path.

You can't say yes. He's your hotel guest. You're attached enough already.

But she couldn't say no either.

She *wanted* that time with them both. For however long they were in her life, she wanted to enjoy it. And if that meant one more meal, then one more meal it would be.

'Yes.'

'Tomorrow?'

'Tomorrow?' She sounded breathless, her pulse racing with a strange mix of excitement and trepidation. 'So soon?'

'You really don't know Lily if you think she'll wait a day more.'

She gave an anxious laugh. He had a point. And doing it tomorrow meant less time to panic in the meantime. 'Okay...tomorrow it is.'

'Great!'

His grin made every anxious flicker worth it. She wanted to make him happy. She wanted to make Lily happy. And if it made her happy too...

'Are you sure it's just Lily who's impatient?' she teased, hooking her arm through his.

'What can I say? She has as many of my traits as her mother's.'

He didn't pale or tense up over the mention of Elena and she took the change to be a good sign, an encouraging one.

'So, aside from impatience, what else does she get from you?'

He gave another laugh. 'Stubbornness, a dictatorial manner, and she's frustratingly independent, messy…'

'Wow—please tell me her mother gave her some softer qualities, else you'll have a monster on your hands when she hits her teens.' She was purposely light and teasing with it, but she wanted to know more about Elena. More about the woman who had secured his love so completely and given him a beautiful daughter.

His laugh was soft, reflective. 'Luckily she does.'

'Like?' she pressed gently.

'Her mother's heart for one, her carefree spirit, impulsiveness, sparkle obsession… The list goes on.'

She smiled at the ease with which the details flowed from him now. 'It's an interesting mix.'

His murmured agreement came from deep within his chest.

'You must miss her…' she said quietly, giving his arm a squeeze and looking up at him. 'Elena?'

He met her eye briefly and there was so much in that one look, but she couldn't label it. It wasn't grief, it wasn't pain… It looked more…bewildered, uncertain. 'We knew each other a long time.'

That was an interesting way to put it. 'How did you two meet?'

He turned away, his eyes on the passing cars now as he went quiet. So much for her not wanting to bring back his pain. 'Sorry, you don't need to talk about her with me. I shouldn't pry.'

He surprised her with a laugh as he stopped walking

and shook his head at her. 'After all I've prised out of you tonight, that hardly seems fair.'

Her laugh was awkward as she realised the truth of it. 'Fair point. You did get my life story—which has been untold until now, I might add. But still, it's okay if you don't want to.'

He studied her for a moment, searching her gaze, and she wondered again if he was surprised by their behaviour. Not only in their actions but their honesty too. She almost asked when he started to walk again, taking her with him.

'We were placed in the same foster home when we were thirteen,' he eventually said.

'Thirteen?' Her heart pulsed; they'd known each other for ever... 'You were both so young.'

'Yes.' His eyes stayed fixed on the road. 'She'd been in care for nearly as long as me.'

'Did neither of you get adopted?'

'No,' he scoffed gently. 'At first there was hope that I'd return home to my mother and Elena to her parents, but it never happened.'

'I'm so sorry.'

He shrugged. 'They had their reasons and then my mother was no longer around, so it wasn't an option.'

She couldn't bring herself to admit that she'd read about his mother, but he likely knew it anyway.

'What about Elena's parents?'

'Her father's in prison, as far as I'm aware, and her mother remarried. Last I knew, Isla had a whole other life— kids, family, all of it. Not that Elena ever became a part of that life again. She was an adult by the time her mother had sorted herself out and by then...' His voice trailed off.

'By then she had you?'

He gave her a soft smile but his eyes were sad, haunted. 'Yes.'

'She was lucky to have met you.'

He scoffed at that, his rejection making her frown. How could he even doubt it when he'd so obviously given them both a better life?

'Does Elena's mother see Lily?'

'She saw her once, not long after Lily was born. Elena wanted to try and forge some kind of a relationship. Becoming a mother herself made her realise that it wasn't a bond so easily forgotten, and she hoped Lily would help bring them back together.'

She could hear the bitter ring to his voice and knew that wasn't how it had gone down. 'But it didn't?'

'I think Isla saw Elena as a reminder of a past she wanted to forget. She was still young; she had Elena at fifteen.'

'Fifteen?'

'Far too young, which is why we understood her fear, her difficulty, her avoidance of it all, but…'

'But she still didn't want to know?'

'It wasn't so much that she didn't, I don't think. More that she was torn between her old life and the new. She had a husband by then, two children and another on the way.'

'Poor Elena.' She squeezed his arm tighter. 'It must have been hard seeing her mother so settled with a new family.'

He gave an awkward shrug and she knew he was trying to make light of something that still hurt.

'Isla did come to her funeral, but… I don't know, too little too late, I guess.'

'Does Lily know her?'

'She's knows of her, but she was just a baby when they met. It would be nice if things were different. It's not like Lily has any other grandparents…'

'Do you think you might try again in the future?'

'Perhaps. It was all too raw at the funeral. She left her number with me and asked me to call but…'

'You haven't got around to it?'

He sighed. 'Is it awful to say I haven't?'

'No, not really.'

'It's not that I haven't thought about it; it's just…how do I know I can trust her to stick around, to let Lily become attached and have her walk away again? I don't want that guilt on my shoulders too.'

'Perhaps you could visit her, talk to her about your concerns. I think you'll know if she's ready to be a part of Lily's life.'

'Maybe…' He glanced down at her, his eyes soft and warm, reeling her in. 'Thank you for this, for understanding and listening.'

'No need to thank me. You've done exactly the same for me.'

'Be that as it may, thank you.'

'Then thank you too.' She smiled up at him, her happiness swelling as they walked ever closer together. 'I really have enjoyed tonight.'

'Me too,' he murmured, and her smile grew.

Ahead, his driver had spied their return and approached them with an umbrella in hand. It reminded her of the rain that had started to fall; it also reminded her of who Jack was outside the happy little fantasy bubble in which she walked. But it didn't burst it, rather it made her smile further because, for a fantasy, she really couldn't write it better than this.

'Thank you,' she said to his driver as he positioned the umbrella over them for the remaining distance to the car.

'You're welcome, ma'am.'

She had to stop the little giggle that wanted to escape. *Ma'am.* Never had she been called that before.

They settled into the back of the car. This time there was barely a hair's breadth between them, and she started to wish she lived further away, that the traffic would be heavier, that the fancy black car would break down—anything to keep her in it for longer. With him.

But, of course, it wasn't to be and as they pulled up outside her apartment she had to ignore the sudden sadness that had the chill of reality setting back in. Of her empty apartment that would greet her and the memories she wouldn't be able to fend off.

'This is me…' she said, stating the obvious but floundering with what she was supposed to do now. What was the etiquette for saying goodbye on a date that wasn't a date?

His driver opened her door and she turned to smile back at Jack.

'Thank you for a lovely evening.' And then, before she could think otherwise, she leaned in and pressed a kiss to his cheek, her body coming alive against the warmth of his. She breathed in deep and pulled back.

'Sophia?' He reached for her hand.

'Hmm?'

His eyes fell briefly to her lips, their depths dark and glittering, and she wondered if he would kiss her. She wet her lips, waiting, wanting, and then he seemed to shake himself out of it. 'Shall we come by and pick you up about ten tomorrow morning?'

'Ten? A bit early for dinner, isn't it?'

'You got me…' His thumb stroked across the back of her hand, the simple caress drawing her eye as the power of it took over her senses. 'I thought I might be able to sneak that under the radar.'

She laughed, the sound high and giddy as she read the reasoning behind his words and couldn't quite believe it. 'As much as I'd love to, I'm working a half day tomorrow…'

'On a Saturday?'

'The hotel doesn't stop just because it's the weekend.'

'Of course.'

'I can get away about two though, if that works for you? Here, take this…' She pulled away to rummage through her bag and took out a scrap of paper and a pen. She quickly wrote down her number and passed it to him. 'Just in case you change your mind, or something comes up.'

He took hold of it, their fingers lightly brushing and neither moving away.

'It would take a sudden blizzard to stop us going out with you, Sophia.'

She found herself tongue-tied and getting drawn into his steely grey eyes that seemed to mirror everything she was feeling. No matter how fantastical that idea was.

'But, luckily for us,' he said, the husky edge to his voice impossible to ignore now, 'we're all in the same building, so not even that excuse will hold.'

She smiled softly. 'So true.'

'I'll meet you in the foyer then? Just after two?'

She nodded.

'See you then, Sophia.'

'Goodnight, Jack.'

His smile was slow as he leaned back into his seat, taking her number with him. ''Night, Sphea.'

She grinned at Lily's name for her and shook her head, sliding out of the car and thanking his driver too.

She was still smiling as she walked through the foyer, up the flights of stairs and unlocked the door to her apartment. Still smiling ten minutes later when she had a cup of hot cocoa wrapped in her hands and breathed in its rich, comforting scent. And even when she climbed into bed, her mind awash with thoughts of him, her body too alive to sleep.

She'd been worried about the past creeping back in, bringing the sadness with it, but with Jack on her mind there was no room for it.

It wasn't a long-term fix, but she could certainly make the most of it…for now.

CHAPTER SIX

'ARE YOU SURE she's definitely coming, Daddy?'

Jack smiled down at his daughter and retied her tartan scarf for the umpteenth time. 'Definitely—she's just finishing up and then she'll be with us.'

'I hope so.' She looked to the row of wellies at her feet. 'I think we should have bought different colours *and* sizes. What if she doesn't like red?'

'How can she not like red when it's the colour of...' His words fell away as he glanced over his daughter's head to see Sophia enter the hotel foyer, her smile lighting him up inside. She'd changed out of her workwear into jeans and a winter coat ready for their outing, its deep red colour setting off both her hair and her eyes. Stunning didn't even come close. 'Looks like you can ask her yourself, kiddo.'

Lily spun on her heel and gave a little squeal of delight as she ran straight up to her, her dark curls bouncing around her shoulders and her scarf trailing behind once again. 'Sphea!'

Sophia dropped to her haunches, her arms outstretched ready to take the cuddle Lily was reaching out for. She squeezed his little girl to her, her eyes lifting to find him over Lily's shoulder and he felt himself grin. She had only been in Lily's life a couple of days but it seemed like more; he felt something shift inside of him. Something he couldn't latch onto or understand. Then her gaze fell to the row of wellies at his feet and her amused frown tickled him into a laugh.

'We bought you something,' Lily said as Sophia fixed her scarf for her.

'You did?'

Lily nodded and took Sophia's hand as she straightened up. 'Come see.'

She started to drag her along and Sophia looked from Lily to him and back down to the wellies again.

'We went for a few different sizes,' he said, 'but hopefully one of these pairs will fit.'

'You bought me *wellies*?' Her blue eyes sparkled as she looked up at him, her glossy pink lips stretching wide. 'I don't think anyone has bought me wellies before, not since I was a child at any rate.'

'Well, it's not a blizzard out there,' he said, recalling their conversation the night before, 'but it's certainly been raining cats and dogs.'

'Cats and dogs?' Lily frowned. 'That makes no sense, Daddy.'

Sophia laughed. 'You're right, it doesn't, but I still can't believe you've bought me wellies.'

'Well, Daddy said you like muddy puddles too.'

'Did he now?'

He gave a shrug. 'It may have come up in conversation.'

'You need to try them on, Sphea, then Daddy can ask Alice to take the others back.'

'Alice?'

'My PA and general life organiser.'

She smiled. 'You really shouldn't have.'

'Technically, I didn't.'

She shook her head, her eyes wide with some unknown thought, and then she looked at the wellies and to Lily. 'Do you have a size six there?'

'I'll find it,' his daughter declared, pulling out the right pair quicker than he could even say anything.

Not that he knew what to say because every phrase that entered his head seemed too inappropriate and...*gushy*. It was a word he had never used, let alone attributed to himself. And he could be neither of those things, particularly in front of Lily. But he wanted to tell her how lovely she looked, how much they'd been looking forward to this outing, how much—

Stop, just stop.

'Here you go…' Lily lifted the pair of shiny red wellies high above her head. 'The colour matches your hair and Daddy got me a matching pair too!'

'Thank you.' Sophia smiled down at her, her expression so unguarded with affection for Lily. He could be excused for getting wrapped up in that same look, surely. It had nothing to do with him softening towards her, nothing whatsoever.

He'd hardly been soft with Elena, hardly let such emotion in at all until he'd first held Lily in his arms.

'I'll just go and put my shoes away.'

She turned to leave and Lily grabbed her hand. 'Wait!'

Lily bent low and picked up a small bag, offering it out. 'Daddy got you welly socks too!'

'He did?' Sophia's brow lifted, her eyes widening further on another laugh. 'How thoughtful…'

'Sorry if it's too much…' he started but she shook her head.

'No, not at all. I won't be long.'

She was still shaking her head as she returned, her eyes dancing bright and blue as she pulled a knitted beige bobble hat from her pocket and slid it on. 'Let's go before those ominous grey clouds return.'

'Higher, Daddy, higher!' Lily squealed as Jack pushed her on the swing and Sophia watched on.

The play park was relatively quiet—people avoiding the wet equipment, she supposed—but it meant Lily could hop from one thing to the next, no jostling for best position, and she was keeping them both on their toes as she rushed about.

They'd done jumping in puddles, they'd done ice cream in the freezing cold, and they'd made themselves sick on the roundabout and enjoyed the grown-up slide, which had produced waves worthy of a log flume, much to Lily's delight, not so much Jack's. He'd managed to get a shower of it to the face as he waited for her at the bottom, something which had evoked fits of giggles from both Lily and Sophia, and no matter how he'd frowned at them they couldn't quit it.

Even now, Sophia was still grinning and laughing, her cheeks and belly aching from the effort.

It was such a perfect afternoon, perfect and so different to how she'd spent the previous weekend and the weekend before that. Memories of Amy haunted her as they always did this time of year but it was so nice to be out in the fresh air and not be worrying, not be anxious.

She'd known Jack would prove to be a distraction and though she knew he and his daughter were a fleeting presence in her life she couldn't stop herself from taking pleasure in every second.

'Hey, Soph, what are you doing here?'

Oh, God.

She turned to see Samantha, her friend and next-door neighbour, heading towards her, her son Noah scooting along in front, and she felt her cheeks flush.

'Hi, guys!'

She could sense both Jack and Lily watching her and her smile felt forced, her voice too. It was one thing enjoying her time with the McGregors, but it was another to merge her fantasy life with the real.

She embraced Samantha and gave her a kiss to the cheek, ruffling Noah's hair too. 'You've come to enjoy the park?'

'Yeah,' Noah said, his blond hair escaping from beneath his knitted beanie so like his mum's; his grin was wide and showed off the gap in his front teeth.

'Gotta get out while the sun is shining,' Samantha added,

her head tilted towards the swings, her eyes wide and gesturing. It was obvious Sophia was with them. Why else would she be standing there watching them like some oddball? She was going to have to introduce them; the alternative was even more awkward. She only had herself to blame too—bringing them to this park, her local park.

She brushed her hands down her coat and took a breath, looking over to Jack and Lily, who were clearly waiting on her to say something. Jack looked mildly curious but Lily looked strangely apprehensive.

'Jack, Lily, come and meet my friends...' she called out, trying to relax her smile and her voice, both of which were supremely difficult with Sam making goo-goo eyes at a grinning Jack. Sophia nudged her subtly in the side, saying between her teeth, 'You're married.'

'Nothing wrong with looking, Soph,' she returned under her breath.

Lily hopped off the swing with a leap but soon shied away behind the legs of her father as they approached, her usual confidence non-existent.

'This is my friend, Samantha, and her son, Noah.'

'Nice to meet you, Samantha.'

Jack held out his hand and her friend was quick to shake it.

'Oh, Sam, please.'

Her friend giggled and the sound had Sophia's cheeks flushing deeper, even more so when Sam's eyes flitted from Jack to Sophia and back again. She was so in for it next time Sam had her alone.

'Jack is a guest at my hotel.'

'A guest, you say?' Sam's voice was drawn out with various other possibilities running rife through her gossip-charged brain.

'Yes,' Jack confirmed as Sophia's brain screamed at her

friend to quit whatever she was thinking. 'My Lily has taken quite a shine to her.'

And speaking of Lily, the girl was still hiding behind Jack's legs. Sophia ignored her internal panic and crouched down to the girl's level, wishing to put her at ease. 'Hey, Lily, you and Noah are the same age, you know.'

She edged out just enough to look at Noah beneath her lashes.

'Hi, Lily.' Noah grinned at her, all confident and a total contrast to the shrinking violet Lily had become. 'When's your birthday?'

'The twenty-eighth of February.'

'Oh, cool. Mine's next weekend. You having a party?'

She looked up at her father and Sophia caught the faint grimace on his face.

'I don't know,' she said, her eyes back on Noah.

'Do you want a go on my scooter?' He pushed it out towards her. 'I can show you some tricks if you like?'

She bit her lip and looked from Jack to Sophia, before looking back to Noah. 'I don't think I'd be very good on one.'

'Why not?'

'I've never been on a scooter before.'

Noah's brows disappeared into his hat. 'You're kidding, right?'

Lily turned the colour of her wellies. 'No.'

'Come on, there's a ramp over there—I can show you some moves. Don't worry, I won't make you do it too, not unless you want to… I can help you, if you like?'

'Go easy, Noah, love.' Samantha rested her hand on her son's shoulder. 'Lily's only just met you.'

Noah shrugged, his grin wide and widening further when Lily smiled at him.

'I'd like that.'

'Cool!'

'So long as you have the time, Sam?' Sophia asked her

friend, half wishing Sam had some place else to be, because this felt too real, as if Jack could really belong in her world if she let him in.

'Sure we do. Dan's had to pop into the office, a last-minute hiccup with a high profile project; you know that kind of thing.' She rolled her eyes dramatically. 'Best he gets it sorted and then we can at least enjoy tomorrow in peace.'

'Great—thanks, Mum. Come on, Lil!'

Noah started scooting away and Lily looked to her father and then to Sophia. She was nervous, unsure of herself, and Sophia's heart ached for her.

'Noah's good fun, Lily, you'll see,' she encouraged her softly. 'Go on, we're coming too.'

The little girl started off in his direction, glancing back over her shoulder twice just to be sure they followed and then she was fully focused on Noah as he whooped his way around the ramps, her shyness gradually falling away as he called out to her and involved her.

It was strange to see Lily stripped of her confidence. She glanced at Jack as they followed them across the park and though he watched his daughter there was no indication he thought anything amiss...unless she recalled the grimace he'd given when the birthday party had been mentioned.

Sophia would hazard a guess that the answer to the birthday party question was a no. No party. No celebration with kids of her own age. And though she knew he meant well, would he see that Lily was actually missing out on things that were considered a normal part of growing up?

A real childhood, with playdates, friends, fun and laughter.

She didn't doubt how happy Lily was with her father, but she couldn't ignore the fact that the little girl was missing out on playing with children her own age. Her shyness with Noah a sad result of it.

'So how long are you staying for then, Jack?'

Sophia pulled herself out of her thoughts at Samantha's conversation starter. She needed to keep her wits about her. She wouldn't put it past her friend to say something completely inappropriate that would have Jack wishing for the ground to open up and swallow him whole. Or, worse, running in the opposite direction and taking his dear, sweet Lily with him.

It was an outcome she should perhaps be grateful for, but it wasn't gratitude that made her chest ache at the idea.

The Italian Jack had chosen for dinner that evening was bustling, but his request to add two to the reservation had only resulted in a twenty-minute delay and the kids had decided the extra time would be perfect for sampling milkshakes at the bar.

Even now they were thick as thieves, laughing about something as they sucked on their straws, barely coming up for air. Quite a change from the Lily who had hidden behind his legs at the park…

'This really is very kind of you both, letting us gatecrash like this,' Samantha was saying. 'I think Noah had resigned himself to a day with just me and him.'

'Nothing wrong with that,' Sophia told her. 'Mother-and-son time is awesome too.'

Samantha twirled her straw in the mojito she'd opted for, her face losing some of its exuberance. 'I'm not so sure. Not when it's becoming routine that Dan has to work Saturday and miss out on his footie practice.' She gave a little sigh but then smiled. 'Still, he's promised to make up for it tomorrow and that's better than not at all.'

'Well, his loss is our gain,' Sophia said, gently shoulder barging her friend. 'And in the meantime you get to enjoy our scintillating company and pizza.'

'That's true.' Samantha gave her a grin and looked back to the two kids who sat opposite each other, leaning forward so that their heads were practically glued together as they talked. 'I think Noah's certainly found a firm friend there; just a shame you're not stopping longer, Jack.'

He felt that same weird tightness in his chest, a sense that the sand was flowing too quickly through the hourglass, but he masked it all with a smile. 'We'll be back in London at some point… We'll have to keep in touch.'

He looked to Sophia. Would they keep in touch too? And what did he really hope to achieve by doing that?

'Mum!' Noah suddenly turned to them. 'Can Lily come to my party on Saturday?'

Samantha looked to Jack. 'She's more than welcome. He's just having a few friends over to play some party games and eat far too many E numbers to count.'

'She's not lying about the E numbers,' Sophia warned him. 'Choose wisely.'

He laughed as Lily pleaded, '*Please*, Daddy!'

'Okay, okay, I don't see why not.'

Sophia and Samantha both smiled at him.

'What can I say—she has me wrapped around her little finger.'

'Nothing wrong with that, Jack,' Samantha said, nodding her approval.

'No, nothing at all.' Sophia's voice had a softness to it, kind of wistful. He caught her eye and she quickly shifted her attention to Samantha and party preparations, food and things that Jack really knew little about.

He *was* a good father now. He knew he was—he put Lily first in everything. But party planning, kids' get-togethers, games…there he was lacking.

And did that mean Lily was too?

He spent the rest of the meal listening to both sides of the table, mentally taking notes and accepting that perhaps it was time for a change. He just had no idea where to start.

He was still pondering it long after they'd taken Sam and

Noah home, Sophia heading back to the hotel with them, thanks to a pleading Lily who wanted a bedtime story. Not from him, but from her.

The alarm bells were starting to ring in earnest. How long could they keep up the association before Lily became attached? And if she did become attached, what did that mean for the future?

He approached Lily's door, his bare feet quiet on the marble floor, and listened. He could hear Sophia's soft, dulcet tones as she read from Lily's latest book, felt the soothing effect of her voice over himself too and he no longer questioned his daughter's choice. Given the option, he'd opt for Sophia to read to him too.

He reached the gap in the door and stilled; his heart caught in his chest. Sophia was in his place, fulfilling the role he had done almost every night for the last three years. She was lying on Lily's bed, her arm hooked around Lily, Baby Bear tucked between them as she read.

He dropped back a little, wanting to remain inconspicuous, wanting nothing to disturb the perfect scene before him. He could see Lily was drifting off, her eyes slowly closing before snapping wide again. She was doing her best to stay awake, but tiredness was winning out. And Sophia was doting on her. Every now and then she'd nuzzle into Lily and place a kiss to her brow, stroke her hair or brush it from her eyes. They looked so perfect together, so…normal.

He told himself it was because he wasn't used to it. That it had been so long since he'd witnessed anyone else in this role.

He told himself it had nothing to do with his feelings towards Sophia.

He also told himself he was a liar.

He settled against the doorframe and just watched, a slight smile lifting his lips as he let the vision work its magic over him. He couldn't deny that a part of him wished this was the norm. That Lily had a mother and he had a wife, and all was merry and bright.

Only he knew the truth of it. Life wasn't like that. It wasn't all roses and happily ever afters.

He worked hard to be able to provide for his daughter; he worked hard to ensure that money was never an obstacle, but he couldn't control life outside of that.

And he couldn't control his heart either. He wasn't capable of loving another like they deserved to be loved. He could love Lily, he could be there for Lily, but over and above that…no.

He'd tried once with Elena and failed.

He'd witnessed too many failed marriages before that too, lived with too many messed-up kids who were the unlucky result of such marriages and he had no interest in exposing Lily to that kind of life. It was safer just the two of them; there was less that could go wrong, fewer variables at play.

And now you sound like you're talking about a business deal…

But then he had a head for business. He'd promised Elena, sworn on her dead body, that he would do everything to make amends for what he'd done. That he would keep Lily safe, he would love her and cherish her, and be there for her. He had no room in his life for more, for someone as beautiful and enchanting as the woman now cuddling his sleeping child in her arms.

A weight settled in his gut as he pushed himself off the doorframe and made his presence known, realising as Sophia caught his eye that, regardless of his promise and all that he had sworn to live by, a small part of him wished things could be different.

It was the same part that wasn't ready to let Sophia out of their lives just yet.

'Hi,' he whispered.

'Has she gone?'

He nodded, his smile filled with the warmth persisting in spite of his mental turmoil. 'I'll help you.'

He crossed the room and leaned over the bed, lifting Lily's heavy head from Sophia's arm so that she could slip out. He laid his daughter back down and Sophia pulled the quilt higher up her body, tucking it beneath her chin. He leaned in to kiss his daughter's head and ended up being head to head with Sophia as she'd gone to do the same. Their eyes collided and in that one look he saw so much, felt so much deep inside.

His eyes fell to her lips, the urge to kiss her so natural and strong that he was lucky she pulled back, lucky she'd seen sense where he couldn't.

He kissed his daughter's forehead and straightened up, reminding himself of the promises he'd made and why.

Only the reasoning was starting to feel woolly, less reasonable...bordering on monastic even.

Sophia padded out of the room, a move he sensed rather than saw as his eyes were fixed on his daughter, his mind focused on the reasoning that had always seemed so solid.

He already felt so much for Sophia, so much that he could hardly get a handle on it, and though he was sure it had a lot to do with Lily's feelings for her, it didn't help.

Maybe they just needed to agree on expectations now to avoid any future confusion. Set some ground rules even. Chaos at work was the result of mismanagement, so maybe he just needed to lay down the law in his personal life and protect both Lily and Sophia.

Who was he kidding? He wanted to protect himself too.

It had been harrowing losing Elena, a woman for whom he'd cared deeply but hadn't loved as she'd wanted, as she'd deserved. He was convinced he was wired wrong, that being stuck in the system for so long had screwed him up emotionally. Even Elena had thrown as much at him on many occasions; virtually every fight had come down to his inability to care, to think of her enough, to empathise.

And he'd come to believe she was right, but now he wasn't so sure. Whatever Sophia sparked in him, it was new and it was different, and it scared him half to death.

But not enough to run the other way...

CHAPTER SEVEN

'YOU REALLY ARE a natural.'

Sophia looked up at the sound of Jack's voice and felt her cheeks colour, as if she'd been caught doing something she shouldn't. But she was only guilty of curling up on the L-shaped sofa that dominated the living area in his penthouse suite.

This wasn't her domain though. As much as she knew this suite like she knew her own home, she didn't belong, not like this.

But she felt as if she did.

She'd felt it when she'd been lying next to Lily, reading her the story. She'd felt it all day as they'd laughed and joked and enjoyed the company of her friends. And she felt it now... It was only the rational side of her brain telling her it was all still fantasy.

'A natural?' She cocked a brow and let her eyes fall to the empty glasses hooked in his fingers and the bottle of red he carried—the very rare bottle of red that would have been pulled out of the cellar especially. *Definitely* all fantasy.

He offered her a glass and she took it, wetting her lips. She shouldn't be taking it; she shouldn't be letting this evening continue now Lily was asleep. But the sound of the deep red liquid hitting the glass told her otherwise. Her tummy fluttered with a mixture of nerves and desire...

But she did want to talk to him about Lily, and it was as good a reason as any to stay longer.

Still, she wasn't fool enough to think it was her only reason.

'You're a natural with kids, with Lily,' he explained as he poured his own glass and set the bottle down on the large glass coffee table. 'You looked completely at home reading her a story.'

He joined her on the sofa—not close enough that she could feel the sofa dip but close enough that her entire body came alive with awareness of his.

She took a sip of the wine and used its soothing warmth to unblock her throat and calm the flutters taking off inside. She felt unbearably hot and cursed her own stupidity for lighting the gas fire that ran along one wall. She hadn't been able to resist it though; it was her favourite feature in the immense suite, that and the view. And she had been cold before his arrival, cold and on edge about the tough conversation she wanted to have and no idea how to broach it.

'I used to read to my sister,' she murmured, her eyes lost in the flames as she divulged an honest piece of herself and remembered happier times.

'Mum and Dad worked long hours so I'd often take over the bedtime routine—bath, teeth, bed and book.' She risked a glance his way and became transfixed. The grey of his eyes, warmed by the glow of the fire, shone as the pulse in his jaw ticked, his face oddly tense.

She wet her lips. 'Sorry to take your place tonight.'

He shook his head. 'You think that worries me?'

His voice was husky, laced with some emotion that she couldn't quite place. No, she could; she just didn't want to because it suggested he cared and the idea of that only led them down a scary, unknown path.

She smiled tentatively and gave a small shrug. 'I'm not sure.'

He took a breath, his eyes falling to his glass. 'No, it's nice that she wants you to read to her. What…' His eyes came back to her, soft, concerned. 'What bothers me is your relationship with your family. You miss them.'

She was so surprised by his turn in focus that she

didn't know how to react, let alone what to say. She shook her head.

'You do, Sophia; it's written in your face when you talk of them. You're so haunted by her loss that you'd rather avoid them than try to forge a relationship of any sort.' He paused, his eyes scanning her face. 'I know I shouldn't compare, but it would kill me to lose touch with Lily, and I think it's slowly eating away at you too.'

'Yes, but I don't know how to fix things. I don't even know where to begin...'

'You just need to be honest with them, talk to them. Yes, it'll be different to how it was, but a new relationship is better than none. And you need to do it while you still can, while they're still around.' He shifted closer, adding quietly, 'We both know how short life can be.'

She took a shaky breath. She knew he was right, knew it and yet she hadn't been able to make that first move. And her parents... Well, they'd given up making the first move long ago.

'It wasn't your fault, Sophia.'

His voice rasped with emotion, its rough edge working over her body like a caress and a hug in one. She felt the spike of tears, felt her throat close and tried to swallow, but it was no use; they were coming and there was nothing she could do about it.

This wasn't what she wanted. She wanted to talk about Lily; she wanted to make him realise that his daughter needed to be around other children, not have some ad hoc therapy session with the man she could so easily fall for... fall for and never have...

She pressed her trembling fingers to her lips and tried to nod her head in response, to let him know his words had hit home. She felt his arm slip behind her, the warmth of his body as they came together, and she didn't know whether she leaned in or if he'd moved, but she was in his arms, her head tucked beneath his, her body shaking as she let go.

'She was in my care though; she was my responsibility.'

'And you were no more than a child yourself.'

'I was old enough to take care of her and…and…' She couldn't finish it; the tears were too much, the sob shuddering up through her. 'I'm sorry.'

'Please, you don't need to be strong with me, Soph. It's okay to let go.'

She gave a scoff. Strong? It was hardly how she saw herself.

He leaned away to place his glass on the side, came back to take hers next and then his arms were around her and she couldn't pull away. She was too comfortable, too soothed, too lost in his scent and inviting warmth.

'I'm sorry I've upset you, but I couldn't let you leave tonight without saying something. Blame it on me being a father: Lily will never know her mother. Yes, she has a picture by her bed. Yes, I talk about her, what she liked, what they did together…but she'll never have real memories of her, she'll never know her for herself. She has me and I'll do all I can to be enough.'

I'll do all I can to be enough…

She took a deep breath, his words hitting so close to what she wanted to discuss that she needed to regain her control, to make him see.

'You're a good father.'

He gave a gentle laugh, the move making her head lift against his chest.

'You *are*…' she insisted.

'But? Why do I sense there's going to be a but?'

She pressed herself off his chest to look at him, needing him to see that what came next wasn't designed to hurt him or criticise him; she just wanted him to see the truth. 'But Lily needs more than just you.'

His eyes narrowed as his body tensed beneath her fingers. 'Look, Sophia, I know things between us...between us are... I don't know what they are...but I have no place in my life for a woman, for a rel—'

'That's not what I meant,' she choked out, shuffling back on the sofa as she swept her fingers over her damp cheeks and felt them burn and pale in an instant.

'It isn't?'

She shook her head, wondering how he could look disappointed as well as flummoxed when he'd been midway through lecturing her on how they could never be. She knew that well enough on her own. The last thing she needed was to hear him state it in black and white.

He raked his fingers through his hair and blew out a breath. 'Of course. Sorry, I just assumed.'

'Well, you can take your assumption and shove it where—' She pursed her lips tight, her eyes wide in horror at her own outburst. She couldn't remember the last time she'd lost it quite so badly, but then she couldn't remember ever being as embarrassed as she was right now. 'Just because you're used to women willing to hop into bed with you doesn't mean you can count me amongst them.'

Well...he could but he would never know that.

'Is that really what you think?'

'It's not what I think; it's what I know. I'm not about to follow suit.'

'I wasn't referring to *your* lack of desire for me.'

Oh, God, even the word *desire* from his lips had the heat pooling in her lower belly. She straightened her spine, lifted her chin. 'No?'

'No, I was referring to the fact you think women in general are—how did you phrase it?—*willing to hop into bed* with me?'

She could feel her cheeks re-colouring, the warmth whipping through her limbs. This was dangerous territory and so far from the conversation she actually wanted to have.

'If that truly is what you think…' he murmured, low, teasing, his eyes probing hers and reading far too much; he was too near, his body still too close despite the distance she had created '…I find it interesting that you declare yourself…immune.'

Immune!

She was so far from immune it was laughable. And now wasn't the time to laugh. Now was the time to run. But not until she'd spoken to him about Lily.

'So…are you, Sophia?'

'Am I what?' she said, breathless, unblinking, immobile.

'Are you immune to me?'

Jack raked his eyes over her. From her over-bright eyes, drowned out by her pupils, the freed strands of her auburn hair framing her flushed cheeks, her lips parted with the denial she couldn't quite utter. To her soft woollen jumper and denim-clad legs curled beneath her upon the sofa and hiding her fluffy-socked feet—socks *he* had bought her, a first—and *never* had he desired a woman more.

He didn't need skimpy lingerie, fancy dresses, heels, or make-up. He simply needed her. Like this: honest, vulnerable, open. He was captivated. And it meant he should be ending this conversation, not encouraging it.

But could he let it go…?

'Are you, Sophia?' *No, he couldn't.*

She wet her lips. 'You can't ask me that.'

Even her voice turned him on, her words emerging all breathy and heated.

'I think it's good to know where we stand.'

She wet her lips again and his restraint almost snapped. He wanted to taste those lips, wanted to hear her confess that she wanted him, that she wanted him like he did her.

'It doesn't matter whether I want you; in a week you will be gone and that will be that.'

'Be that as it may, it doesn't mean we have to deny it.'

Her eyes flared and his entire body tingled with the need to reach for her. To stroke her cheeks, feel their heat beneath his palms, feel that pulse point at her throat tick beneath his fingertips. He reached for his glass, desperate, needing to keep his hands busy, needing to take a second.

As he drank his wine she watched him, the air fizzing with the unspoken and all the things they could be doing. Her body was so still that if it wasn't for the faint sound of her breathing, the movement of her chest, he'd think she'd turned to stone.

'What are you saying, Jack?'

Her question was as quiet as his glass touching down on the polished surface and as he leaned back he turned into her, close enough that their knees brushed. He didn't miss her sudden intake of breath as the contact zipped through her, just as it did him.

'I'm saying that I want you, Sophia.'

'Jack...' another whisper, accompanied by the tiny shake of her head '...we can't. You even said it just now.'

'I said I didn't have time or, rather, the place in my life for a relationship,' he expanded. 'And the truth is I could never be the man for you, Sophia. You deserve to be loved.' His eyes lingered over her face, taking in all that he had come to...come to what? Come to feel something for? To desire? *No*. It wasn't all desire, but it couldn't be what she would want it to be, what she would need. 'You deserve to be put on a pedestal and adored by a man worthy of you and, as much as I would like to be that man, I know I'm not.'

'How can you know that?'

'Because I've been married, I've been loved and...' He shook his head, the sadness overwhelming. How could he tell her that he hadn't been able to love Elena back in the way that she deserved? Lily's mother, of all people. How could he tell Sophia the cold-hearted truth of how he'd failed her?

'I know I could never take Elena's place,' she said and he could see his own sadness reflected back at him. 'I wouldn't want to.'

'You don't understand, Sophia.'

'What don't I understand?'

'I never *loved* Elena.' His chest tightened, his heart crushed within it, and he saw the second his words hit home, the sudden change to her pallor, the tremble to her lips. 'Not in that way.'

'Of course you did. You looked out for her, you worked hard to make a life for you both, you made Lily, you married her...' She floundered, refusing to accept it.

'I cared for her deeply and I wanted to protect her. I wanted to save her from the life we'd found ourselves in. But I wasn't *in* love with her. I couldn't return her love in the same all-consuming way she loved me. I was devastated when she died—devastated that she'd been taken so young, that she would never see our daughter grow up, that she had died miserable and alone because of me.'

The guilt clawed at him now, the chill pushing out the illicit heat of seconds before.

'I'm sure that's not true.'

'It is.' He hardened his voice and his stance now. 'I'm not a good man, Sophia. I'm not a man you can fall in love with, I'm not a man you should invest your time in. I love that you have brought so much joy to Lily, that she's had this time with you and your friends. But you and I, we can never have a future.'

'You *are* a good man, Jack,' she whispered. 'I know we can't have a future; I understand that. I'd be a fool to think otherwise. But all these things you're saying to me, they're not true. I can't believe them—I won't.'

'Elena did. She believed them through and through, and

she would know. She knew me for fourteen years and the last words I had from her were thrown at my answerphone. If I hadn't deleted them I could play them for you now, then maybe you'd believe me.'

She shook her head, the tears returning to her eyes and he knew they were born of sympathy, of pity, and he deserved neither.

'She called me a cold, heartless bastard, and said that if I loved my work so much I could forget coming home, that night or any other for that matter.'

She flung her hand to her lips, but her gasp beneath her fingers was still audible, the shake of her head more severe. 'You can't believe that...you can't.'

'Oh, I believe it all right. If not for the accident, if she hadn't died, she would have left eventually.' He threw back more wine and felt the bitterness, the sadness crawling through him. 'Because she was right. I didn't deserve her. I didn't deserve either of them, and then fate played its hand...' He shook his head. 'Elena never deserved that.'

His body shook, his lungs struggling to take in air. He hadn't cried. Not even when the news had been delivered. Not even that first night back in the empty house when he'd cleared away the untouched dinner. Not even at the funeral. It had all been confirmation that Elena was right. He had no heart and he was incapable of love, bar that which he felt for his daughter.

He was so lost in the rising grief he didn't sense Sophia move, not until her arms were wrapped around him offering the comfort he had so willingly offered her when she'd spoken of her sister. But she deserved it. He didn't.

He pushed himself up off the sofa and out of her hold. He raked his hand over his face and clenched his jaw as he fought back the wave of tears. *Tears!*

'I don't deserve your comfort or your sympathy, Sophia,' he bit out. 'She was right. I didn't love her, but I do love

Lily and I will do right by my daughter. I will always do right by her. Outside of that…' he looked down at her, his eyes pleading with her to see the truth '…I can't.'

She stood up slowly, her eyes not leaving his. 'I'm not asking you to give me anything, Jack. No promises, nothing.'

He could believe her as he looked into her eyes and saw her sincerity for what it was. She reached up her hands and cupped his jaw, soft and soothing.

'Truth is, Jack, I've never wanted a man, never wanted to kiss a man, not like I do you.'

'And you shouldn't.'

'But I do…' Her eyes lowered to his mouth and returned twice as fierce, twice as needy. 'I want you to kiss me, Jack.'

'But I—'

'I don't want more…' She stroked one hand back, her fingers tantalisingly soft in his hair. 'I want to be there for you now, in this second. I want you to realise you are worthy of more than you know, I want…'

Her lips brushed over his, finishing the sentence for her, and he couldn't hold back any more. He wrapped his arms around her, pulling her tightly to him. His head slanted to take more of her kiss, to swallow up the blissful moan she released, his own groan just as powerful, just as needy.

He couldn't remember ever feeling more alive, more out of control. It was heady, intense, scary. He dragged his mouth away, her name leaving him on a pained whisper, and then he kissed her harder, his hold tighter. He needed her to be sure, to know what she was taking on.

'Please, Jack, I want this.'

He found her lips again, his tongue feasting inside, teasing at her own. He felt the shiver that ran down her spine beneath his fingers, felt the way she curved her hips against him, and he didn't doubt her, not for a second.

'Even if we only do this once,' she said against his mouth, 'I want you to be my first.'

My first…

He jumped back as though burned, dragging in a lungful of air.

She was a *virgin*.

Their conversation over dinner that first time… She'd never, not once…?

He'd been Elena's one and only. To be Sophia's too… His gut lurched as he spun away from all her flushed glory. How could he?

Because you're a cold, heartless bastard, that's how.

'You need to go, Sophia.'

'But… Jack?'

'Now, Sophia, just go!'

Before I pull you back to me and take all that you are offering without a backward glance.

Before I ruin what's left of my soul and yours with it.

Before history repeats itself and this time Lily will witness it all and realise what a failure her father truly is.

There was silence behind him. She hadn't moved and this time he looked at her, projecting all the hardness and self-loathing he could. 'Please, just go.'

She blinked once, twice, then shook her head and scrubbed her heated cheeks. 'You know what, Jack, maybe Elena was right. You have no heart, none at all.'

And then she was gone, her words pulling him apart inside. It was all he deserved and more.

But it didn't make it easier to bear. It didn't stop him wanting to run after her and plead for her forgiveness, to wish that life could be different, that he could be different.

He picked up his wine glass and necked the remainder before pouring another. He stared into the ruby-red liquid as though it possessed all the answers and felt the cold settle around him, inside him.

He was alone, very much alone, and he'd never felt more so.

CHAPTER EIGHT

Sophia was avoiding him. He knew it and she knew it.

She'd managed to prevent any chance meeting in the foyer all week by avoiding it all together. She'd not returned any of the missed calls and messages he'd left and the closest they'd got to any interaction had been a note she'd left at Reception for him with the details for Noah's party. Today's party.

Heaven help her...

If only she could have backed out of going, feigned illness, or told Jack that he wasn't welcome. But she couldn't lie, and she wouldn't let her messed-up love life get in the way of Lily enjoying this time with the other kids.

She stared at Sam's inviting lilac door with its ornate yellow frame just like the one out of *Friends* and took a deep breath. It would be fine. There would be no scene, not in front of the children, and with any luck he would have dropped Lily off and fled.

All perfectly fine.

She rapped her knuckles on the door and tried to stop the near constant playback from starting up again in her brain.

With the devastating realisation that he was more tormented by Elena's death than she had ever thought possible came the fact that she cared more than she should. That even though they'd barely met, she'd already been reeled in so completely. And though he claimed he was incapable of having one, he was suffering with a broken heart. One that had been well and truly trodden on by the words Elena had thrown at him in a fit of anger.

And she didn't blame the poor woman. She'd learned enough from Jack to understand the kind of man he was.

She knew work would have filled his days and most likely his nights too. But he had done it because he cared, because he *did* have a heart, and he absolutely *did* love.

She also knew she had to apologise to him. She'd lashed out, her words callous and unkind, but then she'd not been thinking clearly. She'd been so hurt by his rejection, embarrassed by her confession that she wanted him to be her first, only to have him reject her. It had crushed her. Made her feel foolish and stupid.

It wasn't until she'd slept on it and replayed it all that she'd understood he'd done it out of concern for her; he'd done it out of the goodness of his heart, not the lack of one.

She shuddered even now as she remembered the whole scene, wishing she'd never divulged that secret. It hadn't been easy to tell him the first time around, and having him label her as too naïve, too innocent to be...to be what? *Defiled* by him.

Maybe if she hadn't been so honest things would be different now. Maybe they'd have made love all night and every night since. Maybe they'd have made a pact to spend every spare private moment together, entwined like the images her dreams taunted her with.

She felt her cheeks colour and her body respond to the idea, and of course the door was opened at that precise moment.

'Sam, I'm so sorry— *Jack!*'

She squeaked and gulped, the sight of the man before her colliding with the naked one still rampant in her heated thoughts.

'Hi...sorry. Samantha has her hands full with the rabble so I said I would get it.'

'You did?' she blurted.

'I figured it would be you since everyone else is here. The kids that is; all the parents have dropped and run.'

'And you didn't want to do the same?' *Oh, please, why couldn't you have done the same...?*

'No, I'm not one for just leaving her places.' His frown told her he thought she was crazy to even suggest it. 'She's either with me or the people I employ to take care of her.'

'You're kidding, right?'

His frown deepened. He was just as incredulous as her and she realised too late the error of her words. Of course he wouldn't entrust Lily's care to just anyone. Samantha hadn't earned his trust and neither had she. And it stung, overtaking her thoughts of an apology, the things she had wanted to take back from the other night, replacing it with more anger, more hurt.

'Well, for your information, Jack,' she bit out, 'Lily *is* safe with us, regardless of what you might think to the contrary. Now, if you'll just excuse me...'

She needed to get out of his company before she did something she'd regret, like say something else that she'd need to take back once she'd calmed down. She lifted Noah's present to her chest, an extra barrier between him and her, and made to go past him but he reached out, his hand gentle on her arm.

'Hang on one sec...please.'

She looked down the hallway to the crack in the door through which she could see the kids playing and hear their excited chatter as they talked over one another and the music that played in the background.

'What is it, Jack? I'm late enough as it is.'

'I didn't just stay for Lily, Sophia.' His voice was soft, ardent, and she could feel her resolve wavering as her gaze met with the warming sincerity of his. 'I wanted to see you.'

She wet her lips. 'You did?'

'I've been trying to all week but...'

She looked away, her cheeks pinking up. 'I know, I just—I just wasn't ready to see you again.'

'I understand that, but I wanted to apologise.'

'Apologise?' She frowned at him. 'Why?'

'Because I shouldn't have backed you into a corner.'

'You didn't—'

'Let me finish. I wasn't fair on you. I just wanted you to understand why.'

'Why what?'

'Why there could never be an us.'

She started to shake her head.

'I didn't do a good job of it,' he continued. 'Of any of it. I didn't want to push you away, but I felt I had to, for your own good, not for mine. Do you understand?'

Understand? Her eyes flared and her body stilled. Of all the patronising, chauvinistic, belittling... She dragged in a breath.

'I understand *perfectly.*' Her eyes darted between the empty outer hallway and the bustling room ahead, wanting no one to hear what came next as she poked him in the chest. 'You used my V plates as reason to reject me. You think I'm not woman enough to take what you're willing to offer and walk away in one piece. Well, I'll have you know, Mr Up-Your-Own-Behind McGregor, I am a woman who knows her own mind, and when I say I want you I mean it.'

His eyes widened with every word, his mouth parting. She'd shocked him. Good.

But now she couldn't tear her eyes from those lips, those tantalisingly full and extremely kissable lips, because now she knew how they felt and could remember every last detail.

Her belly fluttered alive, her limbs filling with such lustful warmth she was scared her knees would buckle.

'Just because *you've* lived that little bit more than me, Jack, it doesn't mean you get to tell me what I should and shouldn't want.'

'Sophia, do you have any idea of the effect you have over

me?' He raked an unsteady hand through his hair, turned away from her and came back, then reached for her and stopped. 'I want to kiss you so badly right now, and I don't care who sees!'

It wasn't what she'd expected. It wasn't anything close, and before she could really think about it she was reaching out for his jumper and grabbing a fistful as she pulled him into the outer hallway. Noah's present was crushed between them as she pressed her lips to his. Hungrily, she moved over him, *her* mouth driving it, *her* tongue. There was nothing soft or sweet about her now. She wanted him to know she was all woman and she knew her own mind and would take what she wanted.

As soon as his hands lifted to her hair, his lips softening beneath her own, she pulled back and stared him down. 'Just because this is new to me, Jack, it doesn't mean I'm not a quick learner and it *doesn't* make me weak.'

And then she left him, his clothing still ruffled, his hair too as he sucked in air and she walked into the flat to join the lively party ahead. She took a moment to pat down her appearance, to wipe her lips and catch her breath. Samantha would likely think she'd applied an extra layer of blusher, not kissed the face off Lily's egotistical and far too appealing father.

As for the apology she owed him, that would have to wait until later. If he dared to be alone with her again.

What had she done?

'Sphea! At last!' Lily ran up to her, her face aglow, her happiness adding to the endorphin rush already in her system and she grinned wide.

'Hey, kiddo, you having a good time?'

'The best.' She nodded fiercely, her arms wrapped around her legs.

'I'm glad.'

'Yes, where've you been, Auntie Sophia?' Sam's tone

was loaded. 'It's lucky Jack hung around else it would be utter carnage—I'm talking swinging from the chandelier stuff.'

Sophia laughed. 'You don't even have a chandelier.'

'Yes, well, at least you're here now. Drink?'

'Please.'

Samantha disappeared off to get her one and she sought out the birthday boy amongst the kids huddled into the living area. 'Hey, Noah, I've got something for you here.'

She lifted the present up so he could see it and he bounded over. 'Thank you, Aunt Soph!'

'You're welcome,' she said, bending down as he gave her a hug and a kiss to the cheek. 'Happy birthday!'

He took the present and raced to the sofa, his friends and Lily all circling around him as he opened it. She looked back in the direction of the door, to where Jack still was. What was he doing?

'Here...' Sam appeared at her side, a glass of fizz in each hand and offered one out to her. 'Drink this; we're going to need it.'

Sophia laughed but gratefully accepted it, her eyes back on Noah as he ripped through the packaging but her head returned to Jack and his absence. She also knew Sam had noticed, the way her friend's eyes kept flicking to her, trying to read her, and any minute now she would ask, *What have you done with Jack?*

She threw back a gulp of fizz and pondered her answer. *Sorry, hon, I think I just accosted him in the hallway and now he's run for his life.*

'You okay?' Sam eventually asked. 'You've looked strangely flushed since the moment you walked in.'

Sophia almost choked on the bubbles. *Trust Sam to say it how it is.*

'I'm fine.'

'You sure, 'cos you've only gotta say the word and I'll go sort him out.'

She gave Sam a warning glare that was half *Thank you* and half *Don't even think about it.* She just prayed Sam didn't come right out and say something to him.

Maybe she shouldn't have spilled her all to her friend last Sunday. But when Sam had turned up on her doorstep at the crack of dawn, a tasty bag of fresh pastries and two coffees in hand, with a please-let-me-live-vicariously-through-you look in her eye, Sophia hadn't been able to keep her mouth shut. And, to be fair, Sam had been a good listener, a good listener who'd sympathised greatly with the nature of her predicament, but also advised in no uncertain terms that Sophia should be in it for the fun and shouldn't expect more. She'd also been quick to add that should he hurt her she'd go after him with her—

'Nutcracker at the ready, Soph...'

She looked to the doorway and, sure enough, Jack had returned...

Jack leaned back against the wall and counted to ten, then twenty...then thirty because there was no way he was walking back into a kids' party in this...situation. He glanced down then breathed some more. His tent-like situation wasn't the worst of his problems either. It was the fact that he'd been so close to suggesting they end this the one way he knew how: in his bed.

And then what?

She'd have given him her virginity and he would fly away to his next destination—in this case Tokyo—like it meant nothing.

No, just no.

Then why was he still so torn?

Because you want her and you know she's different; you just don't understand why.

And it was his job to understand everything: the people he did business with, the people he employed, his daughter. But Sophia was an enigma—the power she wielded over him, the all-consuming need she sparked.

Maybe he really had been off the dating scene too long. He'd had plenty of offers over the years, but none had tempted him. Not like this. And again, there was the problem—it was her. He wanted her and no one else would do.

Was he really worried about her and her innocence, or was it his own ability to move on that he doubted?

He shook off the crazed thought and headed back inside. Sex could be just that. Sex. It didn't need to be complicated with more so long as they were honest from the outset.

He would let Lily have her fun, enjoy time with her peers and when it was all over he would take this up with Sophia. They would thrash it out until they both understood what the other wanted from this and there'd be no overstepping that agreement.

He couldn't deny that the prospect excited him far too much to let his worry back in. There would be time for worry later, much later, when he was far away from London and the past.

'Ah, Jack, thought you'd got lost between here and the front door for a second,' Samantha teased, turning away and picking up a chilled bottle of beer. 'Here's one I prepped for you.'

She walked up to him, her eyes seeing far too much, he was sure. What exactly did she know? Had Sophia talked to her? And what was she thinking now as she narrowed her gaze on him? Why did women *have* to talk?

'Cheers!' she said, offering up her drink.

'Cheers.'

He chinked the bottle against her glass and took a long pull of the cold liquid, realising not only how much he needed its cooling temperature but that he hadn't drunk straight from the bottle in a long time.

He heard a giggle behind Samantha, an easily recognisable giggle, and he looked over her head to see Sophia's sparkling blue eyes on him.

He raised his brow at her. 'What?'

'Nothing…just the sight of you slumming it with the rest of us, no champagne in sight… It tickles me.'

His eyes didn't leave Sophia's laughing ones; the urge to kiss her was overwhelming. 'So, it tickles you, does it?'

He stepped around Samantha and headed towards her. Her eyes flared, her smile turning wary. 'Uh-huh.'

'If you want something real to tickle you, I'm game.'

She backed up. 'You wouldn't dare?'

'Wouldn't I?'

She backed up some more, finding her thighs meeting the side table that sported plastic cups, juice jugs and a birthday cake.

'You've nowhere to run, princess.'

She was laughing and serious at once, the conflicting dance making her all the more appealing, all the more flushed. 'Lily! Lily! Come and rescue me. Your daddy's going to tickle me.'

'Coming, Sphea!' came his daughter's battle cry, followed by an all-male cry from the rest of the mini-partygoers and suddenly he was attacked, legs, arms, neck, the kids doing their best to take him down. He laughed, swinging this way and that as the kids giggled and cheered each other on.

Sophia relaxed as she realised she was safe, her hand reaching out for his beer bottle as he passed it to her shortly before hitting the floor. And then he became a crawling tickle monster, being tickled and tickling back with more children than he could count.

'Go easy on him, kids,' Samantha cooed. 'We don't want to scare Lily's daddy away altogether.'

Sophia laughed, her genuine amusement lifting him inside and making all manner of bruising from the overzealous tickling he was taking worth it.

She definitely wasn't scared or fearful of him, of whatever this was, now. Her behaviour, even her words on the doorstep, told him that. And if she wasn't scared, then why should he be?

They were grown adults going into this with their eyes wide open... What could possibly go wrong?

CHAPTER NINE

'THANKS SO MUCH for sticking around to help me clean up, guys.' Samantha pulled Sophia into a hug. 'Dan will be home just in time to enjoy the magic of the delayed sugar rush.'

'And two extra kids too. You're brave to add a sleepover to the mix!' Sophia laughed, pulling back to look her friend in the eye. 'You're such a good mum.'

'Or crazy,' she joked. 'I'm not sure which.'

Samantha turned to Jack and pulled him into a hug too, surprising him with the gesture if the wide-eyed look over her friend's shoulder was anything to go by.

'Thank you, Jack. It's not often the dads stick around; you're a bona fide modern father.' She patted him on the chest as she released him. 'I'm *très* impressed.'

Sophia forced back the mental retort that he'd only done it because he didn't trust either of them to take care of his daughter. It was bitter and, in truth, though it might have factored in his decision to stay, he'd clearly had fun. More importantly, so had the kids. And he'd been a fully fledged part of that fun. He hadn't stood in the shadows keeping watch; he'd got involved and been a huge hit with all of Noah's friends. A huge hit with Sam too.

As for Sophia, well, she already knew there was no hope for her...

'It was a novel experience.' He rubbed the back of his neck. His smile was...*bashful*. And making him all the more appealing with it. 'Enjoy the sleepover.'

'I will. I have wine and I'm leaving Dan in charge!'

They all laughed, save for Lily, who tugged on her daddy's hand. 'I wish I could sleep over.'

Samantha scooted down to give her a squeeze. 'With *three stinky boys*, you really don't, but you never know, maybe we can sort something for another time. I'd be glad of the female company.' She looked up at Jack with a smile. 'She's always welcome.'

'Yes, well…' He cleared his throat and placed his hand on Lily's shoulder. 'I think you're right, tonight's not the night for it.'

'But some other time, Daddy?'

'We'll see.'

'That means no.'

Sophia took pity on him and said, 'I might have an alternative idea.'

Lily looked at her, all hopeful.

'If your daddy agrees, you could sleep at mine?'

Lily beamed, her hopeful gaze now set on her father.

There was a crash from inside the flat and Samantha winced. 'Right, on that note, I'm leaving you guys to it. I just hope that noise has nothing to do with Dan's latest construction model!'

She dashed inside and closed the door, leaving Sophia and Lily looking up at a shell-shocked Jack. 'Well… I… what, tonight?'

'Sure.' She shrugged. 'I have no plans, the guest room is made up, and we can watch the latest Disney film and eat ice cream, just like any good sleepover. Maybe I could even paint your nails?'

Lily let out an excited squeal and started bobbing up and down. 'Please, Daddy, please, pretty please, pretty, pretty please.'

Sophia was pushing him. Deep down she knew it. She was toying with his trust boundaries and almost willing him to fail. Because if he failed, it would make it so much easier to keep some distance between them. To let him go in a week's time and not wonder what if.

'Daddy...' Lily tugged on his hand some more. 'Please, I've never had a sleepover.'

'I'm just not sure how it would work.'

'It's really simple.' Sophia smiled up at him. 'Lily and I get the quilt off the bed, plonk ourselves in front of the TV and eat copious amounts of ice cream, pausing only to paint our nails.'

'And me?'

Her smile became a confused frown. 'You?'

'Where would I fit into this sleepover?'

'You'd like a manicure too?' Her voice was elevated, her panic obvious.

'Oh, yes, that would be fun!' Lily blurted, nothing amiss in her world. 'I could paint yours, Daddy, you could do Sphea's, and Sphea could do mine.'

Sophia spluttered, unable to keep the weird choking sound in. This was *not* what she had in mind. But it clearly worked for Jack, whose face had lit up dramatically.

'Something wrong, Sophia?'

'No,' she hurried out.

'So, can we, Daddy?'

'If Sophia is happy, then I'm all for it.'

'But...but I only have the one spare room. You'd have to share or take the sofa.'

'The sofa is good enough for me.'

'Right... Okay then, sleepover it is.' She turned in a dazed fashion and headed to her apartment across the hall, hearing Lily's laugh following her.

'Isn't it funny how Noah has two friends staying over and now Sphea has two as well, Daddy?'

'Yes.' Jack chuckled. 'Very.'

She could feel his eyes burning into her back and caught the husky edge to his voice. *Funny* was not the word she would have used.

Dangerous. Yes.

Funny. *No.*

When I say I want you I mean it...

She'd really said that. Really, really said that. Against this very wall, just a few hours ago…promising him so much and now…now he was about to have a sleepover, at her place, with his *daughter*… No, no, *no!*

Clever move, Sophia Lambert. Clever and stupid and so messed-up.

She'd wanted him to trust her with Lily. She'd wanted him to feel comfortable leaving his daughter with her, just her. Not only for Lily's sake so she wasn't missing out, but because, though he might not trust Sam, he *should* trust her.

And instead she'd ended up with both. Daddy and daughter. In her apartment. For a night!

What exactly was the etiquette for a sleepover when the child came with their father and you wanted that man so badly you propositioned him outside a kids' party?

She had no idea, but she'd better work it out sharpish and make sure he knew whatever it was too.

Jack stood back as Sophia slotted the key in the lock. Somewhere at the back of his mind there was an almighty reel of panicked nonsense telling him this was a bad idea. But right now his daughter was happy and he…well, he was curious.

He wasn't even sure that was the right word, but when Sophia had had him pinned to the wall and taken what she wanted with the promise of—

He quit the recollection as she turned to look at him. Here it came, the excuse, the get-out clause. He could sense it in the nervous flicker of her lashes, her sweetly parted lips that she dampened and ran her teeth over…

'Did you—?' She broke off, colour streaking high across her cheekbones. 'Did you want to go back to the hotel and get some things?'

Things? He frowned, then stood to attention just as quickly. *She means clothes, you idiot!*

Her brow lifted. 'Like clothes…toiletries…' her eyes flicked to Lily '…Baby Bear?'

Lily gasped. 'Baby Bear! I *need* Baby Bear.'

'No problem. I'll call Ms Archer, ask her to pack a bag and get it couriered across.'

'Of course. Couriered over…right.'

'If you'd rather we arranged it for another night…?'

'But, Daddy, we leave in seven sleeps. When will we have time?'

'Seven sleeps?' Sophia repeated, her hand still resting over the keys in the lock. He wanted to deny it, to say he had longer, that they had no intention of leaving yet, but that would be a lie and served no purpose other than to make her, and thus him, feel better. It wouldn't change the inevitable. The takeover deal was almost done and dusted; they had no reason to stay. None at all.

'Yes, we fly Saturday afternoon.'

She lowered her lashes and took a small breath. 'Then tonight it is.'

She pushed open the door and flicked on the lights, the soft white walls giving off a warm ambience as opposed to the grey Samantha had opted for next door. Lily raced in behind her and started poking her head through the open doors.

'It's just like Noah's!'

'Yes.' Sophia smiled at her, then turned to Jack, her lips softening a little and doing something weird to his chest.

'Are you sure—?'

'Where am I sleeping, Sphea?' Lily bustled up to them, interrupting his impulsive need to check she was truly all right with this.

'Come on, I'll show you.' Sophia offered out her hand and Lily grinned at her, her obvious affection for this woman who'd only been in their lives a week chiming with his own. 'While Daddy makes his important call to Ms Archer...'

'Yes, right, I'll get on with it.' His voice sounded gruff, his chest too full to breathe properly. He smiled to hide it, but he wasn't so sure he'd succeeded, not if the questioning look Sophia sent over Lily's head was anything to go by.

'Okay?' she mouthed.

He nodded quickly and turned away, pulling his mobile from his jacket and dialling Ms Archer. Ever efficient, she answered promptly and he was done in five. It took him another five to compose himself enough to join the two women who had put him in this alien position. Their chatter was incessant and he only had to follow it to find them in the open-plan kitchen-cum-diner-cum-living area.

Sophia was warming something on the hob while Lily sat on a stool at the breakfast bar which separated the kitchen from the rest of the space.

'I've had one request for a fully loaded hot chocolate,' she said, looking at him over her shoulder. 'What can I get you?'

He slipped onto the barstool next to his daughter. 'What's a fully loaded hot chocolate?'

'It's topped with marshmallows and cream, Daddy.'

'Sounds good.'

'You fancy one too?'

He could hear the surprise in Sophia's voice and laughed. 'Why not?'

She shook her head. 'You're full of surprises, Jack McGregor.'

'What? Can't a grown man indulge once in a while?'

That high colour was back in her face and this time he knew it was the thoughts at play in her head, thoughts that he'd triggered by the double meaning of *indulge*. She gave him a small smile and went back to stirring the milk in the pan. Next to him Lily was sifting through what looked to be mail.

'Hey, don't be so nosy, kiddo.'

'I'm just looking.'

'That's precisely my point.'

'It's okay,' Sophia said. 'It's just the junk mail I didn't have time to go through at work. It's mainly brochures and stuff. Sometimes there's some interesting—'

'Wow! Look at this, Daddy!' Lily had a brochure spread out before her, her eyes like saucers as she pointed one of her small fingers at what looked like a giant bubble. 'You can stay in one of these and look at the stars *all* night!'

He grinned. 'Looks like fancy camping to me.'

'But look at the sky, Daddy. Does it really look like that or have they just done something with a computer to make it all…fancy?'

'That's the lights of aurora.'

'Aurora?'

'Aurora borealis, the northern lights.'

'Bore what? It looks like magic.' She lifted the brochure and turned it this way and that, her eyes wide, fascinated. 'Magic in the sky.'

'It's amazing, isn't it?' Sophia said to her as she pulled mugs out of a cupboard and scooped chocolate powder into each.

'Have you ever been?' Lily asked.

'No.' She stirred the milk into the cups. 'I'm not good with snow and to see it at its best you need to go in winter.'

'I love snow!'

Sophia gave a soft laugh. 'Most kids do.'

Her voice had turned distant, her eyes on the task in hand but unseeing. Was she thinking of her sister? The memory of that tale sent a shiver running through him now and the impulse to reach out for her was overpowering.

'Can I help?' he asked, coming up behind her, his hand gentle on her lower back.

She gave him a smile that didn't quite reach her eyes and his chest ached for her, his own smile filled with understanding, compassion.

'It's okay; I'm almost done.' She went back to the hot chocolate, squirting in cream and sprinkling on marshmallows with a dramatic flourish designed to hide it all. *'Voila!'*

She lifted two of the mugs and carried them to the counter, while he scooped up the third.

'These are impressive.'

She quirked a brow at him. 'You can say it.'

'Say what?'

'They're a cardiac arrest in a cup.'

'A cardy what?' Lily said, her brow wrinkling as she reached out for the one nearest to her and her eyes became fishbowls once more.

Sophia grimaced at Jack as she mouthed a *sorry* and he just smiled at her. 'Don't worry, I don't think even that would put her off.'

She blushed. 'Can't have a hot choc without all the trimmings. It's criminal.'

Lily laughed. 'Now I get it—cardy arrest. You are funny, Sphea.'

He laughed and shook his head. 'Isn't she just?'

Sophia looked to him, her own laughter sparkling in her eyes. He lifted the mug to his lips, felt the cream tickle at his nose and saw her eyes lower to the sight, her blush deepening. What wouldn't he give to know what she was thinking? 'You want to explain how you drink it?'

'I quite like watching you work it out.'

He cleaned off the tip of his nose and watched as she closed her mouth over a marshmallow and some cream and felt his body tighten. His hand clenched tight around his mug.

'Mmm, it's so good,' Sophia murmured. 'How's yours, Lily?'

'Perfect,' his daughter said, sticking her finger straight in and scooping up the topping, then popping it into her mouth with zero elegance. Mood officially killed. 'Dee-licious! Isn't it, Daddy?'

'Yup.' Not that he had tasted yet...

They all moved to the small dining table and Lily dragged the brochure into the middle of them, the double-page spread open with the bubble-like hotel room surrounded by woodland and the aurora lights flooding the sky. There were images all the way around it showing the various sights Iceland had to offer: waterfalls, the black sand beach, the basalt stacks, geo-thermal pools, geysers... It really was a sight and his daughter was clearly fascinated.

'It's such a great concept,' Sophia said, spying his focus. 'Being able to sleep under the stars, all warm and cosy with a three-hundred-and-sixty-degree view of it all.'

And yet she wouldn't go because of the white stuff also liberally sprinkled throughout the shot. He leaned closer to her, his arm brushing against hers. 'It is incredible.'

'But is it real or have they just made it up?'

'What, the bubbles or the sky?'

'It's all real,' Sophia said, her finger swirling over the bubble in the picture. 'This is in Iceland.'

'Iceland? Have I ever been to Iceland, Daddy?'

'No, neither of us have.'

'I'd like to go some time.'

'I'm sure you would.'

'Could we all go?'

Sophia choked on her chocolate and turned away.

Jack decided that there was no way to answer his daughter's impulsive question so instead he asked her another. 'What was your favourite bit about today?'

Lily pressed her lips together, looked to the ceiling and

hummed. 'All of it! Having friends to play with—Noah has so many friends—and then when we all jumped on you and that was so funny.'

'Funny for you maybe...' he rolled his shoulders '...my body isn't so sure.'

Lily laughed, giving him a playful shove. 'You were great, Daddy. I'm lucky to have a daddy like you.'

His chest swelled, even his eyes pricked, and then he caught the warmth in Sophia's gaze and he was hooked.

'But we have a problem...'

He dragged his eyes to Lily, surprised by her sudden downturn, even more so by her solemn frown.

Uh-oh.

'How do I get friends for my birthday party in Tokyo?'

CHAPTER TEN

'A SLEEPOVER AT the age of thirty—who would have thought it?'

Jack's voice was low as he tried not to disturb a snoozing Lily who was lying between them, propped up on pillows with the blanket covering them all.

'I still can't believe she roped us into getting the sofa bed out just to watch the film.' Sophia didn't look at him as she said it; her eyes were fixed on the TV screen and not on the proximity of his. It was too snug, too easy, lying like this with the lights down low, the TV playing a movie she could remember nothing of, and all in her own domain.

It was easy to forget who Jack was. From the moment he'd got on all fours at the party and rolled around with the kids, taken a slop of cream to the nose with his unmanly drink and cosied up on her ancient sofa with her well-worn tartan blanket, she had lost sight of what was real. Because she didn't just want him, she realised; she wanted so much more.

'I think I was too busy worrying about her upcoming birthday I'd have agreed to anything.'

Now she looked at him and saw the lines of concern creasing his face as the colours of the TV danced over them. 'You're really worried about it?'

'It's not just today. I've been thinking a lot about what you've said, about her having no base and being unable to set down roots or make real friends of her own.'

'I'm sorry.' She felt guilty even though she knew she'd been right to raise it. 'But I think it's important for her to have all that, although I know it makes things difficult for you.'

'Perhaps.'

'Have you thought more about speaking to her grandmother?'

He sent her a quick look and sighed. 'Yes. I have. And I will. It won't be easy, but I think it's worth a shot.'

'From what you've said she'll likely have aunts and uncles close to her own age, family that she can play with, grow up with.'

'That would mean coming back to the UK.'

'And you're not ready for that?'

He worked his shoulders into the pillow behind him, under the pretence of getting comfortable, but she had the feeling it was more to mask the pain of what that thought brought.

'It's not going to be a quick fix though; it's not going to help with the imminent arrival of her birthday.'

'No, I guess not. Do you have to go to Tokyo? Perhaps you could stay longer...' She couldn't stop the spark of hope, the idea of having them around longer too appealing to ignore.

'You could borrow Noah and his friends?' She gave a teasing smile. 'They'd love to see you again, I'm sure.'

He laughed, the sound sending a shiver of delight through her. 'It's an idea... I just wish things were different.'

He went quiet, his eyes distant, and she reached over to place a reassuring hand on his above the blanket. 'It seems to me that you're on the right track though. This time next year things *could* be very different for her.'

He gave her a small smile. 'Thank you.'

'For what?'

'For making me see sense.'

She laughed softly. 'I didn't do anything.'

Their eyes caught and she felt that connection between them sizzle to life. 'You've done more than you could possibly know.'

Her lips parted as she tried to take in air, to cope with the warmth spreading through her body. 'I'm glad I could help.'

'Me too.' He looked to Lily between them. 'I'd best get her to bed.'

She nodded, removing her hand to look down at his sleeping daughter, who had the brochure of Iceland open and pressed into her chest. 'She's beautiful.'

'You both are.'

'Jack…' She shook her head, half brushing off his remark, half treasuring it as she picked the brochure up and climbed off the bed.

'Just speaking the truth.'

She couldn't stop the smile that touched her lips or the way his words turned her insides to a soft, gooey mess as she took the brochure and the empties into the kitchen and placed them on the counter. It felt so surreal having them here…and at the same time so right. She'd never thought herself lonely before, but when they left she just knew it would be different.

She lifted the brochure Lily had loved so much and flicked it open to the double-page spread, placing it down on the counter and tracing her fingers over the see-through dome, the bed with the family of three sitting upon it gazing up at Aurora and the stars.

'She's out for the count,' Jack said, walking back into the room. 'Didn't even murmur when I tucked her in.'

Sophia didn't look up. She was too lost in the image beneath her fingers and the idea that was forming.

'I know what you can do for her birthday,' she rushed out in whispered excitement. 'And she'll love every second. And you won't need an instant family or instant friends to do it.'

She sensed him frown. 'What?'

She slid the brochure across the counter to him and tapped a finger on the picture of the dome. 'This!'

He laughed. 'It's a great idea, but surely it'll be fully booked by now.'

'The resort is new. I only have the brochure because I'm in the industry. They're running some special launch stays prior to their grand opening. I could put in a call, see what there is?'

'I don't know...'

'You saw how much she loved it and you know how much she loves the stars. Even if you don't see the northern lights, she'd be in her element with the snow, the waterfalls, the amazing scenery... She'd love it all.'

He ran a hand through his hair as he looked down at the brochure and then grinned. 'You're right, of course you are.'

'I'm always right,' she teased, looking up into his eyes and realising how much closer she'd stepped as she'd worked on convincing him.

'Is that so?' He turned into her, his hands reaching for her waist, and she had no desire to pull away. This was what she wanted. What she needed.

She leaned into him, her 'Yes...' a whisper, a plea, as he bowed his head and she tilted her own back. His lips brushed over her own, her sharp inhale a striking contrast to the softness of his mouth and its coaxing pressure.

'Sophia...' He parted her lips with his tongue, brushing against hers with teasing intent. As if he was savouring her, exploring her, drawing her out, the inner desire that she'd never known existed until now, until him.

She raised her fingers to his chest and felt his warmth, the hard muscle beneath his jumper, and travelled higher still until her hands were in his hair, holding him to her as he took the same journey over her body.

She was aching, an incessant, thudding pang spreading through her lower belly that promised so much pleasure.

He broke from her mouth to travel along her jawline, his stubble teasing the same path, his tongue, his teeth—

oh, yes. She clung to his head, her own arching back as he brushed against her ear, his lips teasing with his words. 'Never have I wanted someone like I want you.'

'Take me then, Jack, please,' she sighed against him, her breasts pressing into his chest, her leg hooking around him to draw him closer, to hold him near. 'I need you.'

And he needed her too. She could feel his hardness pressing urgently against her, could feel his desire rising with her own, his breath as short. He came back to her mouth, this time hungry, his tongue plundering, and she was ready, willing, waiting. She gave it back to him in return, leaving him in no doubt as to how much she wanted this.

He grabbed her by the hips and lifted her onto the counter, wrapped her legs around himself as he came back to claim her lips.

'This is crazy,' he rasped against her. 'Crazy and out of control.'

'Crazy but so good.' She pulled his lips back to hers, her hands dropping to the hem of his jumper as she tugged it over his head and leaned back. She had to see him. She needed to. His dark skin glowed in the light of her kitchen, the sheen of perspiration reflecting in the light, his short breaths rippling his pecs. 'You're beautiful.'

He gave a gentle scoff. 'I'm a man.'

'So?' She looked up into his blazing greys, so dilated with desire, and the next words came out gruff with her own need. 'You're still beautiful.'

And then she was kissing him again, feeling his hot hands on her bare skin as they slipped beneath her jumper, her nerve-endings coming alive, savouring every sweep of his hands, every light brush of his fingers as they smoothed beneath the band of her bra. She was losing her mind—it was the only way to describe the intense rush of feeling inside her.

'I want you, Sophia.' He yanked the jumper over her

head, her hair tumbling around her bare shoulders as he threw her jumper to the side.

'I want you too.'

He lifted her from the counter and walked her to the sofa bed, easing her down before stretching out beside her, his mouth hot against her lips, her neck. Her hands raked down his back as he travelled over her skin, making her writhe and plead. 'Please, Jack, please.'

She wanted to say more, so much more. She wanted to say, *Be my first*, wanted him to know what that meant to her, but he already knew. Just as she knew the reminder would stop him, as it had before, and so she clamped down on her bottom lip and told him with her body what she wanted.

'Come with us, Sophia—come with us to Iceland.'

Her eyes shot open and she gazed down at him, hardly daring to believe the question and knowing at the same time that she couldn't. The thought, the idea of being surrounded by her fear, by the past, by the snow... She shook her head and shifted beneath him to remind him of her body, of what she wanted in that moment. What he so wanted too.

'You can't ask me that, Jack. Don't ask me that.'

He raised himself up over her, his elbows planted either side of her body to bear his weight. 'Why not?'

'Because I can't. *We* can't.'

He kissed her until she was breathless, panting. 'Why?'

'We don't even know they'll be available for her birthday yet.'

'That doesn't matter. They will be available at some point and I want you to come.'

She shook her head, the emotions clawing at her throat and her chest, making it hard to breathe. 'We both know this has to end and that the longer we spend together with Lily, the more likely it is that she will become attached too.'

His eyes were so serious now as they blazed into hers.

The 'too' spoke volumes; it told him that fear protected her own heart, but did it protect his, as well?

'That's not the whole truth, is it?' he pressed, probing for more, probing for her to admit that she feared being faced with her past. All it took was one harmless-looking snowflake, the ice forming over her windshield, and the shivers would start.

'It's enough.'

He shook his head, one hand stroking her cheek and catching a tear she hadn't known was there. 'You need to stop living in fear of your past, Sophia.'

He kissed her to soften his words and she clamped her eyes shut over the rising swell of emotion within. 'You've taught me that; you've made me realise that avoiding a base, avoiding London, is running from it. And by doing it, Lily has suffered.'

She kept her eyes closed as the tears refused to stop. He was right. She'd been a hypocrite to tell him the same and not realise it was exactly how she'd been behaving all along.

'Come with us. Not because I ask you, not because it would make Lily happy to have you there... Come because you want to. Come because you are ready to move on from it.'

She nodded, her eyes still clamped shut.

'Look at me, Sophia.'

Slowly she did as he asked, her hands coming up to gently stroke his back. 'Come because you want to be with us.'

She wet her lips as she stared up into his eyes. She saw so much—so much that she could almost believe, almost convince herself that it wasn't just her falling hard and fast. It was him too. And that was what had her kissing him so hard that she could barely breathe and he reciprocated, his arms slipping around her as he rolled her on top of him.

He pressed her away just long enough to ask, 'Is that a yes?'

'Yes, Jack, it's a yes.'

He didn't know what to think, didn't know how to be rational about this, to talk himself down from what he was about to do. The truth was he wasn't capable of clear thought. He wanted her more than he had ever wanted anyone, and it felt so right, so natural, so impossible to resist.

He rolled her back underneath him and kissed her, the emotion taking hold of his heart and driving every move he made. He was caught up in her, in what she brought to both him and Lily. And he wanted more. More sense of family, of belonging. He could feel the shift underway inside him, the beginnings of hope for a future, the possibility that maybe he could love her as she deserved and accept such love in return.

That was why he'd pleaded with her to come to Iceland. He knew the magnitude of what it meant for her personally to face her fear, and he knew he wanted to be right by her side when she took that leap.

He didn't know what the future held, but he knew that this was what they both wanted.

He deepened his kiss, one hand smoothing down her front to find the button of her jeans as his other stroked through her hair. He stripped her layer by layer, himself too, with the sense that it wasn't just their bodies being exposed but their hearts too.

You do this and you can't go back. You do this and you're promising more.

He bowed his head, his eyes shut tightly against her naked beauty. 'Sophia…'

He dragged in air, fighting for control over his desire. She answered him with her hands in his hair pulling him to her lips, her bare legs wrapping around his lower body, urging him closer. 'Please, Jack.'

He could hear the lust thickening her voice, the lust and so much more…

'Jack?'

He lifted his head, opened his eyes to see hers glistening back at him in the low light of the TV and his heart pulsed in his chest.

'Are you sure? There can be no going back, no…'

She released his hair, smoothing her palms around to his cheeks. 'Yes, Jack, I want it to be you.'

His breath rasped out of him, a bittersweet happiness choking up his throat. He moved away to seek out his jeans, his wallet, and the protection he had there. He took it out, sheathing himself, all the while feeling her eyes on him, the strength of her need, the sense that this was right, that this was what they both wanted keeping him moving.

He came back to her, their gazes locked together, a thousand words passing between them as he moved slowly, merging their bodies, surrounding himself in her. He wanted to say so much, promise so much…but it was all he could do to control this, to keep it slow.

He felt her resistance, felt her stiffen beneath him and the tension locking her legs tightly around him. He stilled, sweeping his hand over her hair, his nose brushing against hers as he whispered, 'I don't want to hurt you.'

Her eyes glistened further as she shook her head, her legs drawing him in. 'You won't, Jack. You're not.'

She kissed him—kissed him until he could think of nothing but claiming her heart as she had his, forcing out the guilt that tried to break in anew.

You won't hurt her… You won't hurt her… You won't…

Sophia clutched her glass of water to her chest and stared at the kitchen clock. Three a.m. glared back at her. *Three a.m.*

and there was a gorgeous naked man asleep in her sofa bed and she was sitting at her breakfast bar, freshly showered with her PJs on and wishing she could climb straight back in with him.

Hence why she was looking at the clock and not at him. Because the temptation was too great and the risk that she would fall asleep again, only to have Lily wander in and find them, was too high.

It was bad enough she'd fallen asleep the first time, bad enough that they both had, but it had been blissful in the aftermath and she had been too content to move. As had he apparently.

And when she'd woken up to Jack's arm locked around her middle and the initial shock of being in bed with a man had passed, she'd found herself cocooned in his body warmth, soothed by his gentle snore, his scent, and she hadn't wanted to move. She'd let the night play back to her, along with the soreness of what they had shared, and her whole body had flushed with reignited heat and a strange bashfulness.

She'd been torn between staying and showering, and in the end it had been the thought that Lily could wake up that had spurred her into moving. It was one thing for Jack to wake and see her in that tangled mess, but not Lily. She wasn't sure where this turn in their relationship had left them, but she knew it wasn't in a solid enough place for Lily to learn of it.

Tomorrow—*no, later today*—they could talk. They could agree how they should be for Lily's sake and—

'Elena!'

She almost dropped her glass as he cried out. She looked back to the bed, to where he writhed and rolled, his arm flinging out, his face creased up in pain as his chest heaved.

She put the glass down and shot across the room, reaching out for him as she lowered herself to the bed. It didn't matter that it was another woman he called for, another woman who haunted his dreams; she was the one who could be there for him.

She cradled his head against her hip and gently shushed him, her fingers stroking through his hair, thankful that his features started to relax and his breathing settled.

She looked up to the hallway, to where her bedroom door lay, and knew it was useless now; she was his captive whether he intended her to be or not.

'Elena… Elena…' He writhed against her, his dead wife's name on his lips, and though she didn't want it to, her heart ached anyway. Was this how it was for him every night, Elena haunting his dreams? Or had what they'd shared triggered it?

And if it was the latter, what did it mean for them?

If she were to believe what he had told her, he'd never loved Elena, not in the way he felt she deserved. But he'd also said he could never feel for Sophia what he felt *she* deserved.

She thought about all he had said to her, about his request that she join him and Lily in Iceland, that she face her fears with him by her side. Surely that had to mean he felt more? Wasn't that why she'd wanted him to make love to her, why she'd wanted him to be her first, because regardless of what he felt for her, she knew she already felt so much more for him?

Her fingers stilled over his hair, her eyes intent on the sight of him lying beside her.

*Felt so much more…*she really did…it was too late to stop it, to hit rewind.

And even as she accepted it as fact, she knew she couldn't tell him, not yet. He wasn't ready to hear it. He would sooner run the other way than accept that another woman cared for him.

She wasn't scared of Iceland, the snow, the past. She

was scared of the future and the knowledge that what she wanted above all else was a life with him and Lily.

Jack woke with a start to the smell of bacon cooking and his daughter's excited giggle.

'Do it again, Sphea, again!'

'Shh, you'll wake your daddy!' Sophia laughed as she said it, turning to smile down at Lily before lifting her gaze to him and freezing mid-movement, a frying pan out-stretched before her. One second, two, and then her eyes softened into his, her smile lifting anew. 'Too late, he's up.'

'Daddy!' Lily raced across the room and he just had time to lock the blanket around his hips before she launched her-self into his arms. 'Sphea's flipping pancakes!'

'She is?' He grinned at Sophia over his daughter's shoul-der and saw her cheeks flush pink, like they so often did. He felt his heart blooming to life, the extent of what he felt for her hitting him full force. He waited for the panic, the worry...but there was none.

'I am.' She swept her forearm over her head to brush away the loose strands that fell around her face and turned back to place the pan on the heat. 'Can't have a Sunday morning without pancakes and bacon.' She glanced at him over her shoulder. 'Hungry?'

'Ravenous.' And he was, for so much more than food and, judging by the way her brows lifted, the way she ran her teeth over her bottom lip, she knew and felt it too.

Lily wriggled in his hold. 'Are you naked, Daddy? Didn't Ms Archer pack your pyjamas too?'

The innocent question had a foreign surge of heat spreading over his own cheeks... *Oh, dear.* 'I was very hot last night.'

He heard Sophia choke down a laugh and he tickled his daughter, her own laugh masking the telling one from the kitchen. 'Now, why don't you finish helping Sophia, while I freshen up and chuck on some clothes?'

'Okay,' she said on a ripple of laughter, her hair bouncing as she raced back into the kitchen.

'There are fresh towels in the bathroom,' Sophia said to him, her voice softly luring him over. He wanted to go to her, to place his hands on her hips and draw her into a morning kiss, one that was sure to rouse his body far too much and also give Lily the wrong impression.

Wrong impression?

What was the right one? What should he tell Lily about them? It was one thing to be spending this time together now, but how would it look when Sophia came to Iceland with them? How did he want it to look?

He showered quickly, throwing on some fresh clothes and returning to the comforting sounds and smells of the kitchen.

'You're just in time, Daddy! Look I've made a face...' She pushed her plate at him. Sure enough, there were two maple syrup blobs and a strip of bacon for a smile.

'Impressive.'

'Here's yours,' Sophia said, sliding a plate towards him, her skin delightfully pink from cooking, the brush of flour across her cheek teasing him. He reached out and brushed it away with his thumb, catching the way her breath hitched, her lips parted, and had to fight another urge to kiss her.

'You had a little flour...'

She traced the path of his fingers with her own, his need mirrored back at him. 'Thank you.'

'No, thank you.'

'Do I have any flour, Daddy?'

He lowered his gaze to his daughter and laughed; her timing was impeccable. 'You're covered.'

He rubbed both her cheeks with gusto as she wrinkled her nose and made a funny noise.

'All better,' he declared, planting a kiss on her forehead and pulling up a stool before reaching for his plate. 'This looks amazing.'

'It won't beat the hotel breakfast,' Sophia said, 'but it'll certainly fill a hole. Coffee?'

'Please.'

She moved away and poured a freshly brewed pot into two awaiting mugs, returning with them both and offering one to him.

'Thank you,' he said, giving her a smile of gratitude that went so much further than breakfast. He had so much to be thankful for. So much that he couldn't put into words in front of Lily, not yet, but soon. Hopefully, very soon.

First, he needed to reach out to Elena's mum, to see if there truly was a chance for Lily to know her grandmother and her family.

Second, he needed to get Iceland booked and make his daughter's birthday one to remember.

And three, he needed to get his head around his feelings for Sophia, because now that he'd glimpsed how complete his life could be with her in it he didn't want to let it go. He wanted to make this work. He wanted to be worthy of her. He wanted to love her.

Which was lucky since he already did...

He shook his head at his own ramblings, his grin ridiculous, he was sure, but as he forked up a healthy chunk of pancake he realised he was actually too content to care.

CHAPTER ELEVEN

IT HAD BEEN over a week since Sophia had seen Jack and Lily, but it felt like so much longer.

They'd spent every evening together following that night, right up until their departure for Tokyo. Sophia would finish work and head up to the penthouse just in time for bath and bed, and sometimes Sophia would read, other times Jack, but it was always the three of them squeezed into the one bed with Lily and Baby Bear in the middle.

There'd been no more sleepovers though, much to Lily's disappointment. Work and it being a 'school night' were the excuses given but, in reality, Sophia knew they were trying to take things slow, to keep Lily from getting hurt, to hold themselves back too.

Everything was moving too fast, her own feelings for him—for Lily too—growing out of her control and with it came the fear. The fear of pushing him away, of confessing too much and having him run. The fear of the past, of his experience with Elena coming between them regardless of the seemingly comfortable happiness they had found.

Their 'us' was just too fragile.

And it wasn't just the fear of losing him; she would be losing Lily too, and the very idea had her tummy turning over and her feelings for him trapped deep inside, her lips sealed around them. Unless she was kissing him of course... She warmed even now with the thought, the remembered caress of his mouth over hers, the way he could coax her entire body to life with just the sweep of his lips, the stroke of his fingers...

'We're here, Ms Lambert.'

She jerked alert, a startled sound erupting from her

throat as Jack's driver spoke into the silence. She met his eyes in the rear-view mirror, grateful he didn't look as if he'd noticed her teeny outburst or the crimson flush sure to exist in her cheeks now.

'Thank you.' She glanced out of the window and frowned. *Where's here?*

They weren't in the airport departures drop-off zone, that was certain; in fact, they were a good distance away from the terminal itself. She was about to query it when her door shifted open and she looked up to see Jack leaning in.

'Jack!' Her heart soared, the air leaving her lungs in a rush as she launched herself up, her arms wrapping around him.

A secret—yeah, right; her feelings were written in every movement she made.

'Hey,' he said against her ear, pressing a kiss there. 'It's good to see you.'

He breathed her in and then he lifted his head, forcing her back so he could scan her face. 'I missed you.'

'I missed you too,' she murmured, her eyes welling with her heart and she blinked the dampness away. 'Where are we?'

'My private hangar.'

'You're kidding.'

'Not at all.'

'No, of course you're not.' *What a stupid thing to say—this is Jack!*

'Sphea!' Lily came running up, wrapping her arms around them both and distracting Sophia from her self-deprecation. She crouched down and scooped her into a hug, the elation running through her obvious to anyone looking on. Her secret truly was no secret at all. 'I missed you.'

Lily squeezed her tightly. 'I missed you too.'

'Are you excited for your birthday trip?'

She nodded emphatically. 'Daddy has read your brochure with me every night.'

She looked up at Jack. 'Every night, hey?'

He chuckled. 'She can probably tell you more about where we're going than the people who live there.'

Sophia laughed as she stood back up. It was then she saw the plane with its door open, staff and steps at the ready, the engine whirring through the brisk cold air. 'Is that…yours?'

There you go again with the naïve questions.

'It is.' Jack's grin turned lopsided. 'You ready to see inside?'

Was she? She felt nervous, out of place, suddenly uneasy. She turned away. 'I'll just get my things.'

'It's okay.' He took hold of her arm, bringing her back to him. 'My team will take care of your luggage.'

He offered out his hand and she tried for a smile, interlacing her fingers through his like she had come to do so often before they had left for Tokyo.

Lily took hold of her other hand and she smiled down at her.

'We're going to have so much fun,' the little girl cooed, her eyes bright and happy.

'That we are…' Sophia said softly, her eyes returning to the aircraft as they headed towards it together, the butterflies picking up inside her belly.

She knew she was silly to be surprised by it—the plane, the hangar—but she was. Surprised, awestruck, and deep down utterly unsettled. The opulence was a timely reminder of who Jack was and just how much she didn't belong in his world.

At least in her home, even in her place of work, she was able to forget all this and see him as Jack—*just* Jack. Not the billionaire businessman, the successful tycoon, the man in the press. And even though she feared her feelings for him, she had come to accept them. She'd even started to let in hope that he could feel the same, that there could be a future… At least it felt more realistic when they were away from all this.

I missed you…

Even now her lips lifted at his honest declaration from seconds before, one that she had quickly reciprocated and felt to her toes. His words teased her with that future again. But as she looked around her, taking in his private airfield, his staff, his private car that had delivered her, and back to his heaven-knew-how-expensive aeroplane, that acceptance of her feelings, that hope of a future took a hit.

Because this was the stuff of movies. Not real life.

And even Samantha had been cautious when Sophia had opened up to her about how she felt, about this trip and the possibility of there being more. She was her best friend and she actually *liked* Jack, but still she'd cautioned against getting in too deep, to keep her head out of the clouds and her feet grounded.

She gave a soft laugh as they paused before the steps and Jack eyed her, his own smile cautious. 'Something funny?'

'Just something Samantha said. It's nothing important…' Nothing important but the exact opposite of what she was about to do as she started to follow Lily up into the plane.

There was no turning back now.

And in truth she didn't want to.

'Oh, my, Jack.' She couldn't keep the wonder out of her voice as she stepped inside the cabin and took in the plush interior, a mixture of creams and warm wood with inviting sofas, a large TV screen, a dining table, a kitchen one way and a bedroom at the other. It was as impressive as any hotel room and she couldn't believe where she was.

'You approve?' He slipped off his jacket and hooked it over the back of a leather recliner. He looked so at home, so at ease, and of course he would do; this was his domain. But Sophia…she really didn't know how to feel.

'It's incredible,' she said truthfully.

He smiled. 'Wait until you taste dinner.'

'Please tell me it's pizza, Daddy, and none of that fancy stuff we got last time.' Lily screwed up her face as she said it and he looked to Sophia with an apologetic grimace.

'I'm happy with pizza,' she said quickly, silently pleading, *Please let it be pizza.* Something normal, to help her feel normal.

'You are?'

'Absolutely.' He hesitated a second longer and then disappeared into the front of the plane as Lily clambered into one of the seats at the dining table and threw her bag on top of it.

'Come sit next to me, Sphea.' She patted the seat beside her and started pulling sheets of paper out of her bag. 'I want to show you my drawings.'

Sophia smiled and did as Lily asked, glancing down at the little sketches she started to spread out over the table.

'These are of us in Iceland!' she declared and, sure enough, the pictures were of the three of them doing various different things: sledging, having a snowball fight, building a snowman, lying inside a bubble looking up at the stars…

Sophia's smile grew, warmth spreading inside her chest and pushing out the unease, the uncertainty. What Lily dreamed of married so closely with what Sophia wanted too.

'Dinner crisis averted,' Jack said, rubbing his hands together as he returned to them, his own eyes falling to the pictures and making him pause. She watched his face, watched it flicker with some unguarded emotion and then the shutter fell, his eyes lifting to her. 'It means a slight delay to take-off, but we'll still be in Iceland for a decent time this evening.'

'Lovely.'

He looked back to Lily and gestured to all the sketches. 'You've been busy.'

Sophia could tell by his face he hadn't seen the pictures before and she had no idea how to gauge his reaction to them now.

'It helps when I can't sleep.'

'So that's why I keep finding your torch in bed with you?'

Lily gave him an impish grin. 'I like drawing.'

'And I *like* your drawings…' he slid into the seat beside Sophia, leaning forward to give his daughter a stern look '…but you still should have been sleeping.'

She gave a little huff and pulled out her fluffy pink pencil case, ready to create some more.

'I like them too,' Sophia said, ducking low to speak to her. 'Very much.'

And when she straightened again she felt his eyes on her, her own finding his just as swiftly.

'You do?' he asked softly.

'Yes.' And she knew then that they were both saying the same thing: that they liked it being the three of them, not just on paper but in real life, and hope sparked ever brighter inside.

'What shall I draw next, Sphea?'

She pulled her eyes from his and looked back to the pictures, her eyes settling on the sledging one, and for the briefest of seconds she felt the old familiar pang, the chill.

Jack reached out, his hand settling over hers to give it a gentle squeeze. 'You okay?'

She took a breath and gave him a small smile. She knew he'd picked up on the sudden wave of sadness and as she looked to his creased-up brow, his grey eyes soft with concern, she knew she was more than okay.

'Yes.' And with him by her side she would get through this trip and be all the stronger for it. 'I am.'

He returned her smile but he didn't release her hand, keeping it there as they both offered up ideas to Lily, who evaluated each and every one in the special way she had until she'd decided on a scene involving hot chocolate and a roaring fire.

They settled back like that, Lily drawing, Jack's hand on Sophia's, their chatter innocent enough for Lily's ears and so easy. They caught up on the past week, on what had happened with work, with Samantha and Noah. They ate pizza and played Snap with Lily. Everything was normal and relaxed. She could almost forget they were on a plane, if not for the occasional turbulence and the persistent hum of the engine.

Lily gave a huge yawn and scooted a little closer to Sophia's side.

'Tired, kiddo?'

She nodded and rested her head in Sophia's lap. She didn't ask, she didn't seek permission, she just did it and the move was so telling and touching.

'It's the middle of the night back in Tokyo,' Jack said softly, his eyes on his daughter in Sophia's lap. 'She's been going for hours now.'

'You both have,' she said, stroking Lily's hair.

'She's quite taken with you.'

She smiled. 'The feeling's mutual.'

'She's not the only one.' The sincerity of his voice, so close to her ear, had her entire body warming and her eyes returning to his. Was he saying…? Was he admitting…? She hoped so, so much.

He cleared his throat and looked back to Lily. 'The travelling has really taken its toll this time.'

'It is a lot in a short space of time. Have you thought more about settling somewhere more permanent?' She almost said *London* and realised it was too personal, too soon, and too close to what she wanted deep down for her own selfish reasons.

'I have and we will, soon. I'd like to spend a little time with Elena's family first, to see whether there is something worth saving there.'

'Have you spoken to her mother?'

His eyes turned distant. 'Yes.'

'And?'

His lips curved up a little. 'It was nice. *She* was nice. She also sounded beside herself that I'd called.'

'Beside herself in a good way?'

His eyes met with hers and she could see the lightness in them, the relief. 'In a very good way. She wants to meet as soon as possible. She wanted to go all in—Lily, me, her husband and all three children, and though it was nice to hear her so excited, I'm not quite ready to expose Lily to that all at once.'

'Baby steps?'

'Yes, baby steps. I've decided to take Lily to meet her when we get back from Iceland. Then we can talk about meeting the rest of the family. I want to see how Lily takes to her first. I want her to drive this as much as me, if not more…'

Sophia smiled as she looked back to the girl fast asleep in her lap, her soft snore reaching up to them, her thick lashes, so like her father's, fanned out across her deep golden skin. Beautiful. Angelic. And Sophia felt her love for the little girl swell.

If she was to have Elena's family in her life then all the better, but Sophia wanted to be in that life too. She wanted to be in both of their lives.

'What about you, Sophia?'

'Hmm?' She looked up at him, blinking her surprise; she'd been so caught up in her depth of feeling she'd lost track of their conversation.

'Are you going to try and make amends with your family? To speak to them again?'

She gave a gentle sigh. 'I don't know. It's been so long since we talked properly, so long since…since we lost Amy. Maybe it's too late for us.'

'It's never too late, not while your parents are still alive. I've told you before how much it would crush me to know Lily was somewhere in the world and scared of reaching out to me. To know that you and your parents have that separation because of something so tragic, something that none of you had any control over…'

He reached for her hand that she hadn't realised she'd clenched into a fist upon the table and slowly unravelled it to link his fingers through hers. 'You should try.'

She lowered her gaze to Lily, recalling her thoughts from seconds before, of her love for this child who wasn't even hers by birth, and she realised how right he was. She also realised the part she'd played in the breakdown of their relationship, the guilt she'd put on herself and projected onto them. She'd labelled herself as guilty and convinced herself that they blamed her too. She'd never given them a chance to prove to her otherwise; she'd never given them a chance to get close again.

She took a shaky breath and nodded. 'You're right.'

'I know I am.' He said it so sincerely that she couldn't even laugh at his arrogant acceptance of her words. 'And this trip is part of you facing up to your past with us by your side. If you can do this, you can do anything.'

She turned to him seconds before his head lowered to hers, his lips soft, gentle, as he kissed her. It wasn't heated or desperate or needy; it was giving, the passion coming from the fact he cared for her, nothing more, nothing less, and she melted inside, her heart skipping to the beat of his choosing. The knowledge that she loved him was as obvious as the feelings projected in his kiss. She didn't just care for him, she wasn't just falling… She had long since fallen and as she opened her eyes and looked up into his she was convinced it was there, being reflected right back at her.

'Have faith in yourself,' he murmured as he pulled back and she smiled, leaning into him, her head coming to rest on his shoulder. It was comfortable, relaxed, and just where she belonged.

'I'll try.'

Jack turned and pressed his lips to Sophia's hair, breathing in the familiar scent of her shampoo and realised just how much he'd missed this. Missed her.

And seeing Lily so at home curled into her lap, to see the drawings spread out before him in all their hopeful glory… So much rested on this holiday, on him opening up to Sophia and being honest about how he felt, how, despite what he had said to the contrary, he had come to care for her…to love her.

Sophia nuzzled into him further, her head gradually getting heavy as her breathing levelled out and he smiled; she was falling asleep too.

He wrapped his arm around her, pulling her in close as he checked his watch. They would be landing soon but he could make the most of the next twenty minutes or so, before he'd have to wake them.

He looked back to the drawings on the table, spreading out the pages with his fingers until one in particular caught his eye…and his heart.

He lifted it out from beneath the pile and stilled, his chest both warm and tight. It was a church, in front of which stood a couple, and just like all the others, they were that couple. His dark skin, his dark hair, contrasted with

Sophia's fair complexion and auburn waves, their hands locked together, a little Lily standing behind, her smile too big for her face. It was a wedding. *Their* wedding.

A conflicting sense of hope, fear and love swirled up within him, chased down by panic. Panic at Lily's obvious attachment and the fact that he had let it happen. Panic at his daughter's dream that this would be in their future and he couldn't say for certain that it would be. She'd already lost a mother. If he failed, if this relationship ended, she would lose another parental figure too.

Had he made a mistake?

He'd had the good sense to be cautious with Elena's mother, cautious about exposing Lily to that side of the family in case the relationship fell apart, in case she lost them. But his own connection to Sophia had made him rash.

Yes, they'd tried to keep things platonic in front of Lily, tried to show their relationship was one of friendship and nothing more. But this one picture told them they'd failed. That, regardless of their best efforts, Lily wanted Sophia to be a part of their family...just as he did.

He took a steadying breath and slid the picture back under the stack. He just had to make sure he didn't ruin it.

CHAPTER TWELVE

'PUT YOUR COATS ON,' Jack said, shrugging on his own as the engine to the plane was cut. 'It's going to be cold out there.'

Sophia helped Lily into hers before putting her own on, nerves fluttering up in her belly once more. This was it. Time to face her fears and move past them.

The door opened and the cold night air breached the warmth of the cabin, not that Lily was perturbed. She was already racing ahead, up to the elegant stewardess who now waited by the door for them to leave.

'Thank you for my pizza!'

'You're welcome, Miss McGregor.' The stewardess smiled indulgently down at Lily. 'Enjoy your holiday.'

'I will,' she said, stepping out onto the steps.

'Happy holiday, Mr McGregor, Miss Lambert.'

Sophia smiled her gratitude and stepped out behind Lily. The chilling wind, laced with snow, wrapped around her and she shivered, her hand reaching for Lily instinctively. 'Careful.'

'Isn't it pretty, Sphea?' the little girl said, her eyes wide with wonder as they travelled over the snow-banked airstrip. The darkness meant they couldn't see much further than the airfield, but Lily could see what she cared about and that was the snow.

Sophia swallowed past the wedge forming in her throat, pushing back the memories that threatened, barely noticing that Jack had come up alongside her until she felt the comforting warmth of his hand slipping around her own. She looked up at him, part fear, part gratitude, and the rest was all love shining in her gaze.

And she wasn't afraid to show it, not this time.

'Thank you for this, Jack.' She reached up on tiptoes and kissed his cheek. 'It means so much.'

'Thank you for coming.'

Their gazes locked, the air whipped around them, cold and frigid, but all she felt was the warmth of his gaze, heating her from the inside out and the hope flourishing with it. She couldn't remember a time when she'd been happier or felt more invincible.

It was strange when it all hinged on his feelings for her and they were entirely out of her control. Was it crazy? Or was it just a symptom of being in love?

And if it was the latter she was ready to get used to it.

What if he doesn't love you back? What if all this is a temporary affliction and in a week or two you have to go back to living as you did before?

She couldn't imagine it. She didn't want to.

'You okay?'

His question and the frown tugging at his brow halted her spiralling thoughts and she smiled. 'Never better.'

'Come on, Daddy, Sphea—can you save all the kissy-wissy stuff until later? I want to get to our bubble!'

Their eyes widened at Lily's astute observation and they each gave an awkward laugh.

'Patience, monkey.' Jack affectionately cuffed her chin, but Lily merely shook her head.

'Nuh-uh, it's my birthday trip!'

'She has a point,' Sophia said, feeling the guilt of it. Here she was, wrapped up in her own emotions, hers and Jack's, when this trip was all about Lily and giving her the best birthday possible.

She and Jack could wait—she looked back at him—they really could. She didn't want anything to get in the way of Lily's fun, least of all their romantic entanglement.

It had taken twenty-four years for her to meet the right man; she could at least wait four days before risking it by exposing the truth in her heart.

'Do you think she finally got over the fact that we're not sleeping in her bubble room tonight?' Jack asked Sophia as he sipped from the glass of wine in his hand and tried his hardest not to pull her to him, even though the urge had been with him ever since they'd put Lily to bed.

She smiled around her own glass, her eyes flickering with the flames of the roaring fire that bathed the suite's living area in its ambient glow, a striking contrast to the view beyond the glass. The floor-to-ceiling windows allowed for a seamless view over the Icelandic landscape, atmospheric and beautiful in its own cold, almost brutal way. The snowstorm that had hit shortly after they'd arrived continued to whip the flakes up into a frenzy and gave the impression of a life-size snow globe at work, blanketing the rugged hillside and making him glad they'd arrived before the worst of it.

'She was asleep before her head hit the pillow, and what a waste that would have been if we'd gone tonight. She'll realise that tomorrow.'

He nodded. 'True.'

'And it's hardly the weather for it,' she murmured, cupping her wine glass in her hands, the sleeves of her white high-neck jumper drawn into her palms and making her look far too sweet and vulnerable, and so utterly desirable. 'The forecast looks good for tomorrow though.'

'Hmm?' He'd been so caught up in her he'd missed the last.

'The forecast,' she said, one brow lifting, her eyes dancing. 'I said it looks better for tomorrow.'

He swallowed. 'Yes…yes, it does.'

He was finding it harder and harder to keep both his desire and his love for her in check, but he didn't feel ready to confess all. He had been, but that was before she'd accepted the offer of a separate hotel room.

Now he was starting to doubt so much and being uncertain wasn't an emotion he was accustomed to handling. In business and in his personal life, he depended on his steadfast control, his clear head, his ability to detach himself from the emotional and form decisions, take action based on facts.

With her, it was becoming nigh on impossible to remain detached and to trust his instincts, which he knew were clouded by his own feelings for her.

And the fact was she'd accepted the offer of another room.

He'd booked it while they were apart and he'd done it out of courtesy, wishing her to have the option. But the hope that she would turn it down and admit that she wished to stay with them had been there. It was still there.

'It's not really a hardship staying here either,' she said softly, her eyes sweeping the room, with its salvaged hardwood floors, sheepskin furs and glazed concrete walls. It was an eclectic mix of industrial chic and natural materials working together in harmony to give a sense of high-end luxury.

'You approve?'

'You asked me the same question on the plane...' Her eyes came back to him, her smile teasing.

'I know. Call me soft, but I care for your approval.'

She studied him quietly and he would have paid his fortune to know what was going through her mind. She wet her lips and leaned forward to place her glass on the coffee table formed from lava rock and rich wood.

'I should probably head back to my room.'

'What if I said I'd like you to stay?'

Even in the low light of the fire he could make out the

flush of colour to her skin, the nervous flicker of her eyes as they came back to him. 'If I stay much longer I won't leave and then we'll have some explaining to do to Lily.'

Lily. Was that all she was worried about?

All? You should be worrying too.

But he didn't want her to leave.

'And you need to get some sleep too,' she pushed. 'When was the last time you slept?'

Truth was, he didn't know, not properly at any rate. 'I dozed on the plane from Tokyo.'

'That doesn't count.' Her eyes raked over his face and then he saw it. She was worried about Lily, but she was worried about him too.

'Do I look that bad?'

'Bad, no. Tired, yes.'

He raked a hand through his hair and took a breath. What would she say if she knew the reason was more down to her than the jet lag and all the travel put together? She occupied his mind day and night, keeping him alert, keeping him on edge as he wrestled with what he felt for her.

She surprised him by scooting over to him and cupping his cheek, her thumb grazing against his five o'clock shadow. 'You should take a leaf out of your daughter's book and admit defeat. Get some sleep. We have days ahead to enjoy and I don't want *us* getting in the way of Lily's birthday trip.'

And then she kissed him, her lips soft and gentle and a complete contrast to the fire coming alive inside. He wrapped his arm around her, pulling her close as he sought to deepen the kiss, to take all that she would give.

She was as breathless as he when she broke away, and in no way ready for sleep, but still she said, 'Goodnight, Jack.'

He reached for her hand as she rose. 'Don't go.'

She smiled down at him, releasing his hand slowly. 'I have to, and deep down you know that too.'

Did he? He gazed up at her, his eyes stinging with the effort. He was too tired to analyse, too het up to worry about it; he just knew his instinct was to keep her close.

'Go to bed, Jack. Tomorrow's a new day.'

She pressed a kiss to his forehead and made for the door, looking back over her shoulder to say, 'Move before you fall asleep right there…'

And then she was gone and his eyes were closing, his glass tipping in his hand and acting as the wake-up call he needed.

Bed. She was right; he needed sleep. There would be time for them another night.

And this holiday was about Lily's birthday above all else, just as she'd reminded him, just as he should have remembered too.

Maybe he was more jet-lagged than he'd first realised… jet-lagged and in too deep…

He'd never felt more out of control in all his adult life. Entirely off balance. It was scary, unsettling and enough to have him moving to bed in the hope that tomorrow, after a decent sleep, he would at least have a better handle on it all.

CHAPTER THIRTEEN

'COME ON, DADDY, the car is waiting.'

Lily was hopping from one foot to the other, looking up at Jack imploringly and Sophia felt for her. This wasn't exactly the morning she'd had planned either, especially when today was her birthday.

The first full day of their trip and Lily's birthday breakfast had already been interrupted by a call from London that Jack just had to take and now, over an hour later, he was back on the phone again, dealing with the same issue. Some difficulty with some takeover or other. Not that Sophia could piece it together from the one half of the conversation she could hear but it had Jack scowling down the phone as they stood in the hotel lobby waiting for him to finish.

'Sorry, sweetheart...' he covered the bottom half of his phone as he spoke to her '...I'll be done soon.'

Lily looked to Sophia. 'Can we go outside and play in the snow?'

Sophia felt Jack's eyes shoot to her even as her skin prickled and her stomach twisted. She wet her lips and gave Lily a small smile. 'Let's just wait for Daddy; he won't be long.'

'Lily, just be patient,' he said, and Sophia gave him a grateful look for understanding, even as she felt foolish for her overreaction. She had agreed to come here; moreover, she'd witnessed an entire snowstorm last night and survived it. But going outside in daylight, surrounded by it...it was different.

Lily crossed her arms and gave a little huff.

'Hey, come on, he really won't be long.'

Lily didn't look convinced and if Sophia was honest she wasn't so sure he'd be done soon either since he was pacing back and forth in the lobby now, deeply engrossed.

A family of four chose that moment to come bustling into the lobby, a girl and boy not far off in age from Lily herself. The parents headed to Reception while the two kids laughed their way out of the big glass doors and kicked off a snowball fight just outside.

Lily watched them through the glass, the wistful look in her eye tugging at Sophia's heartstrings.

They moved off soon enough, a car rolling in to take them away, but that look was still in Lily's eye, her hand now pressed up against the glass as she stared out at the stark white landscape.

Sophia looked back to Jack, still pacing, and told herself to grow a pair. This was Lily's birthday trip; she should be more important than some business call. But then, what did she know about running a corporate empire? The leisure industry was bad enough. Maybe this was the way of things for him. It wasn't as if the business world stopped just because he was on holiday. And it was a Thursday after all, hardly the weekend.

'Okay, Lily, let's go play while we wait for your father.' She offered out a hand to her, which she took, her smile worth every nervous flutter.

Jack quit pacing. 'Where are you going?'

'Just out front; we can make a snowman while you finish your call.' She smiled down at Lily encouragingly. 'What do you reckon? Can we make one that looks like Daddy?'

Lily laughed. 'Yes!'

Jack wasn't smiling though. When she looked back to him his scowl seemed less about the call and more her suggestion.

'Don't worry; we'll be flattering,' she said, trying to lighten the sudden darkness in the room.

'I'd rather you stayed here.'

Sophia frowned. Seconds ago, she'd been convinced he was concerned for her, and how she'd feel playing out in the snow with a small child, and without him. But now...

Then she remembered the time on Samantha's doorstep when he'd told her with no hesitation that he wouldn't leave Lily at the party, how clear he'd been about not trusting her with just 'anyone,' and the reason he too had joined Lily for her sleepover ultimately.

But it couldn't be that now? Not after all they had shared, all that had happened between them. He had to trust her... didn't he?

'Please, Daddy.'

He looked to Sophia for backup, but she was too flummoxed and upset and confused, trying to convince herself it was because he was worried about her, even though she knew deep down it wasn't. Maybe it had been initially, but not now.

'We can stay just the other side of the glass,' she offered quietly, ignoring the way her skin now prickled, not with her phobia of the snow—or worse, being responsible for a child in the snow—but with his mistrust of her.

He looked from them to the glass and back again, his frown lifting a little. 'Okay—just keep where I can see you, agreed?'

'Agreed,' she said, now feeling like a child herself, anger sparking. She tugged Lily's hand gently, her death stare for him alone, not that he'd seemed to notice as his attention shifted back to the phone. 'Come on, birthday girl, let's go and have some fun.'

They went outside and she did as she'd promised, kept them close to the glass as they rolled the snow and built their man. With his bulbous belly and a Sophia-fist-sized punch hole for his mouth, two beady rocks for his eyes and a thin stone for his nose.

Lily stood back and laughed. 'It doesn't look much like Daddy, does it?'

Sophia had half a mind to storm back inside and pull his scarf off him just to wrap it around his icy counterpart and complete the look.

Still, in her anger, she'd forgotten all about her own trepidation...

Lily looked through the glass to where her father was pacing again, his scowl still present, his hand caught half-way through his hair. Sophia checked her watch. At this rate it would be dark before they even started their tour and whilst they would still hopefully get a glimpse of the northern lights when the sun disappeared, she'd like to see the waterfalls and the black sand beach in daylight.

She gave him a look through the glass, one which she hoped said, *Don't forget whose birthday it is*, and tapped her wrist, indicating the time. He grimaced and looked at his own, turning away a second to say something down the phone and then he cut the call and strode for the exit.

'Here he comes,' Sophia said, her hands falling to Lily's shoulders as she turned her to face the door and her father now coming through it.

'I'm so sorry, birthday girl.' He raced up to her and swung her up in the air. 'You ready?'

'Yes!' she squealed, her legs kicking excitedly and sending snow flying from her feet.

Sophia smiled at the heart-warming scene, her anger falling away as quickly as it had come. 'First you need to see our snow Daddy.'

Payback...

He looked at the snowman and back at her, slowly sliding Lily down his front until her feet were back on the ground.

'It's you, Daddy.'

'Me?' His eyes flitted from it, to Lily, to Sophia. 'And you think it's a true likeness?'

She eyed him as she pretended to consider both him and their creation. 'Seems pretty good, if you ask me.'

Lily laughed and Sophia grinned up at him. 'If only you'd been able to help, then maybe he'd have been a little less…portly.'

'Is that so?' he said, his eyes twinkling. 'I only have myself to blame then.'

'Precisely. Now, don't dilly-dally; the car has been waiting long enough.'

She turned on her heel and made her way to the slick chauffeur-driven four-by-four hired to navigate the tricky Icelandic terrain, leaving them to enjoy the view.

She knew he was watching her, and felt that kick of admiration in his gaze before she'd looked away. He liked that she stood up to him. Maybe he'd therefore welcome the idea already setting up camp in her brain that he should switch the pesky little mobile *off.*

'I *really* like Sphea, Daddy. Like really, really like her.'

Lily's words reached her and her lips quirked up, her heart fluttering in her chest. *I really, really like you too, kiddo.*

She couldn't hear Jack's response as the driver greeted her, opening up the rear door for her to climb in, but she hoped Jack's had been close to a ditto at least.

She settled into the back seat, watching them as they headed towards her, Jack's eyes locking with hers, assessing, searching. Was he looking for the anger he must have spied in her earlier?

She softened her gaze with a smile, which he readily returned. Fact was, she'd been mad—she was still mad when she thought on it—but she couldn't *stay* mad at him.

They got in beside her, Lily taking up the seat by the window so that she could enjoy every second of the passing landscape, which put Jack alongside her. Close—too close.

No, she couldn't stay mad, which was annoying and frustrating in its own way.

He looked at her, his eyes flitting from her lips to her eyes and back again, their intensity deepening into something else, something more primal and making her tummy contract over a rush of heat.

Not helping...

She looked away, to the back of the driver's head as he climbed into the car and demanded Jack's attention as they ran through that day's itinerary and the impact their two-hour delay had had. *Two hours.* All thanks to his blasted phone.

Jack was exhausted. Heaven knew whether he'd truly slept properly last night. She'd not had a chance to ask him since his phone had rung the second they'd sat down to breakfast. He needed a holiday, a real break. The thing had to go, and she'd speak to him about it the first chance she got.

As for the trust issue...that would be harder to raise. But maybe she'd just got it wrong. She looked to the passing landscape, the snow-capped rocks, the trees drooping under the weight of it all. It was pretty, even if it did coax memories to the fore that she would prefer remained buried.

Maybe it hadn't been his lack of trust in her to look after Lily at all; maybe she was being unfair and overly sensitive because she hadn't trusted herself either. She breathed through the rising knot of anxiety in her chest, flexing her tightened fists as she closed her eyes against the view, and then she felt his hand upon her knee.

She turned to see him looking down at her, the emotion blazing in his gaze reassuring her and letting her know he was there.

Yes, maybe she had been wrong, because if anyone deserved the benefit of the doubt it was him.

ployed Connor years back. The guy had proved his worth over and over, and yet here he was, seeking his approval for another matter.

And then the truth hit him like a slap to the face. Connor was like that because *he'd* made him that way. *He'd* made him seek approval, *he'd* made him ensure that he was abreast of every situation, involved in every decision, *he'd* demanded that involvement instead of bestowing on him the trust his role demanded.

Jack was a fool, a prize idiot. He'd employed Connor to cover his absences, to be him in his absence, yet his controlling behaviour and his treatment of him had resulted in the complete opposite.

'Connor, stop.'

'I'm sorry… Was that not—?'

'No, Connor, I mean stop. I mean follow your instincts. I trust you to get this right.'

'You—*you* trust me?'

He could sense the guy's frown down the phone.

'Yes. I wouldn't have employed you otherwise. Do what you think you need to, get us this deal. I trust you to do what's right for the company.'

'And you?'

'I'm on holiday. Not to be disturbed until Monday at the earliest.'

'Monday?'

'Yes.'

'Right. Okay. No problem, I'm on it.'

'I know you are.'

'Thank you, Jack.'

'I think it will be me thanking you next week, Connor.'

He could sense his number two smiling now as Jack cut the call and looked from one lady to the other. 'Happy?'

'Yes!' they both piped up and he took a gloved hand from each and gave them a squeeze. Content, happy, relaxed…and so very tired. But that could wait. He'd get some sleep tonight. He had a feeling this was a turning point for him—changing his work-life balance and putting his faith in others.

He thought back to that morning and the fear that had gripped him at the idea of Sophia and Lily venturing out alone. No. He wasn't ready for that. A foreign country, the two people who meant most to him in the world. No. Leaving his company in Connor's hands was fine. Acceptable even. But letting these two out of his sight in a country he didn't know. No. Just no.

He gripped their hands tighter, his love for them overriding.

'Thank you for doing that,' Sophia suddenly said into the quiet.

'It's long overdue.'

'Yes,' she said, the vehemence in her voice surprising him. 'Even if it wasn't Lily's birthday, I'd say the same. Everyone needs time off once in a while. Even someone as successful and as invincible as you.'

Invincible? He didn't feel invincible right now with her eyes looking up at him, their sheen, their concern killing him inside.

'I know,' was all he could manage as he fought back the urge to kiss her.

'Good.'

She wet her lips, her eyes scanning his face, and he realised the urge existed within her too and it was enough. Just to know they shared that need, that she cared for him enough to state her approval of his decision. It was enough.

'We are here, Mr McGregor.'

The Reynisfjara black sand beach was unlike anything she'd ever seen before. Not difficult considering she'd barely travelled out of the UK. Even when she'd attended the training courses put on by her company abroad, she'd kept close to the hotel studying, connecting, networking.

And oh, my, how different things are now...

It wasn't just her travel status changing, it was her whole outlook on life, on what was truly important and what really made her happy. How was it possible for so much to change in such a short space of time?

She pulled her gaze from the waves crashing at the base of the rugged basalt stacks out at sea and looked to Jack. She knew the answer well enough. Even with his woollen hat and his scarf wrapped high around his face leaving her with just a glimpse of his sparkling grey eyes, he made her tummy flutter and her heart warm. At his side was Lily, a perfect miniature copy with her curls escaping her hat, her eyes as grey as his, peering out above the edge of her scarf.

It was the two of them who made her keen to do what she could to repair her relationship with her mum and dad. They made her want more out of life, more than just work.

They were studying the grey basalt columns rising out of the black sand, Jack leaning down to listen to his daughter above the roar of the sea, and she smiled. Lily was likely telling him all about their formation, from lava to volcanic rock... He really hadn't been lying when he'd said she'd been absorbing every word of the brochure. And Sophia couldn't be happier to see the delight in Lily's face at every landmark they visited.

It was the perfect birthday, with or without Aurora playing ball tonight, ever more so to know that even now Jack's phone was turned off in his jacket. He'd taken it out as soon as they'd stepped out of the car and Lily and Sophia had both glared at it. But he'd simply smiled and declared he was turning it off, saying that all those he cared about were right here with him and that no emergency would be important enough to change that.

It had warmed her top to toe, just as it did now. She'd

loved to think…she wanted to think…he'd included her in that sweeping comment, but as much as she now knew she loved him, she had to keep her hope under control.

'So, birthday girl,' Jack said, clapping his hands together, 'are you ready to head to our bubble for the night?'

Lily looked up at him, her gloved hand tugging her scarf away from her mouth. 'Yes!'

'Great. Dinner first, though, then bubble.'

She pouted.

'What—you must be hungry? Aren't you hungry, Sophia?'

'We could grab a picnic?'

'Oh, yes!' Lily blurted. 'A picnic under the stars!'

'Aren't you full of great ideas?' he teased, his eyes dancing into hers and making her come alive inside, heat, laughter and happiness all bubbling up. 'I'll arrange for our food to meet us there… Does mean I'll be needing this though…'

He pulled out his phone and they both grinned.

'For food, we can forgive you, Daddy.' Then she hooked her hands in Sophia's and Jack's, tugging them back towards the car. 'Hurry—the sky is still clear… I have a really good feeling in my…what is it Ms Archer says—*waters*?'

They all laughed. And, truth was, Sophia had a good feeling too. But it was less about the sky and more about her companions. Her smile behind her scarf grew, her cheeks aching from the effort. She'd never smiled so much before that it hurt; she hadn't even known it possible. Not before the McGregors, before her life had started to feel so complete…

Jack knew of camping, glamping, caravanning…you name it, he knew of it…but never had he done such a thing.

He stared up at the roof of their bubble for the night and seriously wondered whether he'd lost his mind. It wasn't that there was just the one room, the one bed even, it was the fact that a toilet trip required a dash into the depths of the forest, in the freezing snow with a torch for company. Plus, he was exhausted—all the fresh air, the lack of decent sleep these last few weeks and now...*this*.

'Isn't it amazing?' Lily's voice was breathless with wonder as she twirled on the spot beside him, her head back, her eyes on the darkening sky above.

He looked at the obvious pleasure in her face and forgot every negative thought. This was why he'd booked it. He could have booked a luxury lodge, a glass-framed house, anything but a solitary bubble in the middle of a forest, but this was what Lily wanted. A true experience under the stars with them all in one bed together, and he had to admit, after spending last night apart from Sophia, the idea of it made any amount of 'slumming it' worth it.

'We'd best eat before you get too distracted,' Sophia teased Lily as she rummaged through the bags of food that had been delivered and started to lay out a feast on the bed. Hams, cheeses, breads, fruit...more continental breakfast than evening dinner in Jack's eyes, but so long as the women were happy.

Who was he kidding?

He was happy. As they sat on the bed munching away, their chatter so easy and comfortable, he was happier than he'd ever been. Happier than he'd even known possible, and he knew the cause was sitting right opposite him, her cheeks glowing in the soft light given off by the solitary lantern, her eyes bright and often locking with his, the hint of a smile permanently on her lips, save for when she was laughing and then her whole face lifted, the mood in the bubble right along with it.

'Can we turn the light off now?' Lily pleaded, pushing her plate away and trying to settle back on the bed.

'Let me just get rid of these...' Sophia started to clear everything away and he moved to help her, their hands colliding over the same dish. She smiled up at him, he smiled back, the connection holding them captive.

'Ahem!' Their eyes snapped to a stern-looking Lily, a giggle erupting from them both as she crossed her arms over her chest. 'No kissing allowed.'

'I wasn't.'

'I didn't.'

They both said in unison.

The little girl raised her brow in total disbelief and Jack looked back at Sophia. 'Well, I may have thought about it.'

Sophia laughed and pulled away, taking the piled-up plates with her and flicking off the light.

'Oh, wow!' It came from Lily, but Jack was thinking it, his eyes now lost to the skies above as he lay back beside his daughter and took it all in.

It was majestic, ethereal, out of this world. Stars glittered as far as the eye could see, and swirling arcs of mist-like patterns streaked across the sky, casting an almost eerie glow.

'I feel like I'm in a dream,' Lily said as Sophia lay down next to her, the three of them now in a row. He felt Lily take his hand, saw her take hold of Sophia's too and pull them both onto her chest. 'It's perfect. This is perfect.'

It was. The perfect everything. And surprisingly comfy. He could already feel his body winding down, his eyes growing heavy as he worked his shoulders into the cushiony softness beneath him. He yawned and blinked rapidly, staving off sleep.

'You should make a wish,' Sophia murmured. 'With all those stars above, it has the greatest chance of coming true.'

'I will,' Lily said with a bob of her head, her small hands squeezing at them both.

He turned his head to look at his daughter, watching her close her eyes, her face screwed up in concentration, and then she opened them. 'Done.'

'What did you wish for?' he asked, his eyes catching Sophia's over Lily's head and knowing what he would wish for if he were six again and he'd lived a life where he could believe in such things. He'd make a wish for the thirty-year-old him, a wish likely to be very similar to Lily's.

'I can't tell you that, Daddy. It won't come true if I do.'

'Of course, how silly of me.' He smiled at her, his eyes lifting back to Sophia's and pausing just long enough to let her know his own wish and hoping she too could share it.

'Thank you for the best birthday.'

'It was all Sophia's doing.'

'I know—I *was* thanking her.' And then she laughed and pressed a kiss to his cheek. Turned to give one to Sophia too. Then she lay back and they all stared up at the sky, absorbing the natural beauty Earth had to offer and forgetting how imperfect life could be.

CHAPTER FOURTEEN

'I'M READY!'

Lily's call came from her bedroom just as Jack entered the living area with a glass of wine for her. It was their last night in Iceland and they were back in the hotel suite Jack had booked for the first night. Tomorrow they would be back in the UK and then…and then what?

She smiled to hide her worry and took it from him. 'Thanks.'

'I'll go and get her settled, won't be long.'

She nodded and watched him go, her thoughts no less troubled. They hadn't discussed the future, and Sophia still didn't feel ready to confuse Lily's birthday trip with it. But everything he did, everything he said—it all indicated that he was starting to feel the same.

And the more time she spent with him, the more they shared, the more *I love you* threatened to erupt.

Here's your food, Sophia.

I love you.

Here's your drink, Sophia.

I love you.

I'll get the door, Sophia.

I love you.

She shook her head at her own madness and settled into the couch, enjoying the soothing quality of the wine and the warming fire.

'Hey, Sophia.' He leaned his head around the corner. 'She's asking for you too.'

He gave an apologetic smile and she grinned back, unfolding herself from the sofa and leaving her glass on the table as she joined him.

'It's no problem. I'd like to anyway.' She moved to walk past him and he reached out, his hand gentle on her arm to stop her.

'Sophia?'

'Yes.' She looked up into the warmth in his gaze and felt it again, ever more pressing, ever more urgent... *I love you*.

'Please stay tonight—with us, with me?'

Her heart squeezed in her chest, her body stiffened. 'I...' The refusal died on her lips. She didn't want to leave.

'Please?' He pressed again and she felt her shoulders ease, her heart too. It was what she wanted.

'Yes.'

He pulled her to him, the heat of his body permeating their jumpers, his scent assailing her senses. 'You will?' he rasped.

She nodded, her eyes falling to his lips, and then he kissed her and any remaining doubt ebbed away on a flurry of heat and happiness.

He broke away too soon for her body's liking. 'Sorry, I just had to do that.'

And she could only smile as he took her hand and led her into Lily's room.

She was already in bed, the pillow up behind her, Baby Bear on her belly with her favourite book open and ready.

They climbed in, one on each side, and she looked from one to the other, her grin quite satisfied.

'Happy?' Jack said to her.

'Yes, now I am. Aren't we, Baby Bear?'

Sophia could feel Jack's gaze on her, feel her own lips lift with a happiness she couldn't contain.

'You read, Sphea.' Lily edged the book closer to her and snuggled in. 'You can be my new mummy, can't you?'

Her eyes shot to Jack's, catching his sudden pallor and... *what*—panic?

'I don't think anyone can replace your mummy, darling.'

'No, but I can have two mummies. People do, don't they? I've seen it on TV.'

Sophia's body relaxed a little, but Jack still looked like he'd seen a ghost.

'True, very true,' she said, kissing the little girl's head and starting to read, hoping Jack would relax and Lily would be satisfied with her non-answer. This was what she'd been worrying about—Lily's attachment, the what-if of it not working out, and having seen Jack's face...

But he'd wanted her to stay with him tonight. Surely that meant he wanted more?

More what though? A relationship? Or sex? Was she just filling a hole in that part of his life? He'd been clear about his feelings towards Elena, his inability to love before.

Had she really just been so blinded by her own love?

Her stomach twisted, her throat closing over and straining her voice as she tried to read.

Lily yawned. 'Daddy's turn now.'

She looked to Jack, but his attention was on the foot of the bed, distant, wary.

'Daddy?' Lily nudged him and his eyes snapped to her.

'What, monkey?'

'Your turn.' She passed him the book.

'Ah...okay.' He gave Sophia a quick look, a flicker of something in his gaze, and then his focus was on the book, his voice far more jovial than she knew he felt.

She should slip away now. Before he could hold her to her promise to stay. She started to move off the bed and felt his hand close around her own.

'Stay, please.'

She looked back into his face and in that second she would have done anything he asked, because there was that look in his eye, the look she had come to depend on, the look that said he cared. Even if it wasn't love, it was enough to keep her there, for now.

She settled back down and he pulled his arm around her and Lily, his hand coming to rest on Sophia's shoulder, his thumb gently caressing her skin. He had to care for her.

He had to.

'Sophia…?'

They were walking through the corridor that led from Lily's bedroom to the living area, Sophia in front, him behind, and every part of him just wanted to reach out for her and pull her in. But he could sense she was trying to keep some distance. The fact she was walking ahead without even a backward glance was enough to tell him that.

'Sophia?' he tried again as she reached the sofa and lifted her glass from the table.

Slowly she took a sip and turned to look at him. The fire was no longer lit and the room was dark save for a solitary lamp and it cast a shadow over her face and made her look…sad.

He'd seen her look many things this holiday but that wasn't one of them. 'What is it?'

She shook her head and gave a small laugh, but it was shaky, unsteady. 'I don't know where to start.'

'You can tell me anything…' He stepped closer, pausing when he was a stride away. 'Is it me? Is it what Lily said?'

'It was your reaction when she said it…' She took a breath and it shuddered out of her. 'Look, I'm sorry, I don't want to hurt her. I don't want to come and go from her life like she doesn't mean anything to me.'

'I don't want you to either.'

'But I will if this, whatever this is, doesn't work out.'

'Do you want us to work out?'

She gave a gentle sigh. 'How can you ask me that?'

'It's a simple question, Sophia. Do you want there to be a you and me?'

She wet her lips, her eyes dark in the low light and glistening now. 'I'm a realist, Jack. It doesn't matter how swept away I get by you, by Lily, by all this…' She fluttered a hand around her. 'I can't help but think it will all get taken away.'

'It won't if we don't want it to.'

'But your face when Lily asked…when she asked about me being…you know…'

He shook his head, one hand reaching out for her, his palm soft upon her cheek. 'I felt guilty. I told you before I couldn't love Elena, not as she wanted me to, and she was her mother. She, of all people…'

He closed his eyes and breathed in deeply. He'd never admitted so much to another person, never made himself vulnerable in this way before, but he knew he owed her this. The truth.

He opened his eyes and cupped her other cheek, cradling her face in his palms as he stepped forward to close the remaining distance between them. 'But you, Sophia, you make me feel that way.'

Her eyes shone up at him, her lips parting on an unspoken thought.

'When I'm not with you I think of you,' he whispered, 'and when I am I feel like I've come home, that I'm where I belong. I've never known the kind of happiness I've found by your side.'

'But…' She shook her head, the move so small he barely felt it. 'What are you saying, Jack?'

'Isn't it obvious?' He searched her eyes for what he wanted to see, desperately hoping she felt the same.

'No…'

'I'm in love with you, Sophia.'

She inhaled softly, her lashes fluttering as emotions

flickered in the wide pools of her blue eyes, their colour so mesmerising, so familiar now that he could close his eyes and still they would be there, ingrained in his memory.

'And though it makes me feel guilty and vulnerable and in all manner of ways uncomfortable, I can't deny that I love you.'

'Is this really happening?' She trembled in his hands, her voice hushed.

'Believe it.' He kissed her, wanting her to feel it, wanting her to take his words and claim them for her own. 'Please believe it.'

He scooped her up in his arms, pressing another kiss to her lips. 'Let me show you how much I love you...'

He walked her to his bedroom and laid her down on the bed. Her eyes were unblinking as they followed him around the room, closing the door, turning the lights down low and stripping away his clothes.

'Jack...'

He paused over the button to his trousers. 'Yes?'

'I love you too.'

Her voice was so definite, so very real, and he stripped the last of his clothing in one swift motion, joining her on the bed and claiming her lips with his.

This was what coming home felt like. This was what love felt like. And now he'd found it he had no idea how he'd live without it again.

And if life was kind he would never have to.

CHAPTER FIFTEEN

SOPHIA STILL COULDN'T believe the night's events.

The sun wasn't even up and she was lying awake, Jack's arm across her naked tummy, his even breath brushing over her shoulder as he slept so deeply, so soundly. She knew how tired he was, the travelling having taken its toll, no matter how he tried to fight it, and she felt for him.

But this was a new beginning. They were talking about a future—a future in which Lily and Jack would settle in the UK. Less travel, more stability for Lily, more time for them—the three of them. It was all coming true and she was too abuzz to sleep any more.

The second she'd awoken she'd replayed his words of love, his attentive mouth as he'd travelled the length of her body, demonstrating his love for her in such a way that she had felt worshipped, cherished, loved more than she'd ever thought possible.

He loved her. He truly loved her.

And she was so utterly besotted, with him and Lily.

Life truly could be perfect. She'd never dared to believe, but now she did.

She turned to look at him beside her, felt that love blossom in her chest, her heart feeling so big it was impossible to breathe.

'I love you, Jack,' she whispered, and then she heard it, the sound of movement in the hallway. Lily was awake.

She frowned and strained to listen. Maybe she'd been mistaken. But no, there was the delicate patter of small feet, a brush of clothing against the wall.

Although Lily knew of their relationship—that ship had

definitely sailed—she wasn't quite ready to have her walk in on them naked and entwined.

She slipped out from beneath Jack's arm and picked up her clothes from the floor, from where Jack had hastily deposited them. Her cheeks flushed even now at the memory and she pressed a hand to them, taking a cooling breath as she pulled them on and silently slid from the room.

She found Lily in the living area, her tiny frame dwarfed by the tall glass that currently showcased Aurora and the stars. It wasn't quite as striking as in their bubble, but it was no less mesmerising, and Lily was certainly mesmerised.

'Lily,' she whispered, not wanting to startle her.

She turned to her and smiled. 'Hi, Sphea.'

Sophia pressed a finger to her lips and gave a gentle, 'Shh, your daddy is sleeping.'

She nodded and looked back to the glass.

'I wish we didn't have to leave,' she murmured as Sophia joined her, her voice taking on a sad edge.

'You and me both,' Sophia admitted truthfully. 'But you know the weather is set to turn. There's another storm on the way and the hotel is already preparing for it. If we don't leave now, we might get stuck.'

'I wouldn't mind being stuck,' she said, looking up at her and taking hold of her hand.

Sophia gave her hand a little squeeze. 'I bet.'

'Do you think we could build another snowman before we go?'

'If we have time after breakfast, I'm sure we—'

'No, now. Just me and you.'

'I don't know, Lily…' She looked back towards the bedroom then the clock on the wall. It wasn't the dead of night, but it was hardly breakfast time either, and what if Jack woke and they weren't here?

'We could leave a note on the pillow; that way Daddy'll know where we are,' she said, guessing at the cause of

Sophia's hesitation. 'And we don't want to wake him. He needs his sleep. He doesn't sleep enough.'

Sophia shook her head. 'When did you get so grown-up?'

She shrugged. 'He works too hard and travels too much…but hopefully that will all be different now.'

Her words chimed with Sophia's own hope for the future, for everything they'd yet to discuss but she felt in her heart would happen.

'I hope so too.'

'So can we? One last snowman and maybe a small walk, just to the lake?' Her eyes were wide and pleading and she couldn't say no, she just couldn't.

'Okay, get yourself dressed in warm clothing. I'll go and write the note.'

Lily gave a silent squeal, her hands tight on Sophia's, and then she was running, her tiny feet silent against the wooden floor as she made for her bedroom to get dressed.

Sophia shook her head, her smile so indulgent and full of love. If she could bottle happiness, she'd bottle this right now and make millions.

Only her man already had his own wealth, the happiness and the money and the love.

She shook her head some more as she made her way to the desk to seek out some paper and a pen.

She'd just finished placing the note on her pillow when she heard Lily's soft approach. She looked up to see her in the doorway, hat and gloves in hand, hair still ruffled from sleep. She smiled and placed a finger over her lips, gesturing to a sleeping Jack as she passed by the bed. Lily grinned and nodded.

She paused at the door and gave him one last loving look. 'Back soon, sleepyhead.'

They pulled on their hats and gloves and zipped their coats high as they made their way to the ground floor, passing the skeleton staff on the way with a respectful greeting and a smile. It did feel a little weird to be wandering around before sunrise, but she figured with a skyline like Iceland's they must be used to people heading out at all hours, looking to enjoy the view.

When they reached the main exit, Lily slipped her hand in hers. 'This is really exciting!'

'It is, isn't it.'

And it really was—her tummy danced with it. She wasn't sure whether it was the early hour, the magic of the lights continuing to ripple through the sky or the aftereffects of last night, but she could feel it too. The butterflies, the excitement, the thrill of what was to come.

Jack woke to nothing. No noise. No Sophia. Nothing.

Instead of her warm, pliant body, he had her pillow clutched to his chest, her scent still there but no residual heat, no heat. How long had she been gone?

He shoved it away, blinking against the chilling grey light that peeped through the gap in the blind, and the feeling of unease grew. The sun was up and yet there was no sound from Lily, no sound at all. She wouldn't sleep this late, even when jet-lagged; she was always up at the crack of dawn.

He raked a hand through his hair and over his face. He felt drugged, his head thick with too much sleep and it didn't help his unease. He threw back the covers and rose up, his head spinning with the speed of the move. One glass of wine and he felt like this…though it wasn't the wine. It wasn't even the persistent jet lag. It was the fact she had gone. That after the night they had shared she'd sneaked out without so much as a wake-up kiss.

But maybe he was wrong, maybe his ears were deceiving him, maybe she was in the living area keeping quiet to let him sleep. She knew how tired he'd been and it was just the sort of caring thing she would do.

He tugged on a pair of lounge pants, his feet heavy as he made for the doorway, and breathed in deep, his arms stretching out. Yes, she would be here, and if not here, maybe back in her own room getting ready for breakfast.

He looked through the gap in Lily's door. Her quilt was thrown back, her bed empty. He opened the door further. No sign. He carried on through the suite.

'Hello?'

Nothing.

'Lily… Sophia…'

Nothing.

A chill shot through him, his pace picking up. He got to the living area. Nothing. He turned and checked the bathrooms, the bedrooms again, every last possible space. Nothing.

Where were they?

Breakfast. Maybe they'd gone down to breakfast… *Without you?*

He tried to slow his stride, tried to calm his pulse. There was no need to panic. No need at all.

His mind travelled back three years, to his house all empty, to the plates on the table untouched, to the deathly sound of silence… He shook his head, shaking off the memory, and his voice was gruff as he sought to fill the quiet. 'You're overreacting.'

And still his skin prickled up, nausea swelling with the haunting past. He pulled on his clothes, his hands trembling with the sickening fear and slowing his progress.

'Just take it easy.'

Finally clothed, he grabbed his mobile, the room card and left, his pace picking up once more as he headed for Sophia's room. Maybe she'd taken Lily with her while he slept. Maybe she'd wanted to make sure he was undisturbed. *Yes*, perfectly reasonable.

He knocked on her door. He knocked again. Nothing.

Breakfast. They must be at breakfast.

He made his way downstairs, noting the staff rushing around, a stream of guests flooding the foyer.

'What's happening?' he asked one of the men, who was shucking his coat and shaking it out.

'Our tour had to turn back. The storm's heading this way and it's pretty nasty. Even managed to blow rocks into the car in front of us. Took it right off the road. Luckily no one was hurt.'

He saw the TV screen in the lobby showing the news report with the snowstorm warning, and the hotel staff were putting up signs warning guests against venturing out.

He swallowed. They wouldn't be out there. They'd be in the restaurant.

But the niggle inside wouldn't quit.

He looked through the glass to the looming skies fast approaching.

'Believe me, it's as nasty as it looks,' the guy said, spying his focus.

'Yeah,' Jack said, his voice sounding distant even to his own ears as his blood pounded over it. He turned away and headed to the restaurant, almost running.

Please be there, please, please...

'Just one more snowball?' Lily pleaded, her eyes alive with laughter, making Sophia shake her head indulgently.

'Just one, *please*.'

Just one...one more push...

Sophia clutched her stomach as it rolled with the memory. So vivid, so real, as if she was there now and it wasn't Lily she was seeing, it was Amy, begging her for that last sleigh ride, the last...

She swallowed and closed her eyes as if it would somehow push the image away.

*Amy is gone—you can't change that. It wasn't your
fault—it wasn't.*

It was Jack's voice talking to her, soothing her, telling
her to put the past to bed, and she felt his comfort as though
he were there with her.

'Sphea? *Sphea?*'

She opened her eyes. Poor Lily's eyes were narrowed,
concerned, her gloved hand reaching up to cover her own.
'What's wrong?'

She slipped her hand over Lily's and gave her a smile.
'Nothing, darling. I was just a little sad for a second.'

'We don't have to throw more snowballs.'

Sophia gave a soft laugh. 'It's not that, but we do need
to be getting back. We don't want your dad worrying about
where we've got to, especially with the weather already
on the turn.'

It was true that the wind was whipping up, the sky hint-
ing at the approaching storm, but as she looked from it to
Lily she could see she wasn't reassured.

'You looked sad, Sphea. *Really* sad.'

'It was a sad memory that came back to me.'

'What was it?'

Lily's frown persisted, her loving eyes determined to
get the truth out of her.

'It's a long story.'

'I like stories.'

'Not this one, darling.'

'I can take it. I'm a big girl!'

She pulled Lily in for a hug, more for her own reassur-
ance than Lily's. 'I know you are…'

She inhaled softly, her mind remembering Amy in all her
young and determined vibrancy, much like Lily's, and she
tried to work out a way to tell her that was child-friendly

and not too upsetting. She knew part of the battle was deal-ing with her own upset and not relaying that onto Lily more than she already had done.

And you should talk about Amy. You loved her. She was your sister. She doesn't deserve to be pushed out.

Her lips lifted a little with the thought. It was the most rational, most loving reason in the world to talk about her sister, and it had taken Jack talking sense into her for her to realise it.

The accident had been tragic, and she needed to tell Lily that she'd lost her, but she could also tell Lily just how amazing her sister had been, how special to her she was...

'I had a sister and her name was Amy...'

They weren't there. They weren't anywhere.

And he knew, even before he went to Reception to make enquiries, that they were outside somewhere, heaven knew where.

The receptionist who'd been on the desk to check them in the previous day smiled up at him as he approached, her smile morphing into a frown by the time he stood over her and she could read the worry in his face.

'Have you seen my daughter and...and...' What did he say? His girlfriend—the woman who had taken it upon her-self to go out with a storm approaching, taking his daughter with her? 'The woman who travelled with us?'

'I'm afraid I haven't, sir. I've only just started my shift. Let me check with my colleagues.'

He nodded swiftly. 'Thank you.'

She moved from behind the desk and walked into a room behind Reception. He turned on the spot, scanning all the people, outside and in. People bustled about, prepping for the storm, guests milled about, working out revised plans for the day, but no Lily, no Sophia.

The receptionist returned. 'It seems they went out about an hour or so ago.'

'Out?' His throat tightened around the word as his worst fears were confirmed and he had to swallow to ask, 'Did they say where they were heading?'

'I'm afraid not, sir, but…well, no one asked.'

Of course they hadn't. Why would they? He raked his hands through his hair, took a steadying breath—*think, think…*

'Did anyone see which way they went?'

Her frown deepened, her head shaking. 'But I'm sure they will be back very soon. The storm is picking up and—'

'Cameras? Do you have cameras out front?'

'Well, yes…'

'Can you check the footage, tell me which way they headed?'

'Of course, sir. I'll ask Security right away, but I don't think you should be—'

'Thank you,' he said over her. He wasn't interested in her advice. No one, no storm, would stop him looking for them.

He looked to the glass, to the wind whipping through the trees, the snowfall starting to build and adding to the thick layer already down. Despite the staff's best efforts, even the path out front, the drive to it too, were no longer visible between the high banks of snow.

He started to pace. He couldn't take this much longer. He needed to get out there, start looking. What if the worst were to happen? What if it already had?

'Sir?'

His eyes shot to the desk, to the woman looking up at him, apprehensive now. 'They headed towards the lake.'

'The lake?' he choked out.

'Yes, sir.'

The lake was through the woods, down a steep bank. It would be slippery, iced over… He was already striding for it.

'Sir, you shouldn't. You—'

He wasn't listening. Instinct fired in his blood, drove his limbs, his mind… He couldn't go through this again—he couldn't.

As they cleared the bank and the woods the snowstorm really made itself known, the trees no longer sparing them the worst of it.

'It's lucky we left when we did!' she yelled over the wind at Lily, whose hand was clutched in hers.

Lily nodded but said nothing. It was hard to talk with the snow lashing against their faces, biting into the band of skin left exposed between their hats and scarves, their eyes struggling to stay open.

She tugged Lily closer and leaned forward against it, her head bowed.

'Sophia!'

Jack?

She lifted her head, blinking as she tried to focus. There was a shape in the distance, coming towards them. The closer they trudged, the more she could see. It was him. And…and he wasn't even wearing a coat. She cursed inwardly—*what on earth?*

A sense of foreboding had the icy chill spreading on the inside now, her skin breaking out in a fevered sweat.

'Lily!' His yell was harsh, choked even. *Oh, no…*

'What's Daddy doing?' Lily shouted up at her.

'I've no idea. Come on.'

She tried to quicken their pace but the snow had banked fast and it was almost as high as Lily's legs. She turned into the little girl and picked her up, wrapping her legs right around her as she continued on. But Jack was faster. He was suddenly upon them, his arms reaching out for Lily and pulling her from Sophia.

She looked up and saw everything she feared looking

back at her. His eyes were wide, a terrified sheen covering his dark skin. *'Jack?'*

He shook his head, his eyes blazing as the snow fell thick and fast around them. 'Inside. Now.'

Even Lily knew better than to say anything, but she looked at Sophia over his shoulder, her frown forming anew. She knew something was wrong. Something was *very* wrong.

Sophia followed on autopilot, her heart racing in her chest, her gut plummeting. Was this all because she had taken Lily out? Alone? Without him?

She remembered all the times she had questioned his trust in those around him, his trust in her, and she knew it to be true.

He'd said he loved her. He'd told her he loved her less than twelve hours ago.

But if he loved her, truly loved her as she did him, how could he not trust her?

She followed blindly, her thoughts spiralling out of control, her heart rate too. Everything had been so perfect, so right…and now…now she realised it was all a lie.

No, not a lie. She'd believed him when he'd said he loved her. But hadn't he also said he wasn't capable of loving anyone the way they deserved? And wasn't that exactly what this proved?

She'd been a fool. A fool to believe this was possible. A fool to believe she deserved her own happy-ever-after.

A fool to fall in love and believe she'd be loved in return.

Because what was love without trust?

Not enough.

He knew Sophia followed him. He was as attuned to her footfall as he was to Lily's living, breathing form in his arms, past and present colliding with sickening clarity.

Only Lily was bigger, much bigger now, and Sophia…she wasn't Elena.

He opened the door to his suite and strode in. Her footsteps ceased. 'Come in, Sophia.'

He couldn't look at her. Instead he headed for Lily's room; he needed her warm and very, very safe.

'Daddy, why are you mad?' Lily lifted her head off his shoulder, the concern in her gaze crushing him.

'I'm not mad. I was worried.'

'Because we were gone?'

He nodded and lowered her to her feet.

'But we left you a note…'

'A note?'

He crouched, his hands sweeping over her face, her hair, taking off her hat as he kissed her forehead and held her face close.

'Uh-huh.' She nodded. 'On the pillow, next to you.'

He dragged in a breath. So he'd missed the note. It was likely wrapped up in the bed sheets. It didn't change what had happened, how close they'd been to putting themselves in danger.

'You get yourself into some dry clothes, okay? I'm just going to talk to Sophia.'

'Don't be mad with her. It was my fault. I begged her to take me out.'

He closed his eyes and kissed her once more. 'Off you go.'

She nodded but he could tell she wanted to say more… so much more…and he didn't want to hear it. He rose up and closed her door, turning back to see Sophia still on the threshold, her hat and gloves clutched to her chest, her eyes averted and skin pale.

'What did you think you were doing?'

She started like a frightened rabbit, her eyes coming to

him, wide and glinting. 'She wanted to play in the snow just one last time before...before we left.'

He stalked towards her, his anger fizzing in his bloodstream. 'And you thought that was wise, with a storm on its way?'

He threw a hand in the direction of the outdoors, shaking his head in disbelief. 'Anything could have happened, Sophia. *Anything.*'

'It was...it was f-fine when we left. The sky was virtually clear, the lights were dancing, and Lily... Lily just wanted to play some more in the snow.'

'At the lake! You, of all people, should know better than that!'

He was shaking inside and out as he loomed before her now. He couldn't stop. He was so afraid, so angry. He needed her to see what she had done, to realise the danger in it. If he had lost Lily—*hell*, if he had lost Sophia too... And she looked so tiny right now, so fragile and easily broken, her auburn hair a crazy mess around her porcelain complexion.

He reached for her, gripping her forearms, grateful that she was living and breathing in his hold even as the words tumbled out of him. 'What if you'd fallen, what if she'd slipped, what if you'd cracked your head open on a rock, then what? What would have happened?'

She inhaled sharply, her eyes widening, the tears quick to well. 'How could you say that to me?'

He stared at her, saw the hurt in her eyes, the pain, the anguish, and his stomach lurched. She wasn't seeing him; she was seeing the death of her sister all over again. After all he'd said, after he'd encouraged her to move on, to believe she wasn't to blame.

'Sophia...' He cursed, squeezing his eyes shut and opened them again, his head shaking. 'I didn't mean...'

She pulled out of his grasp, stepping backward, her own head shaking, the tears spilling over. 'You meant it.'

'Sophia, I just… I couldn't go there again, after Elena, after she'd run out…the accident… I have to keep Lily safe…and you, you were out there…'

She was still shaking her head, her whole body trembling. 'You *told me* it wasn't my fault. You *told me* I shouldn't live in fear of the past. You told me to face up to it and move on.'

'I did and you should.'

She was heading for her room now and he was torn between Lily in his suite and Sophia across the hall. 'Sophia, please, come back. Let's talk this through.'

'No, Jack,' she threw at him over her shoulder. 'I fell in love with you for so many reasons…' Her voice cracked and her lashes fluttered over her eyes as more tears escaped, each and every one killing him. 'But being a hypocrite wasn't one of them.'

'Sophia, please, I'm sorry. Tell me what I can do to fix this.'

She shook her head. 'It's too late for that, Jack.'

He stepped forward again as she unlocked the door to her room, desperate, pleading. 'Please, *I love you.*'

She pushed the door open and turned to him. For a second he dared to hope, dared to believe she could give him a chance.

'I love you too, Jack…but without trust…'

She looked away, her breath shuddering through her.

He frowned, his palms outstretched emphatically. 'I *do* trust you.'

He did. He felt that trust all the way to his bones. He trusted her more than he had anyone else in his life, but she wouldn't even look at him, her body shuddering with every breath she took.

'I'm not sure you know how to trust, or how to move on from Elena.'

She took another breath, slower this time, her chin lifting, her eyes raking over him before coming back to meet his eyes coldly. It was admirable even that she could find the strength from somewhere.

'Goodbye, Jack. Give Lily my love. Tell her she can write to me if she likes. I'll find my own way home.'

And then she was gone, the door closing softly behind her, and he knew she meant it. That she wanted nothing more to do with him.

But she was angry, upset; she just needed time to think, time to understand how worried he'd been, why he'd said all he had. *Idiot*. He forked his hands through his hair, leaving them to hang off the back of his neck in desperation.

He should have been more controlled. He should have thought before he'd spoken. But that was just it—he'd been too upset to think.

And he'd hurt her in the process.

Really hurt her.

He turned to go back to his suite, turned again to go to Sophia, repeated the move and knew he had to go to Lily, that Sophia needed time to cool off. And that was the one thing they had—time.

All flights were grounded due to the storm.

He just hoped there was enough time to fix the damage his words had done.

CHAPTER SIXTEEN

THERE WASN'T ENOUGH TIME.

Twelve hours later and he'd learned from the hotel staff that Sophia had checked out and paid for her room. She'd left no message, no details of where she'd gone or how she planned to get home. Domestic flights were still cancelled when his own jet had been given permission to leave and so they'd travelled back to the UK without her, a fact that had Lily refusing to speak to him.

It had been nearly a week now and no word. Lily was still barely speaking to him and he couldn't concentrate on work, on anything. He'd avoided booking back into her hotel, wanting to give her the space she so obviously still needed. But it was becoming more and more obvious she wasn't coming around.

Every message, every email, every phone call, all ignored, and he couldn't bear it any longer. He had to see her. He had to explain. He had to make her see how sorry he was, how right she had been, about everything. He had been living his life in fear of the past, doing everything he'd accused her of doing.

And now he wanted a chance to show her that he *was* ready to move on. With her. If she'd have him.

He checked his watch. It was two o'clock on a Friday afternoon. She was more likely to be at work than at home and since Lily was with Ms Archer studying—something she was far more positive about now that she knew he was finding her a school—it meant he could go to see Sophia alone.

He walked into the hotel foyer and felt his heart pulsing right up through his throat. He was nervous, so nervous,

and being in her space, surrounded by memories of her...
He couldn't mess this up. He just couldn't.

He strode over to the reception desk and the woman behind it smiled up at him. 'Good afternoon, Mr McGregor, it's a pleasure to see you again. How may I help you?'

'I'd like to speak to Ms Lambert, if she's available.'

She frowned, her head cocking to one side as she looked to her computer screen. 'I do believe Ms Lambert is currently on leave. Let me just check...'

She navigated the system as he drummed his fingers on the countertop, hoping that she was wrong.

'Yes, I'm afraid she is away, but—'

'Mr McGregor, how lovely to see you back here.'

He turned at the familiar male voice and saw the assistant manager approaching.

'Andrew, isn't it?'

'Yes, well remembered, sir.'

Jack looked to him with hope. 'You wouldn't happen to know where I can reach Soph— Ms Lambert?'

Andrew's eyes sparkled over his faux pas. Just how much did this man know of him and Sophia? And if he did know, would he still help?

'Come this way, sir.'

He touched Jack's arm lightly and led him off to one side, out of earshot. 'I believe she's in Hertfordshire.'

'Hertfordshire?'

'Visiting her parents.'

'Her parents?'

'Yes. It seems she decided that it was time she spent some quality time with them.'

'She did?'

Andrew's eyes sparkled even more, his lips curving into a smile. 'I believe you have something to do with that.'

'I did?' Jack's own lips quirked up; he'd got something right then. 'Yes, I guess I did.'

'And since she's been there a few days already, it must be going well, don't you think?'

He did think. He really did. But it didn't change the fact that he needed to see her, he needed to put things right between them.

'I did get a message from her confirming that she would be back at work on Monday. I think she intends to travel back this evening, taking the weekend to get sorted out, that sort of thing.'

'She'll be home tonight?'

'Indeed.' He grinned now, his face so full of encouragement Jack had the sudden urge to kiss the man. Instead, he gripped his arms and thanked him.

The old man nodded, his eyes starting to glisten. 'I reckon if you try about eight-ish, she'll be home.'

'Good. Good. Thank you, Andrew. Thank you.'

He started to leave.

'You're welcome…and sir?'

Jack paused midstride.

'Good luck!'

Sophia slotted the key in her lock and winced as her shoulder twinged, her body protesting after four nights in her childhood bed. But it had been worth every broken spring, every minute of lost sleep, to have reclaimed what she'd lost all these years: a place in her family home with parents who clearly loved her and had missed her so much.

How she had been blind to it before she didn't know, but it had taken Jack—*Jack*. She closed her eyes over the pain that tore through her, the ache of loss as acute as any grief, and tried to push past it. Though it was no use. She missed him. She missed him so much it hurt like a physical pain no medication could cure.

She opened her eyes and dragged in a breath as she pushed open her door and lifted her suitcase off the floor.

A hot bath would help; it wouldn't stop thoughts of him, but it would ease her aching—

'Sophia?'

She froze, the voice, the man who had plagued her day and night was so real, so very real.

'Sophia?'

She turned towards it and there he was, standing in the hallway. 'How did you—?'

'Samantha let me wait for you with her and Noah.'

She nodded dumbly. So that was where he'd come from. But it didn't change things… It didn't change the fact that she couldn't be with him.

'Why are you here, Jack?'

He walked towards her. 'Can I come in?'

She dragged in more air, her eyes watering as her mind waged war on her body. One saying yes. The other saying no.

'Please, Sophia, just give me five minutes?' he pleaded, his brow raised, eyes emphatic. 'That's all I need.'

She couldn't fight him. She didn't have the strength for it. She'd played out so many scenarios in her head and none of them could match the reality, the force of her own reaction to him, her need for him to hold her and tell her all would be okay in spite of how much he had hurt her.

'Five minutes, Jack.'

She turned away and headed to the kitchen, leaving her case in the inner hall.

She heard him close the door, his footsteps closing in behind her. He was really here. A week apart and he was now here, in her home. She remembered the last time they had been here, her eyes flitting to the sofa that had been extended out that night. The night they'd… She pressed her shaky fingers to her lips, swallowing back the sob that threatened.

'Look at me, Sophia…*please.*'

He sounded so broken, so strained, his vulnerability impossible for her to ignore as she did as he asked.

'I've missed you so much.' It rushed out on his breath, his eyes glistening with sincerity. 'I am so sorry for everything I did, everything I said. The truth is you were right. I was a hypocrite; I was living in the past, scared of it, scared of everything I couldn't control.'

He stepped closer, so close she could smell his scent, his painfully familiar cologne, and it made her body warm, her throat close over with another wave of tears, of longing, of what she daren't hope for but did anyway.

'It wasn't about my trust in you; it was about my fear of losing Lily, of losing—'

'I would have protected Lily with my life,' she forced out, hating that he could doubt it. 'I never would have put her in danger.'

'I know that, and that's what I'm saying. I trust you to keep her safe, but that day, that morning, I was so scared, not just about losing her, but you too. If anything had happened to *either* of you, I don't know how I'd cope.'

Words failed her. She could only stare at him as he continued. 'Don't you see, Sophia, you are as much a part of me as Lily is? Don't you see that's why I felt guilty about Elena? Knowing that you could become a part of me whereas she… she was Lily's mother, she was my best friend, but she was never the woman I wanted to marry, to make a life with, to make a home with.'

His words teased at her heart, every one of them pushing out the chill and replacing it with the warming beam of hope.

'I do love you, Sophia, more than I ever thought possible. I want to be with you. I want to make a life with you, here in London, or anywhere you want to go, just so long as you are with me. With us.'

He reached out to gently raise her chin, to hold her eye. '*Please* believe me.'

'I do believe you love me,' she whispered. 'But I need you to trust me too.'

'I do…and I'll prove it to you. I can be better. I try to control everything that happens to Lily, who she's exposed to, what she does… Everything. But I'm trying to change. I've promised her she can go to school. I've promised her we're going to have a home. I've promised that I'm going to try and bring you home too.'

She smiled at that. It was small, watery, but it was there.

'You've changed so much since I met you.' He curved his hand around the back of her neck, his touch lighting up the skin beneath and feeding her with his warmth. 'You've faced up to the past, your fears, you've returned to your family—'

She frowned. 'How did you know?'

'Andrew.'

She gave a gentle scoff. 'Figures.'

'Don't be mad with him. I think he knew a desperate, lovesick man when he saw me.'

She laughed softly, her eyes searching his. 'Lovesick?'

'Heartbroken. I'm nothing without you, Sophia.'

Seeing the tears in his eyes tore her apart inside but she was struggling for words, struggling to be rational when all she wanted to do was cave in to the emotions within and kiss him, hug him to her and never let him go. But how could she trust him to trust her?

'You changed with my help,' he said into her pained silence. 'Please credit me with the same ability, please help to make me a better man too.'

He was right, so right. If she could change so much, why couldn't he? She talked about his lack of trust in her, but she needed to put her faith in him too. To believe he could change. That together they could be so much better.

She couldn't hold back anymore. She launched herself at him, her lips claiming his as they parted on a surprised rush of air.

'Does that mean you will?' he tried to say against her lips that were pressed tightly to his. 'You'll give me—*us*—a chance?'

She laughed as she kissed him more. 'Yes,' she blurted. 'Yes.' She kissed him again. 'Yes.'

And this time she deepened the kiss, coaxing his whole body to life as he kissed her back, his arms folding around her and lifting her off the ground. She'd never felt so light, so free, so happy and complete.

She lifted her head, gazing down into his eyes that were so wet and so happy at once. 'I love you, Jack.'

He beamed up at her. 'I love you too, Sophia.'

'Always and for ever.'

'Are you getting all romantic and hopeful on me?'

'Yes.'

He swung her around in the kitchen and nearly took out the pots on the drainer. 'Lily's going to be made up; she's already insisted on being a bridesmaid.'

Sophia froze, her heart pulsing in her chest. 'Are you asking me to marry you?'

'Not right now, of course. I'll prove myself to you first, but when I said all that stuff about making a life together, about you being the woman I want to marry, that's kind of where I was heading…'

She started to laugh. She couldn't help it, his boyish, almost coy expression doing her in. 'In that case, just so you know, it would be yes. Not now, of course, but when you feel ready.'

'When I feel ready?'

She nodded, making an agreeing squeak.

'Are you mocking me, Ms Lambert?'

'I wouldn't dare.'

'Why you…' And then he was tickling her and she was running away, stumbling through the living room as she tried to avoid his wandering hands, the backs of her knees colliding with the sofa, and then she was tumbling over it, taking him with her. Two bodies, all legs and arms entwined.

'Sophia?'

She wrapped her arms around his neck as she gazed up into his flushed face. 'Yes?'

'Shall we get the bed out?'

'I've a better idea. Why don't we actually christen my bed this time?'

He laughed as he kissed her. 'I'm not sure I want to waste another second. A week's been long enough.'

'True…but now we have the rest of our lives together.'

'I love the sound of that,' he murmured against her lips.

'And I love you, Jack…'

She sealed her declaration with a kiss, one that spoke of her love, her trust, her faith in their long and happy future together…and they did get to the bedroom, just much, much later.

EPILOGUE

Two years later

NEVER BEFORE HAD Jack suffered such noise. His eardrums were ringing with it. Laughter, shouting, music playing—it was about all he could do to still smile.

'You know next time Lily asks for a birthday party at home,' he grumbled in Sophia's ear, 'I'm going to suggest Iceland all over again…maybe even the North Pole. I bet it's super-quiet this time of year with Santa on holiday.'

'You said that last year.'

'Yes, well, I clearly forgot what a terrible idea this was. At least Noah only had a handful of friends at his…' He looked over the many, many heads in the room. 'I'm sure she's invited every child she's ever met, plus her entire class at school.'

Sophia merely smiled. 'She's making up for lost time, and don't forget, you did agree to her having thirty.'

'Thirty! I'm sure I didn't.'

She looked up at him. 'You were a little distracted at the time.'

Eddie chose that moment to gurgle in his mother's arms and Sophia gently bobbed him up and down.

'Now I remember, Lily asked me the day we came home with this little bundle.'

'Yes, she's not daft, that one.'

'No, but her dad clearly is.'

Sophia laughed as the doorbell sounded. 'Oh, that'll be Isla and the family. You go and get it and I'll pass Eddie to Mum.'

'Oh, no, you won't,' Samantha said, coming up beside them. 'Your mum has filled her cuddle quota; it's my turn.'

'Are you getting broody again?' Sophia grinned at her friend as she eased Eddie into her arms.

'Good heavens, no. I like to cuddle and go. It's always best when you can hand them back.'

'Amen to that,' Jack said, wincing as a high-pitched squeal bounced off the walls of their Georgian dining room.

'Jack!'

'I'm just kidding, love.'

'Get the door before they scarper at the racket. It's time to get some games going before things get out of hand.'

'Out of hand?' he said, his brows raised as his eyes swept over the room. 'I think it's a bit late for that.'

She elbowed him. 'Quit the ribbing and get the door. Musical chairs will have them contained and entertained in one.'

'Musical what?'

'You'll see.'

'You do know how much those chairs cost, don't you?'

'Almost as much as it cost to have the room renovated, yes. Just relax, Jack, live a little.'

'I'll relax when we have our house to ourselves again.'

But in truth he wore the silliest of grins, because life couldn't be better. He had a happy daughter, a healthy son, a wife he adored and an extended family he'd never thought possible.

He made for the door and halted, swinging back to pull his wife into his arms. 'I love you, Mrs McGregor.'

Her eyes shone up at him. 'And I love you too...even when you're a grump.'

'Ouch.'

'Now, go and get Isla before they run—or, worse, freeze on our doorstep.'

He did as she bade, answering the door to Elena's mum,

husband and three children. There would always be a part of him that bore regrets. The biggest one of all that Elena never got to be reunited with Isla, not properly.

But in his heart he knew she'd be happy for what their daughter now had. The one thing they'd grown up wanting and always thought unreachable.

A real family, full of love, and a place to call home.

* * * * *

WHAT HAPPENS
AT THE RANCH…

CHRISTY JEFFRIES

To specialist Jeremy Colwell, my first baby brother, who arrived to a house already filled with the bossiest and most attention-demanding siblings ever, yet still found a way to become the glue that holds us all together.
I love your morning calls, your listening skills and your steel-trap memory that rivals a herd of elephants'.
No matter how many nieces or nephews or in-laws get added to the mix, you always remember everyone's birthdays and anniversaries and accomplishments.
And you always have the best family stories.

I can't wait until you write a book of your own.

Chapter One

Tessa King never shied away from an army of television cameras pointed in her direction. But she'd never had to face those familiar lenses from the opposite side of her father's flag-draped casket.

Until today.

Tessa took a deep breath and inhaled the competing scents of flower arrangements and breath mints as she eyed the cheap boxes of tissue the First Congregation of Teton Ridge placed in each pew for the thousands of mourners who'd come to pay their final respects.

Of course, not everyone could fit inside the community church built long before nearby Jackson Hole,

Wyoming, had become a popular resort destination. Vice President Roper King could have had a much grander, more formal in-state funeral at the rotunda of the United States Capitol. However, Tessa's father was well-known for bucking trends and doing things his own way. That was probably why he hadn't told anyone but his wife about the pancreatic cancer diagnosis. Instead, he'd let his children and his staff think he was returning to the family ranch for a much needed vacation away from the constant demands of Washington, DC.

While small, this church was the most fitting place to hold the patriarch's final send-off. It was where all of the biggest moments in Roper's life had occurred. His baptism. His first, third and fourth marriages (the family *never* discussed wife number two). The christenings of all six of his children, whom he referred to as his late-in-life blessings. And the announcements of his campaigns to run for state senate and, later, governor of Wyoming.

Despite rising through the political ranks and becoming the vice president of the United States of America, Roper King had always remained humble. Especially when he told people that he'd taken his first breath on the Twin Kings Ranch and that's where he'd take his last.

It would've been nice if you'd told us ahead of time that you already knew the final one was coming sooner than we expected, Daddy, Tessa thought as she stared across the aisle at the rest of her family. She was supposed to be sitting in the front row with her mother and five siblings. However, the last time they'd all been to this church together was when they were young children and everyone could still fit on one of the small wooden pews. Nobody had anticipated the fact that while they'd all grown up, everything else in this town had remained the same. Plus, her network producers had thought it more strategic for her to sit on this side of the church, in the same camera shot as some of the most powerful leaders in the world, so she'd volunteered to relocate.

She should've told the network bigwigs to go screw themselves, but she was currently in negotiations for a syndicated weekly series and these kinds of opportunities didn't come around too often.

So instead of being able to lean against her mother, or even her favorite brother, Duke, for physical and emotional support, Tessa was squished next to the current president of the United States. Normally a distinguished woman, the president's teeth kept making a loud clicking sound every time she shifted her cough drop from one side of her mouth to the other. The president's husband, who sat beside his wife, kept adding her discarded wrappers to the ball-shaped wad of cellophane he was crinkling in his palm. Tessa would have been annoyed at their distracting sounds if she hadn't already caught the First Gentleman consoling the president with a tender hug while they'd waited in the shadows of the church's alcove before the service started. He'd been whispering to his wife that the cool menthol would help limit her sniffling and soothe her throat for the eulogy she had to deliver.

Everyone was mourning the loss of her father, not just Tessa.

Still. She had never felt so alone. She'd been nauseous since the first speaker had started his twenty-minute eulogy and there'd been several speakers since. Even though she'd had absolutely no appetite this past week, she'd gone against her better judgment and forced herself to drink one of her mom's plant-based protein smoothies this morning. Another queasy wave rolled deep in her belly.

Clearly, that smoothie had been a mistake.

There was no air movement in this old church and Tessa could feel her cheeks growing warmer with each labored breath. The wooden pews had been drenched with furniture polish in anticipation of the biggest media event Ridgecrest County had ever seen, and the silky fabric of her couture black dress caused her to slink lower and lower in her seat.

Keep it together, she commanded her aching head as she strategically propped the toe of her black pump against the hymnal shelf in an effort to angle the rest of her body into a more upright position.

Unfortunately, the speakers kept speaking, the president kept sucking on a cough drop to keep from sniffling, Tessa kept sliding lower and the cameras kept rolling.

She needed to get out of there.

Finally, a large white screen rolled down from the ceiling and a video montage began. Photos of her father flashed behind the casket as somber orchestra music played through the speakers overhead. Daddy hated orchestra music and he hated drawn-out affairs like this. Whoever was in charge of this production would've been fired from Tessa's set if they'd put together such a formulaic and frivolous piece.

But then the image on the screen changed to a picture of her father standing next to the diving board at the Twin Kings' pool. Roper King had his hands cupped around his mouth as he called out last-minute instructions to ten-year-old Tessa, who was poised on the springboard a few feet above the deep end. Even though she'd gone on to win numerous medals in diving competitions during her teen years, she still remembered the exact words he'd been saying to her in that picture.

"Don't worry about all those twists and flips, Tess. Just jump high and dive deep."

But it was the twists and the flips that had won her medals. It was also one of those particularly bad twist-and-flip combinations that had cost her a spot at the Junior National Championships. And her diving career. And so much more.

Tessa's fingertips instinctively traced the smooth

scar the surgeon had thoughtfully hidden along her hairline.

Her head began to pound as the video screen went fuzzy. She gulped, but her mouth was too dry to swallow. The walls of the church felt as if they were closing in on her and the flowers surrounding the casket seemed to be doubling in size. This time when she slid lower in the slippery pew, she hoped the ground would swallow her up.

Tessa's throat tightened. There was no way this could be happening now. She hadn't had a full-blown panic attack since that day she'd climbed back onto a springboard after her head surgery. Her rehab therapist at the time had explained that traumatic brain injury could cause anxiety, especially when faced with memories of the past event.

Her brain tried to tell her rising heart rate that she was older now. And nowhere near a diving board, let alone a swimming pool. Yet, no matter how many times Tessa's normally logical mind tried to remind her of this fact, her lungs wouldn't cooperate and she couldn't suck in enough oxygen. Just like back then, she needed to get away from the pressure of failure.

Ignoring the queasiness in her stomach and the shakiness in her knees, she rose from her seat too quickly and tripped over an extension cable as she ran down the center aisle toward the exit. If there were any murmurs from the crowd or any cameras turned in her direction, she didn't know. All she could hear was the blood pounding in her head and all she could focus on were the giant double doors ahead of her. Outside, the crisp January breeze smacked her in the face, but she didn't slow her pace. Tessa made it down the first set of steps before crashing into a man wearing a black suit and dark sunglasses.

"Be advised, one of the mares has left the corral. Appears to be Precision."

Special Agent Grayson Wyatt heard the radioed communication in his earpiece right before the church doors flung open. The Secret Service agency's Protective Intelligence Division had come up with the code names for the members of the King family, and Grayson immediately recognized this particular "mare" as the former vice president's oldest daughter—the one whose face was on TV every night appearing cool as a cucumber as she argued with her adversaries.

Tessa King's code name was Precision, a fact that immediately put Grayson on high alert because the young woman stumbling toward him appeared to be anything but precise.

When she slammed into his chest, Grayson's hands latched onto her upper arms to steady them both.

"What happened?" he barked, scanning the area behind her for any sign of chaos or a mass exodus of people that would indicate a much bigger crisis was currently underway. Yet the only person who had followed her outside was one of the agents assigned to vestibule detail.

"I can't stay here." Her words were rushed and her heavily made-up eyes blinked back her panic. "I'm gonna..." Tessa King attempted a ragged breath but couldn't seem to draw in any air. Instead, there was a low gagging sound in her throat and she heaved the contents of her stomach directly onto the concrete step to the right of his polished wingtips.

He moved to the left before a second heave, which was thankfully less productive, yet kept one hand on her trembling shoulder, trying to block the public's view from a rather indelicate situation. When it seemed as if the vomiting had subsided, he patted his empty pockets in vain, wishing he hadn't foregone the decorative handkerchief when he'd purchased his last batch of suits and ties for this assignment.

Grayson stepped in closer. "Ma'am, do you need me to help you to the restroom?"

Her pupils were dilated and glazed over, her entire body now shaking. She was either high as a kite or in the middle of a medical crisis. Possibly both.

"Ma'am. Can you hear me?"

"So dizzy," she slurred, grabbing onto the lapels of Grayson's suit jacket right as her legs gave way.

There was no time to form any sort of plan. He'd been trained to react to emergency situations—even when he wasn't sure what the emergency exactly was—and his instincts kicked into gear. Grayson easily swung the woman up into his arms. Her eyes were a bit glassy, but her lids were still open, which meant she wasn't unconscious. Yet.

"Wyatt has intercepted Precision," the team leader said over the radio, which transmitted into Grayson's earpiece. While it wasn't the same thing as hearing the words *Code 4* or *All Clear*, it was basically his team's way of communicating that he could handle the situation so that everyone else could maintain their assigned tasks.

"Hate…that…stupid…code name," the woman in his arms gasped between short breaths. Then her head fell against his shoulder as she went completely limp. Getting her medical assistance became his top priority. Unfortunately, the Emergency Response Team was on the rear side of the church building, stationed away from all the people and news crews.

A blinding flash of cameras exploded behind the temporary barricades where several officers from the uniformed division were trying to hold back a small crowd. Quickly adjusting his priorities to include both medical aid and now protective cover, Grayson rushed her to the closest car where she would be out of the line of sight.

"Take us around to the rear of the church," Grayson told the surprised driver in the front as he laid the woman on the narrow strip of carpet in the open area in the back of the car.

As the vehicle pulled forward, Grayson spoke into the microphone attached to the clear wire running behind his ear. "Be advised Precision has fainted. We are en route to the ERT staging area so the medics on scene can examine her without compromising the security of the main entrance or impeding the primary evacuation route with additional personnel."

"Roger that," the supervising agent in charge replied over the radio. "Ambulance is on standby."

There was the unmistakable sound of screeching tires as a white news van swerved in front of them, causing their tense driver to jerk the steering wheel to the right. Grayson's head thumped against the roof and one of the black silk curtains came loose from its holder over the side window. He hoped the guy driving them to safety had been trained in evasion maneuvers.

Tessa's eyes fluttered open and Grayson scanned the parking lot behind them for any additional threats while simultaneously placing his fingers on Tessa King's neck to check her pulse. The skin at the base of her collarbone was warm and softer than anything he'd touched in quite a long time.

"What happened?" she asked. Her full pink lips were slightly parted, bringing his attention back to her face—a heart-shaped face with high, rounded cheekbones that framed a perfectly straight nose. He shouldn't notice how attractive she was, but being observant was part of his job.

The other—and more important—part of his job was to ensure the safety of the First and Second families, as well as the thousands of people gathered both inside and outside of Vice President King's funeral. Keeping the scene from turning into a full-fledged spectacle made his job, as well as the jobs of all the other assets on the multiagency teams, much easier.

Tessa's breathing normalized once she'd gone unconscious, but now it threatened to resume its faster pace. She tried to lift her shoulders, but the vehicle swerved again and her elbows lost their traction.

"I asked what happened." This time her words were more of a command than a question. And in Grayson's experience, rich and powerful people like Tessa King were accustomed to having their orders followed.

Grayson couldn't afford to go into some long-winded explanation and risk losing focus of the paparazzi jockeying for position along the sidewalk. "You fainted outside the church."

"That's ridiculous," she replied, her quick breaths making her nose give a little snort.

Tessa tried to sit up again, but Grayson put a hand on her shoulder. "You better stay low until we get to the MultiAgency Command Center."

"Where?" Creases formed between her brows as she gingerly lowered her head.

He exhaled, still concerned about a possible head injury but relieved she wasn't putting up any resistance to his keeping her out of harm's way. "The place where all the federal and local agencies, like the sheriff and fire departments, come together—"

"I know *what* a MACC is," she interrupted, her eyes likely rolling upward in annoyance behind her closed lids. Of course Roper King's daughter would be well-versed on all the government acronyms. Perhaps this wasn't even the first time something like this had happened to her. "I'm asking *where* it is. As in how much longer do I need to lie here like some sort of hapless victim."

"It's in the big white staging tent set up behind the church. We'll be pulling up to it in about forty-five seconds as long as none of these dumbass reporters get in our way."

"There's already a ton of them coming up behind us," the driver said, using the rearview mirror to give Grayson a pointed look. "This thing ain't exactly built for speed, you know."

"Just keep driving," he told the older gentleman in the front seat. "If anyone gets in our way, run them over."

"Run them over?" Tessa lifted one brow. "I assume you mean the *dumbass reporters*?"

Damn. Grayson had forgotten that she was one of them.

He sighed. "Fine, *don't* run them over. Let them

get close enough to the windows so that they can get a good shot of the former vice president's daughter right after she tossed her cookies all over the front steps at her daddy's funeral."

Tessa squeezed her eyes shut again and Grayson inwardly cringed. Not because of the harshness of his words, but at the unfortunate reminder of the reason they were all there.

Roper King had been a good person and an easy assignment—up until this point. The man had been an admired patriot and deserved to be laid to rest with honor. While the jury was still out on the rest of the King family, Grayson owed it to the heavily decorated military commander, former Wyoming governor and United States vice president to prevent the memorial service from turning into a full-fledged circus.

Tessa squinted one eye open. "I thought you said I fainted?"

"You did. Right after you puked your guts out." Okay, so maybe that sounded a little worse than it was. But he needed to convey the seriousness of the situation to her.

She rolled her head to the side to get a better look at him. "Do they throw in the black sunglasses for free when you buy your footwear at Agents 'R' Us?"

"No." He allowed his eyes to lazily travel down her bare, toned legs until they came to her black suede heels. "Don't they sell functional winter shoes at Divas 'R' Us?"

A small huff escaped her lips before she gave him a dismissive glance and turned her head away, effectively reminding Grayson that he wasn't there to trade insults with Roper King's grieving daughter. Even though she'd started it.

He cleared his throat and directed his attention back to their driver. "See the barricade next to the tent? Pull straight in there. Don't worry, they'll move the barricade for you."

As soon as the vehicle entered the covered confines of the immense outdoor tent, Grayson reached for some sort of door handle, but only came up with a smooth, leather-covered panel.

"My passengers usually don't let themselves out." The driver chuckled as he shifted into Park then added, "They also don't usually do so much talking back there."

"Back where?" Tessa blinked several times before her eyes focused on the long, narrow, curtained windows framing the waiting emergency personnel outside. Grayson kept silent, hoping she'd think they were simply in the backseat of one of the fleet of armored presidential limos.

Apparently, he'd been correct in his earlier assumption. King's daughter didn't appreciate being ignored. This time, though, when she shot up to a sitting position, he didn't stop her because they were finally out of view of the news cameras.

The rear hatch opened and Grayson had never been so relieved to jump out of a car or away from a high-maintenance protective detail. He stood to the side as two medics loaded Tessa onto a gurney.

"Is all of this really necessary?" he heard her ask as he tried to concentrate on the operational radio chatter in his ear. "I'm perfectly capable of walking."

One of the paramedics strapped a blood pressure cuff on her arm as the other bobbed and weaved, using the calculated positioning of his body to politely prevent the reluctant patient from climbing off the gurney. Thank God she was *their* problem now.

"They need you back in front of the church," Grayson told the driver as he slammed the door closed. "Thanks for the lift."

As the black Cadillac pulled forward, Tessa's head whipped around and her sexy pink lips formed a little O as she gasped. When she turned to face him, her angry glare made him take another step back.

"You put me in the back of a damn hearse! What in the hell kind of special agent would put someone in the back of their own father's hearse?"

The swear words that peppered her tirade would have been bleeped out if she'd been on live television, and Grayson knew without a shadow of a doubt that his supervisor and his teammates were going to have a field day with this.

Right before he got demoted to a desk job.

Chapter Two

Tessa was sweaty, irritated—and desperately in need of a little privacy. She didn't want these strangers asking her about her medications and repositioning the oxygen mask every time she tried to remove it. She wanted a hot bath and she wanted a cold beer and she didn't care in what order.

Oh, and she wanted the dark-haired Secret Service agent who kept looking over his broad shoulder at her to go find someone else to rescue. As soon as her father had become vice president, Tessa had purposely turned down the offer of a protective detail. She'd insisted it was because the news station provided her with security if she needed it. Really, though, it was because she'd had bodyguards forced on her back in the days when her father had been governor.

It was bad enough that she'd had to suffer through remedial speech therapy for a couple of years after high school just to be able to say her own name. She'd already been several years older than everyone else in the freshman dorms when she'd finally moved to Georgetown. Having armed state troopers following her to all her college classes hadn't done her social life any favors.

Her upper lip curled in annoyance as she glared at the man who'd caused all this unnecessary attention.

And on today of all days.

Sure it sounded odd that someone who made their living as a television personality didn't like added attention, but Tessa's career was different than her personal life. One was due to recognition for her own hard work. While the other...well, the other merely came from her unearned notoriety based on her family's last name.

If she'd been anyone else, would Agent Rescue have swooped in like that? Of course not. Hotshot heroes like him probably lived for the opportunity to "save" someone famous. Someone who had the power to advance his career.

Tessa was about to ask for a copy of the preoperative report—she was well aware of how government agencies and their protective details worked—so that she could find exactly where it authorized some

rogue agent to commandeer a hearse to save someone who clearly didn't need saving. But a commotion
at the far end of the tent gave her pause.

"What in the hell happened to my niece!" Her
uncle Rider used his barrel chest to push his way
to her side.

"I'm fine," she said, her breath clouding the clear
oxygen mask that had been forced on her. Tessa tore
the contraption off her face. The moment anyone in
her family sensed even the slightest hint of weakness,
their protective instincts kicked into overdrive. And
some of her relatives were much less subtle than others. The last thing she needed was her grizzly bear
of an uncle drawing any more attention to the situation. "There's no need to overreact."

"Oh, I'm the one who's overreacting, young
lady?" Rider lowered his bushy gray brows at her.
"You ran outside with no coat as though a herd of
longhorns was comin' straight for you. So what happened?"

"I just needed some fresh air," she offered, knowing full well the older man was unlikely to fall for
some simplified explanation.

Tessa shoved the clear mask back on her face before her uncle could repeat his question for a third
time. She couldn't answer if she couldn't talk. And it
wasn't as though the paramedics could disclose any
information without violating HIPAA regulations.

"This—" Rider held up the pump of the blood

pressure cuff hanging loosely on her arm "—looks a little more serious than simply needin' some fresh air."

"They're just making sure her vitals have stabilized." The annoying agent apparently wasn't bound by the same privacy restrictions as the medical personnel and his deep voice sent a tingle down the back of her spine. "Your niece most likely had a panic attack."

The tingle turned into a chill at his last two words.

Simply hearing the phrase *panic attack* made Tessa fear she'd succumb to another one. She'd almost forgotten how debilitating an episode could be. How far one could set her back.

After that disastrous dive in high school, she'd been diagnosed with traumatic brain injury and instead of going off to college with the rest of her graduating class, the next two years were spent dealing with neurological damage that affected both her vision and her speech. But with countless hours of remedial speech therapy and physical rehabilitation, she'd overcome the effects of the injury, as well as the panic attacks.

Or so she'd thought.

This was bad. She made her living speaking in front of a camera; she couldn't afford to have a setback now. Or worse, give anyone reason to think that she might have a relapse in the future—especially while she was on the air. Tessa tore the Velcro from the arm cuff before anyone could check her blood pressure, which was now way above where it needed to be.

"Seriously. It's no big deal." She tucked a loose blond strand into the tight bun at the back of her head to give her trembling fingers something to do. "I'll be perfectly fine if everyone around here would just let me have some space."

"I know you're fine, Kitten. And *you* know you're fine. But these folks have a job to do and it's not as if we're in any sorta hurry to get anywhere." Uncle Rider and her father were identical twins. Besides the determined and all-knowing stares of their deep blue eyes, though, they'd never looked anything alike to Tessa…or to most people. And they certainly didn't sound alike.

Both King men had been born and raised on the family ranch in Wyoming and both had served in Vietnam, returning home as decorated war heroes. But that was about where the similarities ended.

Roper had married his first wife during college and then married his second wife only a few years later. Both those marriages had ended in divorce, while his third marriage left him a widower at the age of thirty-nine. After a wild and reckless decade in his forties and two stints in rehab, Roper finally met the much younger Sherilee King, his fourth wife and the mother to his six children, when he was fifty-one.

Rider, on the other hand, never had any children of his own. Plus, he'd just been married once, as far as Tessa knew, and her uncle's ex-wife had been the only person to keep the peace between the equally powerful King twins.

Speaking of her uncle's ex-wife, another commotion rippled through the tent, the unmistakable scent of vanilla and extra-hold hair spray announcing her arrival.

"Aunt Freckles!" Tessa smiled at the older woman who was as different from her own mother as her uncle had been from her father. "You came."

"Of course I came, darlin'." Freckles had teased her peach-colored hair into a curly updo that defied gravity. Her heavily applied makeup didn't do much to diminish the laugh lines and creases that had taken her over eighty years to earn. She bent over to press her bright magenta-painted lips to Tessa's forehead, flashing a paramedic—and everyone else on the right side of the gurney—a view down her low-cut emerald-green dress.

Sherilee King had once described her sister-in-law as an older, bustier version of Dolly Parton, and Tessa now stifled a giggle at the accuracy of the description. When Freckles used the back of her cool hand to smooth the loose strands of hair from Tessa's flushed forehead, though, the giggle nearly turned into a sob of relief.

"Having you here makes…" she started, but

couldn't get the words past the emotion clogging her throat. Luckily, the tender expression reflected in the older woman's bright and knowing eyes meant that Tessa didn't have to say the rest aloud.

"I know, darlin'. Now, don't get my tears started or we'll both ruin our mascara and I only brought one backup set of false lashes."

Regardless of the bright spandex wardrobe and beauty pageant–inspired hairdos, everyone loved Aunt Freckles. Like the small pews inside the church, Tessa's colorful aunt would never change and just having her there made Tessa's pulse settle into a more manageable rhythm.

Finally, Tessa sat up on the rolling gurney, which was beginning to feel more like a rolling prison. "Is everyone already on their way to the graveside service?"

"Not yet," Agent Rescue said, reminding Tessa of his hovering presence.

"I didn't get a chance to thank you for saving my niece." Uncle Rider stuck out a beefy hand.

"He didn't save—" Tessa started, but Freckles pushed a plastic bottle of water against her lips.

"Here, darlin'. You should get some fluids in your system." Her aunt made sure she had a mouthful of water before turning to the man who was still wearing those ridiculous dark sunglasses. "Everyone calls me Freckles. It's a pleasure to meet you, Mr....?"

"Special Agent Grayson Wyatt," he said, taking her aunt's age-spotted hand in his bigger tanned one.

Tessa had to gulp down the rest of her water before she audibly groaned. She didn't care how chiseled the agent's jawline was or how his dark brown hair refused to budge from its precision military hairstyle. Any man who introduced himself using his title like that took things way too seriously. Even if it was his job.

"Great." Tessa swung her poorly chosen high heels off the gurney and onto the floor. "Now that we've met the hero of the hour, can we please get to the limo?"

But before she could stand, the agent had sidestepped Rider, which was quite a maneuver considering her uncle's considerable girth, and had his hand cupped under her elbow. "Take it slow."

A warmth spread along the base of her spine, signaling that her neurological functions were still in complete working order. Despite her recent drink, her mouth suddenly felt extremely dry. Even in four-inch heels, Tessa had to tilt her head to look up into his face. He hadn't seemed so tall in the back of the hearse.

Lord, don't remind her of the hearse.

Special Agent Grayson Wyatt *had* been just as bossy back there, though. And if there was one thing Tessa had always resented, it was an overbearing man.

Make that two overbearing men and a nosy aunt, she corrected when Aunt Freckles asked, "So what in the world happened back there?"

"Here we go again." She tried to roll her eyes, but it brought on another wave of dizziness. Grayson gently slid his fingers from her elbow to her upper arm, his strong hand heating the skin underneath her thin silk sleeve.

Freckles, though, was just as unsubtle as her ex-husband. "Did you really puke before passing out in front of the church?"

"No," she said at the same time Grayson replied, "Yes."

"Are you pregnant?" her uncle asked.

"No!" This time Tessa's voice was the only one that answered, and it was louder and sharper than she'd anticipated.

"Sorry." Rider shrugged then looked at Grayson. "Tessa's younger sister once puked then fainted back when she was pregnant. It runs in the family."

Seeing one of Grayson's brows lift above his sunglasses in speculation, Tessa gritted her teeth. The last thing she needed was for that particular rumor to get started. "No, I am not pregnant. Not that it's anyone's business."

"That's a relief," Uncle Rider said, his mouth barely noticeable under his thick handlebar mustache. "I'd hate to have to break your little boyfriend's perfect little nose for leavin' you unattended in a delicate situation."

At the overt reminder of her boyfriend, a flush of embarrassment spread through Tessa and made her doubly aware of the way the agent's protective grip kept her firmly rooted to his muscular side. Up until this point, Grayson's lips had been in a straight, unyielding line. Following her uncle's threat toward the junior congressman from California, though, his mouth softened and might've even twitched with the hint of a grin.

Tessa had negotiated multimillion-dollar contracts with networks and had made grown men cry during live interviews. She wasn't going to stand by and have her health and her personal life called into question in front of a bunch of strangers.

"I'm not the least bit delicate or in need of anyone defending my honor." She snatched her coat from her aunt's arm and held up her palm when both men moved at once to assist her. "Now, if everyone will excuse me, I need to make my way to the family limos."

Grayson's smirk disappeared as quickly as it had appeared. He put two fingers to the earpiece that could've been broadcasting the University of Wyoming basketball game or the latest Taylor Swift album for all they knew. "Sorry, Miss King. The last limo just rolled out of the church driveway."

"Well, I'm not staying here." She straightened her

spine. "I'm going to the cemetery, even if I have to drive myself there in that ambulance."

Grayson mentally calculated the distance from the medical evaluation area to the parked ambulance on the other side of the staging tent. Not that he thought Tessa could outrun him in her condition, or in those sexy high heels that made her legs look like they went on for miles.

Still. He should probably keep his hand on her upper arm. Just in case she did make a run for it. Unfortunately, when he loosened his fingers, his knuckles grazed the side of her breast and a jolt of electricity shot through him.

"My truck's parked out back, Kitten." Rider King's drawl was slower and more countrified than his twin brother's had been, but just as determined. "If the medic clears you, you can ride with me and Freckles."

Grayson didn't care one way or the other who Tessa King rode with as long as someone else took responsibility for her and she was no longer his problem.

"Agent Wyatt will need to come with us, obviously." Freckles shot a pointed look at Rider before fixing an innocent gaze on Tessa. "Just in case you faint again, darlin'."

A groan of protest caught in Grayson's throat.

"Look—" Tessa took a few steps, jerking her arm away from him "—I'm totally fine."

"I know you're fine *now*." Freckles tsked through her painted lips. "But what if you get weak again when we're walking from the truck to the cemetery? Your uncle and I are both too old and frail to carry you."

"Who you callin' frail, woma—" Rider's protest was interrupted by a sharp, bony elbow to his midsection. He rolled his eyes before clearing his throat. "I guess my sciatica *is* actin' up a bit after being squished in those damn wooden pews for so long."

"Let's go, then." Tessa turned toward the tent exit, a woman used to having others fall in line with her every whim. Too bad her wobbly legs were getting in the way of what Grayson assumed was a normally confident strut.

The couple—who may have been old but appeared to be about as frail as a pair of four-wheel-drive tow trucks—followed her. Grayson's phone buzzed in his pocket and he checked the display screen before falling behind a few paces.

Maddie. She never called when she knew he was working unless it was an absolute emergency. And he never would have answered in the middle of a work crisis if there weren't already two missed calls from her. His heart slammed into his throat and he desperately slid his finger across the screen to answer.

"Are you okay?" Grayson tried to keep the panic

from his lowered voice as his eyes tracked the movement of everyone else in the tent. After all, he still had an unwilling detail assignment to protect.

"Yeah, I'm fine. Was that Tessa King you just swooped up in your arms on live TV?"

His voice sounded gruff, even to his own ears. "Maddie, you know I'm on duty."

"Then why'd you answer the phone?" his sister asked.

"Because I thought something might be wrong."

"You always think something is wrong, Gray."

No, he didn't. But he didn't have time to be suckered into an argument with his little sister right that second. "Listen, I'll call you back when I can."

Grayson disconnected the call as he quickened his own pace, hoping to cover his mounting frustration. Switching back into agent mode, which he'd never really left, he radioed the command center to advise his team of the change in plans and a description of the alternate vehicle. "Be advised, I'll be escorting Precision to the secondary location."

After all, protective detail included *all* members of the King family. Even the stubborn, feisty and way too beautiful ones.

"Roger that," the team leader replied over the radio. "The counter assault team is in position, so ensure that the driver adheres to the motorcade route."

Snipers and agents in tactical gear had been placed at designated locations along the road be tween the church and the private cemetery at Twin Kings Ranch. If Grayson planned to rely on the additional layer of long-range security, he needed to get Tessa on the move ASAP.

Normally, procedure would've required him to ride shotgun, but by the time Grayson had double-timed it to the truck to catch up, Rider was already assisting his eighty-something-year-old ex-wife into the front seat of the cab.

Instead of wasting any more time trying to play musical chairs, Grayson climbed in next to Tessa on the backseat and tried to ignore the long-distance camera lenses aimed in their direction.

"Oh, I forgot. You left your purse on the pew, darlin'." Freckles passed a black satiny clutch thing to Tessa over the headrest. "The president gave it to me after the service. Did you know she and I both went to the same boarding school? Obviously, we graduated in different years—"

"Where's my can of chewing tobacco?" Rider grumbled when he hefted himself into the driver's seat. "I need a dip."

"Suck on this instead," Freckles said, shoving a white tablet beneath the man's gray bushy mustache. "But don't bite into it. Here. You kids have one, too."

Grayson immediately regretted taking the offered peppermint that was strong enough to make his eyes water. But at least the potency of the extra-strength mints kept everyone from talking.

In fact, nobody said a word as the truck pulled onto the street and merged into the long line of pre-screened cars heading out of the small town. Thankfully, now that the public ceremony was over, most of the high-profile guests—including the president and her husband—would continue on to the airport in Jackson Hole, taking most of the news vans with them. Only family, close friends and the approved camera people from Tessa's network had been invited to the private family plot on Twin Kings Ranch where Roper King would be laid to rest.

As more and more cars peeled off for the main highway, Tessa reached into her purse and pulled out a small pink tube. She deftly applied some shiny stuff to her mouth without using a mirror, and Grayson felt a stab of envy toward the little wand that softly traced her lips.

He shifted in his seat and readjusted his sunglasses.

His phone buzzed again in his pocket. This time when he checked the screen, he ignored the inquiring text from Maddie. Responding would only encourage her to send more annoying questions that were none of her business.

When they drove by the guard shack at the entrance to the second-largest privately owned ranch in Wyoming, the posted agents nodded. As the truck passed through the log-crafted gates, Grayson remembered the first time he'd ever been to Twin

Kings. Roper King had paid out of pocket to have all fifty-thousand-plus acres of the ranch reinforced by the Technical Security Division. Despite the added electrical fencing, infrared cameras and bulletproof glass, the property was absurdly beautiful and surprisingly efficient and well run.

After half a mile down a tree-lined driveway, the twelve-thousand-square-foot main house sat on a grassy knoll framed by the famous Teton mountain range in the distance. The stables and barn, on the other side of the driveway, were equally as imposing. Or, at least, they were to someone like him who'd grown up in a tiny subdivision outside Baltimore.

They passed the trail that led to numerous outbuildings such as the cookhouse, the corrals and a pair of matching bunkhouses—one to house the cowboys and one to house the special agents on duty—that seemed to be purposely hidden from view of the main house. It was as though the wealthy occupants didn't appreciate the reminder that they had to share their vast property holdings with the hired help.

Since Grayson had been briefed by the same advance logistics teams every time he'd flown out here on Air Force Two, he knew there were dozens of agents in all-terrain vehicles stationed along the perimeter, also trying to remain out of sight.

It took another mile to wind up onto the snow-covered ridge that held several gravestones and an amazing view of the Snake River. Cars were already parked behind the hearse, and, due to the narrowness of the recently plowed dirt road usually only accessed by horse or ATV, Rider pulled the passenger side of his truck right against the fence line.

Grayson hopped out of the backseat and immediately scanned the area around him for potential threats before reaching to assist Tessa.

"I can do it," she muttered, ignoring his hand as she awkwardly shimmied herself across the leather bench seat. The motion caused the hem of her black cashmere coat to slide up her legs, giving him a glimpse of the toned muscles of her outer thigh. He took a step back and resisted the urge to loosen his suddenly tight necktie.

But not before she caught him looking.

A charming shade of pink made its way up her cheeks as she tried to adjust her dress over her exposed thigh. Unfortunately, she was so preoccupied with her modesty that her high heel missed the side step outside the door and she practically tumbled into Grayson's arms.

This time, though, instead of grabbing her upper arms to steady her, Grayson's hands landed on either side of her narrow waist. Tessa's surprised *oomph* came out in a rush of air and he could smell traces of mint on her breath. She tried to pull away, but he held her in place.

"Take a second and get your footing," he commanded, knowing better than to ask if she was okay or otherwise imply that the mighty and fearless Tessa King needed any sort of assistance.

She stared into his eyes—their faces separated by mere inches—and instead of arguing, she took several deep breaths. Beneath his palms, he felt the muscles below her rib cage contract and expand until they finally relaxed.

"Sorry about that." Her apology caught Grayson by surprise; up until now, she hadn't offered him so much as a "thank you" for rescuing her earlier. "I haven't been home in so long, I forgot how impossible it would be to walk around the ranch in these stupid heels. Especially during winter."

"No worries," he said, trying not to think about how great her legs looked in those stupid—but extremely sexy—heels. If talking about shoes kept her from hyperventilating, he would just have to deal with it.

"Please tell me the cameras didn't catch me nearly falling."

Grayson jutted his chin toward the flag-draped coffin being placed over the freshly dug grave. "Nope, they're pretty much focused on where they need to be."

"Oh God." She sucked in a shallow breath as her eyes followed his. A shudder ran through her body, revealing the emotion she was clearly fighting to hide. "Getting through this might be a bit harder than I'd first thought it'd be."

Grayson had a feeling she was no longer talking about navigating the terrain in her stilettos. Her aunt and uncle had already moved toward the small crowd of people standing near the piles of lavish floral arrangements, leaving him on his own to talk her down before she had another panic attack.

"Take a deep breath in through your nose," he instructed then demonstrated. Grayson used to do the same demonstration for his anxious mom whenever she'd paced the hospital waiting rooms, working herself up as she waited for his little sister to come out of surgery. "Now out through your mouth."

His fingers were still splayed around Tessa's waist and her hands had latched onto his forearms. He didn't want to point out that if any of the cameras turned in their direction, the tabloids would have a field day with the image. That would only get her more amped up.

Tessa's uncle had mentioned a boyfriend. Where the hell was that guy? Why wasn't *he* taking care of her? As soon as the thought went through Grayson's mind, the muscles in his shoulders coiled and something primal surged through his nerve endings.

"I think I'm okay now," she finally said as the minister began reading from an open book.

There were several rows of chairs set under a canopy for the family. He jerked his head in that direction. "Do you want me to walk you over to your seat?"

"Actually, do you mind if we just stand over here?" She gestured to a nearby copse of trees.

We.

A shiver went down the back of his neck. *We* meant team. While Grayson didn't mind being part of a tactical team or a sports team or even a math team—eighth grade state champions, thank you very much—he didn't want anyone getting the idea that he was somehow paired up with Tessa King. It was too chummy, almost too intimate. He was supposed to watch over the family—not get personally involved with one of them.

Unfortunately, by the way she kept her arm looped tightly through his as they stood off to the side of the rutted dirt road, they appeared to be much more than a *we.*

Chapter Three

Tessa remained numb throughout the entire grave-side service. Tears might have trickled down her face when the uniformed soldiers handed her mother the folded flag, but Tessa didn't feel them. And, really, if she were being honest, feeling nothing was so much better than the slew of sensations that had ricocheted and rioted inside her during the church ceremony.

In fact, she'd only flinched when that first rifle blast went off during the twenty-one-gun salute. Luckily, the solid frame of the Secret Service agent wedged against her side prevented her from faltering.

Feeling the weight of everyone's curious stares—most probably sympathetic, though some were blatantly curious—she leaned closer to Grayson and whispered, "I don't suppose you have an extra pair of sunglasses on you?"

He reached up with his free hand and slowly removed the black plastic frames from his face. Tessa swallowed. His eyes were a startling shade of silvery gray and held both a hardness as well as a trace of tenderness. He gently slid the sunglasses onto her face and the dark lenses made her rethink her initial assessment of his earlier high-handedness in her so-called "rescue."

The borrowed sunglasses gave her a feeling of strength, almost like a cloak of invisibility, as she reached down and cupped a cold, damp handful of dirt. For the past two days, Tessa hadn't been able to wrap her head around the fact that she would never see her father again. Staring at the gaping hole in the earth, the finality of it hit her and her empty stomach coiled into a hard knot.

Her dad's arms would no longer wrap her into one of his famous bear hugs. He'd never pour coffee into his favorite mug, the one she'd painted for him that read My Dad Is My Hero. His booming voice would no longer tell her to jump high and dive deep.

This was it. He wasn't coming back.

Tessa's mouth moved as she spoke, but her throat was too raw to say the words out loud. *Goodbye, Daddy.*

She gave one last glance at her father's casket before her brain was finally able to send a signal down through her legs, forcing one foot in front of the other. She'd somehow managed to make it several yards before feeling an unexpected tug on her right arm and a concerned whisper near her ear. "There you are, sweetheart!"

The startled expression that crossed her face didn't come from seeing her boyfriend suddenly appear at her side. She'd walked into the church with Davis Townsend earlier today, before they'd been directed to their assigned seats, and he'd insisted on wedging himself into the pew behind her. In the back of her mind, she'd known he would be at the cemetery. Rather, Tessa's surprise arose from the fact that her left arm was still firmly locked against Grayson Wyatt's side.

The Secret Service agent had taken his protective duties seriously and she'd been so caught up in her own grief, she'd barely noticed that he'd been practically holding her up this entire time. And he didn't seem inclined to release his steadying hold just yet. In fact, his shoulder brushed in front of hers as he pulled her in closer, as though shielding her from a perceived threat.

"Davis," she managed to say, too exhausted to force a smile toward the man she'd been dating for nearly two years. The man her siblings and uncle obnoxiously referred to as Congressman Smooth. "Have you been here the whole time?"

"Of course I have, sweetheart. I rode here in the limo with Duke and Tom." Davis glanced at Agent Wyatt before his pale blue eyes dipped to Tessa and Grayson's joined arms. "Per protocol."

A camera shutter went off somewhere behind Tessa and her left leg buckled.

"I've got you." Grayson's stiff forearm kept her from going down. "Just keep walking. We're almost to the truck."

Davis, who was just as much a pro in front of the lens as Tessa, wiped the concern from his expression and pasted his famous campaign smile onto his face. His teeth barely moved as he lowered his voice and asked Grayson, "Is she drunk?"

"No, *she's* not drunk," Tessa answered for herself. She hated it when anyone, especially men or doctors, talked about her as though she wasn't there. Temporarily losing the ability to speak after a traumatic brain injury tended to do that to a person. "*She* just laid her father to rest and her eyes are full of tears and she is about to throw these ridiculous four-inch high heels into the nearest ravine."

"Okay, well it seems as though you're in good hands with Mr.…uh…?"

"Agent Wyatt," Grayson offered, this time not bothering with a handshake. Probably because his right arm was otherwise occupied bearing half the weight of Tessa's one-twenty-pound frame.

"Right. So then I'll just see you back at the house."

Davis moved in to kiss her cheek, but ended up knocking the oversize sunglasses askew. Tessa could only imagine how silly she looked in the sporty, mannish frames, but she wasn't quite ready to return them yet. Wearing them felt as though she was hiding in plain sight.

"You ridin' back with us, Congressman?" Uncle Rider asked Davis as he and Freckles came up behind them.

"No, sir." Davis cleared his throat and his smile returned. Had his teeth always been that white? "I appreciate the offer, but my understanding is that I'm assigned to family limo number two. Per protocol. I'll see everyone there."

"We have a protocol now?" Rider didn't bother lowering his gruff voice as Davis walked away, waving at someone in the distance. "That's his excuse for ditchin' his girlfriend in her time of need?"

The irony of being an expert political analyst and the daughter of a career politician was that most of her family avoided politics altogether and had no desire to ever hold an elected office. Her mother had been the only person who'd been supportive of Tessa's relationship with the up-and-coming congressman. Even her father had advised her to take things slow, which was why she still hadn't given Davis an answer after he'd proposed last month.

"He means his press secretary organized it," Tessa explained through the headache now pounding against her temples. "You know how things work in our world. Our schedules are so packed and our roles are so complex, things run more smoothly when every event is outlined and every detail planned. Besides, it's not exactly my 'time of need.'"

The disbelieving tilt of Grayson's head drew her eyes to his. His icy stare turned to a steely gunmetal gray—probably the same color as the service weapon likely hidden somewhere underneath his suit jacket. "Could've fooled me."

A shiver traveled down the base of Tessa's neck all the way to her toes. If he kept looking at her like that, no pair of sunglasses in the world would be able to hide the effect his nearness was having on her.

Grayson studied his reflection over the sink in the men's room at the bunkhouse later that evening. Most of the funeral guests had left the ranch a few hours ago and, technically, his team was now off duty. He'd originally been assigned to watch the outer perimeter of the house, but SAIC Simon, the supervising agent in charge, had switched him with Agent Franks. For some unknown reason, Grayson had been forced to stay inside the main house, watching the comings and goings of the guests from the safety of the richly decorated living room.

Oh, who was he kidding? Grayson knew exactly why his assignment had been swapped. The Secret Service always had a security plan *and* an alternate security plan for when something went wrong. Not that anything had gone wrong, exactly. At least, nothing that would cause the supervisor to reassess the placement of the agents.

That meant someone from the King family had specifically requested Grayson be stationed inside. But who?

He knew it hadn't been Tessa since he'd pretty much been within earshot of her since she'd fainted in his arms back at the church. Not to mention, she'd practically ignored him once she was within the safe confines of the plush family palace disguised to look like a ranch house. In fact, he was pretty sure she would've preferred he hadn't been there at all.

The good news was that the remainder of his shift had been uneventful if he didn't count that little skirmish between Tessa's mom and her aunt Freckles over a tray of ham biscuits. Or that annoying dipstick, Davis Townsend, taking a call from his press secretary right in the middle of Rider King's toast to his deceased twin. Tessa's brother Duke had looked ready to peel off his Navy uniform jacket with all those shiny medals and throw blows with the congressman.

Aw, hell.

Grayson gripped the edge of the counter so tightly his knuckles turned white. When had he stopped thinking of the King family in terms of their assigned code names and started thinking of them as

Tessa's relatives? Probably from the second he'd held her against him at the cemetery, staring into her soft blue eyes and breathing in sync with her.

Thankfully, though, the assignment was now over. Or, at least, his portion of it. Even sleeping in this custom-built bunkhouse, which was decorated almost as lavishly as a suite of rooms at a five-star hotel, put Grayson on edge.

Rumor had it Roper King had designed the well-equipped building at his own cost because he wanted the security teams protecting him to feel as if they were at home, too—even when they were hundreds of miles away from their own families. The funny thing was, Grayson would've been much more comfortable with a rucksack and a standard-issue cot out in the middle of some jungle than he was here. While the former vice president had liked to ensure his security teams were comfortable and lacked for nothing, this place was way fancier than the furnished studio apartment Grayson had rented in DC.

And when things were fancy, they were usually a lot less welcoming. Case in point: Tessa King.

At least things had gotten easier as the night had worn on. Surrounded by her family with no cameras around, Tessa had seemed stronger tonight, or at least less fragile. Still, Grayson had remained in the background until the catering crew and very last guest had left, just in case she needed him again. Not that she'd needed *him* specifically in the first place.

He ducked his mouth toward the cold water coming from the faucet and gulped. The water out here in Wyoming always tasted better than anything bottled and sold in the expensive gourmet markets in DC. Using one of the plush hotel-style towels to wipe his face, Grayson reminded himself that any agent would've reacted the same way as he had today and Tessa would have just as easily clung to *that* person for support.

He wasn't special.

In fact, the only reason he'd even been assigned as an agent of "*The Shift*," which was what they called those working the first line of defense in the presidential inner bubble, was that Roper King had personally requested him a few months ago. After ten years of being part of an elite sniper unit with the Marine Corps, and then another three as a sniper for the Secret Service's Counter Assault Team, Grayson was still trying to convince himself that the assignment would be worth it since all the extra overtime pay from the protective detail would help with some of Maddie's medical bills.

But now that the vice president would be replaced with the Speaker of the House, who already had her own detail, many agents were putting in their change-of-duty papers. Grayson just needed to get through this final debriefing session before he followed suit.

He slowly ambled out of the bathroom, not looking forward to the ball-busting, good-natured ribbing that would likely take place around the big table outside the bunkhouse kitchen. Several of his teammates were already smirking over their shoulders in his direction as they hunkered around a laptop screen.

"You see this, Wyatt?" Agent Lopez held up her smartphone.

"See what?" Grayson asked as he headed toward his own bunk, not the least bit interested in whatever video was playing on that laptop or on Lopez's phone.

"They're calling you 'the Bodyguard,'" Agent Doherty said in his strong Boston accent. "Not very original, if you ask me."

"Just be glad they're not calling you the 'Hearse Commando,'" Lopez said, getting a round of chuckles.

They? Who was "they"?

A knot of dread formed in Grayson's belly as he stepped closer to the compact screen.

Aw, hell.

The video of Grayson sweeping Tessa into his arms admittedly played out as more dramatic than it really had been. Not that he could explain that to the million-plus viewers who'd already watched the online video. His eyes blinked at the steadily increasing number of views in the bottom left corner of the screen.

"Aw, hell," he said aloud this time, pinching the bridge of his nose.

"You know the rules, Prince Charming." Franks, who'd returned from his shift on perimeter duty, smacked Grayson on the back. "You make the news, you buy the team a round of beers."

"Trust me—" Grayson shook his head "—there was nothing princely or charming about that extraction. The woman passed out and I happened to be in the wrong place at the wrong time. Any first responder would've reacted the same way."

"She doesn't look passed out." Doherty pointed to Tessa's open eyes. "In fact, she looks downright breathless."

That's right. She'd still been conscious when he'd lifted her, her lids slowly lowering as she'd tucked her face against his shoulder. Only *he* knew the truth—that she'd been in the middle of a panic attack and would've collapsed into a heap if it hadn't been for him. Grayson made a dismissive sound. "Pfftt. Breathless? You've been reading too many romance novels, Doh-boy."

"Don't knock 'em," the muscular Irish kid from Southie replied, not at all insulted by the nickname.

"What about *this* video?" Lopez clicked on another link that showed a five-second clip of Tessa pasted against Grayson's side at the funeral. When her boyfriend approached, Tessa had drawn even closer to Grayson. The caption underneath read Tessa King Throws Over Congressman for Her Bodyguard.

A chorus of snickers and taunts rang out in the bunkhouse. Grayson slammed the top of the laptop closed. "Time to debrief then hit the sack. We're wheels up at oh six hundred."

The videos were just a flash in the pan, he told himself—fifteen minutes of fame and all that. The media would lose interest as soon as some other famous celebrity got married, or divorced, or arrested. After the protective detail officially ended tomorrow, he'd never have to see Tessa King again.

At least that's what Grayson thought when his head hit the pillow that night. But when he woke up at dawn, his supervisor was standing between the rows of bunks.

"Change of plans, Delta and Echo teams," SAIC Simon said before the foggy remnants of sleep left Grayson's brain. "Everyone meet in the conference room in five minutes."

Grayson barely had time to pull a T-shirt over his head, let alone grab a cup of coffee on his way to the soundproof building attached to the bunkhouse.

As soon as everyone was in their seats, Simon uncapped a marker and drew a line down a dry-erase board.

"We've got two new situations this morning. Number one." He wrote the word *Pollywog* on the left side of the board then used the marker to tap on the code name for the youngest King offspring. "Seems as though little Mitchell King Junior had a bit too much to drink last night with the sixteen-year-old daughter of one of the county deputies. While getting handcuffed by said deputy for a drunk and disorderly, MJ decided to fight back and racked up a resisting arrest charge."

Lopez groaned. "Who was assigned to tail him?"

"Echo Team. It's not the first time some eighteen-year-old ditched his protective detail, and it probably won't be the last. But we want to finish our investigation into the matter before the media gets wind of it. That leads me to situation number two." Simon turned back to the board and wrote the code name *Precision* before turning to Grayson. "Seems your little romantic rescue routine yesterday got Tessa King into a whole heap of hot water with her cronies at the press."

"It wasn't a romantic rescue, sir." Grayson sat straighter in the expensive leather chair. "I explained that in our debrief session last night."

"I know you did, Wyatt. But that was before the photo of you ever so delicately sliding your sunglasses onto Miss King's nose blew up on social media."

Grayson ran a hand through his hair. *Damn*. He wished he'd taken those sunglasses back from her yesterday so that he could hide the frustration filling his eyes right this second.

"It wasn't like that," Grayson insisted for what had to be the thousandth time. There'd been nothing romantic between him and Tessa yesterday in the least. Sure, she was attractive, with perfectly arranged blond curls and those soft pink lips and that pulse point right where her collarbones came together in the shape of a little heart—

Whoa. He had to stop his thoughts there—before he began remembering how attractive she was from the neck down.

Someone made a wolf whistle as the digital image miraculously appeared on the wall-size screen behind the head of the table. Scratch that. Tessa King was a helluva lot more than attractive. Grayson averted his eyes from the picture of him staring into her beautiful face right before he'd placed his sunglasses on her.

So maybe it *did* look a bit worse than it was.

"Come on, you guys. The second she got into the main house and away from the cameras, she didn't even know I was there." Grayson heard the words come out of his mouth and prayed he didn't sound as though he was disappointed in being ignored. As a shift agent, he was supposed to blend into the background. He obviously didn't *want* to draw her attention. Or anyone else's for that matter.

"So you think she played it up for the cameras?" SAIC Simon studied him.

"No." Grayson sighed, wishing he could claim

that the whole thing was nothing more than an op-
portunistic stunt on her part. It would certainly stop
all the eyebrows currently wagging in his direction.
"The panic attack was legit. Just ask the medic who
took her vitals afterward. I'm simply saying that the
second she knew she was out of the woods, she didn't
need my support anymore. Like I said last night, I
only did what any other agent in my place would've
done in the same situation. And I'm sure Miss King
would've reacted the same way if Franks or Lopez,
or hell, even Doherty, had been the one to catch her."

Simon shrugged. "Well, it doesn't matter who
caught her. It matters that the media think they
sniffed out a big story and they're not gonna let
go when their teeth are locked into something this
juicy."

Tessa was a news personality and probably on
a first-name basis with most of the press corps.
Couldn't she call them off herself? Grayson fought
the urge to rub his temples. Not wanting to give the
woman another thought, he asked, "What do we care
if the sharks eat one of their own?"

"Because those sharks are currently surrounding the Twin Kings Ranch. Along with God knows
who else trying to get a front-page-worthy pic. It's
like the Wild West of paparazzi and reporters outside those gates right now. Nobody needs me to remind them of how John Hinckley Junior was able to
get so close to Reagan in 1981, do they?" The room

went quiet as everyone thought about how the would-be assassin easily blended in with members of the press right before he'd opened fire on the president. Simon cleared his throat before continuing. "Therefore, Agent Wyatt, as long as there is an ongoing threat to the King family, even if it's only from news cameras, you and half the team are staying here."

Grayson swallowed back several curses as he sat stiffly and listened to the protective intel agents outline the focus of their reconfigured assignment, conveniently titled Operation Snowball.

When everyone stood to leave the room, Simon motioned for Grayson to meet him near the now empty coffee machine. After making sure they were alone, Simon opened his laptop.

"Just a head's up, Wyatt. One of the local uniformed deputies in the staging tent yesterday was wearing their body camera and unknowingly recorded footage of Tessa King dressing you down and questioning your tactical decisions. The sheriff is going to do everything in his power to make sure the video doesn't get leaked to the press, but he already has his hands full, and it's only a matter of time before I have the chain of command breathing down our necks about the possibility of calling you before an inquiry board."

Grayson sighed. "Sir, I know that the hearse was an unconventional choice as far as extraction vehicles, but I stand by my decision to use the closest resource available while simultaneously keeping the primary location secure."

"I'm already writing that in my situation report. In fact, I'm keeping you in place on the ranch because I know I can trust you."

His boss made the decision sound like a reward, while the truth was that staying on assignment was a lose-lose situation. Even if Grayson wanted to tuck tail and run, which he never had before, it wouldn't do him any favors. He exhaled in defeat. "And because removing me from an assignment at this juncture might in some way imply that I was being punished or couldn't be trusted."

"That, too. You're a good agent and, from everything I've seen, you handled yourself with the utmost professionalism under the circumstances."

That may be so, given his supervisor's outside viewpoint. But deep down Grayson knew that he'd allowed Tessa to get too close to him. And while he hadn't acted in a way that technically crossed any professional line, there was no doubt his physical response to the woman had called that line into question. Sensing Simon wanted to say more, Grayson prompted, "But?"

"But…" Simon sighed. "My concern is that Miss King might not see it the same way."

The suggested threat of betrayal settled between Grayson's shoulder blades, as though he was already anticipating the knife to be shoved into his back. He'd saved Tessa from collapsing on those church steps for the entire world to see. Then he'd stayed by her side, intervening before she had another panic attack while literally holding her upright as she paid her last respects to her father. He'd even given her his favorite pair of sunglasses. "You think she'll file a formal complaint about me?"

"You think she won't?" Simon hitched a brow.

Grayson sucked in a deep breath, wishing he'd never been stationed on those church steps yesterday. That he'd never met Tessa King. "The only thing I think is that I really don't know her at all."

"Look..." Simon spoke as he packed his laptop into a waterproof case. "We all liked working with her father, and because of that, I want to give her the benefit of the doubt. But I've been in this business a long time. She's probably going to be embarrassed when she sees herself portrayed in an unflattering light. She's also going to have an entire public relations team working to turn this story around so she doesn't look bad. Hopefully, she can save herself without drowning you—or the agency—in the process. It's been my experience, though, that powerful people will do anything to protect their reputations, including throwing little minnows like us to the sharks in order to save themselves."

Grayson watched his supervisor leave before turning his attention back to the whiteboard at the front of the room. Unfortunately, he couldn't afford to sit here and worry about the outcome of a potential inquiry board or a media feeding frenzy. He couldn't even afford to think about how Tessa was going to react when she saw the videos or whether she would save herself. He had a job to do and the job always came first.

He could only pray that Miss King had a good PR person to get them both out of this mess. Because staying holed up on this ranch, no matter how many thousands of acres it covered, with the beautiful woman was going to be more dangerous than diving straight into shark-infested waters.

Chapter Four

"**W**hy do they always do this?" Tessa shoved her
smartphone across the breakfast table so it would be
far out of her reach. She needed to resist the temptation to scroll through any more pictures of her being
carried away from her father's funeral by #Secret-
AgentSteamy, which was currently the top trending
hashtag on every social media platform in the United
States. And half of Europe.

"Because news sells," Aunt Freckles replied, taking a hot pan of her famous buttermilk biscuits out
of the oven. "And sensational news sells sensation-
ally. I would've thought they'd taught you that in
Journalism 101."

"This isn't journalism." Tessa folded her arms in front of her in an effort to still her twitching fingers. "It's pure voyeurism."

"Can you blame the public, darlin'? That Agent Wyatt looks just as yummy as my freshly whipped honey butter." Freckles set down a ceramic crock full of creamy heaven in front of Tessa. "Get your knife ready because there ain't nothing my home-made biscuits can't solve."

"How did you sneak real butter past Mom?" Tessa peeked down the hallway connecting the kitchen to the rest of the house. Sherilee King's strict vegan diet was more about her waistline and less about her fondness for animals.

"I waited until after the guests left and your mom snuck off to that spot by the river where she and your dad used to go. She needs some alone time. Then I slipped MJ a hundred-dollar bill and the keys to your uncle Rider's truck yesterday afternoon to run into town and get me some."

"Couldn't you have just asked the catering staff to leave those little rectangle packets wrapped in foil?"

"Nope. Your momma gave the caterers strict orders to take every last pat with them when they left. Not that it mattered because I wouldn't dream of messing up my new polish unwrapping those darn things when the butter inside isn't even my brand."

Tessa glanced down at her aunt's long acrylic nails, which were now a different—and brighter, if that were possible—shade than they'd been at yesterday's funeral.

"Besides," Freckles continued, "your baby brother was champing at the bit to get out of here yesterday. I merely provided him with the means and justification to escape."

Tessa's mother must've heard that last part as she walked into the kitchen through the mudroom. "So you're the one to blame for Mitchell Junior getting arrested last night?"

"Arrested?" Tessa dropped her knife back into the ceramic crock. "For what?"

"For being out late with Kendra Broman." Sherilee picked up the warm biscuit already coated with butter from Tessa's plate, smeared on another two layers, then shoved half the thing into her mouth. Crumbs fell from her lips as she mumbled, "Two scandals with two of my kids in less than two days. It's like my heart isn't already breaking enough with Roper gone."

Freckles buttered another biscuit and handed it to her former sister-in-law. "Since when is it a crime for a young buck to spend a little time in the evening with a pretty girl?"

"Did I mention there was some underage drinking involved and Mitchell allegedly took a swing at the arresting deputy? Who also happened to be Kendra's *father*?"

"Did you call Marcus?" Tessa reached across the

table for her recently abandoned phone, intending to call her brother.

"Call him? I've been in his office for the past thirty minutes reading him the riot act. When that didn't work, I reminded Marcus that I suffered through twenty-six agonizing hours of labor giving birth to him. I swear, that boy refuses to listen to reason." Her mom lovingly gazed down at the biscuit that had magically appeared in her hand and sighed. "God, I'd kill for some bacon right now."

Freckles, who had an uncanny knack for knowing what people needed before they even knew it themselves, already had the seldom-used cast-iron skillet going. She caught Tessa's attention before nodding toward Sherilee and mouthing the words, *Stress eating.*

"So then where's MJ now?" Tessa asked her mom.

"Still in jail. Marcus is charging him with resisting arrest. I guess, technically, Deputy Broman is charging him with that. But Marcus is the sheriff and *he* thinks Mitchell needs to stay put until the arraignment this afternoon. *He* thinks his baby brother has been bailed out by his family too many times already and needs to learn a lesson. Apparently, *he* doesn't know that reporters are crawling all over town right now trying to get more dirt on *your*—" her mom pointed the butter knife in Tessa's direction "—little display yesterday."

Tessa inwardly rolled her eyes before throwing out

a half-hearted wave dismissing the accusation. Sure, she could defend herself. Again. Or calmly try to explain to her mother that the so-called "little display yesterday," was exactly that—little. She knew from experience, though, that arguing with Sherilee King was tantamount to waving a red flag in the face of an angry bull, and the woman would not be satisfied until she drew blood.

"I'm serious, Contessa." Their mom only used her children's formal names when she wanted to add that extra bit of drama. "We barely laid your father to rest and already he'd be rolling over in his grave with his children's scandalous behavior."

"Stop getting so worked up, Sher." Freckles flipped over a slice of bacon. "Roper King never let a little bit of scandal get to him. This'll all die down by tonight."

"It'd better." Sherilee jutted her chin toward the jungle-print yoga pants doing nothing to camouflage Freckles's curvaceous backside. "Because if I have to eat my way through any more stress, my rear end is going to end up as big as yours."

Freckles opened her mouth to fire back a response at her sister-in-law and Tessa knew she had to stop the two women before the name-calling made the situation worse. "Did you mention the reporters to Marcus?"

"Yes. His solution was to call the special agent

in charge and request additional agents stay on to secure the ranch."

Alarm bells went off in Tessa's head. She formed her lips to ask a question but the words got caught in her throat. Closing her eyes, she touched her tongue to the roof of her mouth, just like her former speech therapist had taught her. She concentrated and tried again. "Wh...wh...which additional agents?"

"Hopefully, not the one you got into trouble with yesterday," her mother replied, apparently not noticing Tessa's stutter.

"Sorry to disappoint you, Sherilee." Freckles wiggled her heavily penciled eyebrows as though she weren't the least bit sorry. Or disappointed. "But it doesn't look like Agent Steamy is packing his bags anytime soon."

The legs of her mother's chair screeched against the wood-planked floor as she scrambled to look out the large picture window that framed the kitchen table. "How can you tell?"

Tessa, hoping to be less conspicuous, remained firmly planted in her seat. Yet she couldn't help stretching her neck to see around both her mom and her aunt.

An all-terrain vehicle with two men in suits pulled onto the dirt road behind the house, followed by another all-terrain vehicle that parked behind them. The second ATV was driven by a woman dressed in dusty boots, jeans and a flannel shirt. Her leather-tooled belt holding a black-leather holster was the only giveaway that she wasn't actually working with the cattle today.

Climbing out of the seat beside her was a man dressed as though he'd just bought his outfit at the Wild West costume shop yesterday. That turquoise snap-button paisley shirt still had the fold creases in the material, which seemed to strain across his broad shoulders. And he was wearing hiking boots instead of actual cowboy boots. Okay, so maybe his well-worn jeans didn't look so brand-new. In fact, they molded to his muscular thighs like they were made for the man.

Tessa gulped and forced her eyes above his narrow black belt, which didn't boast any sort of ornate rodeo-style buckle most of the other ranch employees wore. Agent Grayson Wyatt had to be the worst undercover cowboy she had ever seen.

Unfortunately, the shiver of awareness racing down her spine reminded her that Grayson looked just as attractive as he had yesterday.

Tessa used one of the monogrammed linen napkins to wipe away the dampness that suddenly appeared above her upper lip. She'd thought she'd put yesterday's panic attack out of her mind last night. But then she'd awoken to both the internet and her mother all abuzz this morning. Now, the cause of the incident himself was walking up to the back porch wearing his brand-new shirt, causing her nerve endings to tingle with the threat of disaster.

Even though she knew it was coming, the loud knock on the kitchen door reverberated in her throat.

"Come on in." Freckles's welcoming grin was as wide as the pit growing in Tessa's stomach.

"Is now a good time for that family briefing?" the special agent in charge asked the three women in the room.

"Well, half of our family isn't even here, Agent Simon. But you already know that since you were down at the sheriff's office earlier." Sherilee's tone was accusatory, as though it was somehow the Secret Service's fault that MJ had gotten arrested.

"Mom," Tessa warned before turning her attention to the SAIC, carefully avoiding looking past him to Grayson. "I'm not sure we need a formal briefing. Dahlia lives in town and Duke and his husband are on the same flight to DC with me this afternoon. It'll just be my mother and my sister Finn staying on at the ranch. Oh, and MJ. When Marcus releases him, of course."

"Oh no." Her mother pointed a butter-smeared finger at Tessa. "You are not flying to DC this afternoon and leaving this bodyguard mess behind for me to clean up."

"What mess is there to clean up?" Finn King asked as she brushed past the four agents huddled near the doorway and planted herself in the center of the kitchen. Finn had probably been wide-awake and out roping calves well before dawn. That was why she was the heir apparent to the Twin Kings Ranch. She was the only sibling fully devoted to working the land. "The steers hate those ATVs, by the way. I'd appreciate it if your agents wouldn't race them pass the chutes on the mornings we're trying to breed."

Tessa had never been as happy for her little sister's take-charge attitude as she was right then. Nothing happened on the ranch without Finn knowing about it. And if Finn didn't want the agents sticking around, they'd be out of there by midday.

Sherilee rubbed the one crease in her otherwise cosmetically enhanced forehead before turning to her youngest daughter. "Maybe if you weren't so busy playing matchmaker with your precious bulls, Finn, you'd know that other *humans* in your family are still going through the grieving process."

"Mom, those bulls pay for all this." Finn extended her arm to gesture from the entire house and its professionally decorated contents to the rolling hills outside. "Besides, us *humans* all grieve in our own way. My way is to continue the Twin Kings' dynasty. Apparently, MJ's is to get stupid drunk with Deputy Broman's daughter. And Tessa's way is to make headlines with Agent Steamy over there."

A warm flush spread through Tessa's face and she refused to address the Agent Steamy comment while the man in question was only a few yards away, his calculated gaze seemingly absorbing every detail in their kitchen. Instead, she smiled at her sister and asked, "Does part of the Twin Kings' dynasty involve stomping through the house like a herd of wild elephants with your muddy boots?"

Normally, their mother would've taken the bait and immediately scolded anyone who dared to track so much as a speck of dirt into her pristine home. But she was too focused on pouring the entire contents of the china cream pitcher into her coffee.

"Nice try, Tess." Finn grabbed a biscuit off the plate and shot Aunt Freckles a wink. "But the only elephant in this room is the one between you and Agent Steamy and the hundred cameras stationed along every fence line hoping to get another picture of you two in a compromising position."

Yep, Finn was very well aware of what was going on at the ranch and she had no problem speaking her mind. She'd inherited their father's love of the land, but not his skills at diplomacy or his ability to keep family matters private. Tessa gave her little sister a warning glance and Finn responded by sticking out her lips and making kissing noises.

"With all due respect, Miss King and Miss King," SAIC Simon interjected. "When the media gets wind of your younger brother's arrest, you're going to have paparazzi rushing the gates trying to get the inside scoop. Several of them have already extended their reservations at the hotel in town because of the, uh—" the supervisor briefly glanced at Tessa "—'Agent Steamy' incident. So even if that situation dies down, like it usually does, we're not comfortable abandoning our post just yet."

Grayson cleared his throat. "Can we please stop referring to me as Agent Steamy?"

"Nope," Aunt Freckles said.

"Not a chance," Finn echoed.

"You two are absolutely incorrigible," Sherilee scolded as she stood from the table, pretending not to see all the flaky biscuit crumbs falling from her tailored silk blouse to the floor. "Agents, I apologize for my *youngest* daughter and my *former* sister-in-law. They both know better than to ogle random men and tease employees of our government."

"Mom, aren't you gonna apologize for your *oldest* daughter, as well?" Finn asked not so innocently. "Pretty sure Tessa knows better than to fall into the arms of strange men, no matter how swoon-worthy they are."

"I didn't fall." Tessa shot Finn a look that promised retribution. "He picked me up."

"Technically, you were on your way down." Grayson's mouth quirked up on one side as he corrected her. And to think she'd actually had a dream last night about that mouth of his—

Tessa snapped to attention, squelching the thought as soon as it began.

"What was that all about anyway, Tessa?" her mother asked. "Usually, you have no problem in front of the cameras. Was it the shoes? I know you're friends with that designer, but the heels were way too high and pointy for those narrow steps."

"It wasn't the shoes, Mom." Tessa assumed her mother had been too overwhelmed by everything and everyone yesterday that she hadn't noticed the not-so-discreet exit from the church. If Sherilee had caught wind of what had actually happened, it would've become an even bigger circus with medical specialists called in. Her mom had enough to worry about as it was. Tessa casually flicked her wrist. "We can talk about it later."

"Was it your foundation garments?" her mother continued, refusing to drop the subject. "You might want to switch to Spanx. They're less likely to cut off your circulation."

"Good lord, Sherilee," Freckles said. "Tessa wasn't even wearing a girdle yesterday."

"I didn't say *girdle*," Sherilee whispered the last word. "That would've been beyond tacky to discuss in front of company."

Tessa, her face flaming and her head pounding, shot Finn a pleading look. *Say something!*

"Oh, come on, Mom." Finn might get a kick out of teasing her siblings, but when it came to anyone else doing the same, she was always the first to jump in and defend them. "Couldn't you tell that Tessa had another one of her panic attacks yesterday?"

"No!" Sherilee gasped and Tessa suddenly wished Finn hadn't been so quick to stick up for her. "When did they come back? I thought you'd gotten beyond all that."

"I was beyond it, Mom. I mean I *am* beyond it. That's all in my pa...pa... In my past."

Sherilee shot to her daughter's side and pressed the back of her hand to Tessa's forehead, as though checking for a fever. "All this stress is too much for you. Your neurologist said this could happen, but it's been so long and you've worked so hard. You should stay on at the ranch. I'll fly the speech therapist out. More press is going to mean more scrutiny. If your stutter comes back, you're not going to want to be in front of a camera."

"Mom!" Tessa raised her voice to drown out her mother's ongoing concerns then gave a pointed look toward the four agents, who had been discreet up until this point. Though, when all of this was over, who knew what any of them would say in their tell-all memoirs?

"Don't shout, Tessa. It'll only make you more frustrated and then you won't be able to get the words out at all." Her mom's heavy diamond ring, the one she hadn't dared remove in over thirty years, threatened to tangle in Tessa's hair. Her mother's anxiety tended to escalate a situation rather than defuse it.

It was a stark reminder that Sherilee was the worrier of the family and Roper had been the soother. Tessa winced when the thick gold band inadvertently thunked against her throbbing temple.

"Oh no. Your headaches are coming back, too."

"They are now," Tessa muttered.

"Leave her be, Sher." Freckles stepped up beside Sherilee and put an arm around her waist, leading the distraught woman away from the kitchen before anything else was said in front of Grayson and the other agents.

But the damage was already done. The words her mother had spoken aloud only echoed the unspoken fears Tessa had fought to squelch last night. Could the recent trauma of losing her father possibly cause a relapse? Could all of those symptoms she'd once overcome after her TBI be coming back to haunt her? While her forehead pulsed with crowded thoughts, the space under Tessa's rib cage felt hollow and she resisted the urge to wrap her arms around herself. God forbid the ever-astute Agent Grayson think Tessa was weak or needed some sort of emotional support. Again.

But Tessa was already exposed. And her mom was right. She should probably consult with a neurologist or someone and get her stress under control before she returned to DC. Before she returned to the lights and cameras in the studio and made another mess of herself on live television.

* * *

Grayson wasn't any clearer during the official family briefing in the conference room than he'd been inside the Kings' kitchen earlier that morning. He knew powerful people liked to keep their secrets, but this family was on a whole other level. So what if the world found out that Tessa King had panic attacks or stuttered once in a while?

And Mitchell Junior wasn't the first eighteen-year-old to get into a little trouble with the law. He certainly wouldn't be the last.

"It seems like it would be a lot less trouble to just give the press their story, then let them lose interest," Grayson suggested to the family members sitting around the briefing room table. "They always do."

"Darlin', this must be your first assignment with the King family." Freckles patted his shoulder sympathetically, as though he was inexperienced or too naïve to understand. "They don't like to admit defeat. It's not in their blood. Hell, Rider still hasn't signed our divorce papers and we've been separated for over fifteen years now."

"It's true," Rider said, pushing out his barrel chest. "Grandma Millie and my Marine Corps drill instructors most definitely did *not* train me to surrender. You were Special Forces like me, Wyatt. You know we fight to the last breath."

Tessa's eyebrows lifted at the mention of Grayson's prior military career, which he hadn't shared with the other civilians in this room. Apparently, though, this family had their own recon team working for them. They probably knew just as much about him as he did about them. For the hundredth time today, Grayson clenched his jaw while wishing he had joined the DEA. Or the FDA. Or any other agency that didn't have to deal with the Kings and their inability to stay on task.

"Let's not talk about last breaths, under the circumstances." Mrs. King sniffed, returning to her role as grieving widow now that there were an additional fifteen members of the protective division team in the room with them.

Grayson had to admit, he'd enjoyed the verbal sparring between the King matriarch and her two daughters earlier in the kitchen. Some of his team members had referred to Sherilee King as a diamond-studded battle-ax. Clearly, they hadn't met the younger King females. Anyone who went against the combined forces of Finn and Tessa King had to be sharp and strong enough to withstand the verbal blows.

His father, a former football coach, had always said iron sharpens iron. *"To be the best, you have to practice against the best."* When it came to verbal assaults, the Kings sure as hell kept each other sharp.

That brought Grayson back to his original train of thought. "My point was that if you hold a press conference and answer their questions, they'll hopefully lose interest and everyone can move on. The

King name is certainly strong enough to withstand the fallout from the scandals."

"First of all..." Tessa finally spoke up. "We already have a public relations team working on how to spin this. Second of all, it's not a scandal. At least the one involving me and you isn't a scandal. Yet. But if they find out that you're still on the property and they think we're in close contact, that's only going to fuel their speculation."

"I agree," Grayson was quick to reply. After all, he didn't want the woman—or anyone—thinking that he hoped to stick around any longer than he had to. "Unfortunately, as SAIC Simon already pointed out, removing me from the assignment would be tantamount to admitting that I—that *we*—did something wrong. Or had something to hide. And clearly that's not the case."

It was important to reiterate that he'd followed procedure and hadn't done anything wrong. He'd overheard the earlier conversation about Tessa's history of panic attacks and her stuttering. It was the second time he'd witnessed the way she'd tried to steer certain conversations away from herself. Obviously, there was something more she wanted to hide. Grayson just didn't want her using him as a shield, hiding whatever secret she had behind him. Or behind his career.

"I'm with Agent Wyatt," Duke King said, leaning back in his leather chair. The second child of the

King family was assigned the code name "Peace-keeper," and after watching Tessa's brother calmly interacting with every member of the family during yesterday's gathering, the name was well-earned. "If *you* make this into a big deal, everyone else will make it a big deal."

"I seem to remember Dad saying the same when you wanted to have a small wedding a few years back. But even he couldn't stop the paparazzi from trying to crash his perfect son's reception."

"Perfect is *your* word, not mine." Duke shrugged. From what Grayson had read about the man in the briefing file, he was a high school football legend, graduated top of his class from Annapolis before flying F/A-18s for the Navy. Hard to beat that kind of resume. Finn pretended to flick a piece of mud off her boot and onto his crisply starched uniform. He glanced at his younger sister. "Knock it off, Runt."

"Make me," Finn said then actually sent a clump of dried dirt flying toward the target of Duke's creased pants.

Duke's husband, Tom, whose similar service khakis had the Medical Corps insignia on the left collar, laughed. "Direct hit."

"Real mature, you two," Duke countered as though he were too important to stoop to their teasing. When Finn turned her head, though, Duke got his revenge by flipping the brim of her Dorsey's Tractor Supply ball cap upward and causing the sweat-stained hat to fall on the ground. Apparently, even a peacemaker had his limits before he'd seek retribution. Not that Grayson could blame Duke for putting an annoying little sister in her place.

Grayson had used to play fight with Maddie the same way before she'd gotten sick. Wait, this was play fighting, right? Grayson asked himself when Finn used the fallen cap to smack her brother's biceps. Duke dodged just in time, though, and Finn's blow landed on Tom instead.

Marcus King let himself into the room and Grayson hoped the sheriff was prepared to get between his squabbling siblings. Or at least steer this sinking ship back on course. Then he heard Sherilee King snort and Grayson braced himself for yet another rogue wave to knock them off course.

"So glad you could take a break from your busy schedule of locking up innocent children and join us," Mrs. King said.

"Mom, MJ is eighteen," Marcus sighed. "He's not a child anymore, and he certainly isn't innocent."

"That's not what his lawyer says." Mrs. King crossed her arms over her chest.

Marcus's eyes narrowed. "You didn't actually hire *her* as his attorney, did you, Mom?"

There were several loud intakes of breath around the conference table and even Duke and Finn paused from their play wrestling to pay attention.

Was there another family scandal in the works?

Stay in your lane, Grayson, he told his throbbing head. Mitchell Junior wasn't part of his assignment. Echo Team could deal with this during the second part of the briefing. He looked at his watch.

Agent Lopez apparently didn't share Grayson's desire to get out of the conference room anytime today and asked, "Who is 'her'?"

"Marcus's ex-girlfriend," Freckles said in a stage whisper that everyone in the room heard. "She was in town for the funeral. Her mother is—"

"Hey, Aunt Freckles," Tessa interrupted. "I'm sure the agents are getting very bored with all our family's drama. They need to get back to…whatever it is they need to do."

Yep. This family had plenty of secrets. And Grayson truly didn't want to be a part of any of it. He cleared his throat, resisting the urge to tell Tessa that "whatever it is they need to do" involved protecting her from overeager photographers and anyone else who might sneak onto their property to get a juicy story. Or do something worse.

Grayson tapped a key on his laptop and brought up the next slide on the overhead screen. "So let's go over the perimeter weaknesses and the procedures for entering and exiting the property at the check-in stations."

Finn groaned and Tessa sank lower into her seat as Grayson spoke.

He tried to keep from looking in Tessa's direction

as he discussed the terrain and the fence lines and potential entry points, but it was difficult to *not* see her out of the corner of his eye. Difficult to *not* think about how she'd felt in his arms yesterday.

When Grayson finished his presentation, he moved to the back of the room and chugged an entire bottle of water. Mentally, he felt as though he'd just hiked fifty clicks through the mountains of Afghanistan. Actually, he'd done exactly that during one of his military deployments and it had been a heck of a lot easier back then. And filled with considerably fewer land mines.

As long as he could shield Tessa from any more unexpected media coverage, though, the whole Agent Steamy story would die down and his mission would be a success. That by itself wouldn't be a challenge. The problem: the only way Grayson could protect her was by staying close to her.

Chapter Five

As Lopez went over her list of Twin Kings Ranch employees and authorized guests, Grayson finally allowed his eyes to roam Tessa's profile.

She was even better looking without all that makeup on, but her mouth was tenser than it had been yesterday. Her blond hair was pulled into a loose ponytail and she was wearing a soft gray sweater and a pair of black pants, which looked both expensive and tight in all the right places.

When he'd seen her in the kitchen earlier, she'd been wearing a loose pair of men's-style pajamas. He'd been thinking about what had been underneath that plaid flannel for the past three hours. Just like he was currently wondering what she was hiding underneath that cool façade of hers. Sure, she was maintaining her perfect composure now, but yesterday he'd seen her go from completely vulnerable to a profanity-laced tirade and back to vulnerable.

It was that tirade, though, that kept Grayson from hopping on the first jet out of Wyoming. He was a professional and he'd done his job. If the video of her yelling at him in the staging tent was leaked, there was a chance he would find himself in front of a disciplinary board. And Grayson didn't do disciplinary boards.

Hell, he'd never so much as gotten a tardy slip in elementary school. And that was saying something considering his dad's job at the local high school started early and his mom was usually busy with his sister and wasn't always available to get him to class. He'd had to learn at a young age to manage his own needs and make as little work for his parents as possible. Then after his dad passed away, he'd not only had to take care of himself, he'd had to help his mom with his sister.

Speaking of Maddie, he wanted to call her back before he went on duty tonight. He checked his watch again.

After another ten minutes with Marcus and Sherilee King exchanging pointed glares at each other across the table—and Duke and Finn physically poking at one another under the table—Lopez finally asked the question Grayson had been waiting for. "So who else will be staying on the ranch?"

"Me!" Finn raised her hand. "In fact, I rarely leave."

"And it shows," Duke added. "You could use a little more socialization."

"Children," Mrs. King said to the two grown adults scowling at each other playfully. At least, Grayson hoped they were being playful. There was no telling with this bunch.

Duke straightened his already straight tie. "Tom has three surgeries scheduled for tomorrow at Walter Reed. Originally, we were going to leave for the airport after the briefing, but now I'm thinking someone should stay and be the voice of reason in this family. Plus, my commander called me unexpectedly this morning and gave me leave for the rest of the week."

"He better have," Mrs. King mumbled, then cleared her throat. "I mean, what a nice surprise. I don't think I could get through this without you, Duke."

"Kiss up," Finn accused, but Grayson noted the younger woman now had her arm linked tightly through her brother's instead of shoving him away. Almost as though she wasn't ready for him to leave either.

Lopez, like a teacher trying to get her rowdy class's attention, tapped the two names she'd written on the whiteboard. "Anyone else?"

"I'll be staying on the ranch, obviously," Mrs. King said. She made eye contact with Marcus and added, "So will Mitchell Junior, once the judge releases him."

"I live closer to town," Marcus told Lopez, wisely ignoring his mother's prediction. "But my twins usually come back here after school when I'm working. I pick the boys up around six in the evening and we sometimes stay for dinner. Unless my mom decides we're not welcome anymore."

"Don't be ridiculous, Marcus. I'd never turn away my own family. Unlike some of my children, one of whom I went through twenty-six agonizing hours of labor with to only have them stab me—"

"What about Dahlia King?" Lopez interrupted, looking down at her binder. "Will she be here at all?"

"Dia," Finn corrected. Grayson remembered the info packet he'd received on the King family. Finn and Dahlia were twins, with Dahlia being older by three whole minutes and regarded as somewhat of the family's black sheep. Or lone wolf, depending on who one asked. "She lives above Big Millie's Saloon in town. Her daughter, Amelia, also comes here after school and for riding lessons, so she'll be in and out."

Sherilee sighed at the mention of the saloon and Grayson realized Dahlia's chosen profession was another bone of contention within the King ranks.

But there was one family member who hadn't responded to Lopez yet.

"And you?" Grayson asked, looking at Tessa. "Did you decide if you're staying or going back to DC?"

"I—I'll maybe stay for another day. As long as Duke is here to run interference for me."

Grayson glanced at Duke in time to see him hold up two fingers as if he was pledging the Boy Scout oath.

"Put her down for at least a week," Sherilee told Lopez.

"I'm not staying for a whole week, Mom." Tessa rubbed at the cute little crevice above her nose. "I have a job."

"Your father died, Contessa. I'm sure your audience will understand if you don't hop right back on the air. I'll speak to your producer—"

"No, Mom. He threatened to change his number after the last time you called him. Besides, it's not just my job. I also have a life."

"Then have Congressman Townsend come visit here. Put him on the list," her mother told Lopez.

"No," Tessa said again. "Don't put him on the list."

"Did you break up?" Rider and Freckles asked in unison. The elderly couple had definitely perked up at the possibility.

"No. Not exactly." Tessa's eyes flicked toward Grayson, but when he refused to look away, she focused on a spot past Grayson's head. "We can talk about this later."

So there *was* trouble in paradise. His gut had been right. At least he still had his instincts going for him, even if his sanity was slowly slipping.

"Keep him on the list," Sherilee King repeated to Lopez before turning to Tessa. "It'll look better for the PR team if he visits and your relationship seems solid."

Lopez shrugged. "We can always take him off if things don't work out."

"Think of it as a hotel reservation," Duke suggested. "Except no charge for a cancellation fee."

"Do you think he's going to dump you after this?" Finn asked, clearly ignoring her sister's request to talk about the subject privately. Or maybe in spite of it.

"Never," Marcus replied for Tessa. "Congressman Smooth loves the limelight and the family connection too much."

"Speaking of family connection..." Mrs. King shot another sharp look at Marcus before returning her eagle eyes to Tessa. "I'd appreciate having as many of my children here in Wyoming for as long as possible. After all, the next time they'll all be under the same roof will probably be at my own funeral."

Grayson shifted in his chair. If *his* mother had laid on a guilt trip like that, there was no way he'd be able to refuse her wishes. But Noreen Wyatt would never go that route. His mother was the most selfless woman he knew, and didn't have a strategic bone in her body.

And right now, Grayson needed to go call her to get away from the constant headache the King family had given him.

"So tell me about the food at this new treatment facility," Grayson said to his younger sister whose face occupied the screen of the laptop. She was twenty-eight years old, but looked more like a teenager in that big hospital bed. "Is it any good?"

"Can we *not* talk about my upcoming procedure for a few minutes?" Maddie replied. "I want to talk about my big brother's picture being posted all over the internet like some sort of prince charming rescuing a damsel in distress."

"Don't let Tessa King hear you call her a damsel, let alone one in distress."

"Tell me about her."

He resisted the urge to make sure none of the other agents in the bunkhouse could hear him. They could sniff out suspicion from a mile away. "Even if I were at liberty to disclose that information, there's nothing to tell, really. I hardly even know her."

"Oh come on, Gray. I'm going stir crazy over here practically waiting to die."

"Maddie, you're not going to—"

"Don't say it. We always promised not to lie to each other." His sister's body might have atrophied over the years, but her silver eyes were as fierce and determined as ever. He'd never seen them lose their light, no matter how grim her prognosis had been. "This treatment doesn't have a guaranteed success rate on someone my age. And even then, I'm only holding off the inevitable a few more years."

"If you would let me finish…" he continued, refusing to even acknowledge any possibility that the spine fusion wouldn't work. "I was saying that you're not going to go stir crazy with that new laptop. Which, by the way, I got you so that you can work on that online masters program. Not so you could run internet searches on me. If you're bored, you need to be studying."

"How can I keep my mind on anything right now? Please, Gray. Give me something to live for."

The familiar guilt twisted inside his chest.

Growing up, he'd been the big brother who'd done all the physical stuff his sister hadn't been able to do. Maddie had been diagnosed with Emery-Dreifuss Muscular Dystrophy, or EDMD for short, when she was nine years old. There'd been no stopping the weakening of the muscles in her shoulders, upper arms, calves and legs. There'd only been physical therapy and sometimes surgical intervention to relieve the stiff joints of her elbows, neck and heels. Surgical release of the contracted muscles sometimes helped, but never kept the contractures from recurring.

They'd known that conduction blocks would eventually start affecting Maddie's heart, disrupting the heartbeat rhythm since the electrical impulses wouldn't communicate between the upper and lower chambers. She'd gotten her first pacemaker two years ago. Now she was having rods inserted into her spine to hopefully keep her walking so she could maximize her physical therapy.

Nothing was wrong with her mind or her sassy attitude, though, Grayson thought before asking, "Where's Mom?"

"I made her go get a coffee down in the cafeteria. You think I'd be using that 'something to live for' line if she was in the room with me? I'm not that heartless."

"Sorry. I've been with the cruise director of guilt trips lately," he said, thinking of Sherilee King. "So I'm a little suspect of everyone right now."

"Right now? Gray, you're always suspect of everyone. It's what makes you so good at your job." His sister's eyes twinkled. "Now tell me about your next assignment. Are you going back to the White House?"

"First of all, you know I can't divulge that kind of information. Second of all, I'm still on my current assignment for an undisclosed amount of time."

"So you're staying on that fancy ranch in Wyoming?" Maddie asked but didn't give him time to respond. "Can you send me pics of the inside of the house? I saw an article about the Kings in *Fine Tastes* and there were all these glossy pictures of a huge mansion made to look like a rustic log cabin. The kitchen was bigger than our entire apartment."

Grayson didn't want to admit that the kitchen was in fact twice as big, if one counted something called a butler's pantry and the separate prep area for catering staff whenever the Kings had a party. "Since when do you read snooty magazines like *Fine Tastes*?"

"Since my big brother insisted on paying out of pocket for only the top-rated specialists. All those plush waiting rooms have magazines like that."

Their mom, who had always been Maddie's sole caretaker, hadn't been able to work full-time after their dad died, so their government-subsidized medical insurance only covered the basics. Grayson would've put them on his own insurance plan if he could. Instead, he worked as much overtime as possible so that his sister could have the best health care possible. And so that his mom could afford to take hotel rooms near the hospitals and pay for meal deliveries when she was too tired to cook after spending the day driving Maddie around to doctor and physical therapy appointments.

Neither Noreen nor Maddie would ever ask him for so much as a dime, but if he couldn't be home to take care of them himself, the least he could do was send a part of his paycheck to help.

His dad had always hoped Grayson would get

a football scholarship right after high school, but he hadn't wanted to waste time on college when he could join the Marines and immediately start earning a paycheck to send home.

"Did the screen freeze?" Maddie asked.

"Huh?" Grayson replied.

"You were just sitting there not answering. I thought the video connection had gone out again."

"Sorry, I was just lost in thought."

"About the beautiful and smart Tessa King?" His sister wiggled her pale eyebrows.

"What? No. I mean other than how she relates to my afternoon shift. Speaking of which, I've got to go back to work. Tell Mom to text me when you get out of surgery."

Maddie shrugged. "Give me Tessa King's number and I'll have Mom text *her* instead."

"The painkillers must already be taking effect if you're crazy enough to think I'd ever give you top-secret information like that."

Maddie's eyes narrowed playfully. "So you *do* have her number."

Actually, he didn't have Tessa's number, though he could get it from the Protective Intelligence Division. "Don't need it. And I definitely don't want it."

"You need *some*one, Grayson. Mom is worried that you haven't dated anyone since Jamie."

Grayson shook his head, trying to dislodge the sting of the reminder. "I *need* to get back to work.

Good luck in the operating room and try not to yell at the nurses this time."

"I didn't yell at that nurse. I politely told her that I didn't appreciate them putting me in a hospital gown covered with pink and purple unicorns. I don't care if they thought it fit me better. I'm a twenty-eight-year-old woman. Not some preteen with stars in her eyes."

"Says the grown adult who is addicted to sour gummy bears." He smiled indulgently. "Love you, Mads."

"Love you more, Gray."

He closed the screen of his laptop, disconnecting the video call. He hadn't lied to his sister. He really did need to get back to work, which meant he had to get his mind right. If Grayson couldn't do his job, then he couldn't provide for his sister, which was the indirect goal of all of his missions. All the hours of training, the overtime shifts, the high-risk assignments came at a physical cost for him, but the financial reward was well worth with it. But that also meant compartmentalizing his family life and his work life, and even his social life—not that he had much of one. He couldn't allow himself to be distracted by thoughts of his sister's medical procedure, or by what the internet was saying about him.

Or the fact that Tessa King had just ridden by the bunkhouse on a horse, without an assigned agent trailing at a distance.

Crap. He'd been in the briefing with her and knew

she'd heard the part about having an agent accompany her everywhere she went. He'd also seen her roll her pretty blue eyes at that particular directive. That meant she must've purposely slipped her tail. Doherty was supposed to be assigned to her this afternoon. Grayson should simply let his fellow team member deal with the woman.

Unfortunately, his job was to protect *all* the Kings. Even the ones who'd been assigned to someone else.

Even the ones who made his muscles tense and his blood heat up.

"I know I told you I'd be back on the air by tomorrow night, Bryson," Tessa told the chief executive of programming at her network. Her agent had offered to make the necessary calls for her, but Tessa hadn't become one of the top political analysts on prime time TV by avoiding the tough conversations. "But a few things have come up and I need to stay in Wyoming another week."

"I told you that you should've planned to take the full week," Bryson Johnson told her before speaking to someone else on his end of the line—probably his assistant. "Get Brett Monroe from the morning roundtable show and see if he can cover the eight o'clock slot this week."

"You know, Brett Monroe didn't do well in focus groups when he covered the gubernatorial debates last summer," Tessa reminded her boss. After all, this was *her* show they were talking about. Her name was in the title. *Bottom Line with Tessa King.* No way was some comedian-turned-breakfast-show host going to maintain the serious integrity of the very program Tessa had built. "I'd go with Juanita Munoz. She covered that election scandal in South America and—"

"Fine," Bryson interrupted. "We'll send Brett up to Wyoming for an exclusive on you and that Agent Steamy guy."

"No, I'm not going to comment on the Secret Service agent who was doing his job. We both know that's nothing but tabloid fodder and our network is better than that."

"Hmm. You might be right. Probably not a good look to be talking about your love life on camera so soon after your father's passing. Plus, if you're hiding out, that'll build up the speculation. As long as you don't hide out so long that everyone forgets about you."

"It's only a week, Bryson," she tried to reassure him, though they both knew that in this business, there was always another big story and a hungry journalist right around the corner. "Besides, it's also not a good look for the network to be spinning my family's tragedy to their advantage."

"Damn, Tessa. I'm sorry. You're right." He paused. "Did you get the flowers we sent?"

"The flowers were beautiful," she replied carefully. There'd been so many arrangements delivered to the church and the ranch, she'd had no idea who had sent what. But all flowers were beautiful, weren't they? And she appreciated the gesture, even though she knew that Bryson was probably more concerned with the potential loss of viewers than with Tessa's personal loss. "So I'll see you in a week."

"Of course. Take all the time you need. We'll schedule your exclusive with Brett for March sweeps instead."

Tessa knew better than to tell her boss that there was no way she was going to do any sort of interview about her love life, especially with someone like Brett Monroe. However, that was a battle to be fought after she secured her next contract. At the end of the day, she couldn't blame her network for wanting to capitalize on her personal situation. It was a business, and they were there to make money. Unfortunately for them, there was no story to sell.

When Tessa got off the phone with Bryson, she sent her agent a text with the contact info for her mother's public relations team. After all, those weren't the tough calls, just the annoying ones.

She could hear Aunt Freckles banging around in the kitchen and, as much as she loved the older woman, Tessa didn't want to be within a mile radius when Sherilee found out her former sister-in-law was making chicken-fried steak and gravy for dinner.

Tessa sat back in the stuffed leather chair in front of her father's desk. She'd come into his office to make her call, but she hadn't dared to actually sit *behind* his desk. This room was her father's sanctuary and there were parts of him everywhere she looked. Pictures of him with celebrities, world leaders and military buddies shared space with family photos and homemade Father's Day gifts.

She picked up a frame with a black-and-white photograph of Roper and Rider when they were only seven years old. The towheaded boys were dressed in matching denim overalls and had their arms over each other's shoulders. Their identical noses were covered in freckles and their wide grins were missing at least six teeth between the two of them.

Tessa's heart tugged at the obvious closeness of the little boys. Even though they'd grown up to live such different lives, there were no two men who had loved her more. She shuddered as a sob threatened to make its way through her chest.

If she were smart, she'd let herself have a good cry and get it over with. But once she started, there'd be no stopping the flood of tears that was sure to come. And who knew who might walk in and see her?

She needed to get outside, to get away from all the memories inside the house. When Tessa had wanted to get away from the stresses of childhood, she'd go to the swimming pool her parents kept heated eight months out of the year and practice her dives. But after her accident, her mom had removed the diving board and Tessa had a feeling that seeing the empty spot where the board used to be would be worse than sitting in her father's study.

In DC, she'd work out to relieve some of the antsiness, but she was pretty sure her mom was with a personal yoga instructor in the home gym right now. And Tessa really didn't feel like being around anyone.

She stood and stretched. The entire backside of the house was covered in floor-to-ceiling windows that framed the glorious purple mountains in the distance. Maybe she should go for a ride. She hadn't been on a horse for a few years and relearning the motions would require her to think about what she was doing, which would be way better than going for a mindless jog where her brain might latch onto any passing thought.

She found a pair of extra boots in Finn's closet and, because they weren't the type of sisters who shared everything, Tessa decided it was better to borrow now and ask for forgiveness later.

One of the stable workers offered to saddle a mare for her, but Tessa declined, needing physical activity that required her to get outside of her own head.

She and Phoebe—Finn had named the mare when she'd been going through her *Friends* phase—started off on a measured pace.

Tessa got the older horse up to a slow canter but, rocking back and forth in the leather saddle, she decided it was *not* like riding a bike. She didn't remember her thighs ever burning this much before. Or needing to stretch her lower back. And she'd only gone a couple of miles or so. This might not have been her best idea.

She turned her head to gauge the distance and caught sight of someone riding up the path behind her. Tessa initially felt relief that she was no longer on the trail alone. Then she realized the person appeared to be even more awkward than she was on the back of a horse.

None of the hired cattle hands wore shirts that bright or sunglasses that dark. An electric current shot through Tessa's legs as Grayson Wyatt drew closer.

"Sorry to intrude, Miss King, but we discussed this in the briefing this morning."

"Discussed what?" she asked, wishing she'd brought her own sunglasses again. Instead, she pulled the brim of her dad's old University of Wyoming cap lower.

"Members of the family shouldn't go anywhere without an escort."

She looked at the Teton mountain range in the distance to make sure she hadn't gone farther than she thought. "But I'm not leaving the ranch."

"Still." That was all he said and she swallowed a groan of frustration.

Not that she needed an explanation. Tessa wasn't about to play stupid with him and pretend like she didn't know full well that someone could slip through one of the checkpoints and gain access to them. It was a vast, sprawling property, not Fort Knox.

She was about to turn around and head back to the stables—her sore forearms gripping the reins certainly would've appreciated that. But she saw how uncomfortable the perfect agent was on his own horse and decided she could suffer his presence a little longer if it meant putting him outside *his* comfort zone for a change.

Tessa snapped the reins and urged Phoebe into another canter, the thrill of regaining control overriding her protesting muscles.

Chapter Six

Grayson could go for hours and hours without talking to a soul. It was one of the skills he'd mastered as a sniper for both the Marines and the Counter Assault Team.

Following Tessa King, he didn't say a word—not even a warning when she rode under a sagging tree branch and almost didn't duck in time. Occasionally, he'd hear another agent on his earpiece, yet for the most part, it was blessedly uneventful and quiet everywhere else on the ranch. By the time she passed the trail that would take them back to the stables, though, she was slouching so low that he wasn't sure how much longer she could remain upright in the saddle.

"Do you know where we're going?" he finally asked.

"Of course I do." She slowed her pace until his horse was beside hers. "At least, I used to. But it'll come back to me."

Grayson didn't need the GPS on his watch to tell him exactly where they were. On the airplane here, he'd studied the trail maps while other agents had studied nearby restaurants that served the best steaks and coldest beers. Plus, the horses had already done at least two circles right past this location today. "There's a creek about half a mile from here. We should probably stop and get the horses some water."

She exhaled and gave a stiff nod. "As much as I hate to admit it, you're probably right."

Instead of pulling ahead of him on her horse so that he could once again follow behind her at a respectable distance, she allowed her horse to remain abreast of his.

"You hate admitting when someone else is right?" Grayson asked then immediately wished he'd kept his mouth shut.

Their roles were already defined and there was no room for crossover. He was the agent and she was the assignment. It wasn't that he felt he was inferior to her in any way—except maybe financially. Nor did he care about the fact they came from two different social worlds. His job, though, depended on them staying in their roles. Walking along side by side once again made them equals and blurred those boundaries between them.

The military had a rule about fraternization between officers and enlisted personnel and, in Grayson's mind, this situation was no different. It would certainly be easier for him to do his job if he didn't have to think of Tessa King as anything other than an assignment.

"I don't mind someone else being right." She exhaled and he tried not to stare at the smooth skin along her neck. "I just hate being wrong."

His mouth twitched. "Are you ever wrong?"

"Only when I told myself that riding this horse would be like riding a bike and that I'd remember what to do as soon as I climbed on. Unfortunately, my thighs and lower back have completely forgotten all the muscle work involved."

Grayson allowed his eyes to trail down her legs encased in snug denim. "Your muscles seem to be doing just fine."

He heard the breath hitch in her throat over the sound of the water flowing through the nearby creek. Grounding his back molars in place, he reminded himself of those damn boundaries. *She's a job, not a woman.*

The problem was he knew how to talk to a woman. He didn't know how to make polite conversation with a job.

"I mean, you haven't fallen yet. Not that you normally fall..." He trailed off when she lifted one eyebrow at him.

"You know, I really don't go collapsing in front of strangers. Yesterday was a one-off," she said then proceeded to dismount with more grace than she probably felt.

Don't look at her rear end, he warned himself as he climbed out of the saddle. But as he used the reins to lead his horse to the creek, his eyes went straight to the curve of her backside.

He cleared his throat and scanned the area for any sort of threat, whether it be a wild animal or a bold trespasser wielding a weapon or, worse, a camera. He radioed in their location and got an update from the command center.

They stood along the bank as their horses drank greedily from the stream. He rubbed his hand along the gray gelding's back and murmured a few words of appreciation to the poor animal who'd had to carry his awkward two-hundred-pound frame this far.

"Chandler likes you." Tessa finally broke the silence.

"Who?"

"Chandler Bing. From the TV show. Finn wanted to move to NYC and share an apartment with all her best friends before she decided to become a cowgirl instead. She named these two—" Tessa gestured toward both horses "—along with several others.

That's why their row in the stables is referred to as Central Perk."

Grayson chuckled, the vibration in his throat feeling unnatural. "My sister is a big *Friends* fan, too."

Maybe when this assignment was officially over and debriefed, he'd be able to share that detail with Maddie. She'd appreciate a stable full of horses being named after characters in her TV series.

"Well, I hope your sister rides better than you." Tessa smirked.

"She used to. Hopefully, she will again."

"Is she okay?" Tessa asked as her cheeks turned a charming shade of pink. "Sorry. Asking personal questions is a habit from work."

Grayson could count on one hand the number of agents and military buddies who knew about his sister's condition. Maddie had hated all the pitying looks and curious stares she'd gotten when their mother or Grayson would have to push her custom-made wheelchair on her bad days. So his way of protecting her was to pretend that there was nothing wrong in front of outsiders.

Yet the concern on Tessa's face was sincere and, after all, Grayson had brought up the subject of his sister.

"She has a rare type of muscular dystrophy. When we were younger, our family went to this camp where kids with special needs got to ride therapy horses.

The place was called Let's Ride and that was their motto. The first time they put her up on that great big horse, I immediately demanded that they get her off. She's always been tiny and her muscles are easily weakened. I didn't think she could handle such a huge animal. But she took to it like that—" Grayson snapped his fingers. "Maddie was doing the jump course by the end of the week."

"And what about you? Did you do the jump course?"

"No way. The only reason I got on the horse was so that I could trail behind her and pull her to safety if something happened."

"Of course. A born rescuer. Did anything ever happen?"

"Not that week." His pointed look conveyed his belief that nothing was going to happen this week, either. At least, not on his watch.

"So did Maddie get her own horse when you guys got home from camp?"

"We lived in a duplex in a subdivision outside of Baltimore at the time. So even if we could've afforded one, there wouldn't have been anywhere to keep it. Or ride it."

"Where does Maddie live now?" Tessa asked. "Maybe there's a nearby equestrian program where she could take riding lessons or at least visit the horses?"

"I found a horse farm an hour away from their apartment in Baltimore. It's supposed to be for children with special needs, but they made an exception for Maddie because she looks like she's twelve years old. She'd be so pissed if she knew that because she hates being mistaken for a kid. Anyway, she used to ride whenever she was wasn't suffering from contractures." And when Grayson could send some extra money home to pay for the lessons. "She's having surgery this afternoon to get a steel rod implanted along her spine. It's not a guaranteed procedure, but if it works, she'll regain some of her mobility and might be able to ride again."

Tessa studied him for several moments and he waited for the questions that were sure to follow. But all she said was, "Your face softens when you talk about your sister. Actually, it softens when you talk, period."

Grayson's only response was to scan the horizon and keep his mouth clamped shut. It'd been easier to do his job when they weren't talking and she wasn't noticing how soft or not his face was.

When the horses finished drinking their fill, Tessa led Phoebe up the bank and toward an old wooden post that might've been part of a fence at one point. Apparently they weren't heading back to the stables anytime soon.

She must've read his mind because she offered,

"I just need to stretch out a few more minutes before I get back in the saddle."

She looped the reins around the post and then did some yoga-style poses. Man, this woman was flexible. She lifted her arms over her head before slowly bending to touch the grass below her boots.

Grayson's throat tightened and he averted his gaze, staring at the icy cold water rippling over the rocks as it flowed down the creek. Was it deep enough for him to fully submerge his head? It was either that or be tempted by the view of her thighs as she lunged deeply, her hips dipping low.

He heard Agent Lopez speak into the radio at the same time he heard the familiar whirl of helicopter blades. Grayson's adrenaline kicked in and he hooked his arm around Tessa's waist and yanked her against his side, immediately rushing her toward the closest oak tree, where the thicker branches provided them better cover.

Tessa wrapped her arm around Grayson's waist as she huddled behind him. He had a feeling it was instinctive, but it threw him right back into his role of protector.

He remained planted in front of her as he walked both of them backward so that she was positioned between him and the thick tree trunk. Placing two of his fingers on his earpiece, he copied the radio exchange then relayed the information to Tessa.

"There's an unidentified helicopter circling the property. No station logo or anything else to identify it from their vantage point. It's currently staying above a thousand feet and isn't showing any sign of landing. Do you know if anyone in your family is expecting a visitor?"

Tessa poked her head around his shoulder. "Not that I know of."

Chandler snorted at something in the sky and then stomped his front foot. The sound of the helicopter grew louder and the horse took off for parts unknown.

Damn.

Of course Grayson's first instinct had been to get Tessa to safety before securing the horse. He was a special agent, not a cowboy. Thankfully, Tessa had tied Phoebe to that post. But the mare tugged against her reins, whinnying as though she was about to run off with her stable mate.

"Stay here," he commanded Tessa before approaching Phoebe with both arms outstretched in what he hoped was a calmness that defied his current adrenaline level. When he reached the loose knot in the reins, the mare used her nose to shake her head away from him. He'd prefer to bring the horse under the tree, but he didn't want to risk her fighting him and taking off after Chandler.

"It's okay, girl," Tessa said, coming around his

shoulder, blatantly ignoring his instructions to stay put. "I'll hold her bridle. You retie her."

The helicopter passed overhead just as he got the reins secured tighter. They sprinted toward the overhanging branches together, but not before he spotted a logo on the green paint. Buster Chop's Chopper Rentals.

Grayson spoke into his mouthpiece, advising the team of the logo and the tail number identifying the aircraft's registration. "A large oak tree is currently providing us with suitable visual coverage for now, and I don't believe our position has been compromised yet."

"Copy that," Lopez replied in his ear. "Be advised local air traffic control hasn't authorized any aircraft to be in our no-fly zone and the unsub is not responding to attempts at radio contact. Intercepting authorities are en route and should be on scene in two clicks."

"I've got a visual of the unsub from the eastern trailhead," Doherty added. "Appears to be a telephoto lens aimed out the open hatch of the aircraft. Maintain your current position."

"10-4," Grayson said and exhaled, somewhat relieved that it wasn't something more deadly aimed out the open hatch. Tessa lifted questioning eyes to his face and he told her, "They think it's a photographer. But it keeps circling the area above us, so something must be giving our position away."

"It's probably a scared horse running around with an empty saddle." Tessa pointed to a field in the distance where Chandler was anxiously galloping in circles. "Poor guy was probably heading back to the stables, but the helicopter followed him and now he's just racing in a loop. I need to go get him."

"Negative." Grayson moved in front of her again and reached behind both their backs to press her against him before she could inch forward. The helicopter dipped lower, making the leaves above their heads rustle each time it dropped down. "We need to stay in position. If the horse is scared, he won't come to you anyway."

"I can't just hide under here," Tessa protested.

Grayson wanted to argue with her, but he knew the exact feeling. He hated hiding when he could be doing something way more proactive to protect her.

The sound of an approaching aircraft—make that two approaching aircrafts—drowned out all other arguments.

"Are those fighter jets?" Tessa peeked around his back to scan the horizon. "So much for pretending like my being at Twin Kings is no big deal."

Even though he knew she was only echoing his own words from the earlier briefing, they still had to follow standard protocol any time their team was actively deployed. "Several military jets are on standby at the nearby airfield. A couple of them were dispatched to remind Buster Chops up there that this is a no-fly zone."

The helicopter must've taken the hint because after several seconds, the roaring engines and blades above trailed off until they no longer could be heard.

Grayson's hand was still on the back of Tessa's waist. He loosened his grip, but she didn't immediately pull away.

"The helicopter is bugging out," he said into the radio before running his palm along her lower spine in what he hoped was a soothing motion. Unfortunately, the feel of her breasts still pressed against his back didn't soothe him. He cleared his throat and then took a couple of steps before shifting to face her. "We should be getting the all-clear any minute and then we can return to the stables."

She turned her eyes up to his and, instead of seeing fear or even annoyance reflected at him, they held a tinge of amusement.

"What's so funny?" he asked.

"Unfortunately, there are two of us and now we only have one horse."

Tessa took pity on Grayson and walked alongside her mare instead of hopping back in the saddle and making a mad dash for the stables. After all, she should have waited for one of the agents to accompany her on the ride in the first place.

Not that she'd needed anyone's protection from

the big bad cameraman hanging out of the helicopter. She did just fine dodging paparazzi back in DC, mostly by pretending that they didn't even exist. However, the Secret Service agency had a job to do—no matter how much Tessa resented their intrusion or Grayson Wyatt's high-handedness.

By disrupting their protocol and leaving without her protective detail, she could've caused a lot more work and worry for the team tasked to locate her after realizing she was gone. These men and women were putting their lives in danger to protect her and her family, and taking off like that without a thought of the added workload they'd face was selfish on her part.

Although, to be fair, she hadn't really gone very far.

"Did you know that we'd been riding in circles when you followed me earlier?" she asked the man walking beside her.

Grayson gave a stiff nod, his boots steadily keeping her slower pace even though she had a feeling he could run to the stables and back before she made it another mile. He didn't seem nearly as exhausted as she felt. In fact, with his shoulders squared off and his head on a swivel, he looked as though he was on a mission and wasn't going to rest until he'd accomplished his goal.

"Why didn't you say anything, then?"

"Wasn't my place," he said, causing a wave of

shame to wash through Tessa. Just because she hadn't wanted him there didn't mean she thought of him as the hired help—someone under her authority who should be seen and not heard.

What happened to that guy a couple of hours ago who'd been talking about his sister and her specialized riding program? Grayson had almost seemed like a real person such a short time ago. But then the helicopter showed up and he'd gone right back into special agent mode. Devoid of expression or even emotion.

Not that a simple conversation earlier meant they were suddenly best friends or anything. Just like the heated looks he'd given her in the briefing room this morning didn't mean that he was attracted to her. An unexpected warmth rose along the back of her neck at the memory and she resisted the urge to lift her hair and fan herself.

Instead, Tessa pulled an insulated bottle from her saddlebag and took a long drink, hoping the cool water would lessen some of the heat coursing through her on this unusually sunny January day.

Normally, she was in command of a situation. In fact, two years ago she'd won the Walter Cronkite Award for Excellence in Television Political Journalism because she hadn't backed down during her interview with one of the most powerful dictators in the world.

It was like playing a game of chess. Getting the

other person talking about themselves was key to them letting down their guard. Once their defenses were lowered, Tessa could usually steer them in the direction she needed them to go.

Not that she needed to steer Grayson into some sort of news-breaking headline. But if she could get him talking—or otherwise acting like a normal human being and not a robotic bodyguard—Tessa wouldn't feel as though she required his protection. Or anyone's protection, for that matter. Even if she couldn't take charge of the situation, the least she could do was put them on some sort of level playing field.

"Do you know that most fish and birds use sun compass orientation to migrate to the same breeding ground years later?" She offered him her bottle of water.

"Was that what you were you looking for today, Miss King? A particular breeding ground?" Grayson asked as he took the bottle. Tessa immediately averted her eyes so that she wouldn't see his lips on the exact same spot where her mouth had been seconds ago. Unfortunately, her eyes landed on his neck and she was so transfixed on watching his throat muscles move that she tripped on a rock.

"My point is that I used to know these trails like the back of my hand. But now, everything about this place seems so different."

"Well, you've been under a lot of stress with your

father's passing and your, uh, family..." He took a deep breath before wisely letting that sentence trail off.

"Drama?" she offered.

"I was going to say 'dynamics.'" He smiled and Tessa's knees grew so wobbly she would've for sure gone down if there'd been another rock in her path. If the press had captured Grayson Wyatt's sly grin, the pictures from the day of the funeral would have been captioned a lot more graphically than "Agent Steamy."

Remembering the press and the reason he was there, Tessa sucked in a quick breath to shore up courage. "Listen, I'm sorry for taking off without an escort earlier. It's been a long time since I've had a protective tail, but I still know the rules."

"Luckily, nobody was in any danger. This time." His warning hung in the air between them.

"Anyway, I just needed to get out of the house and clear my head. I hadn't meant to be gone so long. But, like I said, everything out here looks so much different since I moved away. You could've spoken up sooner if you'd known I was lost."

"And risk being called...oh, what was it you said in the staging center tent yesterday? An 'overbearing, overcompensating a-hole with a hero complex'?"

Tessa flinched. Last night, Marcus warned her that one of the local law enforcement officers in the staging area yesterday had been wearing a body camera on his ballistics vest and inadvertently recorded the whole thing. She still hadn't seen the footage and, unfortunately, with everything else going on yesterday, she couldn't recall the exact words she'd used. "Look, I'm sorry if anything I said offended you."

"I wasn't offended," he replied, his smile long gone. She watched his jaw tighten before he continued. "I was doing my job, by any means necessary."

"I never wanted to be part of your job, though," Tessa said, pushing her shoulders back. She needed him to see that she could protect herself. Of course, how could she convince him of that after she'd been so quick to run and hide behind his broad, muscular back as soon as the helicopter showed up? *Don't think about his back!* Tessa straightened her spine. "I never asked for any of this."

He didn't respond for a few moments and Tessa figured he was back in his silent protector mode. Then he cleared his throat. "Your family made a few comments this morning about you having a history of panic attacks and something about a stutter—"

"Oh no!" Her hand shot to her mouth before she could stop it. "I didn't stutter in that video yesterday, did I?"

He tilted his head to one side, as though trying to figure out how to answer her question while still drawing more information from her. It was a tactic she'd used herself when she interviewed guests on her show.

Tessa tried a different strategy. "You know what? Forget I asked that. Let's talk about something else."

"Like the weather?" Grayson looked up toward the cloudless sky. "It's fifty-eight degrees and sunny. Very unusual for Wyoming this time of year. What do you want to talk about next?"

I want to talk about you! Tessa wanted to yell. *Tell me everything about Special Agent Grayson Wyatt.* Of course, she was better trained than to lead with such an open-ended and personal question. Instead she asked, "How about you tell me where you got that ugly shirt?"

He chuckled, but walked several more steps before finally answering. "I borrowed it from Agent Doherty, the guy with the Red Sox hat who was running the projector this morning during the briefing."

"But you're so much bigger than..." She paused when he turned his head toward her, as though he was suddenly very interested in having *this* particular conversation. A tingling sensation raced through her.

"Not that I was checking out your body or anything," she quickly said then felt the heat return to her neck. "I mean, it just seemed like the shirt was a little small on you. Not that it matters. Some people like tight clothes."

Lord, she needed to shut up.

Grayson's eyes traveled down the jeans she'd found in Finn's closet, the ones that Tessa had to wrestle over her hips a few hours ago. Everything suddenly felt tighter, including her own skin, as she waited for him to answer.

She was one second away from grabbing the saddle blanket and wrapping it around herself like a shield when he finally responded. "My boss wanted us to try to blend in with the other ranch employees and I only packed suits and workout gear because I thought it'd be a short trip."

She suddenly had a vision of the man in running shorts and a sweaty T-shirt, his massive chest rising and falling with each exerted breath—

"I had to borrow everything I'm wearing, too," she blurted out in an effort to shut off the fantasy playing through her mind. "Except my underwear, of course. Oh geez! Please forget I said that. My powers of speech never fail me when I actually need them to."

"I will definitely add that to my list of things I need to forget about you," Grayson said, however, his slow, appraising stare suggested he was doing the exact opposite. That he was, in fact, committing every detail about her to memory.

Unable to withstand the heat from his gaze, she began walking again, ignoring the trickle of sweat between her shoulder blades. She bit her lower lip to keep from saying anything else as they approached the stables. Next time Tessa went for a ride, she would ask the female agent to accompany her. Agent

Lopez at least dressed as though she knew her way around a ranch and horses.

But if she made that request, would everyone think that something had happened between her and Grayson today? That could make the situation worse.

Ugh, Tessa screamed inside her head. Why was she suddenly overthinking every little thing?

Maybe she shouldn't go riding again at all, she thought as she unsaddled Phoebe inside the stables. Duke might be willing to go with her, but he flew jets for a living and thought horses moved too slowly. Which meant that if he went with her, then she'd have to play that stupid fighter pilot video game he'd found in the den. Her brother might be the peacemaker of the family, but only because he was a brilliant negotiator. And as much as Tessa loved spending time with Duke, she wasn't about to pick up a game controller and get virtually shot down by someone who'd been trained on actual jets.

Maybe instead of riding, she could just use the home gym, or go for a long run to stretch out the muscles she'd overused today.

But the following morning, after a heated argument between Marcus and Marcus's ex-girlfriend—who had agreed to be MJ's attorney for his drunk and disorderly charge—Tessa found herself heading straight for the stables again to get away from the drama.

This time, though, she didn't have to wait for an agent to come find her. Grayson was already inside waiting for her.

Chapter Seven

Just like the day before, Grayson followed Tessa at a respectable distance after they set out on Phoebe and Ross, a gelding with a black coat and a spiky mane. Chandler had thankfully returned to the stables on his own yesterday—just in time for the evening feeding—and snorted his annoyance at Grayson before grudgingly taking an apple as a peace offering. The stable foreman assured him the older stallion would be fine after his adventure, but should probably rest another day or two before going on any more rides.

They were only half a mile onto the trail when Finn and Duke raced by on another pair of horses, causing

Grayson's and Tessa's mounts to draw closer together. He could practically feel the gears in Tessa's mind shifting, as though she was contemplating breaking their mutual silence. As soon as her lips opened, Grayson beat her to the punch. "So, uh, how long has your family owned this ranch?"

Of course Grayson already knew everything there was to know about Twin Kings. It was in his preop briefing notes. But maybe if he could get her talking about something other than his sister or his job or why he was still there, then he wouldn't slip into talking about himself. Like he had yesterday.

Tessa took the bait and nudged her mount along. "The King family first settled in Wyoming in the late 1890s. But it wasn't on this ranch. My dad used to tell the story about his great-grandmother, who was on a train heading to Oregon to teach at a school in a mining town there. But her train was delayed in Teton Ridge because US Marshals were looking for several members of the Black Hills Bandits who were reported to be stowaways trying to leave the state."

Grayson might've grown up a city boy in Baltimore, but he was a sucker for a Wild West adventure story. "Never heard of them."

"They were a gang of robbers out of Deadwood, South Dakota. Trains, stagecoaches, banks—these guys weren't picky. Anyway, she fell in love with the town and, after the marshals interviewed everyone on board and sent the train on its way, she stuck around. The story my dad *didn't* tell the public was that his great-grandfather was actually one of the Black Hills Bandits and Big Millie—that would be my great-great-grandmother—had discovered the youngest and most charming member of the gang hiding in her travel compartment on board the train. She'd felt so sorry for the handsome bandit, she didn't alert the conductor. In fact, when it was her turn to be interviewed, she told the marshals that she and the young man had been travelling together since Laramie, which wasn't a total lie. So, she fell in love with the town as well as a notorious criminal who promised that he could change his ways with the love of a good woman."

"And did he change his ways?" Grayson asked.

"Only for the first year. He left her with a baby to raise by herself before he skipped town. Since only single women without children could be schoolteachers back then, Big Millie turned to any means necessary to support her daughter."

"So that explains how Big Millie's Saloon in town got its start," he said before taking a swig from his water bottle.

"Actually, it got its start as a brothel."

Grayson choked on the water.

"Aha, I bet you didn't read about *that* little tidbit in your top-secret King Family file." When she smiled, she had a dimple on her left cheek that somehow made her look softer, less standoffish.

Easy, Wyatt. Dimple or not, Tessa King was still an assignment.

He wiped his mouth with the back of his hand. "I definitely would've remembered those kinds of details. So your great-great-grandfather was a train robber and your great-great-grandmother was a madam. Was King even their last name?"

"Who knows? People reinvent themselves all the time. Luckily, this all happened way before the worldwide web made public records so accessible."

Grayson didn't want to think of the other things— or pictures—that could easily be found on the internet. "So I'm guessing your great-great-grandmother eventually decided to go straight and bought the ranch?"

"Nope. Although, when Prohibition started, she was making so much money selling bootleg, she closed down the upstairs rooms. Little Millie, her daughter, took over the daily operation of what was then the most popular speakeasy in Wyoming. See, Little Millie had fallen in love and gotten pregnant by a local boy who'd died in France during World War One. But since she and the local boy hadn't married before he'd gone overseas, his family refused to accept my grandfather as their heir."

"Hmm," Grayson murmured. He knew he should offer a more sympathetic comment, but he'd save that emotion for after he met with the family's PR team and was convinced the rest of the Kings weren't in the habit of denying responsibility for their actions.

"Anyway, Little Millie, wanting her only son to have more than a brothel-turned-saloon as his legacy, won a thirty-acre cattle ranch in a poker game and put it in Hank's name. When Hank's wife gave birth to a pair of boys, they renamed the ranch Twin Kings."

Grayson pointedly looked around at the wide expanse of meadow and mountains around them. "This is a lot bigger than thirty acres."

"Fifty-five thousand, eight hundred and twenty-two at last count," Tessa confirmed. Grayson didn't own so much as a houseplant, so he couldn't relate. "Over the years, Hank bought out the neighboring ranches and when his sons came home from Vietnam, they steadily acquired more acres and built the ranch to what it was today. My dad was the businessman and the networker, while Uncle Rider was the foreman and the cattle expert."

Grayson nodded. "Okay, this part I know. Rider stayed in the original cabin on the other side of the stables and bunkhouses while Roper built a house fit for royalty."

"Technically, it was my mom who insisted on the house built for royalty. She really likes to play up the last name King." Tessa rolled her eyes.

"Is that why your first name is actually Contessa?" Grayson didn't mention that he'd learned that bit of trivia in the briefing file after overhearing her mother call her that in the family kitchen.

"Hardly seems fair that you know so much about me and my family yet I know so little about your background." Tessa slowed her horse when they approached the same stream where they'd stopped yesterday. "Speaking of which, how did your sister's surgery go?"

Grayson swallowed his surprise. Tessa had been so animated talking about her family's history, he hadn't expected her to shift gears so suddenly. And he especially hadn't expected her to remember anything about *his* family. Really, they shouldn't be talking about families at all. Or anything else, for that matter. But as she dismounted, her blue eyes were full of curiosity and remained fixed on his face. He couldn't dismiss her question without seeming like a heartless jerk.

"It sounds like the procedure went as expected. She's on a lot of pain meds and the recovery is going to be pretty rough. They won't know how successful it was until she's able to start her physical therapy."

This was the part where Tessa would nod politely and start doing those yoga stretches again, her question forgotten as soon as she'd asked it. Instead, she tilted her head to the side, her loose ponytail brushing her shoulder. "I read that sometimes the spine will refuse to completely fuse to the rod. Do the doctors have a backup plan in place in case that happens?"

"You read up on my sister's procedure?" It was difficult to hide the surprise in his voice. So he joined her on the ground before leading his own horse to the water.

"Well, I have a tendency to read up on everything. My dad used to call me his research archaeologist because I like to dig for information." Tessa shrugged, causing a strand of blond hair to come loose and frame her face. "I've always been interested in neurological conditions, though. And, last night, it was either listen to my mom and Freckles argue about the trans fat levels in chicken-fried steak, or go to my room and do some research."

"Oh," was all Grayson could manage to respond, keeping Ross's reins firmly in his hand as the horse drank from the creek. He didn't need another runaway horse on his record.

"Sorry, I didn't mean to suggest that your sister needed a backup plan. Obviously, you should stay positive and I'm sure that everything will be fine."

"No, we're being realistic about our expectations. It's just that..." Grayson paused, trying to think of the most delicate way to put this without disclosing his family's limited finances. "Well, we're taking her condition one day at a time. It's difficult to plan ahead since a lot of the procedures that could ease her conjectures are experimental and not covered by insurance."

"Of course," Tessa said, finally looking away. In his experience, people didn't like to be reminded about uncomfortable things like diseases and disparities in wealth. Just when he'd thought he'd found the way to keep her from asking anything else about his family, she asked, "Has your mom been with Maddie since yesterday?"

His sister's name rolled off Tessa's lips so casually, Grayson had to resist the urge to pretend he was receiving an important communication in his radio earpiece. His toes twitched inside his hiking boots as he forced himself to stay put and not literally run away from the question.

"Would you rather not talk about this?" she asked, concern etched across her forehead. It was one of those pitying looks the hospital staff used to give him and his mom. One of those looks that suggested the Wyatt family wasn't strong enough to go through something so difficult.

His shoulders drew back. "No, I was just surprised that you remembered my sister's name."

"You know the names of all of my siblings."

"Yeah, but it's my job to know everything about you." Heat burned behind his ears and he had a feeling they matched her red woolen jacket. "I mean about your family. You guys are my assignment."

"Are we back to that again? I'm just a job to you?"

He exhaled deeply. "I'm trying to remain professional."

"Then treat me like another professional. Hell, treat me like your coworker. Just don't treat me like I'm some snot-nosed kid you're babysitting."

"Fair enough," he conceded. "We're just a couple of professionals with the same goal—to keep you out of the public eye."

"Thank you." She nodded, her chin seeming more stubborn than ever before. "Now, as your coworker, do you have anything going on in your personal life that might be a distraction from you effectively completing your duties?"

"I always complete my duties." His feet moved into a wider stance. "I don't get distracted."

Tessa lifted one perfect brow. "Even when your sister is in the hospital and you're worried about who might be there taking care of her?"

As much as he resented being on the other side of the interview chair, he respected her tenacity. She must be damn good at her job, because Grayson knew she wouldn't relent until she got an answer to her original question. "My mom is with Maddie in the hospital."

Technically, his mom hadn't been allowed to stay in the hospital overnight, so Grayson had booked her a room at a nearby hotel. But he had a feeling the bed hadn't even been slept in. As much as Noreen Wyatt needed the rest, she'd probably paced the floor all night, calling the nurses' desk every two hours for a status report.

Yet Grayson wasn't going to offer any additional information about his family. And to keep her from following up, he put his palm over his earpiece and said, "Excuse me while I radio the command center and give them a status report."

He walked his gelding back to the oak tree where he and Tessa had hid out yesterday from the helicopter. Grayson called in his location to the agent on communications duty, but, as expected, there was nothing new going on at the ranch. Despite her attempts to claim they were coworkers, the truth was that he was stuck out here on babysitting duty, his job talents being wasted on a woman who could clearly take care of herself.

He almost wished another helicopter would show up. Or that some desperate paparazzo would crash through the barricade at the gate. Anything that would provide some sort of action, something that would require him to prove himself as a trained law enforcement officer.

His muscles were coiled together much too tightly and he needed an outlet.

He could only work out at the gym so many times a day. Some of the other agents were going to go into town tonight after their shift, and Grayson decided he might tag along and give his adrenaline a little excitement. Not that he was one who got a kick out of going to small town bars and drinking with the locals, but it would be too dark to go rock climbing and Finn King had already chewed them out about racing their ATVs too close to the cattle pastures.

"You getting a little stir-crazy over here?" Tessa asked, practically reading his mind.

"What do you mean?"

"Your fingers are twitching and you keep rocking on the back of your heels. Plus, you're no longer pretending to be talking into your earpiece."

"I wasn't pretending..." He let the words trail off when she put her hands on her hips, her challenging stance only serving to draw his attention to her narrow waist. He gulped before forcing his eyes upward. "I keep expecting something to happen. But it's just so quiet out here. Not that I mind the quiet. Patience is normally one of my best qualities."

"Normally?" She quickly seized on the word. At this point, nothing about Tessa King's skills at observation should surprise him.

Being patient was one of the things that made him so good at his job, but admitting that would make him sound cocky. And he didn't need Tessa thinking he was both cocky *and* overprotective. Instead, he asked, "Are you planning to ride for much longer? The command center will want to know our ETA so they can brief the next agents coming on duty."

"We can head back now so you can finish your shift." She put her foot into the stirrup and easily swung up into the saddle. "At least *you* can leave the ranch."

She began to trot away and he had to heft himself into his own saddle, wincing at his sore backside before following after her. As his horse picked up speed, he realized they were almost at a gallop and he had to hold on for dear life. He clenched his jaw to keep his teeth from rattling around inside his head as he bounced at full speed down the trail.

He'd wanted an adrenaline rush, but the looming risk of falling off a horse and breaking his neck wasn't quite what he'd had in mind. Plus, Tessa's riding skills had suddenly returned and she was yards ahead of him, her rear end moving rhythmically as she leaned forward over her mare's neck.

So far they'd established that he wasn't a babysitter or a cowboy. So then where did that leave him when it came to doing his job? This damn assignment was more than testing his patience.

By the time he caught up with her, she'd slowed her horse to walk the rest of the way to the stables, and her chest was rising and falling more rhythmically than her butt had been a few seconds ago. One look at her parted lips and Grayson had to adjust the way he was sitting in the saddle.

Maybe it was sexual frustration or maybe it was how he'd seen his life flash before his eyes when the dirt trail had narrowed over by the canyon a few seconds ago. But before he could stop himself, he said, "You could leave the ranch, too, Tessa. You're not a prisoner."

In fact, his job would be way easier if she left. If she returned to DC.

Her hair had come completely loose and she shoved a handful of curls behind her ear. "That's the first time you've used my name."

He cleared his throat and sat straighter in the saddle. "Sorry about that—"

"Don't you dare call me Miss King," she interrupted, her eyes narrowed. "I think we're well beyond that."

Perhaps *she* was past that. But *he* needed to go back to the formality. He needed those boundaries. "I'll talk to SAIC Simon. I'm sure there's somewhere in town that we can secure in advance so that you can get out of here for a little while."

She waved off a young cowboy who'd eagerly run up to assist her out of the saddle. Tessa King didn't need a man to help her and she was making sure everyone knew it, including him. "Good idea. Tell him I'm going to Big Millie's."

Grayson watched as she led her horse away, her long legs taking purposeful strides, before he realized she wasn't joking.

Crap.

Thanks to his big mouth, now he was going to have to make sure she didn't get into trouble at some old brothel.

* * *

Why in the world had she wanted to go Big Millie's? Tessa asked herself for the fifth time that evening. Probably for the same reason her sister Dahlia had refused their mother's repeated pleas to change the name of the establishment. It made them feel more normal, more human, to have some connection to their family's not so illustrious past.

Okay, so maybe a small part of her had also been hoping to shake up the stiff and quiet Agent Wyatt by suggesting the bar outing. In fact, she'd have bet money that the guy would have declined this particular duty assignment for no other reason than to avoid her.

She'd have lost that bet.

Her sister normally didn't have many customers on a Tuesday night, so it wasn't like Dahlia was losing much business by closing early for Tessa and the ten Secret Service agents—five of whom were off duty—who'd accompanied them tonight. In fact, Dahlia was probably making more money since she'd doubled her prices and added a ten percent private party fee to each check.

Two agents were stationed outside the front door and two were stationed by the door in the alley. Finn and Duke had hopped into the black SUV with them at the last minute, and Marcus said he'd stop by with the twins after their basketball practice. Dahlia was behind the polished walnut bar, but the only people drinking anything stronger than beer were four of the off-duty agents.

Tessa wasn't clear on whether or not Grayson was technically working since she hadn't seen him take any time off. Not that she'd been watching him the past couple of days.

Tonight, like any other time, he refused to sit down, passed on a game of darts and didn't so much as tap a toe to the Garth Brooks's song playing on the jukebox. In fact, Grayson spent most of his time pacing back and forth between the front and rear doors to check in with the other agents. It was hard to ignore him when he kept in constant motion.

The man didn't know how to take a break.

Big Millie's part-time cook was off tonight, so Aunt Freckles, who owned the Cowgirl Up Café in Idaho and was also going stir-crazy at the full-staffed ranch, had offered up her skills as a short-order chef. Dahlia's five-year-old daughter, Amelia, came downstairs from their apartment and wanted to hang out with the adults.

"Have you learned how to make a Shirley Temple yet?" Finn asked their niece who handed Tessa a basket of onion rings.

"Mommy said it's a state law that I'm not allowed to touch the grown-up drinks or go behind the bar with her. So I'm helping Aunt Freckles in the kitchen 'cause I'm only allowed to be down here when we're giving away food."

"When we're *selling* food, Peanut," Dahlia corrected. "If we give all our food away, we won't ever make any money."

"Gan Gan says we have lots of money already, Mommy. She says you could buy me a whole zoo if you wanted to."

Tessa, who was sitting on the same side of the refinished wood bar as Finn and Duke, lifted her brows at their mother's latest attempt to sway one of her children into a different profession.

"But I don't want to work at a zoo," Dahlia said simply. "I want to work here. And when you grow up, you'll get to work wherever *you* want. And do you know why?"

"Because we're smart women who make our own choices, Mommy," the little girl replied with an adorable smile before lifting an empty plate over her head and carrying it back to the kitchen.

Tessa was always impressed with how great a mother Dahlia had turned out to be. She often wondered how she'd do as a parent if she had kids of her own. Or if she even wanted kids at all. Her eyes landed on Grayson across the room and suddenly her rib cage felt unnaturally tight.

"You really were the smartest one of all of us, Dahlia," Duke said before taking a long swig from his bottle of imported beer. "Owning your own business means you don't have Mom calling your boss—

or the Joint Chiefs of Staff in my case—to make them give you the week off with bereavement pay."

"Not until Mom gets the liquor laws changed in the state, which she's probably been trying to do. But until then, Amelia's right. Minors are allowed to be in the bar area as long as we serve food. No matter what some new guy who waltzes in off the street thinks."

"What new guy?" Duke asked.

"The cowboy who just inherited the Rocking D," Finn replied.

"How'd I miss this latest development?" Tessa wondered aloud.

"He's not a real cowboy," Dahlia said a bit too quickly. "And you probably missed it because it's been a weird week with other more important things going on. So what's going on with you and your Secret Service agent over there?"

"He's not *my* agent," Tessa said before biting into a crispy, golden onion ring. "Ouch!" She fanned a hand at her scalded taste buds before swallowing several gulps of frosty beer to ease her burning tongue.

"Careful." Finn scooped the basket of rings away from Tessa and offered one to Dahlia. "The onion rings are almost as hot as your agent."

Dahlia and Finn shared matching smirks. They'd been identical when they were girls, but sometime during high school, they'd gravitated toward separate identities and separate styles. In fact, most people were surprised to find out that the women were sisters, let alone twins.

They may be as different as night and day from each other, but when the twins shared a common goal, nobody else in the family would dare to go up against them. And right now, their goal was to keep Tessa from having any sort of break from the ongoing speculation about her and Grayson Wyatt.

"If I wanted to talk about my love life—" Tessa blew on a french fry before pointed it at Finn "—I'd have invited Mom to come along. Or the countless reporters camped outside the ranch gates."

"At least you *have* a love life." Finn snatched the fry out of Tessa's hand before dipping it into ketchup. "Mom told me I'll never have a boyfriend if I always smell like bull manure."

"I usually don't agree with Mom, but..." Dahlia scrunched up her nose. "If the boot fits."

Finn picked up an onion ring and threw it at Dahlia, hitting the bridge of her nose. Dahlia held up the soda spray hose from behind the bar, her finger hovering over the dispensing button. "Who needs a shower when I can hose you off right here, little sis?"

"Well, I'm going to go make a phone call before I get hit by friendly fire." Duke shoved his bar stool back before standing. "Carry on."

"Do *not* carry on, you two." Tessa cast a covert glance around the room to see who was watching their immature display. She shouldn't have been surprised to discover Grayson's eyes on her. After all, she'd felt the weight of his stare all evening—even when he was pretending to be preoccupied with securing the perimeter. Of course, it was hard to escape his attention when Tessa was sitting in front of the twelve-foot-long antique gilt-edged mirror that ran the length of the wall behind the bar.

"He's a serious one, huh?" Dahlia jerked her chin in Grayson's direction. "Does he ever take a break?"

"Not that I've seen so far." Tessa studied the labels on the long line of beers on tap. "Hey, Dia, for an old brothel-turned-speakeasy, you sure have done wonders with the place. Is that shiplap on the walls original to the building?"

"Yes! It was buried under layers of cheap wallpaper and cigar smoke, but I think it adds a sort of rustic charm."

"She got you." Finn shook her head at her twin. "Are we pretending to be on a home remodeling show now? Or can we go back to talking about Tessa's sexy bodyguard?"

"I'd prefer to talk about anything *but* that." Tessa hooked one of the heels from her borrowed boots in the rung of the bar stool.

"You have a lot of rules, big sister," Finn told her. "How are we supposed to have a conversation if we aren't allowed to talk about anything interesting?"

Tessa looked around for Duke, who normally called his husband on speakerphone so everyone could say hi. Where was the peacemaker when she needed him?

Just then, Violet Cortez-Hill walked in the front door. Violet had been in Teton Ridge for Roper King's funeral and, when MJ got arrested, Sherilee had hired her as his attorney.

Oh, and Violet used to be Marcus's girlfriend in high school. So Tessa definitely owed the woman for taking some of her family's attention off of her.

"Hey, Vi!" Dahlia came out from behind the bar to hug the newcomer. "I heard you were staying in town to help my baby brother out of his latest scrape with the law."

"Much to the annoyance of your *big* brother," Violet responded. "He isn't here, is he?"

"Not yet." Tessa smiled at the woman she'd once expected to be her sister-in-law.

Violet let out a deep breath as she plopped herself onto a gold-leather-covered bar stool. "In that case, I'll take a glass of any wine you already have open."

Dahlia drew a bottle from under the bar just as Freckles breezed out of the kitchen carrying two double burgers loaded with every possible topping listed on the limited bar menu.

"Hey, Aunt Freckles," Violet said. "If I had known you were here cooking, I would've left the courthouse earlier. Did Mrs. King kick you out of her kitchen?"

Violet hadn't dated Marcus in over fourteen years,

however, she apparently hadn't forgotten about the King family dynamics.

"No, darlin'." Freckles wore a crisp white apron over her tight zebra-printed blouse and even tighter jeans. "I needed a break from Rider. That old coot has been getting a bit frisky lately. Trying to prove there's still a little gas left in his tank, if you know what I mean."

Tessa and her two sisters all covered their ears, despite the fact that they should've been well accustomed to the older woman's candid comments.

"Aunt Freckles," Dahlia scolded as she lowered her cupped palms. "We can't unhear those sorts of things."

"You know what's crazy?" Finn asked, as though the last few days had been completely sane and normal. "Big Millie's used to be a place where men would come looking for female companionship. Yet now it's full of us trying to hide out from the men in our lives."

"Who says I'm hiding out from anyone?" Dahlia asked a bit too quickly, using a dishrag to scrub at an invisible spot on the bar. The way she refused to make eye contact with any of them made Tessa realize that something was going on with her sister.

And where had Duke gone? Was he hiding out from the man in his life, too? It was weird that Sherilee had pressured the Joint Chiefs of Staff to give Duke leave, but not Tom, who was also in the Navy.

Especially because Sherilee absolutely adored her son-in-law and got along with him better than several of her biological children. Of course, Tom was also a heart surgeon assigned to the hospital at Walter Reed and always kept an extra blood pressure cuff on hand to assure their mom that she wasn't going into cardiac arrest every time her kids stressed her out.

But before Tessa could subject her other siblings to the interrogation she'd just faced, Marcus's twin boys tore through the front door and ran straight for the billiards table. Their father was right behind them, still wearing his sheriff's uniform. His face was drawn tight, his lips pressed together. He was pissed about something and made a direct line toward Violet. Sensing another argument, Tessa and Finn stood, casually maneuvering themselves in front of their friend.

"Now you've got my sisters protecting you, too?" Marcus asked his ex-girlfriend.

"I only need protection from *credible* threats." Violet rose and stepped forward between Tessa and Finn. "And you, Sheriff King, are no threat."

Grayson appeared out of nowhere and asked, "Is everyone okay over here?"

"You know what this party needs?" Aunt Freckles clapped her hands together like a schoolteacher trying to get the attention of a rambunctious class. She pointed to the jukebox that was now playing a lively classic by George Straight. "Dancing!"

"No, thank—" Tessa's protest was cut off by a bony elbow to her ribs.

"Remember when I taught you kids how to do the two-step?" Freckles might be in her eighties, but the strong nudge at Tessa's back proved the woman was still a force of nature. "Tessa, you go ahead and show Agent Wyatt how to do it."

Grayson held up his hands in protest, which was a big mistake since a second shove from Freckles forced Tessa right into his arms. In an effort to steady herself, Tessa's palms landed on either side of his broad chest. She raised pleading eyes to his, but his irises had grown darker, his pectoral muscles flexing under her fingers.

"Finn, you go with Agent Doherty," Freckles continued, though Tessa was afraid to move her head even an inch to see if her sister complied. She didn't want to risk drawing even closer to Grayson. "And, Marcus, you and Violet can talk about whatever you need to talk about on the dance floor."

Tessa wanted to point out that there wasn't really a dance floor in Big Millie's, but her breath was caught in her throat. Agent Lopez and one of the other agents must've taken pity on the paired dancers because soon everyone who was off duty began moving in a circle across the wood-plank floors.

When she and Grayson remained in place, Freckles stepped up behind Tessa, creating a two-stepping sandwich that forced Tessa even closer to Grayson.

"Here, I'll show you again, darlin'. And step, step, slide. Step, step, slide."

It was either start dancing or be trampled by a determined eighty-something-year-old woman in high-heeled snakeskin cowboy boots.

"Sorry," Tessa muttered to Grayson, who looked more amused than annoyed by her aunt's high-handed antics. "Just get me to the other side of the bar and my aunt will find someone else to bug."

Surely, she and Grayson could stay close enough like this for a few seconds. Then Tessa would be able to get her breathing and her body temperature back under control.

Chapter Eight

Grayson was supposed to be off the clock. Instead of enjoying a long, mind-numbing run or a protein shake after an invigorating weight lifting session in the Kings' custom gym, he was steering Tessa around several tables in some old saloon in Middle of Nowhere, Wyoming.

At least Freckles had moved on to another couple in need of her dance instruction, or her peace-keeping skills in the case of Marcus and Mitchell Junior's attorney.

Grayson kept one hand on the curve of Tessa's waist and the other clasped around the soft skin of her delicate palm. However, making his legs move in sync with hers while still maintaining his space was a lot easier said than done.

"Maybe I should lead?" Tessa suggested after he nearly crashed them into an old-fashioned wooden barrel holding the billiard cues.

"I can do it," he said.

"You need to spin me or swing me or something. Make it look realistic. Otherwise, Aunt Freckles is going to insist we keep dancing until we get it right."

A groan reverberated in the back of his throat, sending a vibration through him. He could feel the heat from her body against his and didn't think he could last another song being this close to her. "Your family always seems to get what it wants."

"You know that expression 'failure isn't an option'?" she asked. He replied by spinning her to the right just in time to avoid a collision with Finn and Doherty, who were showing off some sort of pretzel maneuver in the middle of their path. "I think my family invented that expression."

"So nobody is allowed to fail? Or make mistakes?" he asked, thinking the code name Precision really suited her. Yesterday on the trail, she'd freely admitted that she hated being wrong. She'd also been overly concerned with what seemed to him like a mild stutter, and there was no telling how she'd react if that video footage of her lighting into Grayson in the staging tent was leaked. Even though he still stood by his decision and knew an inquiry board would likely vindicate him, he had no doubt that she wouldn't try to save her own reputation by portraying him to be the bad guy.

"It's not that," she replied. "Mistakes are okay as long as they make you better at winning."

Grayson slowed his steps, his eyes searching hers. "Have you ever *not* won, Tessa?"

She tried to look away, but their faces were too close. Finally, she sighed and he felt her warm breath along his neck. "I've lost something before."

"*Some*thing? Just one?" he asked. Tessa didn't respond for a few seconds. The song had changed to a slower one at some point, but their bodies were still swaying in time together. Not wanting to think about what was going on below their shoulders, he added, "Why do I feel like there's a story there?"

"Why do *I* feel like you could find out anything you wanted about me and probably already have?"

"I only know what I need to know as it pertains to the operation."

She made a scoffing sound, causing her chest to press against his. Heat spread through his rib cage. "That's right. I'm the operation. Not a person. Just a job for you."

"Were you hoping for something more?" He should've stepped back, put more distance between them. But he didn't want her to know how her nearness was affecting him. Hell, he didn't want to admit it to himself.

"Of course not." Crimson color flooded her cheeks and she was the one who took a step back. "It's just weird hearing someone else describe me that way. I mean, at the risk of sounding conceited, I'm used to people knowing about my life. Or at least thinking they know. It's one of the trade-offs of being the daughter of a famous man."

"And for being famous in your own right," he pointed out. "Or did you forget you're on TV every night? You're a reporter. Everyone knows who you are."

"I'm not a reporter. I'm a political analyst."

He raised an eyebrow. "Really? There's a difference?"

"Yes. But it seems like you already have your mind made up about that, too."

"It's not my job to make up my mind about anything. Like I said, my only objective is the operation. Digging for information about your personal life would've crossed one of those boundaries."

Unfortunately, the music cut off right before he said the last sentence. Even more unfortunately, Finn King and Doherty had danced their way right up next to them and overheard his words.

Finn looked down at his hand resting above the curve of her sister's hip. "You and Tessa both could stand to cross a few boundaries, if you ask me."

Doherty let out a bark of laughter and told his dance partner, "You have no idea."

Grayson quickly dropped his arms to his sides as though he'd just been touching a ticking time bomb. And in a way he had. He shouldn't have been socializing with the Kings, let alone dancing with one of them. Holding her body against his…

He cleared his throat. "I'm only following orders."

"Aunt Freckles's orders?" Finn quirked her eyebrow. "I didn't realize you worked for her."

Ouch. Grayson felt the reprimand like a punch to the gut. She was right, though. He didn't work for any of them.

"Leave him alone, Finn." Tessa frowned at her giggling sister, who easily spun away in Doherty's arms. She turned back to face him. "Ignore her, Grayson. You're off duty."

He shook his head. "I'm never off duty."

The words hung between them before he pivoted on his heel and walked toward the exit. He'd go and relieve one of the agents covering the door. The brisk night air would help to cool him down. Besides, getting back on the watch was the best way to ensure his guard didn't slip again.

Tessa tried not to think of the way her body had so easily slid against Grayson's last night when they'd been dancing at Big Millie's. She rarely drank socially—at least not since that party in college when she'd had a few too many and her speech had gotten a little too slurry—so she hadn't expected the craft beer to go to her head so quickly. That was the only reason why she'd allowed herself to dance so close to the sexy agent. The only reason why she'd let his words about her just being part of his operation provoke her into making him prove otherwise.

At least, that's what she told herself while she brushed her teeth the following morning.

Okay, so maybe she had been flirting with him a bit last night. Thankfully, he'd called her out on it, asking her if she'd been hoping for something more between them. Then Finn had come along and made that joke about them crossing boundaries and Grayson had switched right back into serious agent mode—which was what Tessa needed him to do.

One of them had to retain some sense of control.

Tessa waited until she knew both her mother and Aunt Freckles would be out of the kitchen before hunting down a cup of hot coffee so that she could feel slightly more human. A black SUV pulled up in the driveway, but before she could see who exited, Tessa scooped several newspapers off the kitchen table, and a freshly made cinnamon roll, and headed to her father's office. Thank goodness Roper King had always insisted on reading his news in print. She was less likely to run across a sensationalized picture of her in the black-and-white *Wall Street Journal* than she would online. And even though she was in a sense hiding out, Tessa still needed to stay sharp for her job.

The current events of today would likely be old news by tomorrow, and she wouldn't know what exactly she was looking for until she found it. But researching something—anything—gave her a sense of purpose and she always dove deep into anything she did.

After a few hours, though, the tiny letters on the pages started running together and her notes on the yellow pad beside her became impossible to decipher. Needing a break, Tessa took a couple of Tylenol to cut down on the pounding in her temples. She wasn't hungover from the night before, exactly, but she didn't think getting back on a horse today would do her head any favors.

Plus, she didn't want to risk having Grayson follow her again. Or worse, having him turn over the protective detail to another agent. That would mean that he was pissed off with her. It was a lose-lose situation, and the thought of losing always sent Tessa's nerves into overdrive.

Tessa grabbed a pair of sneakers and her wireless earbuds and set off on a run instead. She was only half a mile from the house when she realized that Grayson trailed behind her. Something fluttered inside her heart—or maybe she was just winded from her initial sprint up this hill. Either way, she turned up her music and pretended he wasn't there.

And for his part, he stayed a safe distance behind her.

Good, she told herself, picking up speed until she hit her stride. With each step she took, her thoughts cleared, her control returned. By the time she jogged back to the main house and showered, it was time for dinner with her family. Instead of engaging in the various arguments breaking out around the table, Tessa sipped her way through half a bottle of Cabernet, less worried about her speech slipping since she wasn't in public. In fact, she hadn't had to speak at all with all the voices spouting off around her. Wondering why Duke wasn't at dinner made her drink more.

Unfortunately, the wine and the constant bickering brought back her headache the following morning, and she repeated the same cycle as the day before.

Except, having exhausted her research on current events yesterday, she finally gave in and booted up her laptop. She began scrolling through her bookmarked online articles about traumatic brain injury until her head was swimming.

That afternoon, she set off on another run. Again, Grayson remained several yards behind. It didn't take long for a pattern to develop. For the rest of the week, any time she set off on a run or on a horseback ride—or even a quick trip on one of the ATVs to look at the southern fence line with Uncle Rider—the agent always stayed a respectable distance back.

A comfortable silence had settled between them, as though they were simply a pair of coworkers going about their jobs. It was a good reminder that Tessa was on duty, as well. She needed to work on her speech patterns and vocal exercises and stay abreast of everything else going on in the world. Luckily, fewer and fewer news headlines included her.

Until the day that she was returning to the stables on Phoebe and saw a black helicopter on the small helipad behind the bunkhouses. Grayson—who'd somehow managed to get Chandler to trust him again—raced ahead of her on his noble steed, as though he was going to throw his body in front of hers if so much as a single camera lens came into view.

This particular helicopter, though, wasn't some sightseeing charter for rent. It was an Airbus Super Puma, the cost way above the budget of most paparazzi and local news networks. It was also grounded, rather than being chased away by the fighter jets on standby. That meant whoever had landed it clearly wasn't a threat.

Still, Grayson held Tessa and Phoebe at a standstill by angling his horse right in front of the mare. Cupping a hand over his ear, he spoke to someone on the other end of his radio.

His eyes were hidden behind those damn sunglasses again, but she knew they were inspecting the area around them, taking in every potential threat. When he finally pivoted in his saddle to face her, his mouth was set in a grim line.

"It appears you have a visitor, Miss King."

Tessa's stomach sank. While Grayson hadn't said more than a handful of words to her since the night they'd danced at Big Millie's, none of them had been *Miss* or *King*. Or anything else quite as formal. Clearly, he was back to taking his role as protector way too seriously.

She was about to ask who the visitor was, but the front door of the main house opened and she didn't have to.

Davis Townsend. He'd called a few times since the pictures of her and Agent Steamy—*Agent Wyatt*, she mentally corrected herself—had come out. She'd called back once and ended up speaking to his personal assistant, who'd answered his phone. Then they'd only managed a few texts here and there. Tessa still hadn't formally rejected—or accepted—his proposal of marriage, so she shouldn't have been surprised that he would've flown out here expecting an answer.

"There you are, sweetheart!" he said as he approached Tessa and her horse. The woman she recognized as his press secretary was holding a smartphone at an odd angle, clearly prepared to capture a picture of what Davis probably planned as a loving reunion.

Tessa had been a part of politics for so long, she knew all the tricks. That was why she remained in the saddle, letting her horse walk in slow circles to cool down after the ride. "Davis? What are you doing here?"

"I had a break between town hall appearances and thought I'd surprise you." He planned to run for re-election for his district next November, but she knew he had his sights already set on the senatorial election coming up in two years.

"What's up with Debra?" Tessa jerked her chin toward his press secretary. "Didn't she get the memo about the ranch rules restricting camera access?"

"Oh that?" Davis looked back and gave a hand signal to the woman who quickly slipped her phone into her purse. "She must not have realized that applied to personal devices. After everything that's going on in the press, though, I understand you being hesitant about being photographed. Speaking of the press, I figured it's been long enough that I should come out here and put those rumors about you and that—" he hesitated "—bodyguard of yours to rest once and for all."

She snuck a peak at Grayson, whose stoic face didn't reveal that he'd just heard every word, even though he'd moved a few yards away and was maintaining a professional distance. At some point during the week, the agent had gotten a more suitable shirt—denim with snap buttons—and real boots. He could almost pass for an actual cowboy to the untrained eye.

Davis's eye, of course, was very untrained. Or,

as he often pointed out, he met so many people on the campaign trail, it was difficult for him to always put a name with a face. Sure, he could easily recognize the big donors, the top news executives and the political powerhouses. Yet, he could never remember the names of restaurant servers or event staff or even a few of his interns. A trait her father would've openly commented on if he'd witnessed it—and not favorably. She had no doubt that Davis was currently assuming that Grayson was just another cowboy working her family's ranch, which meant he wasn't worthy of a second glance.

Tessa swallowed her embarrassment on Grayson's behalf. "Davis, I'm sure you remember Agent Wyatt. Agent Wyatt, you already know Congressman Townsend."

"Of course." Grayson, who was still cooling down his own horse and probably had some sort of set of rules about shaking hands with anyone while he was on duty, barely nodded. "Although we weren't formally introduced last time."

"Last time?" Davis tilted his head, the confusion obvious along his very tanned brow. Was that bronzer?

"Feel free to refer to me as *that bodyguard*." Grayson's face remained perfectly devoid of expression as he repeated the congressman's earlier description. "Or Agent Steamy. I'll answer to both."

"Aha!" Davis smiled his most charming smile,

as though he wasn't the least bit embarrassed to be called out on his mistake. "Forgive me, Agent Wyatt. I didn't recognize you out of uniform."

"Should I take the mare back to the stables for you, Miss King?" Grayson asked. He knew full well that she always insisted on being the one to give Phoebe her rubdown and oats after a ride.

"No, thanks," Tessa said, then turned to Davis. "I need to take care of my horse. You can wait for me at the main house if you want."

Davis's eyes darted between her and Grayson. He kept his smile in place, but Tessa sensed the jealousy vibrating in the air. After all, he'd already admitted that the only reason he was there was to put to rest the rumors about her with another man. Besides, having busy careers on opposite ends of the country meant that they were used to going months at a time without seeing each other. His being here after barely a week could mean only one thing. He was a desperate man making a desperate last-ditch attempt to maintain the appearance that all was well between them.

But it wasn't. And she couldn't—wouldn't—pretend.

"I'll help," Davis said and walked alongside her.

It was just as well, Tessa decided. She needed to put the man out of his misery once and for all.

She slid off her mare and loosened the cinch before leading her toward the stables, which housed almost one hundred horses at any given time. During herding season, which lasted from sunup to sundown, each cattle hand used at least two different horses a day so the animals weren't overworked.

Once inside, they passed the stock horses, the show horses and the trail horses. The rows of stalls were aptly named with little wooden signs Dahlia had once carved during summer camp. In addition to the Infirmary and Central Perk, there was also Shady Acres, a retirement community of sorts for horses of an advanced age, and Alcatraz, where they kept the animals that hadn't been amenable to riders or any sort of training—yet. Uncle Rider refused to ever give up on a horse.

"Is your bodyguard going to be within earshot of us the whole time?" Davis asked, jerking his head over to the grooming station at the other end of the row.

"He's a Secret Service agent, not a bodyguard. And his horse needs to be rubbed down, as well. If you don't want him here, you can offer to clean out Chandler Bing's hooves yourself."

Davis looked down at his well-manicured hands. "I just wanted a few minutes to ourselves so that we can talk about our announcement."

Tessa's stomach dropped. She really should've had this conversation with him earlier. But her father's funeral hadn't seemed like the appropriate time for the discussion and she hadn't wanted to do it over the phone or by text.

"What announcement?" Tessa asked, knowing full well exactly what he wanted to announce.

"Our engagement. I was going to fly my personal jeweler out here to the ranch, but your mother said there were some issues with your younger brother right now and the Secret Service had you guys on lockdown."

"That's right. I don't believe I saw your name on the original list of approved visitors." Probably because Tessa herself had been the one to strike his name from the list. Apparently, that had been the right call considering Davis had been going behind her back to plot with Sherilee.

"I'm a United States congressman, Tessa. The Secret Service works for m—the government," he corrected himself at the last second before looking over his shoulder to see if Grayson was within hearing range.

Interesting that he claimed his status as a congressman rather than his status as her boyfriend to explain why he should be there. But then again, she wasn't at all surprised.

"About that engagement, Davis." Tessa loosely tied the horse's reins to the edge of the watering trough before hefting the saddle off her. "You know, I never actually accepted your proposal."

There seemed to be very little in Tessa's life that she had control over at that exact moment, but she'd be damned if she was going to give up control over who she planned to marry. In fact, she was rather annoyed by Davis's arrogance in showing up unannounced and assuming otherwise.

"You never declined, either," he pointed out.

"I never really had time to respond at all," she said, although she'd been sitting out here on the ranch with absolutely nothing but time. Tessa ran her hands down Phoebe's legs, checking for possible injuries and swelling.

"So you want to wait longer before we get engaged," Davis stated rather than asked. She'd first met him when he'd been newly elected. When he'd been filled with bright ideas and shining promises, still fresh off the fight of a hard-won election. In the past two years, though, he'd eased into his position, and it was comfortable having a boyfriend who was just as busy as she was. A guy who didn't mind showing up on her arm for public appearances when their schedules allowed it, yet never insisted on going on actual dates or doing all those couple-type things that neither one of them had time for.

Somewhere along the way, though, Tessa had failed to notice the transition in his personality, the rise in his ego. Or perhaps she just hadn't cared because she too had been so absorbed in her own career. They were more like companions, or even colleagues, rather than significant others. When they were together, they talked about current events and their jobs and everything else but themselves. In fact, most of the things Davis knew about her could be found on her Wikipedia page. Grayson, after only a few days, already knew way more about Tessa than that. The sudden realization made it easier to finally say what had needed to be said for several months.

"No, I don't need to wait any longer." She pushed her shoulders back and faced him. "I'm not going to marry you, Davis."

"Is it because of him?" He jerked his head toward the other end of the aisle, where Grayson was hosing down his horse.

"No, I should have told you when you first asked. I let things go on too long and...well, like I said, there never seemed to be any good time."

"But what about the media reports? All the speculation and gossip is going to haunt my upcoming reelection bid."

An unexpected chuckle burst out of her throat. "The fact that you're more concerned with your reelection bid than with a broken heart is evidence that you never really loved me in the first place."

"People like us are too busy for love, Tessa. Sure, a big romance might make for a nice story, but there're more important things than that. Like our careers. Besides, being together makes sense. We get along and we run in the same circles. Really, it's a win-win for both of us. You're the brainy one with the family connections and I'm the charming one with the people skills," he said, not realizing how utterly uncharming he sounded at that exact moment. "Together, we could've gone farther than Roper King could have ever hoped."

Her stomach turned over. She knew their relationship had mostly been based on appearances, but she'd thought there'd been at least a mutual respect there, as well. It shouldn't have surprised her that she was just a step on his career ladder. A big step, but a step nonetheless.

"My dad got exactly as far as he wanted, Davis. And, for the record, he hated people who needed to use someone else to get ahead."

"I was never using you." His eyes narrowed into angry slants. "At least, not any more than you were using me."

"How did I use you?" she asked, crossing her arms at her chest. "I'd love to hear this."

"Tessa King had the reputation of being a cold, cutthroat bitch before I came along. I humanized you. Being in a relationship with me made you at least seem like a real woman."

The urge to deliver a cutting remark threatened to choke her, but she refused to give him the satisfaction of reacting to his stinging insult. Instead she replied in her most dismissive tone. "I think you need to leave now, Congressman Townsend."

"But your mother invited me—"

"Miss King has politely asked you to leave." Grayson had made it to their side of the stables in less than two seconds. "I'll have the command center radio your pilot so you can fly out of here on your own accord."

"Or else what?" Davis's chin lifted.

"Or else we can escort you from the premises in the backseat of the Ridgecrest County Sheriff's patrol unit." Marcus's commanding voice came from out of nowhere.

No, not nowhere. Her brother walked out from an empty stall followed by Violet, her dark hair flecked with several strands of dried hay. Tessa would've asked them what they'd been doing if her brother's eyes weren't so filled with fury.

"Before you make your choice," Marcus continued, "it's only fair to warn you that my squad car doesn't have tinted windows. I'm sure the press stationed outside the gates would love to get a great shot of you back there."

Davis took a step in retreat and flashed that ridiculous fake grin again. "We're good. I was just leaving."

The congressman walked away, with Marcus and Violet following a few feet behind. Marcus probably because he wanted to make sure Davis actually left, and Violet probably because she didn't want anyone asking her what she was doing inside one of the stalls with her ex-boyfriend.

When they were out of sight, Tessa felt the air rush out of her lungs. She smoothed a hand over the mare's damp coat, trying not to notice the slight tremble in her fingers.

"Are you okay?" Grayson's voice was low, his body suddenly close.

"I'm fine." Tessa sniffed and pushed her hair back from her flushed face, sounding anything but composed. "Davis was upset, but it wasn't like I needed you guys to jump in and save me. I wasn't in any danger."

"Then why are you shaking?" Of course Grayson would notice. He was always too damn observant. She dropped her hand and turned to him.

"Because I'm mad at myself for not ending things sooner. I never should've al...al...allowed—" She forced the word out, but the effort made her close her eyes. She put her tongue on the roof of her mouth and counted to five, but the sound of the helicopter's engine, followed by the slow churn of the propeller, saved her from having to finish her sentence.

She turned back to brushing Phoebe, concentrating on the smooth strokes until the mare stomped her foot as though to say, *Enough. Take me back to my stall so I can get away from you crazy humans and eat.*

After caring for her horse, Tessa turned to the mundane tasks of cleaning the bit and bridle, reorganizing a row of leather reins in the tack room and even polishing the saddle.

"I'm pretty sure he's gone now," Grayson said

from the door of the tack room. "You don't have to keep hiding out in the stable."

"I'm not hiding from Davis Townsend." Tessa rolled her shoulders in circles to loosen the tension she couldn't seem to shake. When Grayson kept staring at her, she finally sighed. "Everyone but my mom has been predicting our breakup for a year now. I didn't want to give any of them the satisfaction back then. So now I'm hiding out from my family and all their I-told-you-sos. Plus, I'm so damn mad at my mother for inviting him out here in the first place, I need to cool down before I say anything I might regret."

"How long will that take?" he asked, looking at his watch.

"Probably a few weeks." She yanked the elastic band from her hair and massaged her scalp. "Look, you don't have to stay here and babysit me. If you're off duty, you can go do…whatever you do in your free time."

"I'm never—"

"Yeah, I get it." She rolled her eyes as she cut him off. "You're never off duty."

He smirked, the rare quasi smile suddenly making him seem less like a robot. Tessa had a sudden urge to see the man relax for a change and let down his guard.

"I'm going to make your job easy then, Agent Wyatt. Mr. Truong, our stable manager, keeps a cold six-pack of beer in the back of the tiny fridge in his office. I'm going to go borrow a couple of bottles, along with the keys to one of the ATVs. Then I'm taking a joyride up to Pine Top Point. You can either go back to the bunkhouse and recruit another agent to trail me, or you can go back to the bunkhouse to see if you can find us a bag of chips and maybe some of those homemade sandwiches Aunt Freckles keeps sending out to you guys by the trayful. Either way, I'm leaving here in five minutes with or without you."

Chapter Nine

Technically, he'd gotten off duty halfway through the horse ride. But Grayson hadn't been about to leave Tessa alone with that blowhard fiancé of hers. In fact, after Davis Townsend had left, Grayson found reasons to hang around the stables, telling himself that he was remaining on standby, just in case Tessa needed him for something. Even if it was only to vent.

But she hadn't broken down crying or gone on a rampage or done any of the other things he would've expected a woman to do if the man she loved had just called her a cold, cutthroat bitch. Personally, Grayson had wanted to shove his fist in the guy's face, but had to settle for diplomatically telling the jerk to get lost.

In fact, Tessa hadn't seemed all that bothered by the breakup. Judging by that accidental stutter, she'd been more embarrassed than anything else.

Clearly, she hadn't needed Grayson to swoop in and rescue her. Nor had she needed the comfort of her family, who most definitely would've given her a hard time about not dumping "Congressman Smooth" sooner. Tessa had simply wanted to get away from all the drama.

So then why was he currently clinging to the roll bar of the two-seater ATV as she raced along the dirt trail that wound up to Pine Top Point?

Maybe because he just simply needed to get away from his job, too.

As she hastily shifted gears tearing along the rutted path, he felt himself slowly shift from the role of agent to the role of...friend? No, not friend, he corrected himself when Tessa hit a large rock in the road and sent them skidding sideways before regaining control of the steering wheel. Advisor.

"Are you sure you don't want me to drive?" he yelled above the revving engine as she took another steep incline at Mach 4.

"No. Just hold on to the beer and make sure none of the bottles fly out."

It was hard to hold on to the beer when he also had to brace himself from slamming his head against the roll bar. These jacked-up golf carts weren't made for men his size.

When they finally reached the top of the trail, Tessa shut off the engine but left the keys in the ignition. Grayson waited until she'd climbed out of the driver's seat before slipping the keys into his pocket. The sun would be setting in less than an hour and there was no way he was letting her drive down the hill in the dark.

"Thanks for bringing the food," she said as she grabbed the bag of sandwiches from the metal lockbox strapped to the back of the vehicle.

"I didn't have time to wrap them up, so if it looks like someone lost a cafeteria food fight in there, you can blame that on your refusal to stay on the road."

"We're on a ranch, Grayson. Roads and trails are only suggestions out here." She weaved her way through a wall of overgrown fir trees. "Come on, we have to hike the rest of the way."

He caught up to her quickly and, after winding through fifty yards or so of trees, the peak of the mountain gave way to a flat grassy spot and the most amazing view he'd ever seen.

"Whoa," he said, suitably impressed. "You can see the whole ranch from up here."

Or at least the western half of it. The sun was sinking behind the Teton mountain range in the distance and the sky couldn't seem to decide if it wanted to be purple, pink or orange.

She set down the bag of food and then surprised him by plopping herself cross-legged onto the cold ground without so much as a blanket between the long grass and her designer jeans.

Don't think about her jeans, he reminded himself.

Tessa reached up a hand and his first thought was that she was going to grab onto him and pull him down beside her. It wasn't until she asked, "Do you mind sharing one of those?" that he realized she was reaching for a beer.

"Sorry," he said, shoving the cardboard case at her.

She set the six-pack on the grass and twisted off the top of one before passing the open bottle to him. "Are you ever allowed to sit down on the job?"

He hadn't officially been on the job for the past three hours. He'd even left his earpiece and his duty weapon back in the bunkhouse. Otherwise, he never would have accepted the beer. But there was a hand-held radio in the ATV, along with an emergency kit and a holstered rifle mounted inside the lockbox— just in case they ran into an unfriendly bobcat or grizzly bear. So as long as he had only one drink, he was still well within regulations.

Just to be safe, though, he sat a few feet away from Tessa, careful to keep the bag of food and the remaining six-pack between them. They were lucky they'd caught a break with this unusual warm weather—or at least warm for Wyoming in January. All the snow had melted and they weren't expecting more for another week or so.

He racked his brain for something to talk to her about that didn't include the off-limit subjects. Normally, Grayson could sit in the quiet for hours, but that was when he was working. Right now—he took a sip of the craft beer that wasn't quite as cold as when they'd set out—he was off the clock.

Grayson preferred to operate in terms of black and white, however, being around Tessa King was like being surrounded by every color in between.

His mind struggled with the distinction, with those boundary lines of being on the job and off the job. On duty meant suits, eating on the go and conversations with Doherty on his radio earpiece. Off duty meant sunsets, beer and making conversation with pretty women. He took another long gulp, then leaned back on his hands, taking in the incredible view.

"So." Tessa finally broke the silence. "In the past week, you've pretty much seen me at all my worst moments."

"I thought you didn't want to talk about the breakup. Or your family," he added.

"You're right," she said, then lifted the bottle to her lips. His own mouth went dry and he forced himself to look away. "So let's talk about you."

"Or we could talk about your job," he suggested,

thinking he would lead her into a neutral subject that would interest her.

"We could," she answered. "But I'm more interested in finding out about your family. What's Maddie like?"

The unexpected question took Grayson aback. He was so accustomed to people focusing on Maddie's medical condition, it was almost jarring when they wanted to know about her as a person.

"Well... She's smart. Like, wicked smart. She loves art, making it and studying it. In fact, she's working on getting her online degree in art history. She loves candy and Jane Austen books and all of the Rocky movies. She once wrote an English paper about how *Rocky* was the ultimate love story and the boxing was only secondary to the plot."

Tessa laughed. "I'd have to agree with her there."

Grayson shook his head but continued since he was on a roll. "Maddie's witty and sarcastic and nosy as hell. But she's also kind and caring and loves giving advice. Even when it's unsolicited."

"Like what? Give me an example of her unsolicited advice."

He immediately thought of his sister's comment that he needed someone and hadn't really dated since his divorce. But he didn't feel like sharing that with Tessa. So instead he said, "She thinks I work too hard."

Tessa's grin widened. "I'd have to agree with her on that, as well."

"Says the woman who rarely takes a day off. Even when you're supposed to be relaxing on the ranch, I know you're still spending a lot of time in your father's study behind that computer screen."

"I've got to stay sharp on current events. The rest of the world is still going on out there without me. When I return to work, I've got to be ready to jump right back in and hit the ground running."

Grayson respected her for her dedication, but felt a weird sensation zip through him at the reminder that she'd be going back to work soon. He took a drink to wash the feeling away, then asked, "How'd you decide you wanted to be a political analyst?"

"Well, it wasn't my original career choice." She took another drink.

"Yeah, I think I read somewhere that you were training for the Olympics at one point."

"You can't believe everything you read." She gave a half-hearted smirk; her reference to the reason why they were still in Wyoming wasn't lost on him. "But I don't want to talk about that, either."

"Then let's eat," he suggested, because at this point he was out of conversation topics and he was getting hungry. Plus, he knew better than to drink on an empty stomach.

He rummaged around in the bag and pulled out two different brands of chips. Then he tore the brown paper along one side, turning the bag into a giant place mat. "Your choices are a turkey and Swiss on wheat—or at least partially on wheat since the contents shifted midflight. Or there's a roast beef and cheddar on some sort of roll. I can't tell under all that mustard."

"Gotta go for the mustard," she said, taking the foil-wrapped package smeared with the yellow condiment.

He dug in to the turkey sandwich while she only took a few bites before setting hers down. She licked her fingers and Grayson almost groaned before shoving his remaining food into his mouth and shifting a few more inches away.

Tessa cracked open another bottle, took a small sip and then asked, "Have you ever gone through a public breakup, Grayson?"

A knot formed below his sternum and he wished he hadn't eaten quite so fast. He swallowed the rest of his beer to wash everything down before answering. "I haven't ever done anything publicly. I keep my private life private."

He hadn't meant the words to be an insult, but her lips tightened all the same. "Fair enough. How about a regular breakup? Ever been through one of those?"

He sucked in a breath, twisting the bottle in his hands, unsure of how much or how little he should say.

Apparently, he must've taken too long to answer

because she suddenly gasped. "Oh my gosh! I don't even know if you're married or not."

As much as he wanted to keep things professional between them, Grayson couldn't deny that there was a mutual attraction. If she was thinking about him in all the same ways he was thinking about her, then it wouldn't be fair to let her believe she was lusting after someone else's husband.

"No." He shook his head, keeping his gaze straight ahead. "I haven't been married for a long time."

"But you were. That means your breakup must've been a way bigger deal than the little falling-out you witnessed back at the stables." She paused, as though she was waiting for him to agree. But before he could respond, she caught her breath again, her eyes going wide. Reaching across the remains of their picnic, she clasped his forearm. Even through the canvas material of his borrowed work coat, he felt the heat of her touch. Her voice was full of concern when she said, "Unless your wife passed away. I'm so sorry if—"

"No," he said a bit too abruptly then cleared his throat. "Nothing as tragic as that."

He took another drink of his beer, mostly so that he had a reason for breaking their physical contact. But the crinkled lines above Tessa's nose meant she wasn't quite convinced he didn't have some sort of sob story to tell. And the determined gleam in her eyes meant she wasn't going to stop asking questions until he offered up something.

Grayson shrugged. "My ex-wife was a nurse. One of Maddie's nurses, in fact. Jamie quit her job, though, when I got stationed overseas, so she could come with me. She wanted children right away, but I wasn't ready. I figured we should have plenty of money saved up so that when kids came, we could pay for anything they might need."

"That's understandable, considering..."

"My sister's medical needs," Grayson finished for her. "That was the other half of the equation. Not only were we living off just my paycheck, I also needed to send money home to my mom and Maddie. I was never a big spender, so it rarely crossed my mind that I should be using my money for anything besides the bare necessities.

"After a while, though, Jamie resented the fact that we were going without so that I could keep sending money home. I explained that it didn't seem fair for me to go out for a good time, living it up, when my sister was stuck in a bed or a wheelchair most of the time. Not that it was fair to Jamie, either, I guess. Although, she knew going into the marriage that I'd promised my dad to always look after my sister."

"Your dad passed away?"

"Yes. When I was still in high school."

"I'm sorry." Tessa reached her hand across to his arm again. This time, Grayson held still, trying to ignore the comforting warmth. He'd rather talk about his divorce than the loss of his father, so he returned to the story.

"Anyway, there was a new medication on the market that I thought would help Maddie. But her insurance wouldn't cover the monthly cost, which was about the same amount we were paying for rent.

"Jamie, being in the medical field, thought the medication wouldn't work anyway and would end up being a waste of money. We had a huge fight. She didn't appreciate the fact that I couldn't afford to take her out to dinner because I was using all my overtime pay on trial medications and horseback riding lessons. And I couldn't really blame her. She was putting her life on hold so that I could take care of my sister. Not that I ever asked her to give up her job, but I guess she realized that Maddie would always be my priority over everything else. We parted ways, and..." Grayson shrugged. "Last I heard, she remarried several years ago and has a couple of kids now. So things worked out for the best."

He felt the weight of Tessa's stare as she studied him. A bird chirped from one of the trees in the distance; otherwise the air was thick with their silence. Then he heard a rustling sound and looked down to see that she'd moved the remaining chip bags to the other side of her so she could scoot closer.

"Thank you." Tessa patted his upper arm the way a friend would console another friend. After a few extra pats, she moved her hand up to his shoulder and gave him a reassuring squeeze. Grayson tried not to think about the electrical current that followed the same path. Or the way there was suddenly fewer beers and fewer feet between them.

"For reminding you that things will work out for the best?" he asked, trying to stay perfectly still despite her body leaning closer to him. Her palm absently made slow circles between his shoulder and his biceps.

"No, for sharing a part of yourself with me. I know it goes against the rules about mixing your professional life with your personal life. Whenever I'm around you, I always feel like my life is such a mess, while you're so perfect and calm and in control. It's nice to know that you're a human just like the rest of us."

"Tessa." Grayson's voice was low and tight in his throat. "If you keep stroking my arm like that, you're going to find out exactly how human I am."

Tessa recognized the hunger in Grayson's eyes. It matched the desire whirlpooling through her own bloodstream. The muscles in his biceps flexed under her palm and instead of pulling away, she trailed her fingers along the coiled ridges until she got to his sculpted shoulder.

Just a few more seconds, she told herself as her hand memorized the contours of his upper arm under his thin jacket. That's right. They were both wearing jackets. They were fully dressed. It wasn't like she was actually having skin-to-skin contact with...

Oh hell. Somehow, Tessa had maneuvered herself closer because her fingers were now brushing against the warm skin of his neck. Grayson's nostrils flared slightly, but he remained perfectly still as she pivoted toward him, her leg brushing against his. When had she risen to her knees? Had she crawled over to him? Was she that desperate to touch the man?

She couldn't gauge how much distance she'd closed between them because she didn't dare break eye contact. Their faces were only inches apart, his steel-gray gaze practically daring her to move in even closer. Her heart thumped frantically behind her rib cage as she accepted the challenge.

Tessa traced her thumb from his neck to his jaw, stopping just below the curve of his bottom lip. Grayson lifted his hand to her hip, but instead of pushing her away, he held on tighter.

"Tessa," he said so low, so deep, it sounded like more of a growl than a warning.

Her entire body was buzzing with anticipation. Of what, she didn't know. Tessa hadn't felt this alive since her last free-fall dive.

She sucked in a ragged breath, telling herself, *Just a little more.* After all, the whole point of her staying on the ranch in the first place was to ensure that she could handle her physical responses in emotionally charged situations. Was there a bigger test than right this second? A more perfect opportunity to prove to herself and to Grayson that she was in complete control? For just a few more seconds. Long enough for her to get a little bit closer...

Tessa brought her left knee over his lap, boldly straddling him, silently daring him the same way he'd dared her. Both of his hands captured her hips, his fingers digging into the soft flesh under her jeans.

"Grayson?" she asked.

His mouth was so near, she could feel the heat of his breath as he responded. "Yeah?"

"My life is about to get messy again," she warned before molding her lips to his.

She angled her face slightly before taking the kiss deeper, inviting his tongue to explore her mouth. And, oh how he explored everything she offered. He gripped her hips tighter, positioning her directly over his arousal, and then pulled her against him. Pleasure skimmed the surface of the juncture between her thighs and she ached to feel more. He wrapped one arm around her waist, holding her in place while his other hand trailed up her flannel shirt, his thumb easily slipping the buttons free until she felt the cool air whisper against her overheated skin.

She gasped, causing his mouth to break free long enough to blaze a path of hot kisses down her neck and toward her breasts. His thumb edged the lace of her bra lower until one of her tightened nipples sprung free. Grayson's tongue darted out and Tessa's fingers shot through his short brown hair, holding on for dear life as she threw back her head and moaned.

Heat surged through her core and she pressed herself closer to his hardened length.

Grayson groaned before tearing his mouth away from her exposed breast. "Tessa," he said, his breath coming out in short bursts. "We have to stop."

"I know," she agreed before reclaiming his lips under hers. *Just one more kiss*, she told herself as she surrendered to his skilled tongue again.

His hands framed her face and he gave her lower lip a final nip before easing her away from him a second time. Luckily, the sun had already set, making it easier to mask her disappointment. However, Tessa sensed that the growing darkness would soon give way to growing regret. Especially because in her effort to prove that she was in control, she'd totally lost control.

Her attempt to school her expression was wasted, though, since he was busy making quick work of returning her buttons to their proper holes. Grayson Wyatt, taking charge again. Although, this time it was for the best since her fingers were trembling too much to get the job done.

If she couldn't be in charge of her emotions, then she would have to settle for being in charge of the conversation.

"Don't you dare say something about crossing

some sort of professional boundary," she warned before peeling herself off him and rising.

"It also crosses an ethical boundary. You just broke up with your boyfriend. You were vulner—"

"Stop right there." She held up her hand. "Don't even say that word. I'm not weak, Grayson. I don't need to be protected or coddled. And I'm certainly not in mourning for a relationship that was already broken."

Dang. Mourning was the wrong word to use in this situation and he immediately seized upon it. "But you are still grieving your father."

"True. Although, there's something about our physical connection, about the way my body responds to you, that reminds me that I'm still very much alive. And don't deny that your body wasn't responding just as much to me."

He stood, his jaw tense, his jacket on the ground in a crumpled heap behind him. Tessa barely remembered sliding the outer layer off his shoulders. She only remembered her need to touch as much of him as possible.

"My body should be better trained than that, though." He dragged a hand through his hair, which she'd properly mussed only a few moments ago. "I love my job. Normally, I'm pretty damn good at it when there's not a beautiful and witty woman outrunning me on her horse. Getting involved with you while I'm on assignment is a distraction I can't afford."

Tessa shoved her hands into her back pockets, causing her still aching breasts to thrust forward. While she understood his position and even respected it, a tiny thrill shot through her at his admission. "So I'm a distraction?"

He stepped toward her then gently tucked a strand of hair behind her ear, allowing his thumb to linger against her cheek. "The very best kind. But to do my job well, I have to be thinking clearly at all times. You and your family deserve me at my best. No matter how much I want to strip off every single article of clothing you're wearing and see the real woman underneath, the fact remains that I'm on assignment right *now*."

A shiver of delight raced along her spine and she smiled at him, a challenge forming on her lips "That implies that there will come a time when you aren't on duty. A time when this assignment is over."

"When that time comes, Miss King, there won't be a couple of layers of denim between us. I'll lie back and let you call all the shots." Grayson's promise caused a fluttering sensation deep within her belly. He picked up his coat and dug the keys out of his pocket. "But in the meantime, I'm in the driver's seat."

Chapter Ten

A week went by with Grayson and Tessa pretending that nothing had happened between them up at Pine Top Point. He thought he'd done a pretty good job of returning to business as usual. He'd even kept a straight face when Doherty asked why the new shirt Grayson had been wearing that night was missing two buttons.

Despite a slight surge of reporters the day after Congressman Townsend left, there were fewer and fewer white vans camped outside the gates. It could have had something to do with Duke King returning to his ship after his leave ended. With all those late-night phone calls on the front porch, the most levelheaded member of the King family definitely had something he wasn't sharing with his siblings. Perhaps the press had caught wind of it and followed him in search of a bigger story.

In fact, if things remained this quiet, they wouldn't need as many agents stationed on the ranch any longer. That meant Grayson could finally be done with *Operation Snowball.*

He was passing the stables on his way to the bunkhouse on a Tuesday afternoon when he caught a glimpse of Tessa heading out for her daily ride, a task that Grayson had ensured one of the other agents now covered. As much as his body was aching to be alone with her, his brain was telling him that he couldn't risk a repeat of that crazy make-out session last week.

"You can't ride the horses today," Finn yelled as she came tearing out of the stables, nearly mowing down Grayson in her attempt to reach her sister.

"Why not?" Tessa asked.

"The vet is finishing up the inoculations."

Grayson hadn't seen a veterinarian here earlier. That kind of information would've been on the visitor's log at the command center, where he'd just gotten off duty. Had his team missed something? The last thing he wanted to do right now was to stop and listen to their conversation, but there was no other agent around to confirm things and his investigation senses were tingling.

Tessa lifted a brow. "*All* the horses?"

Her sister looked over her shoulder at the entrance to the stables, probably hoping nobody came out to refute her lie. "It makes it easier to keep them all on the same yearly schedule for shots."

"Ugh!" Tessa stretched her arms over her head. "Mom keeps following me around with an open laptop and asking me when I'm ready to have a video conference with her public relations team. She's insisting that I make a statement to the press before Davis puts his own spin on our breakup. I need somewhere to hide out."

"You want to go to Big Millie's instead?" Finn managed to steer Tessa toward the house.

"I've been there almost every night the past week," Tessa argued. "Except for Thursday when Dahlia closed early for personal reasons and I babysat Amelia for her. Our niece insisted she had a new dog, but I think she was imagining it. Or maybe *I'm* imagining things. Either way, I'm going stir-crazy out here. I think it's time for me to go back to work."

"Have you been cleared by the neurolo—" Finn clamped her lips closed when Tessa gave her a very pointed look and then not so subtly darted her eyes in Grayson's direction.

Now, that was interesting, he thought to himself. Was Tessa under the care of a neurologist? As far as he knew, there'd been no doctors—animal or human—on the ranch in the past week.

Freckles chose that exact instant to walk out onto the front porch. Although, from what Grayson had observed of the older woman these past couple of weeks, she'd probably been standing behind the front door all along, strategically planning her entrance into the conversation. "You know, Tessa, your uncle tells me there's a new state-of-the-art indoor pool over at the rec center. I hear there's a diving board and everything."

Grayson was close enough that he could see the goose bumps rise above Tessa's wrists. "I'm not going diving, Aunt Freckles."

Yep. Aunt Freckles and Finn were definitely up to something.

"Of course you aren't. I was just thinking you could go do some laps. I'm sure Agent Grayson here and his team could call ahead to the rec center and get you a couple of hours by yourself."

No, Agent Grayson here wanted to get back to the bunkhouse and take a nap before he covered the night shift for Lopez. He certainly didn't want to stand by and watch Tessa King wearing nothing but a skimpy swimsuit as her athletic body glided through the water.

However, an hour later, before he was about to get behind the wheel of the black SUV, Freckles grabbed his elbow and whispered in his ear, "Try to get our girl up on the diving board."

Our girl was sitting in the backseat, her face devoid of expression. Only the subtlest clench of her jaw told him that she was upset about something—probably about the fact that she'd once again allowed herself to be cajoled by Finn and Freckles into doing something she was avoiding. Even though he was curious about whatever it was she wanted to avoid, Grayson was determined to keep his distance.

Two other agents rode along in the vehicle with them, so at least he wasn't alone with her. When they arrived at the local rec center, which, thankfully, had already been closed to the public for the evening, Grayson and Doherty went in first to clear and secure the H-shaped building. The main entrance and locker rooms were in the center of the H, the gymnasium running the length of one of the sides and the indoor pool running the length of the other. The only way to access the pool was through the locker room hallway or through the reception area. There was no rear exit, which made it easier for surveillance but more difficult if they needed to get out of there in an emergency.

Not that anyone was anticipating an emergency at some community rec center in the middle of Wyoming. Grayson rocked back on his heels, shaking off another wave of restlessness. Not every assignment could be action-packed and heart-stopping, he reminded himself.

"Indoor pools give me the creeps," Doherty said after they radioed Agent Talib to advise her that it was clear to bring Tessa inside. "It's unnatural to have this much water under a roof. It smells like weird chemicals and everything echoes in there. I'm going to post up by the front entrance."

Agent Talib was already in place outside the locker rooms to make sure nobody came in through that entrance, which meant Grayson got stuck inside the pool area with Tessa, the scent of chlorine permeating the dense air.

The lights were bright, buzzing overhead as Tessa lapped through the water. She swam a few lengths then stopped at the deep end and lifted her goggles onto her slicked-back hair. "You don't have to stand there the whole time watching me."

"I'm not *watching* you," he pointed out. "I'm scanning the area for possible threats. Sorry if you occasionally come into my field of vision."

"Right." Tessa adjusted her goggles, but not before he saw her roll her eyes. "Well, when you used to watch me on my rides, you'd actually get on a horse and pretend to at least be participating in the activity."

"I can't scan for potential threats from inside the pool."

"Please. We're in an enclosed room with no windows." Tessa used a dripping arm to gesture around the four tall walls surrounding the Olympic-size pool. "The only way in here is past the other two agents stationed at the doors. Do you really have that little confidence in your colleagues?"

"Someone has to remain inside. Besides, you shouldn't swim alone without a lifeguard on duty."

"Then swim *with* me." Using her open palm, she sent a spray of water his way.

"I didn't bring a suit," Grayson argued.

"Grab one from the lost and found." She pointed to a large metal-wire bin in the far corner.

He scrunched his nose. "That sounds pretty un-hygienic."

She easily pulled herself out of the deep end, water sluicing from her body as her wet feet slapped along the deck. Her voice echoed off the tiled walls as she walked toward the lost and found bin. "Don't worry. The gallons of chlorine they dump in here will kill off any potential germs."

Germs were suddenly the last thing on his mind as he got a full look at Tessa King's toned legs, which were bare and slick all the way up to the blue spandex material barely covering the firm rounded curves of her backside. His throat went dry.

Tessa, hopefully oblivious to his body's reaction to her in a swimsuit, grabbed a pair of neon-green shorts boasting a wild print of frothy piña colada drinks and pink umbrellas. She held them up triumphantly as she made her way back to him.

Grayson shook his head. "Those look like they

were purposely left behind on a Hawaiian cruise ship by a retired NFL linebacker."

"Hmm." She squinted through one eye as she tested out the elasticity of the waistband, looking from the shorts to Grayson's lower torso. "Might be a few sizes too big. I think I saw a Speedo in there that would work better—"

He snatched the swim trunks out of her hand. "I'll make you a deal. I'll wear these ridiculous things— the Speedo is a no-go—if you teach me how to dive."

Grayson knew there was a reason Freckles had mentioned the diving board, and he wanted to find out why. Even if it meant sacrificing his pride and donning the tacky swim trunks, their obnoxiously bright print making him suddenly wish he had his sunglasses.

Tessa's eyes shot to the high dive and he saw the muscles in her neck working as she gulped. Yep, there was definitely a story there. She wrung the water out of her hair, but not before he saw the tell-tale twitch of her fingers. "What do you mean *teach* you how to dive? The great Agent Wyatt doesn't already know how to do something?"

Of course he knew how to dive. It was part of the combat swimmer stroke course when he'd trained for special forces. But if she didn't already know the details of his training, he wasn't going to volunteer the info. "My mom used to take me and Maddie swimming when we were growing up because it helped Maddie with her physical therapy. But our neighborhood pool didn't have fancy diving boards like these."

That was true enough. Maybe it was his subtle reminder of his sister having a medical condition. Or maybe Tessa just really wanted to see him shirtless. Or maybe she really felt awkward with him watching her while she swam alone. Either way, she inhaled deeply and stuck out her hand to shake on the deal. "Fine."

As he walked into the locker room to change, he explained to Agent Talib in passing that he wouldn't have his radio earpiece in for a short time. She'd replied, "Take as long as you want. I told SAIC Simon we didn't need three agents for this job, but Doherty insisted that you'd want to come along as an extra."

Damn, he thought, cinching the drawstring in the waistband and double knotting it to keep the swimsuit in place. Doherty had likely been in on this plan with Finn and Freckles all along.

When Grayson walked out of the locker room, Tessa was back in the pool, treading water. Her goggles were on the deck where she'd left them, which meant that when he approached in his borrowed suit, there was nothing to obscure her eyes as they widened at the sight of his bare chest.

She bit her lower lip, blatantly staring at the area below his neck. His skin tightened over his already tense muscles and heat spread through his bloodstream.

This is a bad idea. He didn't trust himself around her when they were both fully dressed. How could they be this close to each other in nothing but their swimsuits and keep their hands to themselves?

Unfortunately, it was too late to turn back now. He jumped into the water in an effort to cool off his overheated body and almost lost his shorts.

"Okay—" he nodded toward the board "—show me how to dive."

"You said 'teach,' not show. You go up on the springboard and I'll stay down here and talk you through it."

He should've known that she'd try to outsmart him. He used the side ladder and only one arm to haul himself out of the pool, the other hand still clutching the loose elastic of his shorts. Grayson walked onto the end of the diving board, prepared to belly flop on this whole plan if he had to.

Tessa gave him several instructions of how he should lean over at the waist or bend his knees or move his toes closer to the edge, but he purposely misunderstood everything she said and ended up jackknifed as he tumbled into the water.

The second time he got up on the board, he over-corrected and actually *did* do a belly flop. The red skin on Grayson's stomach stung as he walked back to the board for the third time. He swallowed his pride, along with his penchant for honesty, when he said, "I just don't understand what I'm doing wrong."

His first two attempts had taken so long, she'd given up on treading water in the deep end and was now sitting on the edge of the pool. "You're bending too much at the waist and then pulling your head up too soon."

"No offense," he said, totally intending to offend her. "But I feel like I could do it if I had a better teacher."

"You don't need a better teacher. You need to focus. I'm telling you what to do and you're doing the exact opposite."

"No, I need someone who isn't too afraid to get up here and show me."

She narrowed her eyes at him. "I'm not afraid."

"Prove it."

She stood and he had to force his gaze away from the top of her bathing suit, the clingy wet fabric showing the clear outline of her hardened nipples underneath. She brushed by him as she climbed the steps to the board and a shiver of excitement raced through him.

"Keep your arms over your head like this. Your fingers should hit the water before your head." She gave him several other instructions, but never actually left the board in demonstration. In fact, the longer she remained on the edge, the slower her voice became. "Jump high with your legs and d-di...di...dive—"

She shook her head as though to clear it. That's when he realized the rest of her body was trembling.

"Tessa?" Bypassing the rungs on the ladder, he jumped directly onto the board. "Are you okay?"

She stood at the edge, staring at the water. Her legs were locked together, her hands stiff at her sides. But still, she shook.

"I'm walking toward you," he said quietly, not wanting to spook her. "Give me your hand. I'll help you climb down."

"I d-don…don…" She paused and he had no doubt she was doing that thing where she closed her eyes any time she stuttered. "I don…don't want to climb down."

"Do you want me to stay up here with you?"

Tessa's nod was so slight, he thought he'd imagined it.

"I'm right here, behind you," he told her. "I'm not going anywhere."

This time, her nod was stronger. He could see her shoulder blades expand as she drew in a ragged breath. He realized that he'd been holding his own. "That's right. Just breathe."

They inhaled and exhaled together several times.

"I'm going to stand behind you, just in case…" He didn't want to say *panic attack*. The mere suggestion that she wasn't in control might send her into a tailspin. "Just in case you lose your balance."

She didn't object, so he moved closer and slowly

wrapped his right arm around her waist. "Here, lean back against me. I've got you."

Tessa's body was rigid, but at least her breathing remained controlled. After what seemed like several minutes, he felt her begin to relax against him. Her fingers rose to cover his hand, the one that was firmly planted above her belly button.

"I'm okay," she said, taking a few more deep breaths.

"You want to start backing up? I'll help you climb down."

"No," she said. "I need to get through this. I can do this if you're with me."

"I'm not going anywhere," he promised. Their skin was already dry and he worried that a chill would set in if they didn't either get out of these wet suits or back into the heated pool soon. "Tell me what we're working through."

"I need to dive." Her voice was still a little shaky, but determined.

"Okay, we'll dive together."

"No way." She managed a weak chuckle, but at least she was relaxing. "You're horrible at it."

"I was faking it," he admitted.

She rolled her eyes. "I know."

"So then why did you come up here to show me?"

"I needed to come up here for myself. I thought that if I had an audience, I could go through with it."

"You want to tell me what this is all about?" he tried again.

She sighed, then leaned her head back against his shoulder. "I used to be a diver. I was on the junior national team, training for the Olympics."

"I thought I'd read something in your case file about Olympic training, but I didn't know what sport."

She released a shuddering sigh of what sounded like relief. "Good to know my dad was able to keep some things covered up."

"What happened?"

"I had a bad accident my senior year of high school. It wasn't even during a meet or at practice or anything. Some of my teammates and I were messing around at the pool at Twin Kings. My mom had thrown one of her parties to celebrate us making the regional finals. 'Jump high and dive deep.' That's what my dad always told me."

Something clicked in Grayson's mind. Those same words had caused her to start stuttering earlier.

"But I was showing off. I went to do a backward arm-standing double somersault off our springboard. It's a dive that should only be done from a platform. I couldn't hold my position because the board dipped too low and when I overcorrected, my head hit the edge on my way down. I blacked out immediately and sank to the bottom of the pool. When I woke up from my coma, I was in the hospital. It was almost a week later."

Having experienced numerous hospitalizations with his sister, he knew exactly how terrifying that must've been for anyone, let alone someone so young. "That must've been scary."

The top of Tessa's head hit his chin as she nodded. "I couldn't see at first and thought I'd gone blind. And I couldn't talk, which was even scarier because I had so many questions. The surgeon explained that I had a TBI—traumatic brain injury. After a few days, my vision came back and I thought my speech would return just as easily. I could think of the words, but I couldn't make my tongue form them or my mouth say them. It was like there was a disconnect between my brain and my vocal chords. I spent almost two years in speech therapy relearning how to talk."

He knew the woman was tenacious, but he'd had no idea the obstacles she'd had to face to make it to the top of her profession. "And now you're on TV every night, talking in front of millions of people."

"That's the thing. My career depends on me not making any mistakes on the air. But suddenly I'm having panic attacks and stuttering, and everything that I've worked so hard to overcome is coming back full force."

"You're worried you're going to have a setback."

He brought his other arm around her waist, wishing he could use his body to comfort hers.

"In college, I tried to get back on the diving board and that's when I had my first panic attack. The fear was so intense that it caused me to regress, and set me back about six months in speech therapy. So when I had that panic attack at the funeral, I thought…"

"You thought it was happening again."

"Exactly. I let everyone think I was staying on at the ranch because of that whole Agent Steamy business. But that wasn't the scandal I was worried about. If I can't speak on the air, Grayson, my career is over."

He kissed her temple. "This isn't a relapse. I've seen you verbally spar with your family, and me, and anyone else who has tried to keep you from doing what you want to do. When you're confident and you believe in yourself, the words flow out of you and nobody dares to argue."

This time her chuckle was a little more natural. She'd made it through the worst part—admitting that she wasn't as strong as she pretended to be.

"So, what do we do?" Grayson asked, his lips still near her ear. "How can I help?"

Tessa exhaled loudly. "My dad always said we need to conquer our fears. Failure isn't an option."

"So, what's your fear?"

"Right now, it's jumping off this stupid diving board."

He laced his fingers through hers. "Hold my hand. I'll jump with you."

"That's even more dangerous. What if you crash into me?"

Grayson glanced down at the water. They were only a couple of feet above it and nowhere near the concrete edge. "You want to go first and I'll make sure you don't fall?"

"I don't know." He could feel her rib cage expand and contract under his hand.

"Then we'll just stay up here until you know."

"You're freezing, though," Tessa said.

"How do you know?"

"Because your nipples are so frozen, they're cutting into my back." Her shoulders wiggled against his chest.

"If you keep talking about my nipples," he whispered into her ear, "the rest of me will warm up a lot more quickly."

She laughed, but then her tone changed. "Okay, I'm going to do it." The resolve in her voice was clear.

"Warm me up? Or dive?"

"I'm going to jump off of here holding your hand. Feet first. Then, if I can do that, I'll try to dive. By myself."

As much as he wanted to keep Tessa in his arms,

he knew he had to help her get through this internal battle. "Okay. I'm going to squeeze in beside you. When you're ready, count us down."

She clutched his hand as he lowered his arm. Then, when they were side by side, he slipped his other hand into hers. He didn't say a word, even when they stood like that for at least thirty seconds. Grayson was beginning to think they'd both be going back down the ladder when she finally spoke.

Her voice was a little shaky, but she didn't stutter when she said, "Three... Two... One."

Silence pounded in Tessa's ears as she felt her body sink lower, her heart beating in her throat as she opened her eyes under the water. She blew out a stream of bubbles, noting that nothing had affected her vision this time. Grayson was beside her, although he'd released her hand and was holding up those silly piña colada shorts. She smiled to herself as she kicked her legs toward the surface.

"You did it!" Grayson used his free arm to dog-paddle to her.

"I did it," she repeated and wrapped her arms around his neck. The exhilaration racing through her body was so intense, she couldn't contain it. Tessa kissed him, but she was grinning too much to take things any further.

His smile must've equaled her own because she'd never seen Grayson look so happy. Who would have thought such a silly accomplishment of jumping feet-first off a diving board could inspire so much joy between two people who barely knew each other? Yet, seeing how proud he was sent a liberating shot of satisfaction through her. Tessa had a sudden urge to make him even prouder.

He spun her around triumphantly then asked, "Did it feel good?"

Their legs brushed against each other's as they kicked in place. "Not at first," she admitted. "It felt scary. But then it was over as soon as I jumped. It's more of a relief than anything."

"Do you want to try it again?" he asked.

She nodded and swam for the side railing to haul herself out. "You stay there. I'm going to jump to you."

She was like Marcus's twins when they'd been toddlers, wanting the thrill of the jump yet simultaneously wanting the safety of someone catching them. The second time she went up on the diving board, she still paused for too long at the edge and felt the fear threatening to overrun her body.

"You've got this." Grayson held up his arms. "Jump toward me. I'll get you."

Tessa closed her eyes and leaped off with both sets of toes pointed perfectly down. She didn't sink as far this time and quickly resurfaced.

Grayson, true to his word, was less than an arm's length away from her. "You hardly made a splash."

The third time, she added a bounce before going straight in. The fourth time, she did a forward flip, not quite ready to go headfirst yet. Tessa did several more jumps, each time seeing Grayson's encouraging smile as soon as she resurfaced.

She lost count of how many times she went off the board but, finally, she was ready to try an actual dive. Tessa stopped halfway across the springboard. She took a deep breath and counted off how many steps she would need. One, two, three. Feet together, then bounce and lift. Her arms went up, her muscle memory overriding every anxiety. Without thinking about it, she pivoted midair, her head coming down and her legs straightening upward.

Not only did relief course through her, along with a tiny tremor of pride, Tessa experienced that tingling thrill that used to make her come alive when she was at a dive meet. She came from a family of overachievers. But diving was *her* specialty. It was her skill and made her stand out as her own person, not just another King. She hadn't realized she'd been chasing that same thrill, that same rush of accomplishment, since…well, since her last diving championship.

She heard one of the locker room doors creak open and turned her head in time to catch Grayson waving off Agent Talib. Tessa looked at the digital clock hanging next to the giant timer on the back wall.

Eleven twenty-seven. She blinked the chlorine out of her eyes to make sure she was reading the red numbers correctly.

"Why didn't you tell me how late it was getting?" she asked Grayson, who'd been treading water the entire time. He hadn't so much as swum to the edge for a break.

"Because I liked watching you." He kicked his way closer to her. His eyes were full of pride and perhaps something more. But it certainly wasn't exhaustion.

"We should probably get out," she suggested. Tessa's adrenaline levels were still too amped up to think about being tired, but she knew the exhaustion would set in soon enough. She swam to the ladder, but he didn't follow.

"You go ahead," he told her, a trace of pinkish color appearing on his cheeks. "I'll stay here for another minute or two."

"Why?" she asked before it dawned on her that he was using both arms to cut through the water to keep afloat. If he wasn't holding on to his shorts, then how were they...?

She looked toward the bright green, white and pink material crumpled in a heap at the bottom of the deep end. Her cheeks flooded with heat when she brought her eyes up to his. "Are you, um...?"

"Tessa?" He said her name as a warning and goose bumps spread along her wet skin. It reminded her of the way he'd warned her before that mind-searing kiss several nights ago.

"Yeah?" she asked, her voice raspy to her own ears. The only thing keeping her from seeing the man in all his naked glory was some lapping water. Awareness zipped through her, heightening her senses.

"There are two agents on the other side of that door."

"Right," she said, yanking her inappropriate thoughts back to reality. Ignoring the soreness in her muscles, she hauled herself out. Tessa had a feeling that if she wanted to, she could've tempted him into another kiss, or something more.

Unfortunately for her libido, though, she respected the man's principles too much to take advantage of him when he was naked in the pool.

As she grabbed her towel and headed for the women's locker room, she realized that by diving tonight, by overcoming one of her lingering fears, she was one step closer to returning to work. As soon as she left Wyoming, Grayson would officially be off assignment.

She would probably never see him again. Their lives were so different, there would never be a reason for their paths to cross.

But.

If she ever got the chance to pay him back for how

much he'd helped her tonight, Tessa hoped that she would be able to do so in person. And this time, she wouldn't let the rules get in the way.

Chapter Eleven

When Tessa informed the agents that she'd be returning to the community rec center the following evening, Grayson brought his own swimsuit. While she probably didn't need him in the pool with her again, he wanted to be ready just in case.

However, after Finn and Freckles arrived in the SUV behind them, there was no way he was about to get into the water with an audience there. Still, Grayson observed the situation from his self-designated position near the no-lifeguard-on-duty sign as she did a series of several dives, each one more complicated than the last. Each one also eliciting hearty whooping and clapping from her sister and aunt.

"Don't know why Sherilee was so nervous to come see this for herself." Freckles's voice was surprisingly quiet for once, although the acoustics made everything echo. "Tessa looks fantastic up there."

"Mom thought MJ was going to join a prison gang after spending one night in the Ridgecrest County drunk tank," Finn replied to her aunt. "When it comes to her kids, she's too much of a worrier and stresses out everyone else around her. It's better for all of our anxiety levels—especially Tessa's—if she doesn't come watch."

Grayson had no business voicing his agreement, but he did send up a silent word of thanks for small favors. Tessa might never return to her pre-Olympic-level diving form, but at least she was attempting the twists and flips with increasing boldness and determination. With her family there and her focus restored, she'd barely managed to glance in his direction, clearly no longer needing his emotional and physical support.

He clasped his hands behind his back uselessly. Tessa's renewed sense of confidence would motivate her to return to her job soon, which would allow him to return to his. Or, at least, his real job, rather than being a glorified watchdog. Plus, he really needed to look in on Maddie. While his mom kept him updated with the daily doctor reports, there was always that nagging worry in the back of his mind that both she and his sister were putting on a brave front just so he wouldn't stress about them.

There was a light at the end of this assignment tunnel, and Grayson waited for the calm sense of relief to settle over him the way it always did when he'd successfully accomplished a mission. Instead, an unexplained ball of loneliness formed in the pit of his stomach, growing each time Tessa jumped off that diving board.

The following night, Dahlia and Marcus both brought their kids to the community rec center to swim, turning the place into a King family pool party. Watching the twin boys chase each other across the slippery wet deck as Marcus argued with Violet in the shallow end made Grayson wish he'd brought a whistle.

By Friday night, Sherilee King must've overcome her own fears stemming from Tessa's accident because she arrived at the rec center pool with four more agents in tow, along with enough pizzas to feed half the county. The woman could barely stay in one place because she was too busy pacing and wringing her hands every time Tessa was up on the high dive. Whenever her daughter resurfaced, though, Mrs. King's face lit up with both relief and pride.

"You gotta eat, Agent Wyatt." Aunt Freckles passed him a paper plate filled with two slices of deep dish loaded with melted cheese and nearly every topping offered at the Pepperoni Stampede, the local pizza parlor in the small town of Teton Ridge.

"Thanks," he said, accepting the plate and letting

the scent of garlic and spicy sausage remind him that he'd only had a protein bar for lunch.

"I should be the one thanking you," the older woman said, tilting her peach-colored tower of curls at Tessa up on the diving board. "You're the one who got our girl back on her horse, so to speak."

He ignored the tingle of pride pulling his shoulders back and bit into the first slice. If he kept his mouth full, she wouldn't expect him to respond. Grayson knew when someone was fishing for information, especially when that someone was the least subtle person he'd ever met. Still, he wasn't about to discuss Tessa's TBI or her fear of having another panic attack, even if it was with her well-meaning aunt.

But Aunt Freckles was like a dog with a bone. "SAIC Simon told us there'd be a family debriefing tomorrow morning. I'm assuming that can only mean that you're all pulling up stakes and heading back to Washington."

Actually, Grayson had put in a request for a few days' leave so he could travel to Maryland first to check in on Maddie and his mom. He hadn't put in his official transfer request yet, but was hoping to once they cleared out of Twin Kings. Luckily, he was saved from answering.

"You're not even offering anyone the Garden Party pizza, Freckles." Mrs. King took the plate holding Grayson's remaining slice from his hand

and swapped it out for a one containing a triangular shape of mixed veggies held together by a layer of underseasoned, edible cardboard. "Too much lactose and processed meat will just clog you up and slow you down, Agent. Plant-based foods are the way to go. You'll thank me later."

"Sherilee, you can't just steal a man's food like that," Freckles chided.

When Mrs. King showed no sign of returning the swapped-out paper plate to Grayson anytime soon, Freckles used her brightly manicured fingers to snatch his stolen slice of supreme pizza back from her sister-in-law and dropped it directly onto his plate. Now he had a total of three pieces of pizza— or at least two and a half since he still had his original slice in his right hand.

Despite the past three weeks, these women were still in the throes of an absurd power struggle, and their family and half of the agents were smart enough to stay well clear of them. Grayson had no desire to be one of the pawns in this pizza saga and took a discreet step backward, his exit strategy already in place.

"Hold on a second, Agent Grayson Wyatt!" Mrs. King reached for his elbow.

"You don't have to be so damn formal all the time, Sherilee." Freckles rolled her eyes so dramatically, he worried that one of her false eyelashes would stick to her penciled eyebrow. "Just call him Agent Wyatt.

Or better yet, Grayson. He's practically part of the family by now."

Whoa. A shiver of discomfort zipped down Grayson's spine. He didn't *want* to be considered part of the family and squared his shoulders as professionally as possible before addressing Mrs. King. "Agent Wyatt is fine, ma'am."

"I apologize for my sister-in-law, Agent Wyatt. I think all that aerosol hairspray has gone to her head." Mrs. King made a tsking sound. "She isn't very good with boundaries."

"Gimme a break, Sherilee." Freckles stage-whispered out of the corner of her heavily painted lips, "I apologize for *my* sister-in-law, Agent Wyatt. She never wants anyone to know she grew up in a run-down trailer park in Laramie, so she tends to overcompensate with the whole 'lady of the manor' act."

"An act?" Mrs. King snorted a very unladylike snort. "That's rich coming from a woman who'd rather serve hash browns and unwanted opinions than use her famous surname to actually help her community. Because heaven forbid anyone associate you with that founding family whose name appears on various hospital wings, Ivy League campuses and the Declaration of Independence."

Wait. Grayson's eyes flew back and forth between the two older women. He'd once seen Freckles listed in Rider King's file, but he'd simply thought she was just some café owner from Idaho. He hadn't put two and two together and realized she was part of *that* family.

Before Grayson could ask, Freckles waved a hand in the air—the rows of colorful plastic-beaded bracelets on her wrist clinking together—and asked, "Are we gonna stand here arguing about our dead ancestors or are we gonna show Agent Wyatt our appreciation for helping Tessa get her head on straight?"

Neither, Grayson prayed.

"I'm just glad you're admitting that something other than your high-calorie comfort food you 'prescribed—'" Mrs. King's jeweled fingers made air quotes at the last words "—is what helped Tessa."

"Maybe if you ate something sweet once in a while, you wouldn't be such a..." Freckles continued the argument as Grayson turned all of his focus to finishing his pizza.

Outside, it was nearly thirty degrees and the forecast was calling for the first snowstorm of the new year. Maybe Grayson could offer Doherty a case of beer and tickets to the Red Sox home opener if he'd switch posts right this second. Nah. Every other agent on duty would rather be knee-deep in a blizzard than be trapped in a steamy, chlorinated room with these two battling sister-in-laws.

Grayson scanned the indoor pool, hoping one of the King siblings would come to his rescue. Unfortunately, the cavalry had been dealing with these women way longer than he had. That meant they knew better than to get caught in the cross fire.

As the petty insults flew back and forth, Grayson's mind zeroed in on a sudden realization. None of these King women fit the mold of what society expected. Sherilee King was the overly dignified one, yet grew up in a trailer park. Freckles actually came from an even more famous family with obscene amounts of wealth and privilege. Dahlia had a degree in interior design but owned a former brothel. Finn could've been mistaken for a college cheerleader yet single-handedly ran one of the biggest cattle operations in the state of Wyoming. And then there was Tessa...

Grayson was barely skimming the surface on the hidden depths Tessa kept well guarded. Nothing in the prebriefing files and intelligence reports had prepared him for any of this. This whole family had gone from code names on a chart to very real people with very real backgrounds and personalities. And if he stayed around much longer, the very realness of Tessa would make it that much more difficult for him to file everything away and forget it after the final post-op briefing.

"So, Agent Wyatt?" Mrs. King waved her palm in front of his face and Grayson snapped to attention. "I was hoping you'd have a moment before the briefing tomorrow morning to meet with Sonya."

He shook his head to clear it. "Who's Sonya?"

"She's the head of my public relations team."

Grayson twisted his empty paper plate in his hands. He was familiar with the army of assistants and press secretaries on the former second lady's staff. None of them was named Sonya.

Freckles must have sensed his confusion because she clarified, "Sherilee hired Sonya to help with Mitchell Junior's situation."

Grayson remained motionless. "But that assignment falls under Echo Team. Don't you want to meet with Agent Franks?" Franks had been assigned to MJ the night of his arrest, and had later been assigned to tail him to and from court for his arraignment, as well as around the ranch after he'd made bail.

"Of course. There's just one pesky little issue we need to wrap up."

"What issue is that?" Grayson's lips pressed flat.

"My son Marcus informed me there's a video of Tessa exchanging words with you in the staging center outside my husband's funeral. Apparently, Congressman Davis's assistant has made several inquiries about the footage."

A chill went down Grayson's spine. He immediately knew what this was about.

"I was there." Freckles jerked a thumb at her chest. "Trust me, there wasn't much exchanging on Agent Wyatt's end. Just Tessa cussing up a blue streak and giving him holy hell for taking her for a ride in her daddy's hearse."

"Could you please not make it sound so crude?" Mrs. King's forced smile looked more like a grimace. "Anyway, I'm concerned that the video might not show my daughter in the most favorable light."

It really didn't show either Tessa *or* Grayson in a favorable light. Especially because Grayson was the one being accused of not following proper protocol and might possibly have to answer to his superiors at an inquiry board.

Grayson's stance widened as he prepared to defend himself against a still unknown threat. "Ma'am, it's my understanding that the video was obtained from the body cam of one of the Ridgecrest County deputy sheriffs. As long as nobody tampered with the footage, it's an accurate portrayal of the events as they happened."

"I understand how the recording was acquired, Agent. My concern is the reason why the congressman is so interested in accessing it."

"Well..." He tilted his head, knowing no other way to put this delicately. "The video is a matter of public record. I don't see how the sheriff could keep it from him."

"Oh, public records go missing all the time," Mrs. King replied, and Grayson really hoped she wasn't about to suggest something illegal. "But not in Teton Ridge and not while my son is in charge. Hell, Marcus put his own brother in jail. There's no way he'd 'accidentally misplace—'" she used the finger quotes again "—the video just to protect Tessa's reputation. So, while I might not be able to get rid of it myself, there's always a way to spin things to one's advantage. After all, I haven't gotten to where I am today without being proactive."

A muscle spasmed in his clenched jaw as Grayson easily guessed Mrs. King's so-called proactive route. There was no way she'd spin anything to *his* advantage. But before he could ask her for clarification, Rider King yelled across the pool.

"Hey, Sherilee, I told you I hadn't lost my favorite bathing suit!" The old man waved the bright piña colada–printed shorts over his head like a battle flag as he walked toward them. "Although, I have no idea how they ended up in the lost and found basket at the rec center."

"You sure did," Mrs. King told her brother-in-law, but her smile didn't quite reach her eyes.

"Hey, wifey." Rider wiggled his bushy gray eyebrows at Freckles. "I'm gonna throw these things on real quick and then I'll meet you in the hot tub."

"Stop calling me *wifey*, you crazy old man," Freckles shot back. Then she winked at Grayson before following her ex-husband to the men's locker room.

"I told Mitchell Junior to get rid of that tacky bathing suit years ago," Mrs. King told Grayson as she waved at one of her grandsons who'd just executed a perfect cannonball. Then she lowered her voice. "Let this be a lesson to you, Agent Wyatt. Nothing ever stays hidden unless you hide it yourself."

The woman soon found another agent in need of her plant-based Garden Party pizza, but Grayson wasn't quite ready to breathe a sigh of relief just yet. There was no doubt in his mind that Sherilee King intended on saving her daughter's reputation by throwing him under the bus. He had no idea how she'd do it, but she clearly thought he was foolish enough to be an active participant in her plan.

And for what?

Was his career really worth Tessa suffering a little bit of negative press? She worked in the media, herself. It was her own colleagues who'd gotten her into this situation in the first place. Being at the Twin Kings Ranch these past few weeks almost made him forget how much he hated all these powerful people with their mind games and their publicity stunts. Almost.

Grayson didn't think his jaw could get any more rigid, but it did. He just needed to get through one more day. Then he could close the file on this family for good.

Tessa hadn't been able to get Grayson alone since that first night at the pool when he'd convinced her to go off that diving board. Something had clicked in her brain that evening, and each night that she'd gone to the pool, she grew more and more convinced that she was ready to return to work.

Sure, she might have another panic attack at some point down the road. Nothing was ever certain when it came to traumatic brain injuries. Yet, Tessa was now armed with the confidence that she could face the fear and work through it.

She was done with hiding out and being shielded from the world's reaction to an injury she might never overcome. In fact, she'd spoken to her boss yesterday and planned to be back in the studio by Monday evening. That meant today would be her last day at Twin Kings.

Tessa stepped out of the shower and saw a text alert on her smartphone. Her mom had sent today's agenda to all the siblings. There was a family briefing planned for eleven o'clock and a conference call planned with some PR expert named Sonya at one. Tessa still didn't see a need for the public relations team just yet. What she did see a need for, though, was talking to Grayson one-on-one.

The digital clock on her phone read 10:08 a.m. and she tapped at the screen with her thumb before realizing she didn't even have his number in her list of contacts. Her legs grew restless and she couldn't get dressed quickly enough.

Her last relationship, as well as the one before that, had been conducted mostly through texts and emails and video chats. Yet all her interactions with

Grayson had been in person. It was a weird feeling to realize that in less than twelve hours, she wouldn't be able to simply walk outside and have him magically appear. She wouldn't have any way of getting in touch with him after today.

Maybe it was for the best.

Sure, she'd kissed the man and shared some of her most personal secrets with him. However, as much as they'd talked about something physical happening between them when his assignment was officially over, was she truly ready to go there? Once she returned to her own life, all of these feelings that had been building inside her would likely run out of steam without him there to fuel the fire.

Still. She needed to at least say goodbye to him without an audience. Tessa couldn't afford to leave any loose strings untied—she'd learned her lesson after Davis—and they both deserved the closure. Plus, she wanted Grayson to know that he'd been an instrumental part in her getting through the past three weeks.

Leaving the main house, Tessa kept close to the line of trees that ran the length of the road between the stables and the bunkhouse. Did her attempts to be discreet really matter, though? Everyone on this ranch was always watching. Hell, she'd been shadowed almost half of her life by either bodyguards or Secret Service agents or paparazzi. She strode into the middle of the path to walk the rest of the way. There was no sense in sneaking around now.

She lifted her hand to knock on the bunkhouse door, not wanting to barge into the agents' private retreat, the only place on these fifty-five-thousand-plus acres where they could get away from the members of the King family.

Doherty, the agent who always wore a friendly smile and a Boston Red Sox cap, opened the door. "Hey, Precis— I mean, Miss King. The briefing isn't here. It's in the conference room next door."

"I know." She swallowed down her embarrassment and straightened her shoulders. The trick was to act as though it was perfectly natural for her to show up at the bunkhouse unannounced. To act as though *they* should've been expecting *her*. She wasn't Sherilee King's daughter for nothing. "I'm looking for Agent Wyatt."

"Right," Doherty said, stepping aside. "I think I saw him in the kitchen. Make yourself at home."

The agent left and Tessa let herself into the bunkhouse, which appeared to be empty. The beds were neatly made and several stuffed duffel bags sat on the floor at the end of the bunks, as though the inhabitants had already packed for a quick departure. Tessa's stomach sank when she was presented with the evidence of how eager everyone was to leave Twin Kings.

Prior to today, she'd never needed to enter this

particular building on the ranch and now she had to take a guess as to which side housed the restroom and which side housed the kitchen. She made her way through the open floor plan until she came to the alcove that held a large dining table.

She was at the swinging door that must've separated the kitchen from the living quarters when she heard Grayson's voice. "Is the doctor concerned about the rod?"

"No," a woman's voice responded, sounding a bit echoey and delayed. "They said it sometimes takes longer to fuse, depending on the patient. Maddie is older than most of the people she's operated on, so her bones are already fully developed. We knew going in that it might take longer."

That must be Grayson's mother on a video conference call. Tessa should turn around and leave, but her feet wouldn't budge. She'd been researching EDMD since Grayson had first told her about his sister, and her curiosity wouldn't simply vanish just because it was the polite thing to do. Or because HIPAA regulations required it.

"I knew we shouldn't have waited so long," Grayson said, his voice tense. "She should've had the procedure done years ago."

"Stop beating yourself up, Gray," the woman replied, then made a yawning sound. "You can't work thirty hours of overtime in a day that only has twenty-four hours in it. If it weren't for you, Maddie wouldn't have even been able to have the surgery in the first place. Let alone any of the other treatments you pay for."

"I just hate it that you both are going through this and I'm not there to help, Mom."

Tessa could imagine the stiffness of his jaw. It was how he always looked whenever he wanted to fix something or when something was holding him back.

Oh no.

A wave of realization smacked into Tessa, and her hand flew to her mouth.

She was currently the "something" holding Grayson back from being with his family. She'd been selfishly hiding away on the ranch, licking her wounds and trying to overcome the aftereffects of her TBI, while all of the agents assigned to babysit her—especially Grayson—needed to return to their real lives.

"I know you're not allowed to give us details about your assignment, Grayson, but Maddie said she thinks it should be over soon. You'll come and see us afterward, right?" His mom's voice held a trace of optimism despite all the setbacks life had seemed to throw her family's way.

"As soon as I get the green light, I'll be on a plane to Baltimore," Grayson promised, and Tessa cringed knowing that the supposed green light would come as soon as she was out of his life. "Is now a good time to talk to Maddie?"

There was a pause on the other side of the door and then some mumbling from his mom, who was maybe talking to a nurse or someone else in the hospital room. Tessa was already gripped by so much guilt for being the cause of Grayson missing out on time with his sister, she didn't need to add eavesdropping to the list.

She glanced at the clock on the wall as she debated whether to leave. The briefing started in ten minutes and she wouldn't get a chance to talk to Grayson alone if she didn't wait for him here. She was about to turn from the door and linger by the entrance to the bunkhouse when his little sister's words stopped her.

"Hey there, Agent Steamy. How's the beautiful and talented Miss King?"

"You know that I'm not at liberty to say, Mads. But if you want to ask her yourself, you can."

Grayson swung through the door right then, holding an open laptop in front of him. Tessa's cheeks flooded with heat, her eyelids stretching into wide circles. Of course he'd known that she'd been there, on the other side of the door. The man had a sixth sense when it came to her, always appearing when she wasn't expecting it.

Tessa held up her palms, madly waving them back and forth as her eyes implored him not to turn that laptop around. He tilted his head and lifted the corner of his mouth. The knowing dare coming from his eyes suggested that if she didn't want to be a part of the conversation, then she should've walked away instead of listening in.

Grayson swung the laptop screen around, and Tessa summoned every ounce of professional stage training she possessed to fix her expression from one of mortification to one of pleasant surprise. "Hi! You must be Maddie."

"Oh my gosh!" The young woman blinked several times. "It really is you. Mom, it's really her."

"Hello, Miss King!" Mrs. Wyatt's face appeared on the screen as she squeezed in next to her daughter's hospital bed. "I'm a big fan. I watch your show whenever I get the chance. It's a pleasure to meet you."

"It's a pleasure to meet both of you, as well. Grayson has told me so much about you." Tessa realized her mistake as soon as she saw the smaller woman use her elbow to nudge her mother.

"Grayson?" Maddie squinted at the camera. "My brother, Grayson, talked to you? About us?"

Tessa chuckled, relieved his tendency to be tight-lipped wasn't because of her. "Well, it was like pulling teeth to get him to talk, but we've had a lot of downtime up here on the ra—"

"Our location is classified information." Grayson slapped his hand over the speaker, and in doing so, brought himself next to Tessa so that they were now side by side, facing the laptop.

Maddie rolled her eyes. "I'm pretty sure everyone who has access to a TV or the internet knows where Tessa King has been hiding out these past couple of weeks."

This time, it was Mrs. Wyatt using her elbow to gently nudge her daughter. "What Maddie meant to say is that we watched your father's funeral and, like the rest of the world, we're very sorry for your recent loss."

"Thank you." Tessa replied to the condolences somewhat robotically because she was still stuck on the two words causing her guilt to resurface. *Hiding out.* She was the reason this young woman didn't have her brother by her side in the hospital. Clearing her throat, she changed the subject. "So, Maddie, how are you feeling? Grayson told me you had surgery recently."

Should Tessa have mentioned the surgery? Maybe Maddie Wyatt didn't want some stranger knowing her personal business. Tessa tried not to cast a questioning glance at Grayson as she waited for the other woman to respond. Luckily, she didn't have to wait long.

"Well, the recovery is taking way longer than I was hoping. I went home last week, but then I got super sick and my surgeon was worried about infection, so they readmitted me to the hospital and put me on this mega antibiotic. I'm feeling better now, so it looks like the doc will let me start physical therapy soon. If the procedure works and the rod fuses to my spine, I'm hoping to get back in the pool soon. Maybe even go for a ride on one of the horses at this equestrian center out in the country. Have you guys been doing any riding?"

"*I've* been riding. Your brother has been…" Tessa tapped a finger to her lips. "Well, I don't know what to call his technique on the back of a horse."

When Maddie grinned, even on the screen, Tessa could feel the joy radiating off her. "It's called clinging to the saddle for dear life as he yells at everyone to slow down."

"I'm not that bad." Grayson smiled at his sister and Tessa's heart turned into a puddle.

"Man, I wish I was up there with you guys in Wyoming," Maddie said. "I'd love to see all your horses."

"Perhaps when you're feeling better, we can…" Tessa trailed off as Grayson's elbow lightly pressed into her upper arm, a warning of some sort. Perhaps there was something about his sister's prognosis he hadn't wanted to share.

"Listen, Mads. We have a briefing meeting in about three minutes," Grayson said, immediately filling the silence. "We have to go. I'll call you tomorrow."

"Fine," Maddie replied. "It was nice to meet you, Miss King, even if my brother won't let you make any promises to me about visiting when I feel better. Love you, Gray."

The young woman was extremely astute. An invitation to come riding on the ranch was exactly what Tessa had been about to offer. And she had a feeling that was exactly why Grayson had cut her off.

"Love you, too, Mads. Give Mom a kiss for me," Grayson added at the last second, but the screen had already gone dark.

With the call disconnected, an awkward silence hung between them. Tessa rocked back on her heels, debating whether she could pretend that she'd stumbled into the bunkhouse instead of the conference room by mistake.

"So—" he tucked the closed laptop under his arm and turned to face her "—were you looking for me?"

They were alone amid the rows of beds. After she'd been caught eavesdropping on his private conversation. There was no denying her breach into his personal space. Tessa took a deep breath and came clean. "Yeah, I was hoping to talk to you before the briefing."

"Is it to tell me that you're going back to DC tonight?" he asked, his face perfectly devoid of expression one way or another. "Your network is already running an ad promoting your return on Monday night."

Tessa knew he didn't think very highly of her job, which was part of the reason she was eager to return to it. She needed to put some distance between them before things went too far.

She needed to make sure that her attraction to him wasn't based on the fact that he'd protected her time and again. That he'd been the one to rescue her, even from her own fears. For all she knew, she could simply be suffering from some sort of damsel-in-distress syndrome. Hooking up with the bodyguard was such a cliché, and Tessa was much too analytical for something like that. If she was going to have sex with a man, she had to be sure it was for the right reasons. And she couldn't be sure of that until she was back to being on her own.

"I'm flying out tonight. But before I left, I wanted to thank you for..." *Don't say* rescue, she warned herself. It would only remind them both of how much she'd needed saving and skew the already uneven power balance between them. At the same time, she truly was grateful to him. "I wanted to thank you for everything. I know that you gave up so much in your personal life to stay on longer at the ranch. I also know you had to deal with a lot of teasing with that whole Agent Steamy thing."

"That's part of the job description," he replied, and her chest sank from the hollowness of his words. At least he hadn't said that he'd been paid for putting up with her. That would've been more insulting than anything.

Closure, she reminded herself. *Tie those loose*

strings. She inhaled and continued. "Anyway, I know we talked about what would happen between, uh, us when you were officially off duty. But I don't want you thinking that I'm going to hold you to that."

"Don't worry." His eyes turned to a stormy gray as he crossed his arms in front of his chest. "I copy you loud and clear."

Reaching out, she placed her palm on his forearm and felt his muscles flinch underneath. Great, now she'd insulted him. She dropped her hand. "I'm not saying that the attraction is no longer there. I just need to be smarter about how I act upon it."

Grayson's eyes scanned the room, always on the alert. "Perhaps the smart thing to do would be for you not to act on that attraction at all."

"Possibly," she admitted, realizing that maybe his own attraction was waning now that he no longer had to swoop in and play the hero. "The thing is, not only am I still grieving, I also just came out of a very public breakup. Even though it was a long time coming, if people think I jumped from one relationship to another, they'll be questioning my emotional state."

"We certainly can't have that." He stared at his watch, as though he was already bored with the conversation. "Is there a public relations person for ending things with the bodyguard, as well? Because I don't know if I can take another meeting with your mother and Sonya What's-Her-Name, no matter how hot the kisses are between us."

Tessa's brows slammed together, but before she could respond, there was a loud knock outside the bunkhouse. Agent Doherty cracked the door and yelled inside, "Briefing starts next door in thirty seconds."

She couldn't promise that their attraction would last once they left Wyoming. Even if it did, she couldn't promise that any sort of physical relationship would be worth the price they'd both have to pay publicly. So Tessa held her tongue as she followed him to the conference room.

Luckily, she didn't have to promise him anything. Her flight left before she got the chance to see Grayson again.

Chapter Twelve

Grayson flew back to Washington, DC, for a formal debriefing with his entire unit. As SAIC Simon had predicted, the internal affairs department wanted to review the incident at Roper King's funeral, the one that had led to Grayson meeting Tessa.

He had to sit through several interviews and at least two screenings of the video of Tessa lambasting him over his procedure. The inquiry board informed him they'd let him know the results of their investigation when it was completed. Of course, there was no time frame for how long that might take, but Grayson took solace in the fact that he was being allowed to operate with Delta Team's protective detail while he awaited their decision.

Grayson enjoyed two days' leave with Maddie and his mom before being called back for another assignment. This time, his team was traveling to Philadelphia to protect a group of foreign heads of state sightseeing the birthplace of Independence.

The dignitaries and their aides had their own security teams and all were staying on the top floor of the Ritz-Carlton. The Secret Service agents were a secondary line of defense and their RON—remain overnight—status meant they were doubling up in rooms on the floor below. Grayson had drawn the short straw and been paired with Doherty, but luckily they were working opposite shifts and he didn't have to put up with the man's snoring. Or his wisecracking.

Until the night Doherty returned to the room unexpectedly to dress in his undercover clothes.

"Change of venues tonight," Doherty said as he stopped at the hallway closet to hang up his suit jacket. "The prime minister's daughter talked her old man into taking her to a Sixers' game. If I show up to the arena wearing a button-up shirt and tie, someone might mistake me for one of the coaches."

Grayson squinted at Doherty's five-foot-seven-inch frame. "I'm pretty sure nobody's going to mistake you for a basketball coach."

Grayson lounged on top of the bed, still fully dressed from his earlier shift, waiting for his roommate to finish changing in the bathroom so that he could take a shower. He turned on the television set and half-heartedly began flipping through the channels.

Grayson froze when he landed on Tessa King's perfectly polished image on the screen. Her hair was in a tight bun and her makeup was thicker than it had been on the ranch. In fact, she almost resembled a totally different woman than the one he'd spent time with on Twin Kings. He was so focused on analyzing her controlled posture and the way she kept eye contact with the camera that he didn't even hear what she was saying.

Unfortunately, he also didn't hear Doherty exit the bathroom. "You gonna go out tonight or are you just gonna stay in and make cow eyes over your girl, there?"

"No." Grayson cleared his throat. "I was actually looking for a local news station, but all the channels on these hotel TVs are never the same. And she's not 'my girl.'"

He aimed the remote control at the screen, but instead of turning it off, he turned up the volume. Tessa's voice was strong and precise, and sent a wave of awareness through his bloodstream.

"Right." Doherty slid his holstered duty weapon onto his old leather belt. "Have you talked to her since Wyoming?"

"No." Grayson managed to keep his voice neutral while he fumbled with the remote again until he found the mute button. It wasn't like Tessa had slipped him her phone number or told him to stay in touch before she'd gone wheels up.

"Uh-huh. So then you probably don't know that she's here in Philadelphia right now?"

Grayson's head snapped up. He looked between Doherty and the television that showed her talking, even though he could no longer hear what she was saying.

"It's not a live broadcast, Agent Steamy." Doherty retrieved his Red Sox cap from the top of the dresser. "That episode was prerecorded."

"How do you know she's in Philly?"

"Because I'm a Secret Service agent and it's my job to know things." Doherty straightened his earpiece as he crossed the room to the door. "Plus, I saw her name on the reservation desk's computer when I ran the guest list against our security threat database."

Grayson's muscles tightened. "You mean she's staying here at this hotel?"

"If you're asking out of a personal interest, then I can neither confirm nor deny that. But if you're only interested because you feel a certain professional courtesy toward her—say for example you wanted to advise her that the ice machine on her floor was out of order—then I'd tell you she's in room seven nineteen." Doherty chuckled knowingly as he walked out the door.

Grayson jumped to his feet and paced the room, trying not to glance at the hotel telephone on the desk. It had been over three weeks since he'd last seen Tessa. He didn't dare show up at her room. For all he knew, she could be in town to meet some guy. Grayson wasn't about to knock on her door only to be greeted by her date. His fingers dug into his palm before his brain reminded him that Tessa King was no longer his concern.

Although—he allowed his eyes to land on the phone—she'd probably appreciate him calling her to warn her that he was there, as well. Just in case they ran into each other in the lobby or something. He wouldn't want things to be awkward between them if he caught her by surprise.

Before he could talk himself out of it, he had the receiver in his hand and punched in seven-one-nine on the number pad.

It rang twice before she answered. "Hello?"

Grayson's heart thumped behind his rib cage. "Miss King?"

"Who is this?" she asked without confirming her identity. Clearly, this wasn't the first time someone unexpected had gotten access to her room number.

"It's Agent Wyatt."

He heard the catch in her breath. "Grayson?"

So much for keeping things from turning personal. And, really, there was no longer any reason why they needed to maintain that professional boundary. He scrubbed a hand over his jaw and decided to leap clear across that once blurry line.

"Do you want to go get a drink?"

Grayson half expected her to show up in the bright red tailored suit and sleeked-back hair she'd been wearing when she'd been on his TV earlier.

So, an hour later, when Tessa walked into the nearly empty neighborhood bar down the street from their hotel wearing jeans, riding boots and a soft green knit cap over her loose blond curls, his heart beat faster. Now, *this* was the relaxed version of Tessa, the one he'd spent so much time with on the ranch.

"Hey," he said, rising from his seat.

He'd hoped the place would have some discreet booths tucked in the back where they could talk privately. Unfortunately, when he'd arrived, his choices had been several vacant stools lining one corner of the massive black-lacquered bar or a handful of tall tables stationed directly in front of the plate-glass windows. Knowing that it could seriously affect their careers if the press caught wind of them being there together, Grayson had chosen the corner where she wouldn't be on display to anyone passing by outside. Not that many people were out for a casual stroll this late on a blustery February weeknight.

She must've read his mind because she immediately scanned the room as though looking for anyone who might recognize her. It was nearly ten o'clock on a Tuesday night, so the place was empty except for the bartender and a guy in a bright green Eagles hoodie who only seemed interested in the car restoration show on the TV behind the bar.

Tessa shrugged out of her suede coat and asked, "How'd you find this place?"

"Doherty recommended it. He makes it a priority to know all of the less conspicuous drinking establishments within a fifteen-mile radius of wherever we're stationed."

She pulled off her knit cap and set it on the shiny bar top before running a hand through her hair. Grayson's fingers twitched at the memory of touching the same silky strands over a month ago. Thirty-eight days. Not that he was keeping count.

"So Agent Doherty knows we're here?"

Grayson wasn't about to mention that Doherty was the one who'd casually suggested he contact her. "Let's just say he's a wealth of information when it comes to tactical planning and logistics."

The bartender took a break from folding white dishrags and asked for their order. The woman was older, with a stocky build and a disinterested expression. She reminded him of Gunnery Sergeant Haggerty, his senior drill instructor who'd seen everything but, because he'd been closing in on retirement, hadn't wanted to write up any reports.

If the bartender recognized Tessa King, she didn't

let on. Grayson passed the woman a twenty-dollar bill and murmured, "Thanks," after she handed them their drinks.

He nodded at Tessa's plain-looking vodka and soda before picking up his own pilsner. "No beer for you tonight?"

"Nope." She took a careful sip. "It goes down too easily and I wanted to make sure I have a clear head."

Dread crawled through his chest as he waited for her to politely tell him that what had happened between them on the ranch was a one-off. That their fleeting attraction had been the result of forced proximity. But she didn't say anything else.

The guy at the other end of the bar paid his tab and left. The bartender asked if they needed anything before she stepped out back for a smoke. And still, he and Tessa sat there quietly as though neither one of them knew what to say to the other. Maybe having those boundaries of him being on assignment had actually made them both feel safer. Like they could dip their toes in the water, but always had a built-in excuse for why they couldn't fully immerse themselves.

"Are you in Philadelphia for work?" he finally asked, wondering if things were this awkward between Freckles and Rider King when they'd seen each other again. Probably not.

Tessa nodded. "I'm following a lead on a story about election fraud in the next county over. Investigative journalism isn't really my thing, but the whistleblower claimed he'd only talk to me. According to my producer, all that media coverage following my dad's funeral put me in a more sympathetic light and made me seem more approachable."

He finished his icy beer quickly, washing down the memory of Davis Townsend telling Tessa she was a cold, cutthroat bitch. When Grayson had intervened, he'd been hoping the congressman would resist the directive to walk out of the stables, thereby requiring a forced escort.

He flexed his fingers after he set down his empty glass. "I'm glad things are working out for you. Careerwise."

"How about you?" She pivoted slightly on her bar stool. "What brings you to Philadelphia?"

He explained that he was on a protective detail with some foreign dignitaries, but didn't give any specifics.

"So you're back on the job." Tessa studied him. "I'm glad all that business in Wyoming didn't get you into any hot water with your bosses."

"Well, the inquiry board is still investigating." It helped that none of the Kings had filed a formal complaint. "So they haven't taken my badge yet."

"Speaking of your badge..." She took another sip of her drink before moving in closer. Her knee glazed against his and his pulse skyrocketed. "You told me there would come a time when you were no longer on duty."

There was no mistaking the intent in her eyes. It had been the exact same look she'd given him on Pine Top Point. Just like then, his desire threatened to consume him. Unlike then, though, he no longer had to fight to control it. Anticipation raced through him as he flashed a wide grin.

"I am definitely off duty. At least, where you're concerned." He placed his hands on either side of her face and pulled her mouth against his. He stroked his tongue against her lips and when she opened up to him, he kissed her slowly and thoroughly—not caring about his promise to her that the next time they got physical, she could be in the driver's seat.

Later on, they'd have all the time in the world to take turns being in control.

"Grayson?" She pulled back, her lips already swollen and her eyelids half-closed. "Take me back to the hotel."

Tessa's pulse pounded in her ears as she rode the elevator alone to her room. Although Grayson was technically off his shift, he explained that he still had to keep a low profile while inside the hotel and would follow her using the service elevator.

It was for the best, she reminded herself as her fingers drummed against the brass handrail. Neither one of them wanted to risk being seen together in the lobby. Scratch that, Tessa thought as the number for her floor lit up and the doors opened. Being seen in public with Grayson wouldn't be the worst thing in the world. For her, at least. She hadn't been lying when she'd told Grayson that the public's perception of her had changed after the pictures of them together had surfaced.

Tessa let herself into her room and barely had enough time to shrug out of her coat before there was a discreet knock on the door. Grayson stood in the hallway in his jeans and a snug black T-shirt under an open shearling-lined coat, his gaze just as intense as it had been at the bar. All the blood rushed to her head and she braced her hand on the doorjamb to steady herself. *This is really happening.*

"Are you okay?" he asked, concern immediately replacing the passion in his expression.

"Grayson..." She moved to the side, refusing to let her knees buckle as she held the door open for him. "I'm no longer the damsel in distress. You don't have to treat me with kid gloves."

"Good." He dipped his head as he passed through the open door, dragging his eyes down the length of her and then back up. As though he was calculating which part of her body he wanted to caress first. "Because the wait nearly killed me."

The next thing she knew, the door whooshed closed with a definite click and her shoulder blades were arching into the entryway wall. Her arms circled his neck and his hands followed the outline of her curves until settling under her rear end. He barely had to apply any upward pressure and she was lifting her legs, wrapping them around his waist as he thrust his tongue deeper into her mouth.

He groaned and pressed closer. Using his body to brace Tessa against the wall, he peeled his hands away from her butt long enough to shrug out of his jacket. She took the opportunity to tug on the soft cotton fabric between his shoulder blades and pulled the T-shirt over his head.

The motion broke their kiss, but it also allowed him to return the favor. Grayson made quick work of her sweater and the camisole underneath. She leaned forward so that he could access her bra clasp and he secured her hips under one forearm as he set her aching breasts free.

He kissed her again, their bare chests coming together. She moaned as tingling sensations shot through her tightly budded nipples. Recklessness coursed through her and she slid her hands over the smooth, warm ridges of his biceps, pulling him in even tighter so that she could fuse the heat of her skin with his.

Tessa had always been so precise, so careful, so controlled. She needed to let go and Grayson was only too willing to oblige her. She nipped at his lower lip and said, "Take me to the bed."

"Not yet," he murmured against her lips. "Next

time, we'll make it to the bed. But right now, I need you here."

He elevated her even higher and spun them toward the entryway table. When he swung her onto the edge, something went crashing to the floor. Maybe it was a lamp, she thought as she felt for Grayson's belt buckle. If he wasn't going to worry about it, then neither would she. Drawing in a ragged breath, she slipped her hands below his waistband. He was hard and ready for her.

Tessa's entire body vibrated with need. Specifically, the need for him to take her hard and fast. Anything slower or gentler would just be patronizing. She was done with him thinking of her as some sort of delicate flower that needed coddling.

Grayson captured one of her calves and pulled it away from his waist just long enough to unzip her boot and yank it off. The other one followed and, in a matter of seconds, his wide palms were skimming both her jeans and panties off her hips, sending them sliding down her thighs.

He withdrew something from his back pocket right before she pushed his jeans down lower. She heard the tearing of the foil packet. Grayson reached between them to sheath his length in a condom then positioned himself at her entrance. A tremor started deep inside Tessa's core and she was afraid she would lose herself before they'd even started.

His teeth grazed the lobe of her ear as he asked, "You ready for this?"

"Please don't stop now," she told him and linked her ankles behind his back.

Grayson entered her swiftly and she gasped, shuddering from the fullness of him. He dipped his hips lower, adjusting his angle, and joined their bodies together again and again. She didn't know where her breathing started and where his ended. The marbled entryway echoed every moan and whimper and sigh. Each thrust brought him deeper, brought them closer.

His breath was hot and fast against her cheek. His skin smelled of soap and eucalyptus, and she traced her lips along his jawline and back to his mouth, the whiskers of his five-o'clock shadow making her tingle even more. He captured her tongue once again and dug his fingers into the curve of her hips, holding her in place as he brought her to the highest peak.

He let out a final groan as he shuddered, his release coming right after hers. When the aftershocks faded, Tessa felt the rise and fall of his chest against hers. Their heart rates returned to a normal pace and he buried his mouth against the softest part of her neck.

Tessa didn't think it was possible, but Grayson lifted her even closer to him. He held her tightly as he walked toward the bed. When he lay down next to her on the white sheets, his finger started a trail at her collarbone, moving between her breasts and dipping below her belly button.

She shivered then offered him a satisfied smile. "Now what?"

"Now—" he moved over her "—I'm going to take my time."

Grayson caught sight of a bruise on Tessa's right hip as she stretched in bed early the following morning. Wincing, he asked, "Did I do that?"

"I hope so." She smiled at him. Her eyes glanced at the bedside clock and she gave him a sly grin. "Do you have time before your shift starts to kiss it and make it better?"

Growling, his hand snaked around her waist and he pulled her to him. But before they could start another round of lovemaking, her smartphone vibrated on the nightstand with an incoming call. He tried to ignore it, but then there were a series of pings as the screen lit up with several notification bubbles.

Tessa sighed. "I should probably get that."

She stretched across him to reach for her phone and he took the opportunity to playfully lick the pink nipple poised directly over his head. Unfortunately, her groan wasn't one of pleasure.

He scooted out from underneath her and saw that her face had lost some color. "What's wrong?"

Instead of replying, she showed him her phone screen and his stomach sank. The image on the screen showed Grayson and Tessa clinging to each other in a passionate kiss. In the picture, he could make out the rows of liquor bottles behind them, the green knit cap sitting on the bar beside Tessa.

He didn't bother asking the question he already knew the answer to. The photo could only have been taken last night, when they'd been so engrossed in each other, he hadn't thought about anything else. Grayson sagged against the upholstered headboard, resting his elbows on his knees as he rubbed at his face and dragged his hands through his hair.

He breathed in through his nose several times as he struggled to bring his frustration under control. When he finally raised his head, Tessa was staring off into the distance. He put his hand under her chin and forced her to look at him. "I'm sorry, Tess. I should've had better situational awareness. I knew the huge windows were a risk and I let my guard down."

Instead of berating him—like she had the first time they'd met—she smoothed his hair off his forehead. "You weren't on duty, remember? It wasn't your responsibility to protect me or my reputation last night. Besides, it's not like anyone could really confirm it's us."

The tiniest flicker of hope spiked through his chest, even as he lowered an eyebrow in doubt.

"Look." She held up the phone again. "It only

shows the sides of our faces and they're all smooshed together..."

Her voice trailed off as her thumb swiped the screen and another image appeared. This time, it was a picture of them turned toward each other, not quite kissing, so their profiles were easier to identify. She swiped again and there they were, facing the camera—wherever it had been hiding—and holding hands as they exited the bar. In the third shot, there was absolutely no question that the people in the photo were Grayson and Tessa.

Damn. His fist clenched the pillow as he fought the urge to throw something across the room. Instead of succumbing to his mounting frustration, he slipped the phone from her hand and brought it closer so he could read the article underneath. His eyes landed on phrases like "bodyguard for hire" and "boy toy" and "Davis Townsend's replacement."

But the worst part of the article was the last paragraph where it listed his name and what exactly he did for the Secret Service, including his office location and team assignment. There was even a picture of Grayson in full tactical gear with several other agents when he'd been on the counter assault team a few years ago.

He was no longer the mysterious Agent Steamy, he realized as his blood ran cold. Not only had his cover been blown, his entire career had been turned into tabloid fodder. It would only be a matter of time

until the press got wind of Maddie and started showing up at her hospital.

"How do you deal with this all the time?" he
asked, unable to hide the disgust in his voice.

"Deal with what? The complete lack of privacy?"
Tessa shrugged, taking her phone back. "I grew up
with it. My dad was in high-profile politics before
I was even born. Being surrounded by cameras
constantly is a tough lifestyle, but it's all I've ever
known."

"Most of your siblings could say the same thing.
Yet you're the only King who sought a career in the
limelight."

"I didn't seek it." Tessa pulled the sheet up over
her naked breasts and lifted her chin. "I majored in
political science because it was a way to understand
my father better, to understand the thing he loved
as much as his family. It turned from researching
to analyzing and, eventually, my dad coming to me
for advice. I'd had a front-row seat to government
in action my whole life and I was good at asking the
right questions and digging for answers. The cameras
were there long before I came along. I just learned
how to do what I was good at while they were already rolling."

"Remember that time you commented on how I
never seemed to be off duty?" he asked then waited
for her stiff nod before continuing. "Well, when does
Tessa King ever get a break to just be herself? Don't

you ever get tired of constantly being on display for the world to see? With always having to fall in line with the public's perception of you whether you agree with it or not?"

Tessa's spine straightened. "Grayson, this is my life. My career. Yes, I chose it. And I'd choose it again because I'm doing a job that I love. A job that I think actually matters. People deserve to have a free press and access to global information. Not all journalists and reporters are like these guys." She pointed to the name of the online gossip rag on her screen.

"I get that. But it's nobody's business whether or not *'Beautiful Heiress Tessa King Slips Off to Love Nest with Sexy Bodyguard,'*" he quoted the headline. "I never asked for this kind of notoriety."

"Grayson, I never intended for you to be the subject of unwanted fame and attention. I don't blame you for being upset. But at the end of the day, this is what my job entails. I want you in my life. However, if you want to have any sort of relationship with me, then this is part of the package."

Grayson tried to latch onto the words he'd wanted to hear since he'd left the Twin Kings Ranch. Tessa King wanted him in her life. The bond they shared was way more than just a physical attraction.

Instead of euphoria, though, it was a bittersweetness that hung in the air between them. Because no matter how much they might want to be together, there was too much keeping them apart.

"Of course I want to have a relationship with you, Tessa." Grayson climbed out of the bed and looked around the hotel room floor for his discarded pants. "I don't want to have to sneak around to have one, either. When we were on the ranch, I fell for you harder than I could've imagined. The problem is that *my* job, *my* life, demands discretion. I'm trained to stay in the shadows and not draw any attention to the people I'm protecting. I can't do my job if the paparazzi are constantly dogging me or flashing my picture all over the internet."

He was also trained to retreat and reformulate a plan once he determined what he was up against. Or maybe this was it. The battle was over and it was time to admit defeat and tend to his wounds.

Grayson finally found his jeans on the marble floor in the entryway. Right next to the upended lamp he'd knocked over when he'd made love to Tessa before they could reach the bed. The memory flooded through him, taking some of the sting out of his disappointment. He yanked his jeans into place, trying not to think of her breathy little pants last night as she'd begged him for more.

Tessa appeared in the entryway behind him, her messy blond curls framing her proud face. She'd kept the sheet wrapped around her torso, but her swollen lips were turned down at the corners.

"When I met you at the bar last night, I'd hoped for a better ending than this," she offered. "I fell for you just as hard. Literally. I'd tried to stay away this past month to give us space so we could figure out who we were outside of the ranch, and what we both wanted. But it looks like this is how things have to be if we both want to keep doing what we're made to do. I'm sorry, Grayson."

"I know." He exhaled. "I'm sorry, too."

She didn't tell him to stay. She didn't tell him that they could work through this together. Most important, she didn't ask him to give up his job or anything else to be with her.

In that moment, Grayson loved her even more.

His phone pinged from inside his jacket pocket, where he'd left it last night. He pulled it out to see an incoming message from SAIC Simon. Just when Grayson thought his heart couldn't take any more blows, another round breached his walls.

"Listen. I've got to go to work." He didn't add that Simon had just informed him he was officially off protective detail now that his temporary celebrity status could compromise the assignment. He didn't want Tessa to blame herself.

Twelve hours ago, he'd never expected them to ride into the sunset together. So then why did it suddenly feel as though he was leaving part of himself behind? Grayson's insides twisted with remorse knowing that this was the end of the road for them. Things had ended almost as quickly as they had begun.

The longing for her, though, would likely never go away.

Tessa stood there, the sheet clasped around her, her shoulders back and her chin high. She may be disappointed, but she wouldn't admit it. Tessa King would dive into another new project in no time.

Before he walked out the door, he gave her cheek one last caress and whispered, "Take care of yourself."

Chapter Thirteen

"No, I haven't heard from him in over three days," Tessa told Aunt Freckles the following Saturday afternoon via video chat from the comfort of the sleek leather sofa inside her Georgetown town house. Freckles must have set her smartphone on the counter while she poured batter into cupcake cups because Tessa could see most of the Twin Kings' kitchen in the background.

She was surprised at the pang of wistfulness for her childhood home. Perhaps it had to do with the fact that everyone in her family was busy today prepping for a birthday party for Marcus's twins. After spending so much time in Wyoming recently, Tessa suddenly felt as though she was missing out on something.

"So he split, just like that, huh?" Freckles called out over her shoulder as she slid a tray of cupcakes into the oven. "Do you know if he's still in Philadelphia?"

Tessa shook her head. "At least, I don't think so. I ran into Agent Doherty in the Ritz lobby the day after we, uh, had drinks." She certainly wasn't going to give her aunt too many details and risk Freckles wanting to return the favor by offering up details of her and Uncle Rider's bedroom time. Tessa shuddered before continuing. "Doherty said Grayson was transferred from the assignment. He didn't say where, and I was too embarrassed to ask."

"What do you have to be embarrassed about?" Freckles asked as she returned to her mixing bowl, which must have been where the phone was propped because all Tessa could see was a close-up view of the Cowgirl Up Café logo across the woman's too tight T-shirt.

Tessa blinked several times before deciding it was easier to focus on the cherry blossom trees outside her window than on her senior citizen aunt's substantial bosom. "Because it was being with me that cost Grayson his job. Or at least his job in the Protective Intelligence Division."

"Darlin', don't you ever apologize for being a woman in the prime of your life. You have physical needs. Heck, we all do." Freckles added with a chuckle, "It's why I keep letting your uncle Rider talk me into staying at his cabin every night."

This was the exact visual Tessa had been trying to avoid. But how could she fault anyone for sharing too much information about their love life? Half the world had seen that intimate picture of Tessa and Grayson making out in some dive bar in Philadelphia.

"Now, I know sometimes men don't always think with the head upstairs." Freckles used a measuring spoon to point at her helmet of orangish-colored curls. "But, from what I saw, that Agent Wyatt is a planner. One of those fellas that calculates risks and strategies and keeps an eye out for hidden land mines. You never pretended to be anyone other than yourself. He knew exactly what he was getting into from the moment he first met you."

Tessa let the words settle over her. "Maybe that's why he seemed to already have his exit strategy in place."

"Then again..." Freckles tsked as she returned to the center island to pour out another batch. "Fame's not for everyone, darlin'. I couldn't wait to leave it all behind the second I turned eighteen. The day after my debutante ball, I hauled butt outta Boston so fast, those Beacon Hill society matrons' heads were spinning."

"I know." Tessa frowned, trying to figure out if

her aunt was on her side or his. Freckles could play a mean devil's advocate. "I don't blame Grayson for not wanting to be a part of all that. Deep inside, I think we both knew that anything serious between us wouldn't have worked in the long run. I guess I was just hoping things could've lasted a little longer."

"If I've learned a little something from my seventy-plus years on this earth, it's how to deal with heartbreak."

"Seventy-plus years?" Tessa's mother glided into the kitchen just then and stopped at the specialty blender on the counter behind Freckles. "More like eighty-plus years."

Freckles flicked some of the flour off her hands and the white powder clung to the back of Sherilee's bright cashmere sweater.

Tessa rolled her eyes at the two women. Maybe she didn't miss home as much as she'd first thought. Normally, she would've called Duke for advice, but he was on a classified assignment.

"I'm not suffering from anything as serious as heartbreak, Aunt Freckles," Tessa said, knowing full well it was a lie. If she hadn't already been half in love with Grayson when he'd been on that diving board with her, then it would've happened when he'd done the gentlemanly thing and given her the space to figure out her feelings on her own.

"When you think about the man, does your rib cage get all tight? Do you spend so much time thinking about what he might be doing that when you walk into a room, you forget why you went in there in the first place?" The loose skin on Freckles's neck wobbled as she nodded knowingly. "If so, it's definitely a broken heart."

"It could also be another panic attack." Her mom dropped a bag of fresh kale as she rushed over to the smartphone screen. "Have you seen your neurologist yet, Contessa?"

"It's not a panic attack, Mom. Or heartbreak. It's just…" An empty feeling, Tessa thought. A feeling of jumping off a high dive and expecting to hit the water but just free-falling into air. She bit back the words to keep from saying as much out loud. "I don't know what it is."

"Uh-oh." Sherilee narrowed her eyes as though she could study Tessa's emotions through the screen. "You don't know what it is because you've never felt it before. I experienced the same thing when I fell head-over-heels for your father. I was young. I'd never been in love before. I thought I had my life all planned out in my mind. Then Roper King showed up and turned my whole world upside down. One minute I was telling myself all the reasons why this older guy with a campaign bus full of baggage was all wrong for me and the next I couldn't imagine spending my life without him."

Tessa didn't like how eerily similar her mother's past experience was sounding to her own. She shook off the feeling. "In this situation, though, I *have* to imagine my life without Grayson. His job and mine just aren't compatible and neither one of us could ask the other to give up so much. Unlike you and Dad, it's just not meant to be."

"Not meant to be?" Sherilee King asked. "You're talking to a girl who went from the trailer park to the Twin Kings to the White House. You think being married to Roper King was a walk in the park? He was a recovering alcoholic and I was a cocktail waitress and half his age. Talk about incompatible lives. You should've heard what the press used to say when we'd show up at an event. But we didn't let that stop us. We didn't throw up our hands in the air and say it wasn't meant to be."

"Wait. You were a cocktail waitress?" Of all the things her mother had just shared, Tessa wasn't sure why she'd narrowed in on that one tiny detail. Maybe it was because of Sherilee's well-known disapproval of Dahlia running Big Millie's. "Dad met you in a bar?"

"He'd fallen off the wagon, so to speak, and I helped him get back on. So contrary to popular belief," her mother gave a pointed look at Aunt Freckles, "it was me who rescued him first. Not the other way around."

"Wow. I never knew that." Tessa let out the breath she hadn't known she'd been holding. "Clearly, Dad wanted to be rescued. And lucky for all of us that he did."

"But?" her mom prompted.

"But, I don't think that's the case with Grayson. He likes his life the way it is."

Sherilee brought the phone so close to her face, Tessa could practically see the hidden incisions of last year's eye lift. "If his job's an obstacle, I could always have a word with the director. He won't ever have to know."

"Oh my gosh, Mom! You sound like a mob boss. I don't want you to have Grayson fired."

"How about we just get him reassigned to something more manageable? Maybe he'd like a desk job once he got used to it. The commissioner over at the Internal Revenue Service owes me a favor..."

"Mom! Stop! You can't fix this. I have to let Grayson go."

"But what if..."

"The best way to get over a man—" Freckles's bright fingernails flashed on the screen before she wrestled the smartphone out of Sherilee's grip "—is to learn and grow from the relationship, no matter how brief it might've been."

"Well, you'd be the one to know, seeing as how you're the queen of brief relationships," Tessa's mother muttered to her aunt.

Freckles thankfully refused to take the bait. "Listen, darlin'. What you need to do is find something good that came out of the affair. What did you learn from it? How are you a better person from it?"

"Or you can always throw yourself into charity." Her mom stuck a spoon into a bowl of chocolate frosting. "That's what I always do to get my mind off things."

Mom shoved the spoon in her mouth quickly, but Freckles had eyes in the back of her head. "Then why don't you go volunteer somewhere, Sherilee, instead of stress eating all my food before this afternoon's party?"

"Because my kids all need me here right now." Her mother continued to list every single cause for stress—no matter how insignificant—currently occurring on Twin Kings Ranch. Each one involved one of Tessa's siblings and whomever they may or may not be dating.

By the time Tessa disconnected the call, she suddenly wished she had her own tray of cupcakes to shovel down her mouth. She walked to the kitchen, wanting to dive into a meal or something else that would take her mind off her heartbreak. *Disappointment*, she quickly corrected herself, wishing her aunt had never used the *H* word.

But the only food in her refrigerator was a three-day-old chicken-and-pesto wrap from the craft services table at work, and half a jar of green olives. Tessa decided to avoid the risk of any lurking photographers camping out in front of the gourmet market down the street and placed an online order for grocery delivery.

Shopping for dinner on an empty stomach had been a mistake, though, she later realized when all the items in her virtual shopping cart totaled over five hundred dollars and couldn't be delivered for almost three hours. Instead of waiting patiently for her groceries, she called her favorite Thai take-out place and the manager promised to have her order of coconut chicken soup and drunken noodles at her front door in less than thirty minutes.

With dinner on its way, Tessa was left to ponder how she could grow from her extremely short-lived relationship with Grayson. She returned to her laptop and tapped absently at the mouse. What did she learn from Agent Wyatt? Other than that little trick he did with his tongue when he…

Focus, she commanded her brain. Opening the internet home page, she tried scrolling through her search history. She really needed to clean out her web browser, she concluded as she looked at everything she'd researched in the past few months. There had to be something in here that might trigger an idea.

She was still tapping at the down arrow when her eyes landed on it.

EDMD.

Maddie's medical condition. Tessa had asked Grayson about his sister at some point during the evening when they'd slept together. He'd told her that Maddie's procedure was showing some signs of progress and allowing her more movement. He'd tamped down Tessa's excitement by reminding her that Maddie would never regain the full use of her muscles. But even Grayson couldn't hide the twinkle of hope when he'd added, "The good news is that the doctors think she might be able to eventually get back on a horse one day."

His words about getting back on a horse replayed in Tessa's mind as she ate her Thai food and researched equestrian therapy opportunities. By the end of the night, she'd scribbled down a slew of notes and had the perfect idea on how to implement both Freckles's and her mother's advice at the same time.

Tessa would use what she'd learned from her relationship with Grayson to make someone else's world a better place.

Grayson hadn't seen Tessa in almost a month—in person at least. He'd caught a glimpse of her on a television set in the lobby of the hospital when he'd been waiting for Maddie to be discharged a couple of weeks ago. Then again last Tuesday when she'd been on location in the Midwest, discussing the aftermath of a multivortex tornado that had left the residents of a poorer community without electricity and running water while a neighboring county with a higher tax revenue had its power restored immediately.

Seeing her on the screen each time made his lungs

seize midbreath, as though someone had sucker punched him in the solar plexus. If it was painful enough for him to watch her from hundreds of miles away, he didn't want to think about how painful it would be if he saw her in person.

When the inquiry board had concluded its investigation and he'd been cleared to return to his team, Grayson had expected to feel a sense of relief. A sense of closure where Tessa King had been concerned. But then an instructor at the James J. Rowley Training Center referenced the funeral incident involving Tessa as a case study in tactical emergencies, and asked Grayson to speak to a class of recruits about unusual protective detail scenarios.

The presentation and subsequent role-playing drills during Grayson's crisis training simulations went so well, the director at the JJRTC invited him to formally transfer to Maryland and become a permanent instructor. The change in assignment was not only closer to his family in Baltimore, it meant that news vans had less access to him on the enclosed five-hundred-acre facility.

While he'd always preferred being in the role of operative—the guy who comes in and gets the job done—he had to be totally honest. Ever since that night on the diving board with Tessa, Grayson had gotten a taste for inspiring others. Now he looked forward to the challenges of training the up-and-coming agents.

Plus, the new assignment came along with his pick of challenging physical endurance courses, firing ranges and bomb detection simulations whenever he needed an adrenaline fix. Intense tactical training and hand-to-hand combat beat a boring six-mile jog any day of the week.

Grayson's phone vibrated against his belt right as he finished his workout on the rope course with the Spec Ops team. He was still catching his breath when he swiped his thumb across the screen to answer.

"Hey, Mads. How was pool therapy today?"

"Forget about pool therapy, Grayson." His sister's words came out in a rush. "Have you seen the pledge drive?"

"What pledge drive?" he asked, digging into his duffel bag for his stainless steel canteen.

"The one Tessa King launched last night on her show. Didn't you watch?"

Grayson almost choked on his gulp of water. He cleared his throat and then unclipped himself from his harness. He didn't tell his kid sister that watching his ex—did Tessa even qualify as an ex if they'd only spent one night together?—made him feel as though a hiking carabiner was clamped around his heart.

"Nah, I missed it."

"Well, she did an hour-long special about neurological disabilities and the need for physical therapy facilities outside of doctors' offices. Grayson, remember that horse camp I went to when we were teens?" Maddie didn't give him a chance to answer. "She had the owner of Let's Ride on her show talking about how it's not just kids that need to be on horseback, or zip-lining through the trees, or rowing across lakes or any of other things that get people rehabbing in the fresh air. And she's right. I mean, it's great for the kids, of course. And I'm all for her raising money for camps like that. But those kids are going to grow up someday, hopefully, and then where do they go? No more fancy unconventional rehab programs for them. No more horses or aquatic centers unless they have the money to pay for them out of pocket."

"Slow down," Grayson told his sister, but should've told his own mind because his head was already spinning. "You're saying Tessa King is trying to raise money for adults with physical limitations to go to horse camps?"

"Not trying to, Grayson. She already did. After only twenty-four hours, the fund she started, called— get this—the Coach Oliver Foundation, has already raised twelve million dollars. She's also lobbying for more insurance companies to cover alternative forms of physical therapy."

He stood motionless as the information sank in. All of the football players at Montgomery High had loved Coach Oliver Wyatt. He'd never told Tessa anything about his father, yet somehow she'd found out and named the foundation after a man she hadn't even met. Grayson's heart went from being squeezed to being in danger of flying out of his chest.

Maddie kept talking and it took Grayson a few seconds to catch up to what his sister had just said. "What did you just say about sweeps week?"

"I said that every other station and newspaper is reporting nonstop about that scandal with General What's-His-Name. But Tessa waited for the peak week during the Nielsen sweeps, when TV ratings are at an all-time high, to use her time on the air to help people like our family. See, Grayson. Not everyone in the media is a vulture out to pick your bones clean."

Grayson chugged more water, as if he could refill the sudden emptiness churning inside. "When did I ever tell you that?"

"The day before the doctors released me. Mom had just seen that article with you and Tessa King kissing in some magazine she'd found in the hospital cafeteria. She asked you if you were actually dating Tessa and you told her not to believe everything she read in the news. Then she told you a picture was worth a thousand words and—"

"I remember," he interrupted before she could get to the part where their mom warned him that being in the spotlight was preferable to him living in the shadows. "I thought you'd been asleep when she brought that up."

"You guys always have the best conversations

when you think I'm sleeping. Like that time you told her that you were enlisting in the military instead of going straight to college, and she told you that Daddy would've wanted you to finish your education. Or that time when you told her that you and Jamie were getting divorced, and she told you that someday the right woman would come along and you'd realize that there was so much more to life than sacrificing yourself to the overtime gods."

Grayson's stomach was now full of both water and guilt. He tossed his empty canteen back inside his bag. "Did you also overhear us the time we were talking about you no longer watching those true crime documentaries because you were the worst detective ever?"

"Nah, I must've been sleeping for real during *that* conversation." Maddie laughed. "Hey, I gotta go. I have an online class starting in two minutes. But make sure you check out the website for the Coach Oliver Foundation."

They disconnected and Grayson hauled his gear and rucksack across the sprawling campus to the dorm rooms where some of the instructors stayed during the week. He couldn't remember the last time he'd slept in a bed that he actually owned.

His mom and Maddie had downsized to a smaller, inexpensive apartment when he'd joined the Marines. Grayson'd had a handful of furnished rental units here and there, including the six months he and Jamie had lived overseas. But he'd lived most of his adult life out of barracks, hotel rooms and bunkhouses.

As he let himself into the dorm and appraised the cheap blue comforter, along with the basic dresser and matching desk, a vision of the main house at the Twin Kings Ranch popped into his head. What would it feel like to actually live in a real home? Not one that expensive or vast, obviously. But one that had been built and decorated specifically for his tastes. One that had Tessa relaxing inside after they'd both come home from a fulfilling day at work.

Grayson took a quick shower—at least these temporary accommodations had a private bathroom—then powered on his laptop. He had a few minutes before teaching his next class and should've spent the time researching apartments in the nearby town of Laurel, Maryland.

Instead, he found himself scrolling through the Coach Oliver Foundation's website. The digital counter on the bottom of the screen kept changing numbers as donations poured in by the minute. Even though he'd once lumped Tessa into the same boat as tabloid reporters on the prowl for a sensationalized story, deep down he'd known she'd always used her media platform for good. Whether it was bringing awareness to those in need, or exposing corporate and government corruption, or interrogating some of the most powerful people in the world, she didn't back down from a challenge. Just like her diving, she did everything thoroughly and with exacting precision.

She also didn't invest herself in a matter unless it was important to her. All this time, Grayson had been so preoccupied thinking about that video recording of her in the staging center tent, and worrying about her throwing him under the bus, he hadn't realized he'd been doing exactly the same thing to her when he'd left her like that.

Tessa was one of the few people who knew that Maddie's care was a top priority in his life. Instead of cutting all ties with him when he'd told her he couldn't date someone with her level of fame, she'd spun that fame to *his* advantage. Or, at least, to his sister's.

That had to mean she still cared about him, right? And maybe if she still cared, there was a chance he could convince her that he'd made the biggest mistake of his life when he'd walked out of the hotel room. Grayson wasn't convinced she'd forgive him, but for the first time in weeks, he was also full of hope.

There was no way to know if Tessa would even consider the possibility of a partnership again after he'd already refused to go into battle with her once. All Grayson knew was that the most successful missions required an advance plan. He picked up his phone and called the only person he knew with a special forces background and a working knowledge of seeking forgiveness from a female in the King family.

When Rider King answered, Grayson cleared his throat.

"Hello, sir. I was wondering if I could talk with you about Tessa."

Chapter Fourteen

Grayson never should have listened to the wily old rancher, he thought as he led his class of recruits across the South Lawn of the White House. The chairs had already been placed in the Rose Garden for an informal awards ceremony, and his students were in attendance merely for observational purposes.

Somehow, Rider King had talked Grayson into convincing his director and the director of the protective detail assigned to the White House that the recruits needed practical, real world application of their training in the most boring of circumstances.

It just so happened that the boring circumstance

Grayson deemed most suitable for the training was one in which former Second Lady Sherilee King was to be awarded the Presidential Medal of Freedom in recognition of her contributions to philanthropy.

Not that anything was all that boring when the entire King family came together.

Briefing all the agents on duty and the president's chief of staff had been one of the most awkward presentations Grayson had ever endured. But if things went according to plan, nobody would know the real reason he'd staged such an unbelievable scenario.

"Precision has landed," Grayson heard in his earpiece as he herded the recruits to the observation area. That meant Tessa was on the premises. But they still had a few minutes before everyone took their seats. It wasn't until he saw the news cameras setting up that Grayson realized there'd be no going back after this.

He spotted Rider King near some foliage outside the west colonnade, the gray felt Stetson he wore for "fancy occasions" making him stand out above everyone else. Grayson strode over to the older man and asked, "Sir, are you sure this will work?"

"Not if Freckles catches me out here, it won't." Rider held out a circular tin of chewing tobacco to Grayson. "Want a dip?"

"I don't mean sneaking out here for a wad of chew." Grayson tried to ignore the pounding in his temples. "I meant this plan today with me and Tessa."

"Considerin' you haven't found any other way to get her attention..." the old man started then shrugged. "I don't see how it could hurt your chances none."

"But won't Mrs. King be upset that we're upstaging her award ceremony?"

"It was Sherilee who thought of this idea in the first place, son. I'm just a good soldier who does what I'm told."

"Oh hell." Grayson looked upward, hoping a freak thunderstorm would engulf him. But the April sky was a clear blue.

Mrs. King walked up at just that moment and used her little purse to swat the container out of her brother-in-law's hand. "Rider King, you know full well that tobacco products aren't allowed on government property."

Rider jumped back. "Damn it, woman, I thought you were Freckles. That sounded exactly like the kinda thing she would say."

Mrs. King's eyes darted back and forth between him and the half-empty tin. She sighed. "Carry on, then."

Grayson wanted to commend the older man on his well-played reverse psychology, but Tessa's mother turned her attention to him instead. "It looks like all the camera crews are in position. Are you ready?"

"I'm ready, ma'am. However, I do have just a few concerns about the execution of this particular strategy."

Mrs. King gave him a chilling look. "You changed your mind about Tessa?"

"No, it's not that at all. I love your daughter, ma'am, and I wouldn't be here right now if I didn't want to be with her." Grayson waited for Mrs. King's pursed mouth to relax before he continued. "Remember when Davis Townsend came out to the ranch to propose to Tessa? Wasn't that your idea, too?"

"Of course it was."

"Well, that didn't work out so well. Why would this time be any different?"

Mrs. King rolled her eyes. "What are you talking about? Davis did exactly what I wanted him to do and Tessa reacted exactly as I'd expected. She'd been dragging that breakup on for way too long and sometimes we just need to rip the Band-Aid off, if you know what I'm saying."

"So you knew she'd break up with him?" he asked, bewildered.

Mrs. King's sigh was one of exasperation. "Obviously. The trick was getting Townsend to bring his press secretary along. Tessa doesn't mind the cameras when it's for work. But she hates all that extra publicity just to show off."

"But then why are we…" Grayson started and Mrs. King swatted at the air, dismissing his confusion as if it was an annoying fly.

"If Davis had truly cared about my daughter, he would've foregone the cameras and kept things private. But he wasn't willing to step outside his comfort zone for her. But you, Agent Wyatt? You're willing to make a real sacrifice. That's the ultimate gesture." Mrs. King looped her arm through Rider's. "Now, let's all get into position."

Grayson looked toward the sky again, wondering if there had in fact been a thunderstorm, because Mrs. King's reasoning left him in a fall-out shelter of confusion.

He should have been comforted by the woman's faith in him and this plan. But no other mission had been as important to him as this one.

He couldn't lose Tessa for good.

"And none of this would have been possible if I didn't have the loving support of my family behind me," Tessa's mother said into the eight microphones affixed to the podium. Shutters clicked all around them, and Tessa fought the urge to look around at the Secret Service agents hovering in the background to see if any of them might be Grayson.

But he was long gone and her plan to get over him by diving into a charitable endeavor had backfired. Planning the fundraiser with Maddie and Mrs. Wyatt only made Tessa miss Grayson all the more.

"Come on up here, kids," her mom said, and Uncle Rider gave Tessa a nudge.

What? This wasn't part of the plan. The president was supposed to award her mom the medal, her mom was supposed to give a brief speech, and then they were supposed to meet in the West Wing reception area for light refreshments and some informal pictures. Nobody was supposed to be called onstage.

Tessa's eyes shot to Marcus who was already halfway to the podium with a sullen MJ in tow. Next, she looked at Dahlia and Finn, who were both refusing to make eye contact with her as they took turns pushing one another to the front of the pack. She finally got Duke's attention.

"What's going on?" Tessa asked under her breath as they joined their siblings. "Mom never goes off script."

"Remember what Dad said the first time he taught you how to jump into an eddy in the Snake River?" Duke replied, but the crowd was clapping politely and he had to pause so that he could smile and wave to the cameras aimed in their direction. Her brother glanced at something behind Tessa and then finished, "Just tuck your knees up and roll with it."

Tessa barely had time to process his words when she felt herself being lifted into the air. An *oomph* escaped her lips as she bounced against a solid chest. Then she saw who that chest belonged to and all the air left her body.

"This gets easier every time I do it," Grayson said into her ear as he turned toward the wall of lenses zooming in on them. He cradled her in his arms as reporters yelled out questions, but the only thing she could hear right that second was her pounding heart. And him. "But I have no problem practicing it over and over again until I get it right."

"What are you doing here?" Tessa tilted her head as she looked between Grayson's face and the entire press corps assigned to the White House. She tentatively wrapped her arms around his shoulders for balance.

"Well, I thought I could go back to my own life and you could go back to yours. But I was absolutely lost without you," he said, and Tessa was glad he was holding her because her legs would've turned to jelly. "So, I'm making another daring rescue. Except this time, I'm rescuing myself."

Another wave of shuttering cameras peppered the air and she lifted her brow. "Isn't this the part where you usually sprint us off to safety?"

"I want them to look their fill and take as many pictures as they need." Then Grayson kissed her, right there in front of her family, and the president and the entire world watching from home. When he finally pulled back, he stared into her eyes as though they were the only two people there. "I love you, Tessa King, and that's not something I ever want to keep to myself again."

Tessa's chest couldn't contain all the pounding and excitement racing through her heart. She'd known that he cared for her, but she hadn't thought he'd be willing to give up everything else in his life for her. "But what about your job?"

"I transferred to the JJRTC to become an instructor. Apparently, the recruits seem to think that my unfounded celebrity status somehow means I actually know what I'm teaching them."

"And the notoriety?" She bit her lower lip.

He hefted her closer to him. "You told me that being with you meant that I had to accept being in the spotlight. It'll be a learning curve for me, and I can't always promise that I'll do or say the right things when the cameras are rolling. But I'd rather be by your side than anywhere else in the world. This is my way of proving it to you."

Tessa pulled his face to hers and kissed him again. "I love you, too, Grayson. I promise to hold on to you this time, to be *your* protector and to try to shield you whenever I can. If things ever get too overwhelming, we can always go hide out at the ranch."

Just when she thought her heart was going to burst, her family closed ranks around them, making the moment even more special because they were all a part of it.

Uncle Rider tugged his cowboy hat lower on his head and asked, "So, who planned the exit strategy?"

"Well, you guys told me I couldn't bring the horses." Finn threw her arms up. "So I thought someone else was planning it."

"Don't look at me." MJ shoved his hands into his

pockets. "Sheriff Big Brother over there is still holding my driver's license hostage."

Everyone began speaking at once and, as her family argued among themselves, Tessa asked Grayson, "Are you sure you know what you signed up for?"

"Not really. When it comes to you and your family, I'm finding that all my rules and careful strategizing can easily be blown off course. You're the only assignment I want, though, so it looks like I'll just have to hold steady."

"Then let's get out of here." Tessa smiled at him before giving him another kiss.

Grayson walked her through the Rose Garden, over the South Lawn and toward the Ellipse. "I didn't want to leave any of the planning to your family, so I took the liberty of securing a transport vehicle for our dramatic exit."

She narrowed her eyes. "I love you, Agent Wyatt, but there's no way I'm getting into another hearse with you."

He barked out a laugh and she felt his chest vibrate against her.

"Don't worry." Grayson nodded toward the helipad. She turned to see the small green helicopter with the Buster Chop's Chopper Rentals logo on the tail. "I got the next best thing."

* * * * *

MILLS & BOON

Coming next month

ITALIAN ESCAPE WITH THE CEO
Nina Milne

'What's wrong?'

'Nothing. Just keep talking. But I think we've been spotted.' Out of the corner of her peripheral vision, she saw someone point at their pod, camera in hand. 'We *have* been spotted.' Her mind went into overdrive, on automatic she appraised the scene. Champagne, private pod, the whole thing shrieked of date night. This was the perfect set up for a launch of their relationship, discovered by accident, it would reek of authenticity.

Instinct took over; and leaning over she kissed him; her intent had been a simple quick featherlight brush of the lips but she hadn't bargained for her body's reaction. Or his. Because it wasn't enough, the sheer giddy sensation whirled her head. After a first startled second where he froze, he turned his body, raised his hands and cupped her face in his hands, the firm cool grasp made her catch her breath.

Then he deepened the kiss, slowly languorously as if they had all the time in the world and Ava forgot where she was; forgot everything except this heady moment in time where nothing mattered except the sweet sensations that glided through her whole body. Then all too soon it was over, the wheel literally stopped turning and Ava realised they were near the top.

As she pulled away she caught sight of his expression, knew it mirrored her own. Shell shock, surprise. All wrong screamed the one bit of her brain that was still in gear. Pull this together. Seamlessly she pulled a smile to her lips and whispered. 'Don't look surprised.' Knew that a photo like that splashed on social media would give away too much.

To her relief Liam got it instantly, leant forward to hide his expression, looked as though he were whispering sweet nothings in her ear and then he moved away to pick up the champagne bottle to top up their glasses, a smile of sorts on his lips.

Ava focused on breathing, sipped the champagne, wished it were the bubbles that were swirling her head rather than the aftermath of the kiss. 'Sorry. I reacted on instinct – I saw an opportunity to make this look real and I took it without thinking.'

'There's no need to apologise – you took me by surprise that's all.' With an obvious effort he cleared his throat, brought his voice to a normal tone. 'What do you think will happen now?'

Continue reading
ITALIAN ESCAPE WITH THE CEO
Nina Milne

Available next month
www.millsandboon.co.uk

COMING SOON!

We really hope you enjoyed reading this book.
If you're looking for more romance, be sure to
head to the shops when new books are
available on

Thursday 7th January

To see which titles are coming soon, please visit

millsandboon.co.uk/nextmonth

MILLS & BOON

MILLS & BOON

THE HEART OF ROMANCE

A ROMANCE FOR EVERY KIND OF READER

MODERN

Prepare to be swept off your feet by sophisticated, sexy and seductive heroes, in some of the world's most glamourous and romantic locations, where power and passion collide.
8 stories per month.

HISTORICAL

Escape with historical heroes from time gone by. Whether your passion is for wicked Regency Rakes, muscled Vikings or rugged Highlanders, awaken the romance of the past.
6 stories per month.

MEDICAL

Set your pulse racing with dedicated, delectable doctors in the high-pressure world of medicine, where emotions run high and passion, comfort and love are the best medicine.
6 stories per month.

True Love

Celebrate true love with tender stories of heartfelt romance, from the rush of falling in love to the joy a new baby can bring, and a focus on the emotional heart of a relationship.
8 stories per month.

Desire

Indulge in secrets and scandal, intense drama and plenty of sizzling hot action with powerful and passionate heroes who have it all: wealth, status, good looks…everything but the right woman.
6 stories per month.

HEROES

Experience all the excitement of a gripping thriller, with an intense romance at its heart. Resourceful, true-to-life women and strong, fearless men face danger and desire - a killer combination!
8 stories per month.

DARE

Sensual love stories featuring smart, sassy heroines you'd want as a best friend, and compelling intense heroes who are worthy of them.
4 stories per month.

To see which titles are coming soon, please visit

millsandboon.co.uk/nextmonth

MILLS & BOON
MEDICAL
Pulse-Racing Passion

Set your pulse racing with dedicated, delectable doctors in the high-pressure world of medicine, where emotions run high and passion, comfort and love are the best medicine.